Migratory Animals

Migratory Animals

MARY HELEN SPECHT

HARPER ● PERENNIAL

NEW YORK ● LONDON ● TORONTO ● SYDNEY ● NEW DELHI ● AUCKLAND

HARPER PERENNIAL

P.S.™ is a trademark of HarperCollins Publishers.

FIRST EDITION

Designed by Leah Carlson-Stanisic
Title page art by Tristan Tan/Shutterstock, Inc.

Library of Congress Cataloging-in-Publication Data
Specht, Mary Helen.
 Migratory animals: a novel / Mary Helen Specht.
   pages cm.
ISBN 978-0-06-234603-2 (paperback)
I. Title.
PS3619.P4365M54 2015
813'.6—dc23   2014025457

ISBN 978-0-06-234603-2

15 16 17 18 19   OV/RRD   10 9 8 7 6 5 4 3

For T

Migratory Animals

PROLOGUE

What Flannery first noticed when she arrived in Nigeria were the towering palm trees. It was like walking off the airplane into a land of giants. The next morning, Flannery, barefoot, crossed her new front yard and stood beneath one of the sturdy palms, her shoulder blades pressing into the grooved trunk. She tilted her chin to look up at the canopy when, suddenly, the tree shook its head at her. A flock of birds swept from the branches, crackling the leaves.

Flannery was on the lam. Ever since her mother's death when she was in college, she'd let graduate school and then various research grants in climate science take her farther and farther from Texas: Wisconsin, Juneau, the Klondike, West Africa. Sometimes she imagined herself as a spider spinning an enormous web, swinging from one corner of the globe to the other, and like the spider, Flannery didn't know exactly what she wanted—until she caught it.

She met Kunle at an outdoor canteen near the Nigerian university where she had been posted on what was supposed to be a brief data-collecting trip. Sitting at an adjacent table with a soda and a worn textbook, he leaned over to her and said, "You should try the palm wine." Kunle wore slacks and a blue button-down oxford, both ironed within an inch of their lives. Trim and preppy, he looked like one of those idealized husbands in films, the kind of man who kissed a beautiful wife before leaving for the office, the kind usually too straitlaced to be Flannery's type.

Flannery first thought to ignore him, remembering the U.S. security officer at the consulate who told her to avoid the mainland. "You mean mainland Lagos?" she asked, referring to the crowded coastal metropolis of flyovers and shantytowns. "No, the mainland," he said, sweeping his arm in a grandiose gesture across the map hanging on his wall, indicating the center of the country where she would be living and working, indicating *all* of Nigeria, except, of course, the two tiny islands where the consulate offices were located.

But Flannery was not built to be frightened of new things, certainly not this handsome man in glasses sitting next to her at a crowded canteen. So she ordered a cup of the palm wine and changed her life.

Flan knew she was in love when, during a dinner at her house a few weeks later, Kunle recited a poem he'd jotted down on a scrap of newspaper that ended with the line, "For winter must not steal a kiss." And then he kissed her, and as he did, he trembled. When she decided to stay in Nigeria and work full-time at the research outpost in Adamanta, Kunle made goat stew to celebrate and gave her a copy of *The Palm-Wine Drinkard* tied with a bow, saying that if she was going to be a white Yoruban, then she should understand her new history. He said, half joking, "This story will tie you to me forever."

In the novel, the protagonist's only and entire job is to drink palm wine, tapped from the budding red fruit of the towering West African palms. When his tapper dies falling from a tree, the drunk makes a perilous journey to Dead Town in the hopes of finding and bringing him back. Flannery was fascinated by a world where drinking palm wine could be a job and where the dead lived in a village down the road.

Reading the novel for the third time, she noticed a line of sweat trickle beneath her shirt, over the vines of star jasmine coiling along her ribs, a tattooed tribute to her late mother's garden. Flannery's own dead were far away, across the world in a place she visited once a year, just long enough to kiss her friends and family on the cheek. On her next trip to the States, Flannery had a palm-wine tree tattooed alongside the star jasmine on her back. At that moment, it seemed easy to ink a claim to such a thing, such a place. It seemed easy to choose a new home.

Five years passed, and without warning, recession hit in 2008 and funding for climate science began to dry up. The research post in Adamanta exhausted its grant money, and Flan's boss was shuttering the operation, going back home to the UK. In order to apply for her own funding stream to keep the post open, Flannery needed lab equipment she couldn't get in Nigeria. She needed to return to Texas for a while—there was no other way, she and Kunle agreed. Flannery's stomach churned at the thought of being in the States for so long, the emotional tar pit of a needy sister, old friends and lovers, a grief-stricken and defeated father. Everything that she'd traded for this sparkling new man, this new life.

On the night before her flight, Kunle took her in search of fresh palm wine. They held hands, walking through the overgrown outskirts of the university campus, wide trails winding through frangipani and hibiscus, the gritty dry-season air cutting through Flannery's mouth and throat. A woman in a bright green wrapper passed them carrying a computer monitor on her head.

"You *oyinbo*s always carry luck," Kunle said, stopping suddenly, nodding up to where a palm-wine tapper perched dexterously atop one of his trees, wearing baggy brown pants and a sweaty tank top, bare feet gripping the trunk. Tappers spent entire afternoons and evenings climbing palm trees—using nothing more than their feet and a thick strip of woven bark to hoist themselves up—tapping into the flowers at the top of the palms and tying plastic jugs underneath to catch the liquid sap.

She and Kunle waited at the bottom of the tree, and when the tapper touched down, Kunle gave him some naira in exchange for the fresh palm wine. They drank from little plastic cups with tin lids to keep the flies out. Flannery imagined she and Kunle were bound in the pages of *The Palm-Wine Drinkard* and that sitting and drinking was the only job they had in the world.

She was reminded of an American teacher she'd met who had taught Thomas Hardy novels in a Nigerian high school in the 1960s and had been surprised to learn that his students had no idea what it meant to kiss. As she sat on a wooden bench drinking palm wine, morose over her own departure the next morning, she asked, "Is kissing un-African?"

Kunle shrugged. "Is not knowing un-American?" He told her that during his undergraduate days he'd dated a girl from an isolated, rural village and that "she'd nearly screamed when I tried to kiss her. 'Why would you eat my teeth?!'"

Before he could finish the story, Flannery reached her hand behind his head, touching her lips to his. It was dusk, and a shadow of bats flew over them in search of insects.

"I can't stand this," he whispered into her ear.

She nuzzled him in agreement.

He squared himself in front of her. "Let's get married."

She raised her plastic cup high in the air.

"I'm serious," he said.

She swallowed the rest of the palm wine. They planned to get married one day, had talked about it, but she always put him off because a wedding would inevitably involve her family and friends from the other side. Kunle was of this place. Of her life in this place. Kunle was untainted by the loss and heartbreak Flannery's family dragged behind it like a lizard's tail. But maybe, she thought now, watching the dimple in his cheek hollow into a smile, this long trip to the States was an opportunity to say good-bye to her old life for good.

"Okay. Visit me in Texas and meet my family." They touched hands, allowing themselves to forget for a moment that travel visas for Nigerians were not quite so simple to obtain. "We'll have one wedding there and then come home and have a wedding here. We'll do it right."

To save money, Flannery usually took a shared car from the bus station in Adamanta to the capital, Abuja, where she then caught a flight to Texas via London. But this time, her friend Mrs. Tonukari insisted on driving her.

Mrs. T was an older Welsh woman who had come to Adamanta with her Nigerian husband in the heady days after independence in 1960. Most of her fellow "Niger Wives" from that time had moved back to their own countries over the years, sometimes with and sometimes without the husband in tow. But not Mrs. T.

Mrs. T shrugged when Flannery and Kunle sat in the backseat, pressing their bodies together like desperate teenagers. The woman had never said explicitly that she didn't approve of Kunle. Instead, she liked to whisper to Flannery over tea about how Nigerian men were incapable of monogamy. Or how nobody in this godforsaken country was incorruptible in the long run.

The car jolted up and down over incessant potholes, Flannery with one palm on Kunle's blue-jeaned thigh, one around the ropy tendons of his neck. They passed women and children selling groundnuts and toothbrushes, a roadside shack with a sign that read MAKE WE TALK INTERVENTION SITE, and the occasional palm tree surveying rolling hills of dirt.

At the airport, Kunle unloaded bags from the jerry-rigged trunk of the ancient Peugeot, and Mrs. Tonukari, wearing a button-up housedress that matched her short old-lady hair, one tooth missing, hands mangled by arthritis, turned to Flannery and said, "It's hard to come back, you know."

Kunle looked at Flannery hard, knowingly, from where he stood on the curb, her rucksack slung over his shoulder. Then, he winked. "I'll be right behind you." This was his first time at a real airport.

Once, when Flannery and Kunle lay sex-sweaty on their thin mattress, he'd asked if, before flying on an airplane, she sent insurance policies from a machine in the airport. Flannery had stared at him, not sure how to react.

"No way, José. That's bad luck. And machines like that don't exist," she'd said, kicking the mosquito net with her foot.

Squinting as the flames from a candle played across his face, Kunle told her he'd read about them somewhere.

"You'll be on a plane one day," she said, "and you can see for yourself."

A year after this exchange, Flannery came across the story of an automated insurance machine in a memoir by the Nigerian writer Wole Soyinka. In the '60s, when he was a young man returning to Nigeria after studying at Leeds, Soyinka wrote about a machine in the London airport where, for a fee, the thing would spit out an insurance policy you could read and sign right there and then drop into a special mail slot.

Flannery ran into the bedroom and showed the passage to Kunle as though she were the one who'd discovered it: "Look. He says he went crazy, sending them to dozens of people. Guys he owed chop to. Family. Anyone he could think of. Other passengers began freaking out, wondering if he knew something about the flight that they didn't."

At the time, she'd stared at Kunle's serious face, with its three symmetrical scars running down the left side, noticing for the first time how he looked a little like the photograph of the young Soyinka on the book's flap jacket: cheekbones like machetes; bony shoulders perched over a girlish waist; liquid body like a dancer.

A harried woman behind the British Airways counter at Nnamdi Azikiwe International Airport looked at Flannery like she was an imbecile when she asked for directions to the automated life insurance machine. The woman handed Flannery a boarding pass.

Sitting at her gate, Flannery closed her eyes, readying herself to face her sister, who would be waiting when she arrived in Austin. She thought: *The only thing that will keep me from coming back to this place is if the plane goes down.*

ALYCE

*T*he ruddy birds arrived inside that slit of morning just before daybreak. It was nearly summer solstice, so the sun came early—before Alyce, who sat holding the image of a looped rope in her mind, felt ready for it.

Alyce was awake because she never slept. These days, every cell in her body was a spring threatening to burst and fly apart like the cuckoo clock in old cartoons. Some nights, like tonight, she fantasized about a noose swinging from the thick rafter that split the ceiling of the cabin. Or she imagined filling her pockets with rocks and walking into the deepest part of the creek. Or pills. Or a fall from the cliff. Or car exhaust. But she wasn't entirely serious. Alyce was a mother. She told herself this: *I am a mother. I am a mother.*

The animals at Roadrunner Ranch didn't sleep, either, going about their insomniac lives on the other side of the cracked casement window. Skunks and rabbits scampered along the fence line. Armadillos dug up worms around the porch. A raccoon knocked one of the bird feeders catawampus.

Listening to the armadillo shuttle forward in the grass outside, Alyce sat cross-legged at the workbench in her studio—really the cabin's sitting room—the back of her pale hand scribbled with notes for a wedding shawl: 2 skeins chen. xtra thin, pck of hks, eyelsh lace. Written diagonally up the inside of her forearm were the mathematical calculations to determine how much cloth, the size of the reed, and how many threads would go in each dent. The wooden table's long indentations were navigated by rows of various bead combinations from her cache, which she kept in the drawers of an old library catalog. But Alyce was not really working. Alyce hadn't really worked in months.

This summer was not the first time she'd been paralyzed by the dark tar pooling inside her brain, but this was the worst it had ever been. Worse than when she had her jaw wired shut at thirteen. Worse than when she spent three months in bed after her eldest son was born.

Baskets heaped with balls of colored silk and wool yarn covered a small table behind her horizontal floor loom, and she dipped her hands into the whites and yellows, closing her eyes, feeling for the softest. Alyce hand-dyed her yarn—in bowls and buckets set up on the porch—because she was obsessed with color: the gullible green of new spring leaves, the piss yellow of old bathtubs. None of her yarn was uniform, but made of subtle gradations: apricot to tangerine to burnt orange. Two weeks before, she'd dyed several skeins using the dried indigo her best friend, Flannery, always brought back from West Africa, and which Alyce first had to ferment to create a deep blue.

Staring out the window just before dawn, as the hidden sun turned the horizon navy, Alyce began to see farther than the patch of manicured lawn out into the field of oak and cedar, eyes half adjusting to the unfolding scene, brain still trapped in the flotsam of sticky daydream, so at first, she wasn't surprised the ground was blanketed by orange half-moons, gentle swells, bright splashes of belly: robins migrating for the breeding season.

There were hundreds, maybe thousands of robins, and they perched on the trees and the fence and on every inch of native grass, transforming the acreage outside into undulating waves of color.

Their bellies were the persimmon of the itchy 1970s sofa in her house growing up, the color of dried blood.

Some of the robins were attracted to the deer corn, and so the thickest concentration of birds was along the jagged line toward the house where Alyce and her dark-eyed sons had laid out the kernels. Alyce knew Texas was on the central migratory flyway; birds returned from wintering in warmer climes, hugging the Mexican coastline, and then flocked into the central United States and Canada where they nested and bred. She also knew the flock of robins was supposed to be beautiful, was supposed to catch her breath with astonishment. Alyce felt nothing.

But her boys would love it. Alyce closed the door to the studio behind her and slipped into her sons' room, waking them in their bunk beds with hands on their shoulders and the word, "Come."

They went through the kitchen and out the side door, then circled to the front of the house, rounding the porch on tiptoes. The birds ignored them. Her sons, Jake and Ian, crouched in front of her in matching blue-and-white-striped monogrammed pajamas, gifts from Harry's parents; Ian cast an occasional glimpse at his older brother, Jake, to confirm his feeling of wonder. That what he was seeing was real.

Living on this ranch was part of Alyce's most recent arts fellowship, and for the boys, everything was new and wonderful. "The leader's named Roger," whispered Jake definitively, pointing to a bird settled on a branch of the only tree actually inside the fenced yard. Ian nodded in agreement.

"Sic semper tyrannis!" Alyce said. The boys ignored her.

Jake was wiry and pale like Alyce, but Ian would be different. He was square and squat, even for a three-year-old, and would grow to have the body of a wrestler, she thought. Alyce hoped that whatever else happened in the years ahead, they would remember this moment and think of her less harshly.

Standing in boxer shorts and a T-shirt, shivering, a hand self-consciously placed on each of her sons' shoulders, Alyce took a deep, full breath in the way her ex-therapist had taught her, but it caught in her throat on the way out as she watched Harry emerge from the other side of the house. He wore a brown canvas jacket, carved walking stick in one hand, tongues sticking out of his un-laced hiking boots. When Alyce looked at her husband, she couldn't make herself feel anger or grief or tenderness or trust.

"Early birds," Harry whispered, standing above his family on the ledge of the porch. She wondered why he said it that way. There was no "up early" or "up late" for Alyce, just a ceaseless groan of semiconsciousness.

"You, too," she said, noticing the stink of her own underarms, the greasy sheen of her unwashed hair as she pulled a hand through its tangles.

"I wanted to hike before the heat. And then I saw . . . this," he said, gesturing at the robins. "Look at them." She could see it in his face, the way the muscles tensed: her husband had been just as hoodwinked as her sons, perceiving something spectral about the robins' movements en masse, about the ways they formed complex patterns, designs the birds themselves could not have understood on more than an intuitive level.

Alyce came from a family of birders, but she had never been in-terested in checking off species from a list or watching them gorge at backyard feeders. Rather, flight itself was the reason she'd majored in mechanical engineering in college, specializing in aeronautics, an unsophisticated science compared to how birds migrated long dis-tances based on the earth's magnetic field, big gliders using the thermal updrafts created during the day, as the heat from the sun rose, and small powered fliers, like robins, preferring to migrate at night when the atmospheric boundary layer was still. Back and forth, back and forth. Just one more way to devour endless days.

Alyce looked at her boys—all three hunkered down, staring out at the field, connected by a web of dumb, guileless awe. Jake and Ian flocked around Harry and each other, forming their own instinctive patterns of flight.

Harry leaned into their sons and said, "We'll have enough robin soup to last the entire winter." The boys' expressions turned first to horror before scrunching up in the way they did to show their suspicion of grown-ups.

Jake turned and explained patiently to his younger brother that the robins were messengers of a magical army. "I'm going to ride one."

"What about me?!" cried Ian. The robins started, jumping slightly to the top of a dance beat, before bolting east in a rush of chirps and feathers, eyes and beaks suddenly obscured by wing. Her sons stood to watch orange puzzle pieces converge and fly away.

As the birds freckled the face of the horizon, Alyce pictured the robins that would fly into the windows of skyscrapers, or become caught in the fuselages of airplanes, or simply run out of energy and fall, unable to fly on.

"Jake is going to be sleepy and cranky at school." Harry began to tie the laces of his boots. "We probably shouldn't wake them up for every little thing."

"It was cool, though. Right, guys?"

"Pretty cool," said Jake, now nonchalant.

"You have a very cool mother," Harry told them, but his voice was strained. He turned to Alyce. "You could have woken me up, you know."

Alyce lay on the grass and looked at the sky and, from this perspective, Harry appeared as a scarecrow, awkward sticks dressed up to create the illusion of human menace.

Harry sighed. "Don't forget. Someone's coming to drop off the tent and chairs this morning," he said. They were hosting Flannery's welcome-home party next week—Harry had badgered Alyce into offering up the ranch.

Alyce closed her eyes. "And there are still boxes to unpack. Food to buy. Dishes to wash." *Breaths to breathe*, she thought. "Have you noticed how we buy food and then eat it, and then have to buy more?"

Harry didn't respond. Alyce opened her eyes and saw the corners of his mouth turned down, the folds in his forehead, the subtle droop of his tired eyelids. For a moment, she wanted to reach out and hug him, but the feeling passed before she could own it.

A scream of delight drew her attention. Alyce sat up. Jake was standing in the yard throwing a horseshoe dangerously close to his brother's head.

"Put those fucking things down," she hissed, and then clasped a hand to her mouth to catch the vitriol before it escaped. Too late.

"Flapjack time," said Harry, and with that, the boys dropped everything and lined up to follow him inside, the Pied Piper of Pancakes. His walking stick leaned against the porch swing, forgotten.

Alyce stayed on the ground for a moment, looking out at the trees and sky, wondering if a few of the robins were watching through the brambled cross-stitch of brush, and like her, waiting anxiously for the cover of night.

FLANNERY

*F*lannery, jet-lagged and half delirious, slumped into her sister Molly's car outside the airport in Austin. They drove past the overturned bowl of pink limestone that was the state capitol building and stopped for lunch at a place called Quack's.

The long narrow bakery echoed with the clanging of silverware and the clicking of computer keyboards; brightly painted wooden tables were shoved close together; dogs, tied to the railing outside, barked as each new person flung open the door, uppercuts of air-conditioning hitting them in the face. The sisters ordered at the counter, then staked out a spot in the corner flush against a bookshelf full of board games. "I hardly slept last night," said Molly. "You're finally here." Her sister was two years younger and six inches shorter than Flannery, with darker hair, bigger breasts.

"I didn't sleep, either," said Flannery. "Dragging myself through Heathrow at three in the morning might have had something to do with that." She interlaced her fingers with Molly's and leaned forward.

"I wouldn't let Dad pick you up—wanted you to myself first," Molly said, "but I did tell him that you and I would drive out to Abilene this weekend. Hope that's okay. . . ." Flannery listened to the stream of words, letting them flow through her, feeling the warmth that bubbled up whenever she first saw her sister, before the bickering and confused feelings resurfaced. "He could come here, but he hates new Austin and just spends all day bitching about the traffic and the yuppies and drives Brandon and me up the wall. Papa's cooking now, you wouldn't believe it, and he's not a total catastrophe. Nothing too fancy, but . . ." Molly put her hand over her mouth and laughed. The two sisters looked at each other.

"Too bad Kunle couldn't come," Molly said.

"Actually, he has an interview at the consulate in a few weeks for a visa and we're hoping—"

"Hey, sorry, but I've got to pee. Listen for our number, Flancakes." Molly almost knocked over her chair as she rose and turned, threading her way through the tables toward the back.

Molly and Kunle had never met in person, just on the computer. Once, when Flannery dragged him into the bedroom to video chat with Molly while she went to answer a knock at the door, her sister asked about the three parallel scars on the side of Kunle's face. Flannery overheard them from the other room.

"All future kings of the Yoruba are born with them. It's a sign of royalty."

"Born with, huh?"

"Only joking. They came from a fight with my brother. Flannery told you I was raised by a pack of lions, *abi*?"

"What?!"

From the hallway, Flannery had cocked her head in wonder. Maybe he believed Molly would think him savage or primitive if he told the truth.

The sandwiches at Quack's arrived in plastic baskets lined with wax paper. Flannery was in the middle of taking a bite when her sister emerged from the bathroom door across the bakery. She saw it in Molly immediately. It struck like a bullet. Her sister walked toward her, swaying a little from side to side, a flashback of their mother, tilting back and forth like a toddler not yet comfortable with how the steps transition one into another.

Molly smiled as she moved forward, oblivious in her amber beads and blue jeans. She was beautiful—she'd always been the pretty one—and Flannery wanted to stop her, to freeze the moment, or at least slow the ticking off of seconds: the red of the bathroom door as it clicked shut; the smeary fingerprints on the display window housing glittery confections; the flick of a customer's wrist as he tossed coins into the tip jar on the counter; the way the coins jangled as they hit bottom.

Flannery closed her eyes. She was shocked, and the most shocking thing was not even this confrontation with the first signs of disease in her sister. It was the realization that, somewhere deep down in the cracks and fissures of her brain, Flannery had known this could happen. But not now. Not this soon. *Wahala*, she thought. Big trouble. She tried to suppress the image of her mother attempting to spoon soup into her own mouth and then throwing the bowl across the room when she couldn't keep her hand from shaking.

Flannery felt a sharp pressure on her back and realized it was Molly's palm beating up and down because Flannery was coughing a little on the sandwich. She blinked hard and spat the mess back into her plate. She inhaled a rough breath.

"You're a tough cookie," said Molly.

"Went . . . down the wrong pipe."

Flannery stared as her sister began eating, and it was like something playing across a television without sound. The way Molly slid a ridged potato chip into her avocado sandwich "to give it more texture," giggling and eating and talking at the same time. How did her sister do that? What was she even saying? It was all Flannery could do to bob her chin up and down, hoping this was the correct response to whatever was being asked, head swimming in recriminations:

Had Flannery really imagined Africa would make their mother's death and all its implications go away? You didn't just blink your eyes, move across the world, and expect the darkness you left behind to disappear. Blink, blink: Flan thought of their mother in her last years, eyes darting one way and another. The inability to maintain eye contact was a symptom of Huntington's disease, but it had always seemed to Flannery like a reluctance to face things.

"You will? Excellent. I know you're moving into that rental, but they'll last in sacks for a while until you get settled. We'll pull them out of the ground in a few months."

Flannery felt the urge to run. She didn't want to be there anymore. She didn't want to look at her sister or talk to her or even think of her.

"Are you listening to me? Mom's iris bulbs have finally split. I'm thinning out the extras this year."

Flannery didn't know how to say she wouldn't be staying long enough to plant their mother's irises here. "I don't know." And then, as though it explained everything, she said one word: "Africa." And yet, despite this pronouncement, her future in the rutted streets threaded with concrete squares and wooden stalls, filled with smells of grilled meat and exhaust, where Flannery had bargained over goods for the last five years, began to glimmer and smear in unreality. Panic set in.

Molly betrayed her hurt feelings with a shrug. She said she had to get back to work but would drop Flan off at the house so she could take a nap.

"I must have forgotten to tell you. I feel horrible," said Flannery, looking away from the steady beam of her sister's gaze. Her baby sister. "I'm staying with a friend tonight. From graduate school. She's teaching at the university now, and I promised . . . a great big house . . . I figured it would be easier. . . ." As she spoke, unsure whether she was making any sense, Flannery stared at the sad, overturned remainder of her chicken and pesto on whole wheat— mangled and falling apart. It was enough to make her want to throw up.

Flannery dragged herself and her luggage (stuffed with cheap gifts, or what a Nigerian friend of hers called "DCC"—Developing Country Crap) down the sidewalk. A row of brick storefronts advertised antiques and used music and funky art painted on recycled wood. Across the street, peach-colored roses threaded through the metal fence surrounding the mental hospital. Trundling along, Flannery passed a corner telephone pole inexplicably encased in a colorful knitted fabric. Yarn graffiti. In Nigeria the Yoruba believed intersections were liminal spaces, thresholds where humans and spirits and ancestors overlapped, and they often left offerings like this at crossroads. Flannery touched the strange handmade fabric and remembered how her mother looked before the illness, knitting and sewing costumes for one of her plays at the community theater, sharp pins sticking from her mouth like weapons and black lace piled in the bowl of her lap.

Flannery eventually found the bar she remembered fondly from her time as an undergrad at Marsh College, a small, nerdy engineering university situated in the neighborhood nearby. The dive bar, which had been frequented by grad students drinking Lone Star and people looking to get in bar fights with grad students drinking Lone Star, was directly above the Burger Tex, and you had to climb up a fire escape to get there. As she dragged her suitcase through the entrance, Flannery saw that El Gaton was a much hipper place now, with walls covered in hundreds of wine bottles sticking out of severe, modern racks. Real wine sounded good. So good. The only wine they drank in Nigeria was sweet palm wine or imported "sangria" from a box.

Soon after she walked inside, El Gaton began filling up with happy-hour patrons, carefree and young, disposable income fattening their wallets, while Flannery ordered a glass of white and then another and then another, occasionally looking around, pretending to be meeting someone. As she drank, she tried not to think about her sister but to focus on her real purpose here—to complete research that would allow her to return to Nigeria. To Kunle, the man she would marry. To the place where they sat outside in red plastic chairs and ate the best melt-your-face-off fish pepper soup, kids stopping to ask, "Are you here on an adventure?" (because white people in movies were always going to Africa on adventures) as she laughed at them and said, "How did you know?"

Flannery was a lightweight these days, and the alcohol quickly made her woozy and regretful. Where was she going to sleep tonight? She shouldn't have lied to Molly about having other plans, but Flannery just couldn't bear the thought of watching her sister all evening. She looked at her bar bill and thought, *Fuck. I could buy a goat for that.* She considered mentioning this to the bartender but decided against it, remembering how Mrs. Tonukari always said nobody on the other side actually wanted to hear anything real. Nigerians never asked about Mrs. T's life back in Wales, and her Welsh friends could never understand what she'd been doing all those years in Nigeria.

The man next to her worked the crossword puzzle in pen. Flannery asked to borrow his cell phone, which he handed to her without looking up. Pressing a finger into her other ear to block out the noise, she dialed Alyce's number, but when her best friend picked up, she sounded shrunken and distant, as though she were talking through a sack.

"Can I stay with you tonight?"

She was answered with muffled noises.

"Ground Control to Major Alyce."

"Sorry . . . I'm distracted. Jake won't finish his green beans . . ."

"Call the gendarmes." Flannery sighed and asked how Harry and the boys were, but Alyce didn't answer that question, either. Instead, she asked, "Are you drunk?"

"Stranger things have happened."

"I thought you were staying with your sister."

"I am, but she's busy with work. You know. I thought we could catch up."

"One problem. I live on a ranch an hour from town now, remember? I can't leave the kids alone to pick you up, and a cab out here will cost a fortune."

"Right." Flannery had the feeling Alyce was trying to set boundaries, to protect her family. As if Flannery was going to come over with a bottle of bourbon and a batch of malaria for the boys.

"Hold on a sec."

Flannery rolled her eyes. Unbelievable.

"Sorry, Flan. Ian's diving off the top bunk again. I'll call you later."

There was a click before Flannery could remind Alyce she didn't have a cell number in the States yet. Alyce, who always had her back. Who had told the speed-addled cabdriver in Spain to pull over and made him sit in back while Alyce drove them through the dark empty streets toward their hostel. What had happened to that Alyce?

At the bar, another drink in hand, Flannery couldn't help herself from peeking at her neighbor's crossword. "Enya."

"Excuse me?" He angled his thick neck toward her, and she noticed the Eastern-bloc-style cap perched in his lap.

"Forty-nine down. They love to use her. It's those vowels."

"Yes." He smiled weakly and wrote it in. Handsome and clean-cut in an old-fashioned way, she decided he looked like Phineas from *A Separate Peace*, or at least what she imagined Phineas would look like—something about his square jawbone and blond hair. Poor, perfect Phineas who fell from the tree or was pushed.

"Phineas," she said. "Things were not always this way. For example, this bar used to be a dump." She almost slipped from her stool but caught herself by grabbing his arm.

A group of women walked in from outside, laughing.

"My name is Ash," he said, as the bartender plopped down a small plate in front of him, a slider with blue cheese dribbling down the side.

When she heard Ash's name, she thought of libraries and quiet, those last two letters forming a *shhhhh*. Don't disturb the other patrons. Don't wake up the sleeping baby. Ash.

"I need a place to crash. What do you think, Phineas-Ash? Do you have a sofa? In exchange, I could teach you a thing or two about crossword puzzles." She knew this wasn't coming out exactly right, but she was sleep deprived and going through reverse culture shock; they were all going to die, but her little sister was going to beat them to it; her apartment wouldn't be ready for move-in until Monday; she felt sick. Flannery vaguely understood that these problems were not on equal levels of importance. Her heart fluttered insistently, trying to beat its way out from under the bones of her chest.

Ash's smile was strained, annoyed, and he lifted his hand to show her the band on his left ring finger. "Wherever you end up," he said, "I hope you're not driving."

By the time the taxi pulled up outside the door of the bar, Flannery could only think of one place she could go. She didn't know the address, but how hard could it be to find?

She waved away the cabbie when he tried to put her things in the trunk, heaving her giant rucksack beside her onto the vinyl seat.

"There's an old firehouse in Clarksville behind Jeffrey's. Do you know it?"

As the cab moved forward, warm air from a rolled-down window blowing across her face, Flannery closed her eyes and imagined being back in Adamanta, the streetlamps dark, no electricity coming from the passing buildings as they sped by on the back of an *okada*. Too late for the buses, so they'd flagged one of the passing motorbikes to take them home instead: Flan behind the driver; Kunle behind her. She remembered how his breath passed along her ear and the side of her face as she leaned back into him. His legs straddled hers, and his hands barely touched her torso as if held there not by muscle but by magnetism. It was joy and movement and freedom in a liminal space, invisible ghosts licking at their heels.

SANTIAGO

Santiago ripped cedar boards with his circular saw, which he kept permanently plugged in on the still-torn-apart first floor, wood shavings and sawdust fanned out in waves. He itched for the day that his fire station would be, as he put it, "fully operational." His own artistic Death Star. His dream was to arrive at work each morning by sliding down the metal fireman's pole in a designer suit. Despite the fact that one of his uncles had been a talented carpenter in Brownsville when he was growing up, Santi hadn't learned to work with his hands until shop class in high school. His father made sure they kept their distance from "la familia," as he called it, with affection; his idea of the American dream did not include a messy family dynamic dragging down his only child's upward mobility. His father was a Mexican who didn't much like Mexicans, and it was only later that Santi began to wonder what that might do to a person's psyche. Maybe it was why his father never left the Valley himself. Or why, once Santiago did get an education (his father whispering the phrase "graduate school" over and over when he came to watch his hooding ceremony), the two of them had seemed at a greater and greater loss around each other.

As Santiago worked, the din from the saw deafened the knocking at first, the subtle sonic emerging slowly, like the distant tapping of a woodpecker in a pecan tree outside, something out of the ordinary but that did not necessarily affect him. Then he thought, *Wait. Wait a second.* He turned off the machine and set it gently down. Someone was banging on the front door. Without allowing himself to rush or hurry, he walked forward, sweaty, covered in grime, calm.

"Those glasses make you look smarter," was the first thing she said, standing in the doorway, her tall body never having fully outgrown the gangliness of youth, wooden bracelets clattering down her wrists. There were dark circles under her eyes, and her breath smelled like hot wine.

Santiago raised the Plexiglas carpenter's visor he'd forgotten he was wearing. "Flan."

For a moment they stood looking at each other in the light of his porch lamp, and then he grabbed one of her bags, turned, and walked back inside. He wove his way through the first-floor construction, moving his body with lightness, as if the whole thing had been planned in advance. As if he'd known all along she was coming.

Santiago motioned for Flan to walk ahead of him up the stairs, his pulse quickening as he watched her. Not an amateur drunk, she treaded slowly up each step, deliberately. Flannery looked like a mess, but when he stared at her she blurred into the nineteen-year-old Flannery whom he'd first kissed on the concrete stairwell outside his dorm room, the twenty-three-year-old Flannery dancing on a bar in Matamoros wearing cowboy boots and fishnet hose, the twenty-seven-year-old Flannery who threw a White Russian in his face and laughed.

She stopped at the top of the staircase and looked at him. "El Gaton . . ."

"I know." He nodded in agreement. "It's full of hipsters now. Looks nothing like back in the day when we used to stop there for a beer . . ."

". . . when we walked the earth. And that Dairy Queen is gone, the . . ."

". . . most depressing DQ south of the Mason-Dixon. It closed three yeas ago."

"I wonder what happened to that guy who worked there. The one always crying into your Blizzard as he made it."

"Breeze. Always a Butterfinger Breeze."

"Right."

Santiago's bedroom furniture consisted of a mattress on box springs, two laundry hampers, and a low dresser of painted metal. He watched as this prodigal, beautiful creature shrugged off her backpack, dragging her gaze over his collection of Jesuses lined up along the dresser. Dashboard Jesus with built-in magnet conferred "blessings"; Thumbs-Up Jesus signaled the affirmative; Zombie Jesus stared emptily; another plastic Jesus wore a gimme cap emblazoned with the letters W.W.I.D.; a "Daily Bread" toaster stood ready to toast bread with the image of Jesus's face; Clapping Dashboard Jesus rotted in its box labeled "Enlightenment on a Spring"; and the Happy Birthday Jesus Tree-Topper doubled as a motion sensor, sounding a tinny alarm as they passed by. Flannery nodded and said, "Nice." She said it like she'd forgotten that she was with him when he bought his first one. Maybe she had.

"Let me show you around."

"Later. Not in the mood for brushed bronze hardware quite yet."

"Yeah?" he asked, with faux concern. It was just like her to march in from Africa with such self-righteousness—as though he and Harry hadn't had to close their shop downtown. As though their college friend Steven's farm wasn't going broke and Brandon's funding at the Climate Institute wasn't evaporating and half the people they knew weren't laid off and stuck in homes worth a third of what they had been. "This is a new America, sweetheart. Recessed lighting and brushed bronze hardware are all we have left."

She reached out and patted his head, as if to say it was all right, and then sat on the edge of his bed and looked at him, eyes glassy. "I could eat anything. Anything at all."

Santiago was proudest of the kitchen with its metal counters and deep sinks, pots and pans hanging from hooks on the ceiling. He decided on puttanesca sauce because it would be fast—tomatoes, onion, garlic, olives, and red pepper flakes sautéed quickly over high heat. He thought about the way Flannery used to chop garlic, hunching over the project, taking forever, but managing to slice each clove in three directions such that it fell apart into perfect, tiny squares. Garlic bricks for the faerie people, she would say.

Santiago didn't try to process what was happening, as though thinking too much might ruin it, focusing instead on the movement of his knife as he chopped. He took leftover penne from the fridge and dumped it into the sauce. By the time he walked back into the bedroom, Flannery was facedown, her clothes still on, passed out. Sighing, he sat beside her and ate the pasta by himself. It could have used a little more salt.

Balancing the plate in one hand, he used the other to pull off Flan's shoes and socks. He had to jerk hard, and this woke her a little. She groaned and turned over. Her eyes fluttered open, unfocused. She poked at his arm and whispered, "Hey. Have you noticed anything weird about my sister lately?"

"Weirder than usual?" he said through a full mouth.

"She picked me up at the airport." Flannery curled into herself like a snail. "She's starting to fall apart. Like my mom. Watch her closely. She loses control of her body . . ."

Santiago sat on edge of the bed, the plate of pasta like a stone in his hands. He didn't move. Flannery passed back out.

Downstairs, Santiago took off his carpenter's visor to rub his eyes, then put it back on. His shoulder throbbed, but he began again, sanding down the corners of the cedar with fast, repetitive strokes. Wearing himself out. Working his mind through Flannery's words.

At first he'd considered calling Brandon, but to say what? *Hey, buddy, is your wife coming down with an incurable disease, by chance?* No. Flannery was drunk. Flannery didn't know what she was talking about. She hadn't been here in forever.

Santiago comforted himself with the miracle of Flannery's presence in his bed. They'd been together on-and-off-again over the years. But not lately. Not since she'd moved to Nigeria, years ago now, avoiding being alone with him whenever she came back on her trips that seemed to last mere hours.

On only one visit did she stay out late at the West Annie Icehouse after the others left, but not so she might go home with him. It was Christmas Eve, and a few of their friends had met at the old bar with its outdoor picnic tables where they could smoke while drinking ice-cold cans of Pearl and escape, for a few hours, the suffocation of family.

"It's been a long transition into friendship," Flannery had said, twisting her hair into a knot, "but we finally seem to have done it."

"Does that mean we can't get naked anymore?" He'd been too proud to reveal the sting.

"There are downsides to everything." She hugged him gently from behind before wrapping her neck in a gauzy scarf and walking away.

What had changed? What had brought her to his fire station? Santiago didn't want the reason to be Molly, because he loved Molly; they all did. But also, selfishly, this wasn't how he wanted to get Flannery back. He wanted her to come back to him out of love. Because she'd finally realized they belonged together.

In the middle of the night, Santiago could no longer keep moving. He unplugged his saw, went upstairs, spread his body out on the polished concrete floor of the entryway, and drifted off into restless half sleep. Through somnolent gauze, he saw his menagerie of bobble-headed Christs, moving in a kind of dance around Flannery's body on his bed, spinning and toggling, and Santiago had the sense they were protecting her or working on her, moving Flannery to remember what was important.

The next morning, Santiago went to the lumberyard. Flannery was still safe in the sleep of the dead and, in his feverish work the previous night, he'd run out of cedar planks. He needed more; he needed something to do with his hands.

Santiago drove past the defunct power plant by the river, morning sun throwing a glare on its loud murals in support of La Raza. This part of town, with its turquoise stucco and Catholic lawn art, reminded Santiago of parts of South Texas, where he grew up.

Fine Lumber and Plywood was in a scrappy neighborhood where every front yard possessed a vicious mutt behind a chain-link fence, and a man at the end of the block sold tamales out of his pickup. Santiago usually bought one pork tamale, one chorizo and onion. The man would reach into his Styrofoam cooler for the tamales, hot and doughy and wrapped in cornhusks, and Santiago would munch on them as he browsed wood. Today, however, his stomach sparked with nervous energy, and he didn't stop.

At the lumberyard, he climbed from his used MINI Cooper and walked toward the glorified tin barn. In moments like these Santi wished he still owned his old truck; it was emasculating to have his lumber delivered. Nobody won but British engineering. Santi suspected the workers sneered at his tiny car, despite his carefully chosen bumper sticker advertising the immortal words of Davy Crocket: *You may all go to hell, and I will go to Texas.*

The prices at Fine Lumber and Plywood may not have been

better than those at chain home improvement stores, but the selection was, and the place wasn't crowded with dazed DIYers. Rough-handed men in Wranglers and carpenter pants pushed trolleys of wood across the concrete warehouse floor, a Saturday morning supermarket for tough guys.

Inspecting a stack of aromatic planks of cedar, he saw that what was left was shitty, the dregs. Maybe he could get a deal on them. Santiago was using the cedar to build a closet in what would become the fire station's master bathroom. Santiago had bought the decommissioned fire station (and MINI Cooper) after his father had died two years earlier—right before the recession forced Santiago and Harry to give up their office on South Congress (and their cute assistant with her severe jet-black bob and tribal tattoos). So the current plan was for Santi to turn the second floor of the fire station into his living space and the first floor into their office and storefront. He was dipping into the firm's rainy-day fund to finish the project, already over budget. But, he figured, what better advertisement for an architecture firm than a knockout industrial remodel?

As he picked up another wooden plank to look for defects, Santiago's phone vibrated. It was Dalia, a woman he'd been dating for a few months. She was warm and slinky and young, barely twenty-three, and they'd met at a hip-hop concert when she passed him a joint. He let it ring. He'd have to break things off with her soon. In the past, Santiago might have strung Dalia along while he waited to see what happened with Flannery. But that wasn't a risk he was willing to take anymore.

"These are the ones I want," a woman's voice behind Santiago announced. He turned to look at the woman standing in front of the cubby filled with zebrawood, a golden heartwood rippling with streaks of black. "These are kick-ass."

"And the most expensive wood here," said the man beside her. Santiago couldn't decide if he was her husband or her contractor.

"Why's that?"

"Because you like it so much." The man shrugged. "The reason anything rare and beautiful costs more."

As the couple wandered off, Santiago shifted on his feet, staring blankly at the yards and yards of regulation-cut timber. Santiago thought about how every single plank in the warehouse would become part of buildings housing human lives. Lives like his and like Flannery's. His eyes scrolled over the words written on the wall in chalk: *Poplar, Pecan, White Oak, African Mahogany, Cypress, Spanish Cedar, Cherry, Alder, Fir.* It was a poetry all its own, and Santiago smiled, deciding he would buy the cedar and the zebrawood, damn the cost. Just because he wanted to. Just because it wasn't what his father would have done. Just because it was beautiful and full of possibility.

MOLLY

*L*ater, Molly would say she began to suspect something was wrong with her on the Friday that cutbacks were announced at work.

That morning she'd arrived to a voice mail announcing the cancellation of the ocean desalination project. Molly managed the laboratory for Water Resources, two labs down from the Atmospheric Ice Lab where her husband, Brandon, worked, and she was one of the first employees to receive official information because she wrote and disseminated all the memos to her lab. She liked to revise the wording of what was passed down from on high to something a little more catchy: "'STOP DOUCHING THE SEA,' says administration. 'Thank you for your attempts to play God by turning salt water fresh. Please focus your attentions elsewhere (or, if not yet tenured, consider a visit to the charmingly minimalist unemployment office at Twelfth and Lavaca).'" Molly kept waiting to get in trouble for these missives, but so far, nobody had said anything.

She swiveled in her chair to grab the memo she'd sent to the printer and handed it to one of the few people in the lab below her in rank, Nathan, a lab tech with a linebacker's build. "Copy this and put it in everyone's box."

"Even yours?" he asked.

She ignored the twitch of her hand. Too much coffee, she thought, and not enough sleep.

Throughout the day, scientists, graduate students, and postdocs filtered through the big push doors of the lab, earbuds pumping music into their heads as they sat at their benches working, entertaining pipe dreams of scientific breakthroughs. Sometimes Molly wandered down the long open hallway to kiss her husband, whom she invariably found scribbling notes in some dark corner, holed up like a rat, face scrunched in concentration. His family had emigrated from Iraq before he was born, and his hair was a glossy black, skin the color of toasted almonds. But in the lab, Brandon transformed into an ethereal entity, a disembodied dance of synapses flitting around the room while Molly tried to keep up, feeling dulled and slow. Whenever she popped her head into his office, Brandon would stop and then explain, rapid-fire, in all its terrifying minutiae, whatever he was working on.

"The short version," Molly might say, sighing the sigh of the scientist's spouse.

He would look up at her and brush his hand along her hairline, flipping over her ponytail. "The short version? Hmmm."

On this particular day she was supposed to have lunch with her sister, but Flannery canceled, claiming to be stuck in HR. Brandon had worked it out so Flan could rent lab space and equipment to do her work here at the Climate Institute, and it was true that she probably faced a monstrous amount of paperwork. It was fine. Molly was an expert at concealing her disappointment.

She ate a granola bar from the vending machine and then did inventory, going through drawers and closets, entering numbers into her spreadsheets, ordering centrifuge tubes, Petri dishes, syringe filters, beaker cups, Buchner funnels, amber vials, capillaries, spring pumps, PH meters, slides and pipettes, methyl ethyl ketone, potassium iodide, and benzocaine. Molly loved her job because she was naturally meticulous. She was certain she loved her job twice as much as Brandon and Flannery loved theirs, despite the fact they were big-shot PhDs doing actual research. Molly had not even considered applying to graduate school, content to coast through college, ultimately falling into a bachelor's of science and a career ordering materials, sterilizing dishes in big silver autoclave machines, preparing flasks of media, scanning scientists for radiation, organizing meetings, proofreading grant applications, and lording over the lab techs.

Maybe it was growing up with a father whose ambitions had been so thwarted. A father who just couldn't understand how he'd ended up an obscure novelist teaching too many courses at the community college, still hoping, even at age seventy, that one of his unpublished manuscripts (which had come to outnumber his published ones) was a breakthrough waiting to happen.

Whatever the reason, Molly set her sights low. She liked waking up and knowing exactly what to expect from the day. And she liked there to be a sound track.

"Whatcha got playing this week?" asked Sanjeet, who was working on a project to determine the effect of polluted rain on underground spring water in the Edwards Aquifer. He was one of the grad students Molly called "the perennials," whose projects dragged on and on, delaying their commencement sometimes for years. Above his computer was tacked a piece of paper labeled THE PERIODIC TABLE OF AWESOMENESS with the boxes of chemical elements replaced by things like Christopher Walken, mullets, ray guns, and bounty hunters. The microscope at the station next to him had a loose connection and someone had posted a sign on its neck: PLEASE DO NOT MOVE ME. I AM A DELICATE FLOWER.

Everything in these lab stations was white, including the chairs and tables and cubbies. It made Molly feel as though she were walking through a cloud.

"Hayes Carll," she told Sanjeet, counting the number of rubber gloves in the drawer labeled GLOVES, PENS, FORCEPS, RAZOR BLADES.

"Sell him to me." Sanjeet was leaning back precariously, chair balanced on one leg, lab coat half on, half off.

"He's the only musician under forty who can pull off a rose-embroidered western shirt," she said, letting him listen to the rockabilly twang on one of her earbuds before closing up the drawer and marking -10 on her clipboard. "You guys got everything you need?"

"We need to buy you a drink," Sanjeet said, nodding to include his "butt-mate"—the graduate student whose bench station was back-to-back with his and whose gray-eyed gaze was intent on his computer screen. "We've been here since six this morning working on a grant application, and it's time to move on."

"I have plans."

Molly had felt awkward around Sanjeet ever since the Climate Institute graduation party the year before when, after too much mystery punch, he'd beckoned her into a corner to show off the half-finished tattoo of Nikola Tesla on his back. In an inexplicable desire to match him, Molly had turned around and, without a second thought, dropped trou to reveal the words scrolled across her ass in a looped script: *Proud to Be in Texas Where Bob Wills Is Still the King.* Sanjeet pretended he didn't remember.

As Molly walked away, trying to negotiate a turn at the Faraday cage, she felt herself slip, feet escaping from under her, and there was nothing she could do but turn her hip so that she landed on its pocket of flesh. From this new position sprawled on the floor, the bulletin board that loomed over her, filled with scientific papers and signs warning of biohazards and radiation, seemed suddenly ominous.

"Look who's already started tippling." Sanjeet grabbed her by both elbows, lifting her up. "What happened, wobbles?"

"Too much energy, not enough fundamentals," she said, trying to smile despite her throbbing hip. Trying not to show her fear. *The janitors did their job too well*, she told herself, staring at the waxed floor.

"Hey, have I ever shown you my moon walk?" Sanjeet started to slide backward. "Check it out."

She watched him dance, Sanjeet's slide moves causing him to recede from where she stood, still a little unsteady, one hand against the wall, the other reaching helplessly into thin air.

FLANNERY

As a child, whenever Flannery tripped and skinned her knee walking up the porch steps, or bit her tongue falling from the monkey bars, or belly flopped sailing off the diving board of the swimming pool in Rose Park, her father would always say the same thing: *You're a tough cookie. Tough cookies don't cry.*

And so she didn't. She became proud of the little white scars adorning her knobby knees as she soaped them in the bath before bedtime. Her mother told her, while putting on makeup before another performance of *Guys and Dolls*, that scars migrated up the body over time, showing Flan the C-section scar on her belly and claiming it had moved there from her foot. Flannery liked this idea and imagined being old with a face crisscrossed by mutilations like the prizefighters on television.

While her sister, Molly, occasionally played tennis at the public courts in their neighborhood growing up, Flannery was drawn to sports with contact. She played defense in soccer, slicing her cleats through other girls' legs; forward in basketball, protecting the rebound with her elbows; and digger in volleyball, her hip bones hitting the floor with a loud smack. She was a tough cookie.

Then, her first heartbreak arrived, initially so painful she thought about nothing else for weeks, carrying around the wrenching loss of a beautiful, delicate archaeology student who had come home to wait tables for the summer in the same Mexican restaurant where she worked all through high school serving plates of warm sopapillas. Months after their breakup, he drove back to visit her during fall vacation, parking his beater in her parents' driveway, long fingers combing through his well-picked Afro.

"Flan." He pronounced it like the Mexican dessert, their own little joke, as he grabbed her into an awkward hug.

She hadn't planned this reaction but, standing there barefoot on her porch, she said, "You shouldn't have come." Because as she'd seen him walk across the lawn, Flannery realized she'd already worked through the pain, discarded it or sealed it off like an oil well whose gush was over. Love, like all wounds, healed easily, she realized. Nothing was really at stake—and not because she thought her life would be short, cut off by the genetic disease that stalked her childhood, but because she somehow felt assured of her invincibility, every new survival another testament to it.

Their parents had encouraged this way of thinking, hadn't they? Hadn't her father told the girls they would be all right? That they had nothing to worry about? Which was why Flannery had been startled by her father's words when she called in tears to tell Papa what she'd witnessed at Quack's.

"I know."

She stopped sniffling. A darker foreboding replaced the tears, which had been made up mostly of fear because part of Flannery had expected her father, with all his stubbornness, to tell her, "No way, José." She thought he would say, "Don't cry. Tough cookies don't cry." But instead, the words that traveled through the phone were, "I hoped I'd be long gone before this happened."

"But, Papa. I thought we didn't inherit the gene. I thought . . ."

"Who told you that?" As he spoke, she imagined him standing in the hallway, crouched over the old beige landline telephone still perched on the hutch, a halo of family photographs above his head. "I never said that."

". . . I assumed . . ." Flannery let her voice trail off, confronted by her own lie.

If she'd really assumed that, then why, in graduate school, had she submitted to a neurological exam and psychological screening before letting a nurse draw two vials of blood, one for the genetic test and one for research? They'd required that Flan bring someone with her when she came for the results, so she told Santiago they were going to the clinic to find out if she was pregnant (and, as far as she knew, he still thought that). At the time, Flannery toyed with the idea that if she came out looking pale, ghastly, he would not think she'd received an HD gene's death sentence but the opposite. The life sentence of motherhood.

In the tiny office, a genetic counselor had showed her the two printouts, one at a time. The first allele: normal. And then, the second allele: normal. Flannery was confused by this way of doing it. Of using suspense. A game show where the alleles were doors behind which the prizes and punishments of inheritance lay in wait.

Returning to the clinic lobby, she'd seen Santiago before he saw her. He was engrossed in a midday talk show, legs tightly crossed, one knee resting on top of the other. Watching him, Flannery felt a wave of guilt for dragging him along, for trying to pretend that she wasn't in this thing alone.

"False alarm."

Santiago neither smiled nor frowned in response to the news. "Let me buy you a beer before I head back to the office." It was the summer between semesters, and she was crashing at his place in Boston while he interned as a grunt on a project with a Dutch architect.

They boarded the number 62 bus as it looped from the North End, with its redbrick and Italian restaurants, back through downtown. Santiago didn't ask why she was so quiet or badger her to reveal what was wrong. Loyalty and lack of judgment: these were the qualities they cultivated in each other then. The stops and starts of the bus jarred them back and forth, their shoulders bumping against each other. The woman across the aisle read something called *The Book of Tofu* as Flan watched historical graveyards flitter by, the pub where you could drink a Sam Adams while looking at his grave marker across the street. Flannery didn't really believe in an afterlife, but she couldn't help think how much better it would be to be buried out here, where American revolutionaries were buried. The dead were not hidden away, but slept among life, Bostonians walking past them on their way to work, right in the thick of things.

A fifty-fifty chance. It was almost too neat, too tidy. Of course the test was negative. Of course she was free of the gene. She was invincible. The fact that Flannery didn't possess the mutation had no effect on Molly's chances one way or the other—Flannery knew enough about genetics to know that. The disease was maddeningly random in who it chose, but Flannery couldn't escape the feeling that her own thick skin, her own ability to heal, was somehow connected to the outcome of the test. That she had sucked up all that was strong and, in doing so, stolen her future from Molly, the family's delicate, rose-cheeked China doll.

On the phone with her father, Flannery began to understand that it might have been the other way around. Their parents never told Molly to be a tough cookie. They indulged and protected her and stroked her hair at night because they already knew. Molly didn't get Huntington's because she was weaker; maybe she was just treated that way because she had Huntington's.

At that moment, Flannery didn't think to ask how her father had known. Or why he'd never said anything before. "Maybe I'm wrong. I was jet-lagged and exhausted. Maybe it's nothing."

"No."

The word was like a hard flick to her sternum. "But Molly never wanted to get tested." Flannery didn't know why she said this, why this mattered. The tests only revealed what was already there.

"Expect erratic behavior," he told her. "Don't indulge it. You'll need to take her to the specialist as soon as possible because they have new drugs to slow the progression."

"But, Papa, she doesn't seem to realize yet."

"Oh." There was a pause. "The worst isn't knowing what is going to happen to them, Flan; the worst is knowing that they know what will happen."

There was another silence, and in that space flashed images of her mother, face resigned as fifteen-year-old Flannery changed her adult diaper, gently wiping and wiping until her mother shook. And Papa breaking his wrist—how it just hung limp like a sleeve—trying to lift her mother from bed because, even near the end, he refused to hire help or put her in a home.

"You have to drive down from Abilene." Flannery would only be here for a few months. She had a job in Nigeria. She had a life there.

"I can't," said her father, in a whisper that sounded very old. "I'm in the middle of something. . . ." Papa spent his spare time writing literary westerns about assholes and tough guys. Once, after another rejection from a New York publishing house, Flannery asked why he never wrote anything based more on his own experiences. "Because I write about lives I never had, lived by men I could never be."

"It's not like she doesn't have a husband," said Flannery eventually, as if they were discussing a problem with a logical solution. "Brandon will be great."

"Absolutely. Of course."

They talked a while longer about nothing, then said good-bye and hung up as though having come to some satisfactory agreement about the sale of a used car, a lemon. Flannery walked to the bathroom and dry-heaved into the toilet.

Flan was not thinking about that phone conversation when Molly and Brandon picked her up at her run-down apartment complex on their way to Alyce's ranch for the homecoming party. No, she would not think about it. She would not search for signs of disease in her sister's movements as Molly jumped out of the car to let Flannery sit in the passenger seat, a rule the sisters had come up with years ago so neither would ever feel like a third wheel.

Instead, Flannery leaned back against the headrest and imagined Kunle, who would be riding a *danfo* at that very moment, crowded four to a seat in the rickety van painted with maxims like "Protected by the Blood" or "No Food for Lazy Man," hurtling down the lawless, crumbling highway toward Lagos and his visa interview at the U.S. Consulate later that week. Kunle hated traveling. He usually chose a seat by the window if he could get it and, when it was his turn to lean back in the seat (it was too crowded for everyone to do so at one time), took his handkerchief and spread it over the lower half of his face, as if that could protect him from the dust and car exhaust and odor of close bodies.

"You're quiet," said Molly from the backseat as they drove out of town on a well-maintained highway where the traffic laws were posted and clear.

Why not say it aloud? "I wish Kunle were here." While she was allowed to roam the globe, he was still a prisoner to his country.

"They'll give your boy the visa. Why wouldn't they?" Brandon tapped her lightly with one hand, the other gripping the steering wheel. She saw him glance in the rearview mirror at Molly, smile their private smile.

Flannery didn't feel like telling them about how few Nigerians made it past the consular officer sitting on the other side of the desk, attempting to judge whether each applicant could be trusted to return home. "Yeah." She sighed. "Why wouldn't they?"

They should have applied for a fiancé visa, she thought. Those visas took months longer, but there was a better chance for approval. Of course, though she would never admit it to Kunle, this way of doing things was a win-win. If he didn't get the visa, people would understand why she had to go back so soon.

There was a saying in Nigerian pidgin: "Body no be firewood," meaning that a body is not meant to be put through all the searing pains and horrors of this life. But when she'd first heard Kunle use the phrase, she'd thought he was talking about romantic sparks, the burn of physical attraction. Love turning your body into sticks of firewood. Flannery told herself she would not forget what it was like waking to the call to prayer each morning, dawn light illuminating a tree of egrets standing sentinel at the edge of the campus pond. She would not forget the burn of her body when she woke in his arms.

Eventually the car drove over a cattle guard, a metal roadrunner soldered onto the open gate, before continuing for what seemed like forever down a curving caliche road. They parked adjacent to a white ranch house. Before Flannery opened the car door, Molly popped her head over the seat, kissing her on the cheek. "You're home." Then, Brandon wrapped his arms awkwardly around them both, kissing the opposite cheek until even Flannery's face betrayed a small smile.

ALYCE

lannery's boyfriend is coming to visit."

Molly announced this abruptly to the people sitting closest to her at the picnic table, including Alyce, who dipped tostada chips into habañero and mango salsa and drank a strong margarita from a plastic cup, letting the sweat bead on her forehead and neck. Even in the shade of the oak tree, languid afternoon turning to dusk, the summer Texas heat was brutal. Alyce turned toward Flannery, her best friend, but was not particularly surprised, merely raising an eyebrow at her to say: *Well, tell us about it, by all means.*

"He's applying for a tourist visa," Flannery said, shaking her head. She seemed withdrawn, and Molly, fingers fluttering nervously in the air, was in a state Alyce could only describe as forcibly cheerful.

"Then, they're going to buy a house down the street and stay forever," said Molly, sweetly, jokingly, sporting red rectangular glasses and a black T-shirt. "Even if I have to keep them tied up in the basement." She was trying to be funny, but there was a tenor of desperation in her voice. It was no secret that Molly was unusually attached to her older sister, which was why she'd ended up at Marsh for college, becoming part of their coterie despite being two years younger, even marrying Brandon, who at this particular moment announced, "And then we can barbecue every Sunday and finally start drinking martinis and sleeping with each other's wives."

"Finally," said Santiago, swirling goopy queso with a spoon. The whole spread disgusted Alyce, who let the flies land on her untouched plate without bothering to shoo them away.

"Glad you guys have it all worked out," said Flannery, sitting bronze cast beneath the sun's rays as they sliced through tree branches, her brown hair and the freckles covering her body adding to a sepia effect. Alyce let her head loll onto Flannery's shoulder as two vultures glided on wind currents far above them, and she tried to feel happy that Flan was home.

The party was made up of old friends, mostly from their college days, many of whom Alyce didn't really see on a regular basis anymore. Kids. Work. Life. Breath.

Steven and his girlfriend, Lou, walked over to the picnic table, and Alyce stood to make room for them, gathering up dirty napkins so they wouldn't blow across the yard and lodge among the dense patch of cedars lining the fence.

"You started gardening." Steven pointed to the small eight-by-four raised bed.

"Harry's idea." Everything was Harry's idea, she almost said. Alyce felt like an outside observer watching people she knew, in that way you know familiar television characters, on an old Zenith. Why was she required to respond? How was it they didn't realize she wasn't one of them anymore?

"Just say no to chemical fertilizers."

"I'm glad you brought that up," responded Harry from across the table. "I actually invited you all out here so you could each take a dump in our compost pile." A whoop came from the porch as someone turned up Michael Jackson's "Billie Jean" on the stereo.

"You should put up a fence to keep out armadillos. They like to eat roots."

"I found an old book in the ranch house that claims armadillos taste like sea turtles," said Harry, eyebrow raised.

"Let's trust the literature."

Alyce had known Steven for as long as she'd known her husband. Steven had been Harry's roommate freshman year and later lived with all of them at Dryden House, the dumpy, ramshackle clapboard perennially rented to upperclassmen on one of the muddled but tree-lined streets bordering Marsh College. After graduation, Steven had been recruited into the vast and ambiguous Dallas consulting industry, the lucrative late-1990s catchall for aimless humanities majors with good grades, but he was laid off after the tech bubble. He'd used his small savings to buy a piece of land near the Austin airport that he named Heavy Metal Farm. Now he raised chickens and grew heirloom tomatoes and other organics ("consulting for the soul") to sell at the farmers' markets, which had become popular since locavores had infested the city. But with the recession, even the fat of the land had gone anorexic. The last time they'd spoken, he'd told Alyce he wasn't sure the farm would last through next year.

Steven turned to her. "Snow White, why are you wearing a jacket? It's scorching," he said. Hair black as ebony, skin white as snow, lips red as blood. Barely five feet tall, Alyce kept her black hair tied in a ponytail these days; she hated the way blue veins had begun to show, a vampiric map, betrayed by her translucent skin.

Alyce looked down at the worn leather blazer she wore over a T-shirt and mismatched cotton pants. "It's part of my ensemble." But really she imagined the sting of the sun like a whip.

"My woman runs cold," said Harry, coming to her rescue as usual. "Her internal thermometer is one of our age's great scientific mysteries."

Beers were wrenched out of ice. Silverware clattered. People hugged Flannery and complimented Alyce and Harry on the food, though Harry had done it all—prepping the house, manning the grill, breaking up fights between the kids—because she was so exhausted. Flannery leaned into Alyce's ear at one point, asking, "Everything okay?" Flannery's homecoming was the only reason Alyce didn't feign illness and just disappear back inside the house.

Alyce tensed, willing herself to act normal and say something, anything. "Steven, aren't you going to tell everyone the real news?" she asked, because she'd been surprised when Lou called her out of the blue two weeks ago, wondering if she had time to make a wedding shawl ("Silk?" "No," Lou had said, "White chenille with eyelash lace. You know. Like yours. Well, not exactly like yours.").

Now Alyce sat still, the attention of her friends successfully deflected.

"Yeah, sure," said Steven, looking at Lou, who absentmindedly picked globs of paint from her cutoff jeans. "I'm in the market for some groomsmen and was wondering if you all knew any good ones."

Soon, everyone huddled around the table, giving their congratulations, jockeying for information. "When? Why now? Is Maya excited?" Steven and Lou had been living together for years. Their daughter, Maya, was almost four years old.

"Instead of groomsmen," said Lou, turning her head so that one long feather earring brushed her right shoulder, "I was thinking of having y'all come down the aisle with Steven in a dancing procession. You know, like the Baraat in Indian weddings?"

"With the Cherokee Nation smoke-signaling Pachelbel's Canon," said Santiago, grinning. Alyce watched late-afternoon light dapple his arm as he reached for one of the napkins stacked beneath a rock. Thin and fine-boned, Santiago had begun shaving his head three years ago when he could no longer disguise his sharply receding hairline.

Some people laughed at Santi, others turned to chat again in pairs and threesomes. They passed around plates of shish kebabs and German potato salad and chunks of crusty bread. They refilled their drinks. Alyce tried to remember what it had felt like when she'd loved these people more than anything.

Watermelon was the only perfect fruit.

Cool and wet. Sweet but not so sweet one felt sick after eating it. The Christmas contrast of the green of the skin and the red of the flesh. In grade school, Alyce and her best friend, Jessica, carried a small watermelon as "provisions" when exploring the back alleys of their Phoenix suburb. Afterward, they would each hold a piece daintily by the rind while red juice dripped stickily down their mouths and chins, pushing tiny black seeds around with their tongues.

But chopping a whole watermelon was a bitch, and there in the kitchen that afternoon, during Flannery's homecoming party at Roadrunner Ranch, she had to press the dullish blade from both ends before the bulging middle finally cracked open. She held up the knife and imagined bringing it down, carving herself into pieces instead. Releasing the pressure to coordinate her limbs as one cohesive body.

Slicing the fruit into smaller and smaller chunks, she watched a pair of finches through the refractive bottles lining the windowsill. The birds at the feeder had recently exchanged their winter camo for summertime, yellow-feathered bellies, and the color caught her eye, jarring and garish. (Her brain automatically calculated the dye combination it would take to re-create.) The feeder was already there when they'd moved in, and Harry kept it filled it with seeds from the feed store off the highway. Now, one pair had built a nest beneath the overhang of the porch, balancing their home precariously atop a rafter.

When Alyce was growing up, her whole family had been so obsessed with birds that being sent into the wild with a pair of binoculars and a laminated identification guide was a rite of passage for every twelve-year-old in the Buckle clan. Letters and, later, e-mails always began with a list of recent sightings ("WOW: A pair of painted buntings made three appearances at the pecan tree feeder last week!!! We're also happy to announce that Ruth is pregnant."); vacations were planned around at least one reported nest of a rare or striking species. Alyce almost fell to her death at age ten when her father encouraged her to climb "higher, sweetie, higher" up a rock embankment where a great blue heron had supposedly laid eggs.

Out the window, the ranch finches were uncharacteristically calm considering all the activity: Steven and Lou trying to dance the tango in the grass, three steps in one direction, dramatic head turns, three steps back; the clank of metal echoing across the yard indicating Brandon and Molly were in the process of losing a game of horseshoes to Harry's cousin and his boyfriend; and the kids, her own two boys and Steven and Lou's little girl, crushing and crowding into the oversized blue-and-green hammock Alyce's parents had brought from Mexico a few years ago as a Christmas present for Harry, who, along with the other guests, was not in immediate view—perhaps off on a walk, she thought. Clouds hung bored in the sky.

Alyce used to adore parties, with this group of friends in particular, but really any sort of party. At one time she thought herself a natural hostess who crackled to life when there were other people drinking, pairing off to gossip, sneaking cigarettes out of view of their partners. Unlike marriage or parenthood, hosting allowed her to dip in and out of various currents, no obligation—the spotlight of attention dispersed through the group like light through a prism. But in time Alyce saw this for what it was, too. Just a party. As transitory and insubstantial as bird-watching. A way to pass the time. Drinks emptied and refilled. Dishes dirtied and then cleaned, dirtied again. Stories told, retold, forgotten. Did you hear the Flaming Lips are playing at Stubb's? Have you read the story in the latest *New Yorker*? How about them Cowboys? Nothing that she'd hoped would fix her—love, motherhood, art—ever had. It was enough to make you want to curl up in bed and go to sleep and never wake up.

But Alyce couldn't hide in the kitchen forever. Sliding the perfectly sliced pieces of the paragon fruit onto a platter, Alyce noticed a walking stick insect lying still along the white door frame, trying unsuccessfully to blend in with the wall. For the creature's sake, Alyce looked away and, in the way all of them had learned to do in one way or another, pretended not to see it.

Just before sunset, Harry was corralling everyone in order to usher them to the small cliff that rose from the other side of the creek. Alyce took him aside, sitting him down gently on the porch next to their sons, who were eating more watermelon, faces a smear of pink. Their boys were both good eaters and Ian, the youngest, liked to give people names based on food. Usually, Harry was "strawberry pancakes" and Alyce "fried eggs." At the moment, she felt her yolky goo leaking like an open wound.

"Harry, do you mind if I stay here? I'm just not up to it. I'm sorry."

Her husband pursed his lips. She could see him trying not to snap at her.

Taking a deep breath, Alyce shook her head to indicate that she was just being silly. She forced herself to stand. "If we're quiet, we might see deer."

"You've been saying that since we moved here," Jake whispered.

Alyce reached out to feather his hair but instead let her hand just float there above his head like a halo.

The group had to walk back up the road, traverse the low-water crossing over the creek, and then cut through a field to approach the cliff from the side where the cedar was penetrable. Behind the house the mowed lawn devolved into wildflowers, big blooming prickly pears and waist-high grasses shimmying in the hot wind. In the meadow was a dried-up pond and oaks and cedars that didn't quite obscure the view of a development springing up along the ridge.

Alyce made a mental list of things on the ranch that could kill you: rattlesnakes, water moccasins, a fall from the cliff into a half-empty creek. These thoughts were shiny coins in her pocket.

As they walked along with the group, Harry handed Alyce a bota full of wine, and she slugged from it, a red trickle running down her chin. It tasted a little like watermelon, she thought. As she handed it back, their hands brushed, and he smiled in the intimate way that made his cheeks crinkle, a smile that said: *Here, this is my gift to you. This party, this artistic fellowship we didn't really need.* He seemed to be smiling the words: *I'm here because I love you.* She tried to remember what it felt like to be in love with him, but she couldn't even recall how long they'd been married. Ten years? Eleven? Her mind felt fuzzy. An image flashed: of Harry, in college, too self-conscious to dance at parties usually, and Alyce plying him with shots and beers, saying, "Bottoms up, baby. Bottoms up," until he allowed himself to be dragged to the makeshift dance floor, Harry grooving slowly like an uncoordinated facsimile of an underground jazzman as he twirled Alyce in circles, she dancing fast and frenetic, tossing her hair, releasing everything into the music.

When the group of partygoers reached the edge of the cliff, choked as it was with trees and shrubbery, they pushed through until arriving at a rock shelf with a view of the falling sun and the house in the distance and the creek trickling below. In front of her, Santiago sat on the furthermost crag, legs dangling off the ledge, prompting Brandon to say, "That's a long way to tumble."

Santiago didn't turn around, and Brandon seemed to realize his mistake, grimacing in self-reproach. Nobody said anything, but Alyce immediately thought of the day two years ago when Santiago's father drove off a highway bridge and into a gorge after stopping by his son's house for a cup of coffee. Father and son had talked about the Rangers' collapse and scooped sugar into their mugs. Alyce was still trying to wrap her mind around it. One moment you're drinking a cup of coffee with your son like it's nothing and the next you roar out of life. She felt an enticing warmth spread through her torso just thinking about it. She walked forward to sit beside Santi along the ledge.

Behind them, Molly stumbled. "Mexican jumping rocks." Her voice slurred a little.

"Molly is traaaashed," Alyce said under her breath to Santi.

The bright laughing chatter of the group behind them meant there wouldn't be much chance of seeing deer or even the turkey vultures that nested along the cliff.

"She's only had one beer, I've been watching," said Santiago, staring straight ahead into the ravine. The skin on his face looked tight, and his eyes—were they watering? "She's her mother's daughter."

Alyce didn't understand what he was talking about at first. Santiago shrugged. "Think, Alyce. Her movements . . ."

Stumbling, slurred speech, hands fluttering like paper birds. Maybe. But Molly was young. So much younger than Molly and Flan's mother had been. The odd warmth Alyce felt grew stronger until her face burned red, her pulse quickening. She looked at Flannery, hunching in front of a small cedar, silent, contained, distant.

Alyce stood and left Santiago on his ledge perch, not yet consciously wondering why he, of all people, was the source of this information but sensing it had something to do with her best friend. She walked behind Flan, encircling her in a loose embrace; they leaned against each other like two poles of a teepee. Alyce shielded her face from the sun as it shone directly parallel to them, stalled on the horizon. Years ago, when Flan's mother was dying, Alyce used to drive Flan, and later Flan and Molly, to Abilene on the weekends, but they'd be so hungover that they'd sleep in and not leave until late in the day, Alyce forced to drive west for hours into the setting sun, squinting hard as Flannery popped cassettes into the tape deck with her foot, long straight hair whipping out the window.

Alyce could learn this news about Molly, and yet her own limbs still moved in the same way, her own breath still traveled in and out of her lungs, air molecules trembling invisibly. Alyce did feel something new, though. Curiosity? She felt legitimately interested in what was going on around her for the first time all day, all month.

"There it goes," said Molly loudly, the sun finally disappearing below the tree line, leaving a spray of lavender clouds behind. It was a nice sunset, though not particularly spectacular, not especially noteworthy as far as sunsets go. Alyce's chest surged with a rare crest of feeling anyway. It was the cliff and the wine and the sunset, but mostly it was the thought of endings glittering strangely in her mind's eye: Santiago's father's, Molly's. Part of the feeling was sadness, a feeling her depression had made as rare as all the other emotions.

As everyone began to switch on the flashlights Harry had handed out before they left, Alyce looked down at her sons lying on the ground, a pin cactus inches from their heads. She saw their spiky elbows and chins; she willed herself to say what a mother would say: "Time to go."

Jake, her firstborn, her lovely little dark-eyed Jake, stared back at her from his position splayed on the ground. Then he said, "I don't think I'm up to it. I'm sorry."

The others laughed at the serious, melodramatic little boy, but Alyce's heart melted into the hammock of her belly. He was mimicking her. Getting attention for being drained and useless and spent. Jake's eyes were muddy pools into which Alyce could not see. Brown, watery pits. And their defiance frightened her.

As everyone else turned to leave, panic rose in the back of Alyce's throat and she rummaged in her bag, hands shaking, for the bottle of Xanax she stashed there for emergencies. The world was making it clearer and clearer: Alyce was bringing her family down.

The old friends walked back to the house in silence, flashlights leading the way, the crunch of footsteps on gravel. At the low-water crossing, droves of fireflies blinked along the creek banks like the pinpricks of light you see after staring too long at the sun.

"Name the speaker," said Brandon as he lugged Alyce's youngest son on his shoulders. "The difference between the right word and the almost right word is the difference between lightning and the lightning bug."

"Andre the Giant," said Lou, sarcastically.

"Mark Twain," three people corrected in unison. Alyce imagined Lou rolling her eyes in the dark, annoyed by this game in which her fiancé and his friends flexed their collected, trivial knowledge.

As everyone dropped into their cars, which then began to trek back down the road toward the gate and the highway and the city, Alyce had a fleeting thought that the line of vehicles looked like a funeral procession following a hearse. Headlights twinkled and dipped.

He washed; she dried. Out the window, the moon shone a circle onto the lawn. The boys were asleep on bunk beds in the room they shared.

Alyce didn't tell her husband about Molly. Not because of any conscious decision to keep it from him, but because it no longer crossed her mind to include him in her inner life. But Alyce did have the sick urge to humiliate Harry by asking him the big questions. Are you happy? Do you think we're decent parents? Are you still in love with me? Instead, she asked, "Remember when Steven said getting married while gay marriage is illegal in Texas was like joining a country club that excludes blacks?"

"People change." Harry kissed her on the shoulder. He was never critical of their friends, never critical of their marriage. He was able to say: Maybe you need help. But never, if you don't get help, I'm leaving. Never, this isn't working. Or let's separate for a while. Because Harry seemed to think you didn't change your life or make dramatic choices so much as, like an infielder, react to what came at you and make the best of it.

And by now he and Alyce were so immersed in the chill he probably no longer noticed it. No longer expected her to respond to his touch like she had before. To fling her arms around his neck and say, "Wear me." To Harry, they weren't unhappy; they were just busy. They had settled down.

"The boys behaved themselves," he said. "Didn't nag for attention." The ceramic plates he was stacking banged on the shelf, and the noise grated.

"Maybe we shouldn't have had them when we did. They'll be so much older than everyone else's kids. Who will they have to play with?"

"Maya. All the other children in the world." Harry hung the dish towel on the handle of the stove, stretching and running his hands through brown hair streaked with white. His T-shirt read LA CRIATURA GORE BAR and was faded and tight around the stomach because he rarely bought new clothes. "I'm going to take a shower."

Alyce didn't watch him leave but listened to his steps, his hand on the bathroom door, the sound of the electric toothbrush. She swallowed the word she wanted to say: *good-bye*.

With the light on above the kitchen sink, Alyce could barely see past her reflection in the window to the yard outside. She imagined walking out the door and sinking into the hammock from Mexico, rocking back and forth in the blue-and-green threads, like waves, like the sea. She imagined floating off, maybe toward her expat parents, who lived in a cold stone house in Guanajuato now and almost never came to visit. She remembered, as a girl, wrapping herself in the long strands of her mother's nearly waist-length hair, and her mother's voice, rarely aimed at her, Alyce, but rather at her parents' many friends, always coming and going, her mother's laugh tinkling in response to things Alyce only partly understood.

She didn't remember her mother reading books to her as a child, but she remembered her telling stories, trying to get Alyce to fall asleep so she could return to the living room where the rest of the adults drank and played records. She remembered her mother telling her the story of the honey-diviner, a bird whose call sounded like "Quick! Quick! Honey! Quick!" and how, if you followed it, the bird would lead you to a stash of honey in a tree nearby. But if you didn't share some of the honey with the bird, it plotted revenge. The next time it came calling—"Quick! Quick! Honey! Quick!"—it led you to another hole, and inside wouldn't be honey but a poisonous snake.

As Alyce finally began to drift off, her mother would lie on the bed and say, "Now my turn," motioning for Alyce to scratch or rub her back. Her mother always wanted something in return, her share of the honey.

Alyce retreated to the studio. Designing Lou's wedding shawl would be another welcome distraction from Alyce's official project, a series of small tapestries reinterpreting William Morris's famous designs, *Woodpeckers in an Orange Tree* and *Strawberry Thief.* Alyce still hadn't chosen between the sketches scattered across her workbench or measured out the yarns on her warping board to create the order for slaying them on the loom.

Since moving out to Roadrunner Ranch for the Women's League fellowship, Alyce found herself uninspired by the weaving project that had landed her the gig. The compositions were so mannered and aristocratic and restrained and, well, lovely, too. But she just didn't particularly feel like making them new. She could put an updated spin on them, abstracting the trees, turning the birds into mechanical, steampunk versions of the real thing—but why? Who really cared? The only reason she'd applied for and accepted the fellowship was because they needed money. They would live free for a year and make extra cash renting out their house in town. Though he didn't say it aloud, Alyce knew Harry, with his and Santi's firm on shaky ground, wished she'd return to engineering, to being the practical one with the steady income and good benefits.

The only tapestry actually hanging in Alyce's studio was a square weave of gray thread, hand-spun from the fur of her first long-haired cat, slowly unraveling on the top and bottom because she never tied it off. It looked like a rain cloud. She'd made the cloth after reading about a weaver goddess riding a shaft of moonlight to impress an official in the Tang dynasty. The goddess shows the man her robe. It is not made with needle or thread. It is perfect. It is where the phrase "a goddess's robe is seamless" comes from, and Alyce wove her own seamless piece of art as a reminder: she, Alyce, was not a goddess. She was only human.

She went into the kitchen to make coffee, scooping two tablespoons from the tin in the freezer and dumping the grounds into the tiny white coffeemaker. She filled the reservoir with water and turned it to brew. Coffee. She thought of Santi's father. One moment you're drinking coffee out of an ironic Hello Kitty mug with your son, shaking your head over the Rangers' disappointing season, and the next you're flying high over a river gorge. Life spilled out of you.

There were so many moments when Alyce was outwardly affectionate toward her young sons but inwardly thinking how easy it would be to walk away. Not easy. But not as difficult as it should be.

As the coffee brewed and gurgled, Alyce's mind turned back to the image of Molly on the cliff, and she probed it again. Some sadness, yes, she'd discovered that already, but the sadness seemed almost perfunctory, like an old habit. Resentment, maybe, because this news would bring to the others a renewed, though tragic, appreciation of life, but not to Alyce. Finally, she realized what the feeling was: part of her, though she didn't yet know how big a part, wanted Molly's future. To have a disease that was real and physical, a comprehensible reason for the pain and an eventual end to it.

Alyce was a mother, and Molly was not. But kids were resilient. They survived all kinds of tragedies, and Harry was a really good father. Surely she was dragging them down. Was it a terrible cliché to think they'd be better off without her? Her son's voice echoed in her head, parroting her, *I'm not up to it. I'm sorry.* She knew she couldn't make it as an engineer anymore, not realistically, not after all these years, and with her gone, at least there would be life insurance. Alyce would be better as a story told before bed, as a memory glossed over with time, than as a real-life, breathing, flawed mother. She thought of how Santiago took his small inheritance and bought his dream: an urban fire station. What could she leave her own sons so that they might be better off than before?

In her studio, surrounded by blurry sketches that made her want to scream, all manner of small beasts toiling away outside the window, Alyce decided to throw away her William Morris drawings.

This decision did not feel like a resolution exactly, but choosing to eat celery rather than rocks. No matter how exhausting it might be, if Alyce truly planned to bow out, she must make something beautiful to leave behind. Something for her sons to remember her by.

She sighed, searching her reserves for a vestige of energy.

Alyce tossed the dozens of filled pages into a far corner of the room. Slowly, splaying her fingers along the thick paper like making a bed, she spread out a new ream over the table, picked up a stub of charcoal with the other hand. She would draw whatever came to mind.

And so she started.

First: a long picnic table. Similar to the one just outside the ranch house where everyone at the party had sat earlier, waving beer bottles and skewers of dead animal. Next, she sketched heads. Ovals and eyes, the arch of a neck. Individual faces took shape and distinguished themselves.

The words echoed in her head: *Quick! Quick! Honey! Quick!* As she drew, she wondered if she could imbue the paper and charcoal with stories from her past. Alyce did not remember what it felt like to be happy exactly—that was like trying to feel the high of a drug the morning after, on the comedown. But if not the precise feeling, she could remember the scenes, the settings, the people involved. She could leave her sons the outlines of what it meant to be happy and hope that they would fill them in. If she could weave a piece of cloth capable of encapsulating the few, small things that had been good about her life, she could give it to Jake and Ian. Then, she might be free to go.

Could she make her sons understand how difficult her childhood had been? That, shy and awkward even in high school, she hadn't felt at home until she'd arrived at Marsh College? Nestled in a historic neighborhood on the outskirts of Austin, with all the streets named after famous authors like Chaucer and Wordsworth and

Dryden, Marsh was known as a nerd school. Some of her classmates used to buy the bumper stickers in the campus bookstore that read I GO TO MARSH, I MUST BE SMART and put them upside down on their cars. The small university had such a big endowment from its founder, who'd hoped to create a Harvard of the South, that if you were book-smart and ambitious, the admissions committee didn't care where you came from or how much money your parents had socked away in a college fund, which was good, because Alyce's folks weren't big savers. And at Marsh, for the first time in her life, she was one of the pretty girls, one of the people others wanted to be friends with. They were her people, her new, real family.

Flannery: Small eyes with long lashes and long straight hair spreading out behind her like a train. Freckles everywhere, splattering off her face and into the air. Chin cocked, confident. Alyce drew her in the cubist style because Flan had the beauty only other women truly appreciate—the tall, dramatic angularity of a runway model, sharp jaw and shoulders, jutting collarbone. She was the first person Alyce met at college, her freshman roommate, and they used to share Flan's upper bunk during thunderstorms.

Santiago: Head bare and shiny. She drew him long and thin and towering, not because he was really so tall but because everything about his body shouted vertical line. Corduroy jacket. An architect like her husband, Santiago had that same pretentious look. She thought he enjoyed designing homes because he was always in search of one—he never brought the same woman around twice.

Steven: Obscured by beard and caveman hair and overalls. Now a self-professed laborer of the land, Steven had for a few years been clean-cut, a doll in khaki slacks. The one to laugh first and longest. She found his new Santa Claus appearance more appropriate, like he'd finally relaxed into himself.

Lou: Her body and hair, both full of puffed-up, wavy lines. Alyce drew her with a garland of flowers on the crown of her head. Her mouth was partway open—she might say anything, she didn't give a shit. Lou hadn't gone to college with them. She was new, though she'd been around for years. She was not yet Steven's wife, but to them she already was.

Brandon: All wild, dark, Middle Eastern hair. He looked like electricity. Alyce drew him gazing at Molly, his hand on her neck. Inseparable. Nothing in his luminous appearance gave away his long days sitting behind microscopes and beakers.

Molly: Heart-shaped face, heart-shaped torso, heart-shaped mouth. Enormous, watery eyes that seemed to look out on everything with equanimity. Her hands placed together in her lap. Dying.

Alyce and Molly had never been close, and Alyce wondered now if part of that might have been because they were too much alike. They were the ones who'd been most conventional, married their college beaus, ended up with mortgages. Molly had always seemed a little dull to Alyce and, frankly, she'd wondered why everyone else was so enamored with her when she followed Flannery to Marsh.

Now she could see Molly's glow. It was the closest thing Alyce had felt to a sexual attraction in years, maybe longer. It was as though death were a powdery film on Molly's skin that might somehow rub off onto her own.

As she continued to draw, hand moving in broad strokes, she imagined her sons' faces behind the paper, absorbing her story into their developing brains.

It was in college when I began to suspect that traces of what would eventually happen to us already ran faintly through every single moment of life. Like quartz through a bed of rock.

Brandon was driving the Honey Wagon, whistling, gliding us through the humid streets away from Dryden House and toward the Jumbodome, the Monster Truck Rally, and first destination of the night.

We were young and afraid of nothing except being left behind. We did drugs out of boredom. We did them for fun. But we also did them for reasons I didn't entirely understand at the time. We did them to be momentarily released from the irony that lay like a waxy film on our skin and tongues and eyeballs. We did them so for once we could say exactly what we meant.

We held hands in a chain, blocking the rednecks and shitkickers behind us, as we walked up the concrete ramp to our seats, where we squirmed and twirled and laughed at everything. We passed red plastic cups of beer from hand to hand. We swayed and yelled as Gravedigger or Eradicator or Carolina Crusher revved their neon-painted engines and jumped and smashed cars in the dirt arena below, our depth perception so altered it seemed the big-wheeled trucks were mere inches from busting into the stands and making a bloody mess of the chanting crowd.

Flannery crawled onto Santiago's lap, and they began to kiss, their lips sucking at each other as he put his hand up her floral skirt and along her dimpled thigh. I leaned over and grabbed her shoulder, yelling into her ear, "I love you guys together!," and so they pulled me from my seat and onto Santiago's lap, too, all hugging and giggling and making fools of ourselves. I did love them.

Steven was gone for what seemed like ages, finally returning with more beers and a dazed group of children. We ran fingers through their hair and said we would never have kids ourselves, but that they seemed all right. They could be our little brothers and sisters and come home with us, we said. We gave them handfuls of popcorn and sips of our beer. At some point, they wandered away.

Molly kept trying to get everyone to look at the lights overhead, and we rolled our eyes at her for being such a trip novice, but she was right. The lights blinked and expanded above us like little broken pieces of firmament.

We left and threaded through the parking lot looking for the Honey Wagon. It was dark. Your father kept saying, "It's gone. I knew it would be gone. I knew it. It's gone. It's really gone." I kissed him hard. We found the Honey Wagon and jumped in through the windows.

We went to a park, the one across from the roundabout with the big triple-layered fountain in the middle. It was after hours, and the water wasn't running. Brandon gripped a pink glow stick between his teeth and held Molly's hand, leading her toward the playground, where they disappeared for a while inside an orange metal teepee. By the time they came back, we were all lying on the grass and on each other's bellies and chests and arms, looking up at the stars. Mooning, we liked to call it. Thinking about how great we would become and about all the ways we were going to change the world.

I began to pluck long blades of the Saint Augustine grass and twist them into a tight braid. I said I was weaving our destinies together. Or maybe it was a nest for the bird I felt I had become, each in-breath thrusting me higher.

Molly sank down beside Flannery and looked up to where we all were looking, into the black and bright. She reached over and took the woven braid of grass from my outstretched palm.

This is where we belong, Molly said. We will stay like this forever, she said.

Yes, we said.

Yeah.

Sure.

Why not?

Yes.

Yes.

HARRY

*L*ying in the dark, his hand straying into the cool, empty side of the bed next to him, Harry struggled to let go of the buzzing thoughts that threatened to keep him awake for hours. It had always been hard for him to fall asleep alone. Harry sneezed. And then he sneezed again.

Harry's mother had taught him two things about the Finnish culture from which they were allegedly descended: the equivalent for "cheers" was "*kippis*," and sneezing twice in a row was bad luck (although three times in a row was good luck in love; four times, good luck in money—which gave one a sense of how the Finns prioritized things).

Harry's mother had been an earnest and active member of the Daughters of the American Revolution, having traced her lineage back to John Morton, signer of the Declaration of Independence on behalf of Pennsylvania and grandson of Finnish settler Martti Marttinen, who'd changed his name to Morton upon arrival in the New World. Despite generations of distance between Harry and his immigrant ancestor—not to mention abiding disdain for his mother's involvement in the uppity DAR—as a young boy, Harry was obsessed by the idea of this faraway place called Finland. Craggy shorelines. Brutal winters. The shape of the country like a hook cast down in water grasping for the lip of a fish. The way the word *Helsinki* dropped and caught in his throat.

In fifth grade, Harry wrote a report on the Finnish sauna, trying to reconcile the images in library books (small outdoor structures made up of wooden slats and rustic *kiua*s and masonry containing heated black stones) with the sauna his oil executive father sometimes went to with clients in the fancy gym in Houston, marbled and filled with small fountains shooting fast spits of water from the mouths of ridiculous statues.

Harry remembered a stern private-school teacher looking over his shoulder, probably suspecting the boy's interest in Finnish saunas was more about seeing nude people than cultural heritage. And even now, Harry himself didn't entirely understand that youthful fascination with Finland, Scandinavia, cold northern Europe. Maybe it was the exotic images of ice and evergreen forests and wolves, so different from the muggy Gulf Coast of his hometown. Maybe because he imagined it as the land of winter behind the wardrobe in the C. S. Lewis books he read growing up—snow glittering like crystals, sleds filled with furs, animals dancing around fires. Maybe it was an innate, genetic attraction to women possessing the contrast of black hair with translucent skin—after all, wasn't that what first drew him to Alyce? Hair as dark as night, skin as white as snow.

In fact, the first thing Harry ever said to her was, "In Finland, that means good luck in love," after she'd sneezed a second time. She was sitting at a nearby table in the dining hall, and he leaned back in his chair to say it. He was lying, of course, but she was lovely and he didn't want to start things off on the wrong foot. Alyce was sitting with Flannery, whom he only knew then as the loud, chain-smoking freshman who lived below him. He figured they drank so much because they'd both been good girls back home.

Alyce always claimed not to recall this first encounter, but Harry remembered it explicitly because he'd done something appallingly out of character: he spoke first. Harry rarely engaged strangers, not because he was a social pariah who froze in the presence of the fairer sex, but because he wasn't good at beginnings. He'd never had to be. He'd gone to the same private school his entire life with the children of his parents' social circle. He didn't remember meeting his childhood friends for the first time. He didn't even remember meeting the girls who would become his teenage girlfriends, his first crushes and heartbreakers. In his world, one's attention just sort of circled the same group of people, alighting on a different face every few months, like a dragonfly jumping from one plant to the next around the same small pond.

In fact, Harry was relieved when his parents bribed him to stay in Texas and go to their alma mater, Marsh College, offering him a Toyota Corolla and a debt-free college experience. He'd applied to many of the same far-flung schools as his buddies—Emory, Williams, Brown—because he felt he should want to leave the state. But he didn't, really. He rationalized staying in Texas by telling himself he would need all the financial help he could get if he was going to make it as an architect. Harry had known since he was ten exactly what he meant to do with his life. It didn't matter that he'd never been especially gifted artistically. He was smart and worked harder than everyone else and assumed that would be enough.

He also justified going to Marsh by promising himself he would study abroad. In Finland, naturally. Then, he heard Alyce sneeze twice, and looked at her sitting primly in the metal chair, her legs in a pretzel like a dancer: pale skin, black slacks, a gray V-neck T-shirt.

Harry never went to Finland. He told his parents the architecture program was too demanding for him to take a semester off, which was partly true. But he was also afraid if he left, Alyce might find someone else to spend her time with. They were living at Dryden House that year. They were nesting.

He and Alyce weren't officially a couple back then, but they had frequent midnight powwows in his bedroom (Harry was the only one with his own room, for which he paid more rent). He explored her body like it was the map of a northern coastline. The dip of her lower back. The low-lying stomach bookended by hip bones, sharp ledges where his fingers got caught up. The elbow. The clavicle. The shoulder blade. She was small and sharp and he claimed her bit by bit.

In those days, Alyce was indefatigable. One project after another: painting the kitchen yellow, inviting a group of Bengali students over to teach her how to make curries, waking Harry up in the middle of the night to say, "I've found us cheap flights to Vegas. Let's go there tomorrow and win a million bucks. Give me your credit card." When did she find time to study? He wasn't sure. Sometimes she scared him, but it was a good kind of scary. Like a roller coaster you know must have been tested but still seemed like it might go off the rails at any moment.

One day he came home to find dozens of copper birds strung from the ceiling above his bed, small as fists with sharp beaks and tails. The light glanced off the metal as they turned faintly on paperclip hangers. They were crude cutouts made with an inexact tool, but there were so many, floating up there all together, that they blurred into something stunning. They flocked. Like a family. Like they belonged together. He lay back on the bed, looked up at them, and thought, *Finland. Alyce. Finland. Alyce. Family.*

MOLLY

*T*wo months ago, when her husband, Brandon, had announced that he'd finagled an arrangement where Flannery could rent lab space at the Climate Institute after her research post closed down, Molly had bought a bottle of prosecco on her way home and proceeded to dance around the house to the Bangles. When they were kids, *All Over the Place* was the cassette her sister used to play again and again on the pink jam box they shared: *I'm going down to Liverpool to do nothing. All the days of my life* . . .

However, Flannery's move to Austin was not turning out like Molly had hoped. As she complained to Brandon one night during the *Dumpster Divers* reality television show they were addicted to watching before bed, Flannery was being distant and weird. Supposedly spending all her time with friends from grad school. Refusing Molly's offer of the irises—as though everyone didn't already know she was going to stay. As though, even if she did end up with Kunle, they wouldn't ultimately prefer to live here.

Molly tried to be a good sport. You still might move back to Nigeria? For good? Really? Flannery liked to remind her that she had already lived there for five years, but Molly still had a hard time processing this fact. Flannery's life in West Africa may have seemed to last years to Flannery, but for Molly it had passed by overnight.

Molly had pictured herself and her sister eating lunch together every day at one of the cheap Thai buffets along the Drag west of campus. In the weeks since she'd been back, however, Flannery worked straight through lunch, only agreeing to meet Molly once at the institute's basement cafeteria where they shoveled down spinach macaroni and cheese off thick plates still warm from the dishwasher, brown cafeteria trays stacked up on an extra chair. The windowless room was depressing, the floor coated in yellowed linoleum.

After minutes filled with the sound of their chewing, Flannery said, "I burned you some of my Fela Kuti bootlegs. You liked that last Afrobeat stuff I sent, right?"

Molly nodded.

"When you and Brandon visit Nigeria, Kunle and I will take you to the Shrine."

"I thought Kunle was a snake-charming, Bible-beating, Holy Roller who rejected indigenous religion?"

"Africa Shrine," Flannery said. "Where Fela played before he died. Where Femi plays now." She told Molly she had never seen anything like the shows there. Dozens of the best musicians in West Africa playing until dawn. Dancers covered in paint and intricate beads and towering headdresses, shaking their hips and shoulders so fast to the music they become a blur of color and texture. They stomped and sang and glistened in the lights. Then, like a heartbeat, they just stopped.

Molly nodded, reaching for Flannery's plate to stack on top of her own. "Maybe we'll make it someday." But she didn't mean it.

After dumping their dishes into the plastic tub, she turned to her sister. "I was thinking we could drive to Abilene next weekend and visit Papa." Molly didn't need to say out loud that it was the thirteenth anniversary of their mother's death.

Flannery stopped walking, her expression flat, unreadable. "No," she said, as if it had been a random question: Do you have to go to the bathroom? Do you have change for a five?

Molly opened her mouth but nothing came out. What was going on with her sister?

Flannery began to walk away, but before she opened the door to the stairwell, she turned to Molly, who thought she caught a flash of contrition cross her sister's face. "I talked to Papa the other day, and I think he wants to be alone this time. We'll go up another weekend."

Molly nodded. She didn't understand, but she didn't press. She deferred to Flannery. She had no desire to go home without her sister.

Waiting for the elevator, Molly remembered when they were kids, returning from Rose Park on their bikes, swooping into the driveway one after the other to see Papa packing the trunk of the car. He was wearing white sneakers rather than cowboy boots. His out-of-town driving sneakers.

"We leave in fifteen. Grab your jackets. There's going to be a cold snap."

Snaps on pants, snapdragons in a pot on the porch, snapping her fingers, which she couldn't do nearly as well as her sister. Cold snap. Molly had rushed to get her blue jean jacket covered in NASA patches, not because she understood the temperature was dropping, but because they were going to Dallas again and she wanted some sort of protection from whatever it was that made everything different there: Uncomfortable. Awkward. Sad.

Even then, Molly knew her family vacations were not like most people's. Since she could remember, when her family left town, they traveled in her parents' used Pontiac three hours east on winding Interstate 20 to the sprawling white medical center in Dallas.

Did she understand back then why her mother had to go there? Molly remembered asking her father about it once—early on, probably, though she couldn't be sure. Why? Why were they always going to the hospital?

Papa had told her, "To be witness. To be witnesses to each other's lives."

It was one of her father's many cryptic statements from which she and Flannery were forced to piece together their own meanings.

Their mother said very little on these road trips, napping and looking out the window, flipping through a plant catalog, while their father played cassettes of Larry Blevins's *Town and Country Christmas Bluegrass Jamboree*. "Where should we stop for lunch, y'all?" their father, trying to be upbeat, would ask after they'd gone through Fort Worth and were approaching Arlington, the Ferris wheels, roller coasters, and water slides of the big amusement parks taunting them on both sides of the highway. Molly pressed her forehead against the window glass until the passing structures were nothing but blurs of primary colors.

"Dairy Queen," said Flannery, flipping her long braid back and forth. Flannery always knew what she wanted. They weren't normally allowed fast food, but Flannery's tone of voice implied they deserved it, that this was a shitty way to have to spend a weekend, and that lunch at Dairy Queen was the least their parents could do.

Molly didn't remember their mother smiling on these trips. Was it because she knew her smile was slowly becoming a grimace? That gummy snarl that eventually claimed all the faces of people with Huntington's? Or was there just no reason to?

Back then, when they were alone, Molly begged Flan to retell stories of their mother before. Her older sister claimed their mother used to star in plays at the local theater, which was in the round with big gray bleacher seats. This impressed Molly because Abilene was her whole world, and this theater, where they sometimes went to see pageants and musicals at Christmas, the apex of local sophistication and grandeur. Flannery claimed their mother had sometimes taken them along to a performance, allowing them to sit backstage and eat sandwiches, and that the other actors doted on them, teaching them dance steps and painting their faces with stage makeup. Molly had no memory of these events, but she believed Flan. She believed her sister that the golden age of their family had passed.

When Molly opened the door to her house, a stucco bungalow covered by a tin roof that didn't match but was too expensive to replace, Brandon was sitting at the kitchen table looking intently into a dirt-encrusted cardboard box as the last of dusk light filtered through the miniblinds.

"What do you suppose this is?" he asked, holding up an oddly shaped orange-and-green gourdlike vegetable from the box.

"Magic pumpkin." She dropped her keys into the ceramic bowl on top of the antique secretary desk.

He tilted his head, considering it. "Sautéing it in butter wouldn't cook off any of the enchantment?"

"No way."

When they received their weekly box of produce from Steven's farm—Molly and Brandon owned a small community share—it was often filled with exotic varieties of vegetables that they didn't really know what to do with.

"Smothering it in cheese might not hurt, either."

Santiago was coming to dinner, and they had a few hours to kill before Lucinda Williams took the stage at La Zona Rosa. As Brandon washed and put away the vegetables, Molly slipped down into the rocking chair. Out the window, she watched her neighbor across the street soap up his sedan, suds overflowing out of the driveway and running down the street, a green garden hose snaked around his feet. There was a sycamore tree in the man's front yard that reminded Molly of her childhood home, of the two sycamores she and Flannery used to climb until eventually both trees died from a fungal disease when she was a freshman in high school, leaving the front yard empty and burdened with sun. When they'd climbed the trees as girls, she on one and Flan on the other, they pretended to be inside fairy castles, draping gold blankets over themselves like capes and smuggling their parents' champagne flutes to use as wands. Flannery always wanted to be the good fairy, forcing Molly to be the bad one. Secretly, Molly hadn't minded. It gave her an excuse to say mean things to her sister.

The rocking chair creaked beneath her. It was old, an antique from Molly's mother's childhood. Most of Molly and Brandon's furniture was hand-me-down. After her mother died, Papa hadn't wanted to be constantly confronted with so many memories in his Abilene house. Flannery lived out of a backpack and took nothing, so Molly and Brandon commandeered the round table and matching chairs carved with images of wind and clouds, the rocking chair, the secretary desk, the coatrack made of brass.

On their walls were framed album covers from their combined collection of LPs and EPs: the Japanese version of "The Wind Cries Mary," the Andy Warhol Velvet Underground with the peel-away banana sticker, Chuck Berry's first pressing of "Roll Over Beethoven." She and Brandon wanted kids someday, but they were also reluctant to leave behind their present life, free of the clutter of plastic toys, the distraction of whining voices.

This was Molly's most peaceful time of the day, when she read trash magazines surrounded by the smells and noises of Brandon in the kitchen. They liked to be silent, together. Not the sad, empty silence of elderly couples in Denny's restaurants, but a silence that pulsed. Washing dishes, reading in bed, sleepily getting dressed in the morning, all of it like a graceful dance that buoyed her up.

When she and Brandon talked, it was because they had a story to tell. As a joke, once, Brandon's friends had given him business cards with the title "Oral Historian" written in dramatic calligraphy across the front. From the beginning, perhaps intuiting that they'd be together for the long haul, Brandon and Molly parceled out their stories in bits and pieces, dragging some of them out for years, like a television series of their past. One of Molly's favorites was the story of how her husband became interested in cooking.

Growing up in a traditional family, Brandon had cooked only when absolutely necessary—when his mother was sick and his sisters too young to be trusted with the stovetop burners. Then, one summer, he received a small study-abroad grant from the Kurdish American League to visit the region in Iraqi Kurdistan where his parents came from and to live with a host family outside a village near the Iranian border. His parents had no desire to return themselves; their extended family was dead or had left during the Barzani revolts in the late 1970s.

After a hike to the Bekhal waterfall one afternoon, Brandon returned to the stone house to find his host mother crying as she chopped aubergines into cubes on her worktable. He fell in beside her, slicing green peppers and courgettes and potatoes, knowing better than to ask. The lives of Kurdish people were full of things to cry about. Maybe she cried for when they were mustard gassed or for when they were massacred and forced from their homes. Maybe it was for the sons killed or the daughters raped and disappeared. The knife was awkward in Brandon's hand, and his vegetable pieces all funky and oblong.

But as Brandon and his host mother stewed vegetables and kneaded dough, and as the light slanted through the rough, rectangular windows turning everything a pale gold, the woman, her long hair tied back in a flowery scarf, began to sing. Brandon tapped a rhythm out with his foot. They said nothing. By the time the *tapsi* was prepared and the family, which normally annoyed Brandon with their loud talk and strange manners, was sitting around the table sopping up the spicy sauce with thick slices of naan, his host mother was smiling again. So was he.

Sitting in the rocking chair as Brandon prepared food in the other room, Molly thought about calling her aunt in Dallas to see if she would drive down to Abilene next weekend and meet her at her father's house. But no. Flannery said they should wait, and so they would. Molly hadn't talked to her aunt in ages, anyway: since their mother's death that side of the family had fallen off, like a old neighborhood for which you feel affection but never have a reason to visit anymore.

When they were growing up, their aunt's was where they stayed each time they went to the medical center in Dallas, and Molly remembered the brick ranch house as dark and musty with flowery upholstery and thick drapes. There was an antique clock that struck the hour and half hour, and blue-and-white china plates that hung on the wall above the mantel.

Only as an adult did Molly begin to wonder how their aunt must have felt being the one who didn't get Huntington's. The one who made the painful decision not to have children and yet, as it turned out, never even possessed the defective gene. Did she ever wish she could trade places with her sister? Did she ever wish she could take Molly's and Flannery's uncertain DNA strands and fill them with her own purer transcription? Of course, back then, their aunt would not have known for sure she couldn't get the disease; she was still at risk.

Like their mother, their aunt was a gardener, although she loved different plants. When the weather was nice, the two women would drink what their aunt called Texas Snake Bites, cider mixed with Lone Star beer, and sit in the garden having long, meandering conversations.

"She was charming; she knew her bourbon," she remembered their aunt saying to their mother once, "or at least she liked her bourbon." But Molly could no longer imagine who they might have been talking about. She remembered a tiny orange tree and fierce-looking tiger orchids. She remembered the smell of Chantilly.

"Your winter sweet is blooming nicely," her mother said. "And your . . . and your . . . what is it called, the yellow blossoms . . ."

"You know what it's called," Flannery sneered suddenly from where they played a board game on the patio table, no longer pretending she too wasn't eavesdropping. "You grew up here!"

At the time Molly didn't share Flannery's frustration over their mother's many memory lapses and confusions. She was still too young to fully understand what it meant to watch the woman who brought her into the world fade and disappear.

"Yes," said their mother. "It's on the tip of my tongue."

Molly squinted but couldn't see anything on her mother's tongue.

"Witch hazel," said their aunt, nonchalantly. "I thought there wasn't enough rain for it this fall, but it's done better than I expected."

Their aunt was also a big fan of the Dallas Cowboys, "America's Team," and so sometimes, while their parents were at the medical center, Molly and Flannery found themselves sitting around listlessly watching football with her in the afternoons. If Molly let her hand fall between the sofa cushions, she could feel the sudden hardness of the handgun her aunt kept hidden there "for protection." During one trip their aunt was hoarse from a case of laryngitis, and so she poked Molly or Flannery whenever she wanted them to yell in her stead. Flannery was poked whenever the Cowboys did well, and she yelled: "Woohoo! That's what I'm talking about!" Molly was poked whenever they had been wronged by the refs or by the other team: "Bullshit. Total bullshit."

After changing into shorts, Molly rolled out her yoga mat on the back porch, its wooden overhang festooned with white Christmas lights they kept up all yearlong.

Then, she did vinyasas, swiftly moving from one pose to the next in a flow: Mountain, Plank, Up Dog, Down Dog, Warrior Two, Reverse Warrior, Triangle. Tuladandasana, Bakasana, Salamba Sirsasana. She was obsessed with balance poses. She told herself she did them over and over because she enjoyed them, not out of any desire to mask or correct her physical faults, her increasing clumsiness. She lifted her right leg gingerly from behind as her chest dipped toward the ground, her torso twisting to one side as she splayed her left hand to the sky, gaze following. She teetered but managed to stay in it. She breathed deeply. Half-Moon.

As Molly held a tripod headstand, the blood flushing her brain, an image from her honeymoon in Mexico City floated to the surface. She and Brandon were on their way back from a show at the Palacio de Bellas Artes, holding hands and walking through the long underground subway tunnels toward the train that would return them to Brandon's boyhood friend's apartment, where they would sleep with windows open to a breeze, listening to the sound of the vendors yelling "Tamales, tamales tan ricos," and smelling the faint odor of marijuana plants on the balcony. But then, as they walked forward, the doors of a stopping subway train opened to literally hundreds of teenagers streaming forth in a wave, each holding in their arms the statue of a saint, some of them elaborately carved and enormously unwieldy, others unrecognizable blobs of wood. She and Brandon stood still as the crowd flowed past them in a rush; everything inside

Molly vibrated. She turned to look at her brand-new husband, his wild curls a halo around his head, and she grabbed him around the waist so that her arms too would be full.

Suddenly, images from the Mexico City train station still pulsing through her brain, Molly went light and toppled onto her yoga mat, bashing one shoulder on the way down. She moaned and tucked her knees to her chest. Back and forth, she rocked.

Santiago and Brandon were both alphas in the kitchen.

"I've just never seen polenta cooked this way in my entire life. That's all," Brandon was saying when Molly walked in after her shower. Brandon's nose crinkled like it did whenever he was concerned.

"Well, get ready for the next-level shit," said Santiago, wearing a white apron with the phrase WORLD'S NUMBER ONE GRANDMOTHER written in red cursive.

"One Strawberry Hill Boone's Farm and the latest Juggs says it collapses under that much moisture."

"You boys play nice," said Molly. Brandon walked over holding a wooden spoon, and she opened her mouth to the hot, steaming Swiss chard. "More serrano," she said.

Brandon was the chef of the marriage, but Molly was the one he turned to for spice consultations, claiming she had an unusually good palate for these things. She went along even while suspecting he'd invented this theory out of his Brandonian desire to include her. Molly was really only good at identifying songs on the radio, and the only two things she liked to do in the kitchen were to peel hard-boiled eggs and make guacamole. There was a special satisfaction when the shell of an egg came off in only two or three pieces, or when an avocado was sliced open to reveal the perfect chartreuse of ideal ripeness.

As the three of them sat at the table that barely fit into one corner of the kitchen, Brandon nodded as he took a bite of polenta, a movement that indicated, "not bad."

Santiago put a hand to his shaved head and looked up, something strange in the way he held his mouth. "I thought Flan was coming tonight."

"She canceled," said Molly, scraping butter-roasted "magic pumpkin" off her plate with the side of her fork. "Working late."

"She's meeting us at the show?"

"Nope." Molly looked back at her plate with the dusty rose on it, too self-absorbed with her own sibling resentments to notice that she wasn't the only one disappointed.

Recently Molly had gotten a ticket for reckless driving (she told the officer and her husband she'd been on the phone, though that wasn't true), and so Brandon did all the night driving now. He let Molly and Santi off at the entrance to the club.

The band began on time and played two hours of tragic bluesy rock and country. Molly liked La Zona Rosa because the dirty concrete floor sloped up from the stage, so even being short, she could find spots to see above the bobbing heads of those in front of her.

The front woman was no longer young and beautiful, yet she had that leather-and-zippers aura of eternal cool Molly wished for but knew she'd never possess. The crowd of shitkickers and hipsters and dirty old hippies swayed en masse; Brandon stood behind Molly with his arms around her waist, and they breathed and moved and sweated, a singular beast. Lou and Steven met them there, and they stood nearby drinking beer handed out by Santiago, who made trip after trip to the bar. Onstage, the singer made the word *righteously* sound like gritty exultation.

During the encore, Molly was on her way back from the bathroom, trying to find her friends in the crowd, when she started to get an un-settled, lurching sensation in her stomach—an anxious, shaky, heart-racing panic. The notes from the guitars onstage suddenly seemed stretched and off-key, grating. She put her hands over her ears.

She tried to take a few steps toward the middle of the room, her feet weaving in front of her, and then she stumbled. Her body was disobeying her. Like one of those dreams where your limbs are seemingly trapped in a vat of honey. Some men standing nearby laughed and rolled their eyes: "Hold your liquor, sugartits."

The stage lights pulsed and circled up above like halos. Molly crouched to escape them, focusing her gaze on the littered ground, the crunched plastic cups and wadded-up credit card receipts—confusing clues to a mystery she couldn't solve, couldn't quite wrap her head around. *Good night! Thank you for coming, Austin! I love you!* What was she doing here? Who had brought her to this place, this experience? What was making everything spin? The crowd moved past Molly on their way to the doors, jolting and rattling her, a few of them looking down with abstract concern. She noticed a pair of lanky calves and Converse tennis shoes—Flannery. Flannery was here to save her. But when she tilted her head upward Molly saw orange curly hair and a teenager's face. The stranger slid away into the crowd.

Headaches. Mood-shifting night panics. Tics and twitches and restless limbs. Problems driving and counting money. Loss of bal-ance. They were all symptoms she knew intimately from growing up, from watching her mother die, and yet she'd managed to ignore and deny them all. And Flannery. The way her sister had avoided Molly ever since getting back to Austin. Had it been so clear? No. No. No.

She closed her eyes, remembering the time in Dallas when she and her sister weren't led into the usual waiting room at the hospital with the green plastic furniture that had accrued the waxy film of hours and hours of their boredom. The time they were allowed to go back with their mother into a different space where nurses and technicians bustled around little stations labeling vials and marking paperwork, one of them stopping to take a white medical glove and blow it up like a balloon, handing it to them with a bright smile.

Flannery tossed it to Molly with a look that said, *I'm too old for such a transparent bribe.* But did Molly truly understand it that way at the time? She remembered holding the glove balloon with the tips of her fingers as if it were a crystal ball.

The nurse was preparing to take a blood sample from both girls.

"Why, Papa?" asked Flannery, her hands pushed deep into her corduroy pants pockets.

"To help Mom," said their father.

"But we're not sick like she is."

"Of course not. That's why she needs your help."

Later, days after the Lucinda Williams concert, Molly would do her own research. She would discover that this was before the International Huntington's Association had drawn up guidelines to limit testing of those under age eighteen. In fact, it was not for a test of HD at all, but merely to add their blood samples to a project on the cusp of finding and labeling the exact gene that could eventually predict the future of someone at risk. But already they were close, already they could make a pretty good guess based on the number of CAG repeats on a certain gene. And that, as it turned out, was good enough in Molly's case.

The nurse bound her arm and readied the syringe.

"It will only hurt for a second."

Finally, the group found her sitting on the concrete of the club floor. They surrounded and protected her, Lou's and Steven's and everybody's arms reaching out like one big net. She looked into their eyes—Brandon, Santiago—and did not see surprise; what she saw looked more like grief and desperation. She could almost detect the invisible film that rippled between the land of the living and of the dying. She felt ice-cold, as though she were trapped inside a deep, black hole while warm, living people tried to drag her out, to reanimate her.

But it was too late. As they pulled her up, she let her body go limp. Molly was dying, and it seemed she was the last to know.

SANTIAGO

Santiago looked at the window, fogged and beaded from the humidifier, still expelling its slow mist of water particles up into the room like one long winter breath.

"Since when do you fly-fish?" asked Flannery. It was morning. They were lying on the floor in sleeping bags.

"My grandmother made them." Santiago followed her gaze to the case he'd hung on the wall a few days ago: dozens of colorful and elaborate flies, tiny and twisted with little trails of fuzz and string.

"They're funny looking," she said.

After the scene at the concert, Santiago had left Molly and Brandon at their car, Molly folding herself into the passenger seat in silence. He had taken a cab to the Climate Institute and dragged Flannery back with him to the fire station, where they drank whiskey and paced the floors, crying and wringing their hands. He talked some about his own father's death, but mostly Flannery rambled, spewing bits of stories he had to work to put together, about how her grandfather, her mother's father, had been misdiagnosed with Alzheimer's at first but his chorea was so bad her grandmother moved him out of town. To hide him. How at his memorial service, Flannery saw two of his sisters shaking with chorea, all blamed on strokes or something else. All ashamed to face the truth: they had passed down a death sentence to their children.

Later, when he was too drunk to drive her home, she agreed to stay the night if she could camp out downstairs. He gave her his blue insulated sleeping bag and then zipped himself up next to her in a cotton army-green one that had belonged to his father, enduring the hard floor in the sick hope she would turn to him for comfort. But Flannery slept spiraled in on herself the whole night.

"That one's called a 'Royal Coachman.' That one's a 'Peeper Popper,'" he said, pointing at the flies displayed on the wall. "A 'Humpy Blue.' And . . . I can't remember the rest."

"You never told me your grandmother was into fly-fishing." She lifted her other hand into the air and pretended to catch the flits of sunlight that played on the wall.

"My grandfather fished; Abuela tied the flies. He didn't have the patience for it." Santiago's father had rarely taken him to visit his abuelos at their small tin house on a Rio Grande tributary, where they fished and raised corn and cleaned houses at some of the ranches nearby, his grandmother frying up pieces of queso blanco at the stove and singing songs in Spanish that Santiago never had the chance to learn. Recently Santiago had begun to understand that his father was probably more embarrassed than he was estranged from his parents, critical of their dirt floors and lack of interest in learning English. His father thought their way of life, their poverty, might be contagious.

"Your grandparents were a team," said Flannery, smiling. He loved her smile, how it transformed her otherwise ovoid face, giving it dips and contours, a more complicated landscape. This morning they didn't talk about Molly or his father, but he wanted to turn to her and say, *Well, you must stay now. How could you go back to Africa after this?*

"Would you ever tie flies?" Santiago asked instead, rubbing her shoulder with his thumb.

"Give me a lover and a fulcrum, and I'll change the world."

"Lever." He turned inside his sleeping bag to look at her. She faced the ceiling and her small pink ears stuck out from her hair like seashells.

"Lover. Lover. Lover." Her tone was hard when she said it. Each word a whip.

He thought of the first time he'd laid eyes on her. It was the Night of Decadence party, a bacchanal thrown by Marsh students each Halloween and known for its scandalously clad, drug-fueled dancing—an interesting proposition at a nerdy little engineering school. He saw her walking across the quad wearing nothing but a G-string and pasties, having convinced an art student to paint the rest of her body the white and black of a Halloween skeleton, so naked even her bones showed. She set up a row of tequila shots on the picnic table outside and said to Santiago, "I don't know about you. You look like trouble."

In their sleeping bags on the floor of his fire station, Santiago could feel Flannery becoming restless. He said, "It's Saturday morning. Let's troll the garage sales."

"I have to go into the lab."

"Later."

She bit her lip and shrugged. Santiago took it for "yes."

By midmorning it was already hot, and Santi felt his underarms dampen, which he hated.

"A widow," Flannery said, holding up a plastic turkey. "He was a hunter. He died years ago, but she's only now able to finally let go of all his stuff."

"She cried into his clothes every night, but not because he was dead," Santiago added, "but because she'd cheated on him for years with his twin brother and the guilt was too much." There were stacks of T-shirts and cargo shorts and flip-flops on a foldout table, science fiction paperbacks in a box beneath it. Incense and potpourri and accordion fans.

"And she couldn't tell anyone because the twin brother was the married mayor of Georgetown, until he left his wife of twenty years—not for her but for a stripper from the Yellow Rose . . ."

". . . who was working her way through medical school . . ." He turned an orange-and-yellow hurricane lamp over in his hands.

During the summer when Flannery crashed with him in Boston, they'd spent weekends crisscrossing Cambridge looking for yard sales, stopping to flip through yellowed paperbacks, scratchy LPs, army fatigues, heavy clip-on earrings, scented Christmas candles, teacups with saucers, dolls with missing limbs, rusted wrenches, and big bunches of cloth flowers faded from too many days in the sun. Life's detritus. They did the commuter crossword puzzle over day-old glazed donuts, Flannery sometimes pretending she didn't know as many answers as she did just so Santiago wouldn't become too frustrated and throw the newspaper across the room. He knew this, and he let her. Three down: Sound that might indicate hunger. Mew. Thirty across: One with a growing hobby. Gentleman farmer. When the summer was gone, so was she, not even a mixed tape for him in the mail.

"Santi," said Flannery. "It's boiling. One more, then let's head back." They were only on their second yard. With the app Santiago downloaded on his phone, it was much easier to find garage sales than it had been back in Boston, when they'd had to go aimlessly looking for homemade signs with Marks-A-Lot arrows.

"Right," he said. Flannery always did what she wanted. "We should get something for Molly." He looked around. "What about one of those weird, splotchy hand-dyed scarves?"

"Is she still obsessed with scarves?" asked Flannery, grinning at him. "I love that you remembered that." She leaned over and kissed him on the cheek.

Instinctively, Santiago reached a hand into the messenger bag he always carried slung across his chest, feeling into its depths for the 1950s Dashboard Jesus and fingering the plastic hand that shaped a blessing. He and Flannery had bought it at a garage sale almost a decade ago now. Santiago didn't really believe in these things, in relics or even in Jesus, but something had moved him to slip it into the bag that morning, a talisman in his quest to woo Flannery back, a link to their past before Nigeria got in the way. His father may have let the good life pass him by, but Santiago was not going to make that mistake.

Now was the time, he thought. "Flannery, look at me." He spun her around to face him. "You need to call your sister." Part of him felt guilty for using Molly in this way, but he believed what he said was also true. Molly needed Flannery; she always had.

She shrugged him off.

"You will regret it, Flan, if you don't do this right. I'm telling you."

She looked up at him, and her eyes were slightly altered, moony. He was getting through. Then, she half smiled and looked off in that way that meant the conversation was over.

There was so much else he wanted to say. He wanted to remind her about how she'd stayed up all night at Dryden House helping him finish a model due the next day, sitting hip to hip with him at the kitchen table, painstakingly gluing into position bits of balsa wood and Styrofoam as well as the little plastic figures he included to give it scale, like a bride and groom atop the cake; and how when her mother died senior year, for two weeks straight he played nothing but My Bloody Valentine—her favorite sad band—during his 2:00 A.M.–6:00 A.M. shift at the college radio station. It had been his way of holding her hand, of serenading her grief.

As they walked along, side by side, together, handling goods they had no intention of buying, Flannery turned to Santiago, her mouth open as though she were releasing moths captured inside. Then, he heard the Pavement riff he'd programmed into her cell phone the night before. Her phone was ringing.

She closed her mouth and looked down at the screen. "It's Kunle." And the moment was broken.

As Flannery walked away, Santiago tried not to notice how her face relaxed when she talked to this stranger on the other side of the world. He took his own phone out of his pocket. He had one missed call from a client, Kit Hobbes. As he hit the dial button, Santiago allowed himself to hope the man was calling to give them the green light on his vacation home design job.

"Kit Hobbes. How's life treating you?" he said, trying to sound like Harry did when he talked to big clients. Santi wandered back to his car and got inside to escape the ambient chatter of other yard-sale shoppers.

"A problem, I'm afraid." Kit was an executive for a local organic juice company. Harry and Santi had designed a small home for him that cantilevered over Town Lake on the still-underdeveloped east side of town. They'd only landed the job in the first place because Kit knew Harry's parents in Houston, but he liked their design and promised them more work.

Listening, Santiago cringed as Kit explained that all the insanely expensive copper fittings on the deck were starting to green and crumble at lake level. "I just don't think it's going to hold up."

The copper had been Santiago's idea—it looked stunning—and

that meant he'd have to be the one to fix it, too. It would take a bite out of their account to coat everything with iron.

"I'll have our contractor out there to look at it next week." Santiago tried not to let his voice tremble, to remember that he owned a design firm and knew what he was doing. "And while I have you on the phone, have you thought any more about the Marfa house addition? We have some time opening up and would love to get started."

"Look. You and Harry are great kids. Talented. But that's not going to happen," said Kit as Santiago's brain began to shut down, the voice on the phone sounding farther and farther away. "Our retirement took a hit in the market like everybody's. Maybe in a few years we'll revisit that project, okay?"

Santiago watched Flannery pace the side of the house, laughing and tossing her hair as she talked on the phone. The owners of the yard-sale house were parked in lawn chairs in the shade of the one pecan tree, staring at the customers as if they were thieves.

As he sat in the car, waiting for Flannery, his phone rang again, vibrating against his lap. It was Harry calling this time, probably to check up on things at "the office." Santiago didn't pick up the phone. Not because of the copper mishap—that wasn't good, but it wasn't the end of the world. But because Harry had spent months now working on Kit Hobbes's Marfa house, inspired by the Donald Judd boxes that dotted the West Texas desert. Santiago thought he'd sold Hobbes on the idea when they talked about it last winter, but they hadn't actually inked a deal, which was what Santiago had implied to Harry. Harry was always bringing in projects with his Houston connections, and Santiago had only wanted to do his part. To show that he could make business happen with his talent. Hadn't that always been the dream?

Maybe they could sell the design to someone else, he thought. Santiago watched as Flannery moved toward his car, her phone now hanging dead in her hand. But who else would want to buy the design for a two-room cube in the desert? With one hand, he reached across the car to open her door; with the other Santiago felt again for his plastic Jesus, praying for many things in the only way he knew how.

FLANNERY

When Kunle called her at the yard sale, Flannery felt relief. Anything to take her mind off Molly. Anything to bring back Nigeria.

"Did you get it?" she said before hello.

"Once again, robbed of the Nobel Prize by those bastards in Stockholm."

She snorted. "Did you get the tourist visa?"

"No."

Flannery sucked in her breath.

"They rescheduled the consulate interview for next week." He couldn't hide the disappointment in his voice. "Rotimi's kids are driving me mad—Prosper actually took a piss on me in the middle of the night, poor kid."

Kunle was staying with his brother's family in Lagos, where real estate prices were so high that Rotimi's family had to squeeze into a two-bedroom flat, which meant Kunle was sleeping on a king-size mattress with the children (Praise, Promise, Precious, and Prosper) while he waited for the visa interview. Unlike other megacities, Lagos didn't have satellite slums: the whole place was dilapidated and mired in extreme poverty—or at least that's what Flannery had read in *The New Yorker*. But living in Nigeria one eventually learned to make subtle distinctions between decrepitudes, to consider factors such as the density of trash along the road, how many people were asleep on benches among the market stalls, if any paint had been used on buildings. In areas of town that at first seemed indistinguishable from others, one began to intuit the presence of elite compounds and neighborhoods hidden behind locked gates and cinder-block walls spiked with broken glass.

"And you? How far?" Kunle asked in Nigerian slang. "Have they found your bike?"

"Ha. Even our police don't give a shit about a stolen bicycle in the hood."

"*Abeg*, move somewhere safer, baby."

Flannery's new apartment was a nondescript one-bedroom east of I-35. As much as she liked the idea of dirt-cheap rent and a quick bus commute to the Climate Institute, passing storefronts hawking bright pink piñatas and pulled pork sandwiches, she felt guilty living on the east side, another overeducated Caucasian bringing gentrification and an eventual hike in property taxes. But it was a good thing she'd taken the place—Kunle had a job teaching biology at a public university, but the government hadn't paid faculty salaries in months because of another budget shortfall.

"Your flat sounds like a dump," he continued, pressing the issue. She closed her eyes and tried to imagine him standing next to her in his blue soccer jersey and ironed khakis. "You haven't been there a month, and your bike's already been pinched. It suffers you more than Nigeria." He seemed to have forgotten she decided on a bike rather than the used hatchback she'd been eyeing (much harder to steal) because his father had come down with spinal meningitis, needing weeks of treatment in the hospital, which had siphoned both their savings.

"Technically, it was only the front wheel." There were bigger things to worry about than stolen bike parts. "So don't get a bee in your bonnet. Don't get your knickers in a bunch," she added, hoping to lighten the mood, to regain access to their intimate history whereby she mocked his Briticisms. Most Nigerian schools were taught in English, but an actual British accent was particularly prized, and for those not lucky enough to be "been to's"—people who had been abroad—it was enough to have what was called a LAFA, or Locally Acquired Foreign Accent.

Flannery had been surprised by how, as a white person, she was treated in many places in Nigeria, not reviled as a former oppressor but revered as a celebrity. There was a saying in Nigeria: "Clap like you would for a white." The first time Kunle walked with her through Agbono market at night, buying snacks wrapped in newspaper and passing towers of yam, tomato, T-shirts, and sandals illuminated by kerosene lamps and the occasional lightbulb strung along a wooden frame throwing shadows off the figures laughing and shopping on their way home from work, people began waving at them and shouting "*Oyinbo! Oyinbo!*" or "Mrs. White!" Being in Nigeria hadn't really taught Flan what it was like to be marginalized but, rather, what it was like to be famous, eliciting smiles and shouts with a mere word or touch of the hand. "I don't hate your company, anyway," Kunle had said in response to all the fuss. He liked to present compliments like this, using contradictory negation. "Cockroaches tend to go it alone, so when you see them circling something, you know it must really be good."

"Are you calling your people cockroaches?"

That evening, as they sat on wooden benches drinking bottles of Star, he became obsessed with comparing the color of their skin, placing his forearm beside hers and saying, "You're not really white. I'm not really black. But in relation to each other . . ." as well as making pronouncements like, "Sometimes I look at you and see a beautiful woman, and sometimes I see a slaveholder."

"Why do rich Nigerians put their money in America, but rich Americans don't put their money here?" he asked a different time, pointing to another in a long line of newspaper articles about a Nigerian politician purchasing a second home in Maryland.

"What about me? I buy beer here all the time."

Flannery now wondered if part of her ennui since returning to the States had to do with returning, not only to her sister's illness but also to the quotidian reality of being just one among millions. Nothing special.

"Flannery. You still there?" Kunle's voice sounded small and distant through the phone. "What's wrong? Gist with me."

Flannery stood in a stranger's yard looking at a table of someone else's castoffs, some other family's junk, and she didn't know how to begin to tell Kunle all that was really wrong. That her sister was dying and she wasn't. That she needed to do something for her but didn't know what. That Santiago, with his devotion and lack of judgment, sat in a car nearby looking at her with adoring eyes. That, despite the long hours spent at the lab, she wasn't close to having a proof of principle so that she could return home to him.

Flannery was using advanced computer modeling to predict whether various green barriers planted along the edge of the Sahara might delay or stop the desertification creeping into Nigeria. She was programming her own model, using the derivations her Nigerian lab group had come up with before the research post closed, but so far the results weren't significant enough to convince the National Science Foundation to fund her at the next level. They certainly weren't enough to keep Kunle's homeland from turning into dirt.

Kunle was no longer on the other end of the line. Another dropped international phone call. She clicked the piece of plastic shut in her hand. She looked up at the sky.

It took almost a week for Flannery to act on the sense of responsibility that, after the morning at the yard sale with Santiago, she was having a harder time ignoring. Steven and Lou were moving forward quickly with their wedding, and Flannery and Molly had been asked to help plan the bachelorette party. Flannery tightened the muscles in her abdomen and phoned her sister, offering to pick her up in Santiago's borrowed car. She would be a better caretaker, she told herself. She would rise to the occasion.

The local nonprofit CASITA, which worked to keep immigrant youths out of juvie or foster care and where Lou worked as director of special projects, was staging a fund-raising happy hour where Lou had asked them to meet her. The event was at the private library and grounds of Floyd Falcon, one of the wealthiest businessmen in the state's capital. Flannery had only heard about this place.

After being greeted at the gate by a smiling CASITA intern in a tweed skirt, they spent a few minutes meandering the collection, including the outdoor statuary, poached from all over the world. Falcon had strong ties to defense contractors.

"The owner calls this the Garden of Evil," said Molly, as she led Flannery past larger-than-life statues of Lenin and Saddam Hussein and a bust of Chairman Mao all tucked into perfectly landscaped foliage. "Look, there's Churchill over on the high ground."

And inside, in the library itself, the bounty was even stranger: first editions of Isaac Newton alongside Hitler's personal place settings; the first U.S. Census signed by Jefferson next to a miniature of the atomic bomb "Little Boy" signed by the pilot of the *Enola Gay*.

At one point, Molly turned her mouth to Flannery's ear and asked if everyone knew.

"Everyone?" asked Flannery, though she understood what Molly meant.

"Everyone coming to plan the bachelorette party." Molly was whispering, though there was nobody nearby.

Flannery nodded. Of course, by now everyone knew Molly was sick.

"Once the main business is done, make an excuse and get us out of here."

Flannery nodded but thought: so here it comes again, her role as protector of the ill and dying. To be with someone who had Huntington's was to be on display. As the symptoms became worse, the chorea and grimacing and flitting eyeballs would always create a scene. Always. Flannery remembered being at a baseball game once and her mother not returning from the bathroom. It was Flannery who noticed she'd been gone too long, and Flannery who was sent to find her, which she did: flailing about in frustration in front of a stern-looking cop one level below their seats. Flannery put her arms around her mother to calm her, her mother finally able to sputter, "He thinks I'm drunk." Flannery, not even bothering to address the policeman directly, looked in her mother's twitching face and said, "It's okay. He doesn't understand you're sick." As a teenager, Flannery found it hard not to care what people thought. She found it painful to ignore the world, suffocating to be so needed by her mother.

At the Falcon Library, she gravitated toward the row of death masks in the far corner beneath a shelf holding a hand-sewn first edition of *Don Quixote*. Flannery didn't recognize the subjects of three of the masks, all old men, but the fourth was obvious: Abraham Lincoln. She knew the molds were initially done in plaster, but she couldn't help imagine his stoic, puckered face being slowly coated in liquid bronze, as if to snuff out the last air in his presidential lungs.

"So what do you think?" whispered Lou later, having found Flannery and her sister in the Garden of Evil, putting an arm over the two women's shoulders, a glass of wine dangling from each hand.

"Wonderful in every way." Molly grabbed one of the sloshing glasses.

They found a bench in the garden and sat down. "Isn't there something creepy to fund-raising for troubled kids in such a lavishly fucked-up place?" asked Flannery.

"Yes."

"And shouldn't you be over there schmoozing with all those moneybags rather than discussing your bachelorette party with us?"

"Flan. The moneybags prefer to spend their time talking to each other in a setting that doesn't make them feel guilty about their own lives."

Flannery noticed some of Lou's friends waving from the back porch, making the international sign for "Anybody need another free drink?" before walking over. The three women wore flowery sundresses and various incarnations of what she and Molly used to call "Savior sandals." Like Lou, the three women were unshaven, bursts of black hair beneath their armpits like grass growing from the crack of a rock. It made Flan feel suburban and overly groomed.

They hugged Lou, who said, "You guys remember Flannery and Molly? Steven's friends from college." Flannery had actually complained to Molly earlier, saying they really should have been invited to the bachelor party. Molly told her to be grateful they were invited to anything at all.

Of course they remembered the two sisters. They asked how they were doing. Was Flannery enjoying being stateside? Was Molly . . . ? The conversation stuttered.

"Molly's been doing a lot of gardening." Flannery tried her best to fill the void. "She grows the most beautiful irises. Tell them."

"The irises bloomed months ago. They're dormant now."

From the opposite direction, Alyce arrived wearing loose, rumpled linen, bags and dark circles under her eyes. But Flannery didn't notice this at first, so relieved was she to have backup. Alyce had always been the one who knew how to deal with hard things. In college, she'd been the only one who didn't clam up and turn awkward when Flannery spoke about her mother.

"Sorry I'm late." Alyce shrugged, kissing Flannery and Molly on their foreheads before sitting down. "There was a triple hatchling homicide on our porch at the ranch this morning. The boys are in mourning—wearing black, building a memorial of leaves. The whole hog."

"Have you been inside the library yet?" asked Lou.

Alyce gazed at her hands; she didn't seem to be listening.

"To have your own personal librarian—that's what impresses me," said one of Lou's hippie friends.

"We could all chip in and share a librarian," said another, raising her eyebrows at the man, cute in a nerdy sort of way, strolling the garden, gesticulating wildly as he answered people's questions about the collection. "I could use some help with my . . . shelving."

Flannery noticed Molly's legs shaking a little. And were her cheeks redder than normal? "Let's get you into the shade. I think there's an umbrella in the car. I'll grab it."

Molly's smile was tight. "No, thanks."

The discussion about Lou's bachelorette party wasn't as long and drawn out as they'd feared. By now, these women had done this dozens of times and pretty much agreed: keep it cheap, keep it alcoholic, keep it party bus. If they ponied up for the psychedelic party bus, nobody would have to drive, and they could just barhop until it was time for karaoke.

"Shit," said Lou, standing up from the bench and giving a fake smile to a man in a blue-and-white-striped catastrophe from the J.Crew catalog. "My boss is waving me over to meet that crotchety bitch who always promises to give us money and never does. We're done, right?"

A waiter came around with a tray of raw tuna and cheese croquettes. Flannery started to reach for the food until she remembered that fish was supposed to increase chorea in HD patients. Wasn't it? Or was that just shellfish? And all Molly had had to drink this afternoon was wine, which wasn't good. "Can you bring my sister here some water? And do you have any fruit?"

The waiter, who looked about twelve, nodded.

"It's fine." Molly picked a croquette off the tray.

Flannery mouthed *fruit and water* before the penguin-suited waiter had time to make his escape.

"Don't Milky Way me. You have to take care of yourself," said Flannery, growing impatient. "Don't Milky Way me" was a phrase originating when their aunt offered Molly a Milky Way from a bag of leftover Halloween candy, and Molly lied, gushing and saying it was her favorite when, in fact, she hated them. For years afterward their aunt gave her a Milky Way each time they visited, Molly choking it down with a smile. "You have to stand up for your health. You have to be smart."

"Gosh, sis. That's always been my problem. Never was as smart as you."

Flannery looked to her best friend for some support, but Alyce remained on the bench, placid and half smiling. Lou's other friends were trying not to stare.

The waiter came back with a glass of water and a bowl of grapes, which Molly thanked him for before turning both upside down, emptying the water and grapes onto the grass.

Flannery sighed. "I have to get back to the lab. I'll drop you at home."

"Molly, I feel like having another glass of wine. Do you?" Alyce motioned to the stunned, fumbling waiter.

"In fact, I do." Molly looked at the ground. "Don't worry about me, big sister. I'll catch a ride with Snow White." She held up a hand, a half wave, a dismissal. Flannery nodded before walking back toward the library, with each step the feelings of love and protectiveness for her sister and best friend falling away until her entire body felt calm and numb. A knife slicing through air.

Her cell phone showed a voice mail from Santiago—no doubt calling to kvetch about the bachelor party powwow. They had always been on the same secret team when it came to their friends' weddings, drinking all the free liquor and then making behind-the-back jabs at the wasted money, the bourgeois traditions and sexist rituals. They'd thought they were too good—for what? To register at Macy's for Fiestaware? To grow up? But these days she couldn't help thinking about what it would be like to marry Kunle. To know they would have a future together. To be legitimized and respected by the world as two people with a future together.

Strolling back through the building, buzzed from wine on an empty stomach, Flannery looked to make sure the librarian was turned the other way before sidling back up to the row of death masks she'd seen earlier. She closed her eyes, laid the palms of her hands firmly on Lincoln's creased and handsome face. She tried to imagine what it was like to be dead. She couldn't. She turned around and walked away.

MOLLY

As Molly watched her sister walk purposefully across the garden, past the statue of Mao and the crepe myrtle and the concrete gurgling fountain, she tried not to feel guilty. She didn't deserve to feel guilty. But she did deserve her anger—at her husband for somehow knowing and not telling, at her sister for being so patronizing (and lucky), at the universe for twisting a part of her DNA strand and killing her off too young.

But Molly was becoming weary of blame and sickness, which was all she'd been thinking about for days, sorting her memories and enemies. Now she needed to discuss concrete, physical things one could see or touch or eat. She needed to be here.

As though reading her mind, Alyce said, "The creek at the ranch has shriveled in this heat wave. It's mostly disconnected pools with fish swimming around in circles using up all the oxygen, sitting ducks for the blue heron along the cliff."

"It's funny how living in the city I've hardly noticed it hasn't rained." Molly turned to study Alyce sitting next to her.

"At night the coyotes howl their asses off. I can hear them from my studio." Her legs, so tiny, not like a fashion model but more like a gaunt old woman, were twisted into a cross-legged position on the bench, beige pants swallowing any sign of calf or foot. Alyce was disappearing into her clothes.

"Sounds kind of cool, actually."

"Not as cool as the tracks we run across in the morning. And the scat. It's like being a detective or a tracker: a deer crossed here, a fox quick in pursuit." She told Molly she'd learned how vegetarian scat had seeds in it, carnivore scat little bits of white hair, and that it was hard to tell the difference between fox and coyote because on the ranch they ate more or less the same things. "One of them pinches at the end so it tapers. I can't remember which one though."

"You should write a paper. 'Special Topics in Feces Tapering.' I wonder what a tracker would say coming across my scat: A woman crossed here, obviously on her way back from eating a black bean and corn burrito with a large queso from Taco Cabana."

Alyce didn't even feign laughter. "You know the triple bird homicide? The one I told y'all the boys are in mourning for? I sat on one of the birds."

"Oh God." Molly shivered, even in the heat.

"The blue jay or whatever it was that knocked those three baby titmice from their nest in the roof of the porch, knocked one straight onto my morning-coffee chair."

"And you sat on it."

"The two that were still alive didn't even have fully formed wings yet," she said. She told Molly they just lay on the concrete, squirming helplessly, beaks opening and closing in vain, downy skin wrinkled and bunched up like that of the starvation victims on television news. "I put them out of their misery, swept them onto the lawn before the boys found them. Somehow I thought soil and grass wouldn't make the whole thing seem quite so brutal."

Molly knew this was not normal conversation, but it was nice to focus on someone else's troubles. She had first met her sister's best friend fifteen years ago, when she was a senior in high school visiting Flan for the weekend at Marsh. Flannery and her friends had just moved into the big ramshackle rental on the edge of campus that they called Dryden House and decided to throw a "fancy" dinner party, speaking in foreign accents and pretending their Goodwill plates were bone china. They sautéed gulf shrimp in butter—overcooked and rubbery. Brandon and Santiago struggled with their first rack of lamb—it was too dry, but it was lamb. For dessert, Alyce's coconut cake, her mother's recipe. This was how Molly remembered it.

"Does one use the small spoon for the soup?"

"No, no," said Steven from across the table, his own British accent more Dick Van Dyke than Henry Higgins. "That's for the heroin. You eat the soup with cupped hands—it's all the rage in Montmartre."

Bottles of Boone's Farm Strawberry Hill "wine" from the corner store were liberally poured; Molly's mouth smarted at the shock of sweetness when it hit her tongue.

"Daahling, the finish of this gastronomical novelty is only matched by its faintly burnt hair smell," said her sister, ruffling Santiago's already thinning pelt.

"Even better than the Oriental noodles from a fortnight ago. What were they called?"

"Ramen, my pet. The most significant contribution from the East since gunpowder, or Chinese checkers."

Alyce's black hair was piled on her head that night, pale face covered in shimmery dust. "The weather in this place certainly showcases your orbital mammaries," she'd said, pointing at Molly's chest.

Molly looked down. The window-unit AC was blowing directly on her, and her nipples were erect and showing through her thin T-shirt. Her face turned red.

"Doesn't it, boys?" continued Alyce.

Brandon and Santiago, wine charged, began chanting "Yes. Yes. Yes" at the same time, louder and louder, trying to drown each other out. The reference to her fictional namesake was not lost on Molly, even though she still hadn't actually read *Ulysses* in its entirety. There was an eruption of brief laughter before people's attentions moved onto something else, but Alyce held Molly's eye for a beat longer. Like a good-natured challenge.

Molly didn't think Alyce was trying to be mean or embarrass her or put her in her place. She just said whatever came to her head, and to Molly, there was something liberating about that.

Molly loved the idea of people who performed their way through life as if outward circumstances were nothing but props. People who did not seem to be weighed down by where they came from. Over time, Molly would discover there were all sorts of baggage and sharp edges to these people who eventually became her closest circle. But in that moment, looking at them from the outside, all she could see were lives that existed inside an upturned snow globe. Glittering in the light.

Even in a tight-knit group of friends like theirs, alliances varied, and in college she and Alyce had rarely hung out alone, just the two of them. But now, as Molly stared at Alyce, sitting on a bench in the Garden of Evil, she felt a tenderness emerge and spread, like juice spilled on carpet, for this woman who seemed to have previously unrealized capacities for suffering.

They sat for a while in silence, Molly working up the nerve to do what she knew needed to be done. She set her face to a neutral expression, turned, and wrapped her arms around her sister's best friend, holding Alyce close to her chest and saying in a voice she hoped sounded steely and objective, "Everything will be all right." There would come a time when Molly would no longer be able to hold someone in complete stillness. But not yet.

Alyce returned her hug, and then just as quickly let go, saying, "Thanks," but quietly.

Alyce reached in her purse for a tube of lipstick and applied it without a mirror. She smiled brightly. "Did I ever tell you about the kissing contest your sister and I won freshman year?"

"How did you both win?"

"We were on the same team." She chuckled. "Against Harry and Santiago. They looked like two guppy-fish ten-year-olds kissing for the first time."

The sun started to set, giving the grass a golden wash, everything splashed with Orange Crush. The temperature had dropped to somewhere near bearable. The Garden of Evil was empty except for the two of them and one waiter, who stood patiently by the door to the library like a sentry.

Molly liked to walk the neighborhood around first dark, and Brandon usually went with her—out of that sense of obligation often tied up with love, she thought. These days, she wished he would stay home.

Tonight they walked past the bungalow with its garden lined with bowling balls; they walked past the purple A-frame housing a nonprofit shelter for gay youth, past the corner lot where a man lived inside a small historic church he'd had transported from East Texas. Brandon pointed to a calico curled up on the roof of a sedan.

"Cat," he said. They were always on the lookout for mangy felines napping on porches or beneath shrubs, counting the cats because it was a contest of theirs to see who could spot the most.

Molly frowned, "How many does that make?" They usually held hands on these walks, but now Molly kept hers tucked into the pockets of her hoodie.

"Forty-two this summer. You have ten."

"Maybe I need glasses," she said, but she knew it was because she was a distracted walker. Molly loved scouring people's gardens and landscaping, straining to see in lit windows and spy on families eating dinner or watching television, colored lights flickering off the walls.

Sometimes they spotted green parrots perched up and down a telephone wire, the strange pandemonium of feral, tropical birds that, according to neighborhood lore, had escaped from a pet store and now nested at the university's intramural fields down the road. There was no sign of them tonight, though.

They passed a Latino man in Wranglers picking up pecans and dropping them into a trash bag. It was getting dark for that kind of work, but the temperature was cooler. A few weeks back someone had posted on the neighborhood listserv complaining about people who went around "stealing pecans right out from under our noses" and suggested notifying the police. Molly posted a response saying she didn't think of them as thieves. She preferred to think of them as gleaners.

Molly and Brandon rounded the corner. Molly almost said "cat" before realizing the eyes she saw gleaming from behind a recycling bin were a raccoon's. The beast crouched in the wild overgrown yard where three days ago she and Brandon had stopped to look at several dozen bright red flowers—all willy-nilly over the yard, sticking up out of the grass atop very long stems, like giraffes.

"Schoolhouse lilies," Molly had exclaimed.

"In August?" Brandon said he thought they usually sprang up in September, as their name implied, just after the kids started back.

"Not everything happens according to plan," she said, not trying to disguise the bitterness in her voice. The question she refused to ask hung in the air between them: *How long did you sense I was sick, and why did you keep quiet?*

She'd said the name only once, and that was on the way home from the concert, when she'd turned to her husband from the passenger seat: "Huntington's." They drove in silence for a while. What else was there to say at that point? Though it had gone verbally unacknowledged, had they not lived for years with this shadow darkening around them?

"We'll find the best specialists. The best." He didn't suggest she get tested. He didn't suggest she might be wrong.

Some things changed immediately. The physical world around Molly became glassy and unreal, her smile forced; she and Brandon stopped having sex. Other things stayed basically the same. They woke up each morning and went to work and mowed the lawn and made dinner and walked the neighborhood. Molly still tucked her cold feet under his thighs when they watched television on the green upholstered sofa. She thought about how eventually she would become unable to kiss her husband slowly, luxuriously on the lips. Not that she could bear to kiss him like that now.

She was furious with Brandon. She didn't know how to explain precisely why. It wasn't her husband's fault she was sick, of course, but the look in his eyes when he found her on the floor of the concert haunted her. He must have watched the signs of disease begin to manifest and yet said nothing to her. It felt like living in her parents' house again: dirty, awful secrets smudged on every surface.

Molly started eating more, collard greens and plums and big batches of scrambled eggs, and resting, taking catnaps throughout the day. Her body felt tender, and although she didn't remember any of these being symptoms of early Huntington's, she figured it was probably just her brain catching up with what had been going awry in her body for months, maybe years.

She didn't let Brandon go with her to the dozens of doctor's appointments set off by her diagnosis. She told him there would be plenty of time for him to take care of her. So Molly was sitting on the white butcher paper alone, after what felt like the millionth poke and prod she'd undergone in the past month, when the doctor, a tall woman in her sixties, came back into the room with a strange expression on her face, one Molly had not yet encountered, not even when the woman had handed her the papers for the advanced directives so Molly could decide things about feeding tubes and respirators and DNRs.

"You're pregnant. Almost six weeks." The doctor didn't say congratulations. After a moment, she asked Molly if she understood the implications.

Molly sat in shock while the woman patiently explained things she already knew. That the child would have a fifty percent chance of inheriting the gene. That because Molly was already symptomatic, the pregnancy would be difficult at best, another stress on her already stressed body.

"It wasn't planned." Molly mentally counted back six weeks. It must have happened in the week before the concert. "I . . . can't." She knew it was too late for her to be a mother.

The doctor patted her leg. "I'll give you the necessary referral in that case."

Molly nodded. She was getting good at moving her head up and down in acceptance. No need to smile or respond when you could just nod.

On the way home from the doctor's, she turned the windshield wipers on when it began to shower and then flipped the switch on the radio, searching the dials for an answer. She wanted to hear Lightnin' Hopkins singing "Baby Please Don't Go." Or Bessie Smith's "Nobody Knows You When You're Down and Out." Or Nina Simone's "I Put a Spell on You." Nothing even close. She ended up singing along, against her will, to the Eagles. But her mind was running through different lyrics: Baby, baby, baby.

Last week, Brandon had tried to get her to listen to a series of podcasts he'd downloaded about Huntington's. One of them documented a couple who were considering whether to use new fertility methods to implant only zygotes without the gene or whether to use traditional methods and hope for the best. "How is that even a choice?" Brandon had raged. "What else is science for?!"

Molly didn't feel like going straight home with her news, so she stopped off to see Toni Price play her weekly "hippie hour" at the Continental Club, an old, small juke joint with a red velvet curtain behind the stage. Molly ordered a burger and sat on a stool at the back where she could barely see willowy, long-haired Price for all the fans swaying on the dance floor fronting the stage. Every now and then, the singer put her arm in the air, sparkling with sequins, her voice disembodied and lovely.

She and Brandon had always wanted children, hadn't they? Eventually? When they'd lived in Ann Arbor for two years for his postdoc, they had talked about it some. She'd certainly thought about it more back then, so alone in a city without friends or family. If Brandon had to stay in the lab over the weekend, she sometimes took the bus to a place an hour out of Ann Arbor where you could snowshoe for ten dollars. Once, on the way, the bus left the highway for some reason she did not understand, slithering through the narrow residential streets of a suburb, past what looked like a graveyard for ice cream trucks. The sides of the trucks were painted in sad shades of lime green and ochre, pictures of clowns and words like *lick* and *nuts* followed by exclamation points. There were at least fifty of them, hibernating for the winter, wrapped in chain-link fence, like her, waiting for a time when children would appear on the streets laughing, playing ball, and chasing the thought of wet, sliding ice cream.

When they discussed children, it was always in the abstract, Brandon never pushing for them, Molly saying inane things, like how the world seemed too fragile, people swinging to and fro like tinkling glass ornaments. If she'd known earlier—if only!—she might have kids already. They would be half-grown. They would know her.

Arriving back at the house that day, Molly meant to tell Brandon. She really did. But instead, closing the front door behind her, the words that emerged from her mouth were cold and accusing: "Why haven't you called your parents to tell them about the diagnosis? I assume they didn't know before I did."

"I've been meaning to . . ." His voice strained. They looked at each other without really looking at each other. "I'll do it right now."

She watched him flip open the phone, punch numbers, and immediately greet his mother, who was the type of person who always picked up on the first ring.

Then, there was a brief silence inside of which Molly could imagine her mother-in-law's ritual litany of complaints. Her gout. Her neighbors. Her children.

"Sahlah is a grown woman. Let her alone," said Brandon. "What she's doing is far from child abuse, Mama."

Brandon's sister Sahlah, housewife and mother of two, had recently decided to don the niqab, arriving at his parents' most recent Eid-ul-Fitr dinner wearing the midnight-blue headgear that left only her dark brown eyes and heavily penciled eyebrows showing, outraging Brandon's only marginally religious parents. Molly had been intrigued by how Sahlah's face no longer gave away every emotion. Was her mouth smirking beneath there? Or set in that line of determination she must have used when she was sixteen to get her curfew moved back to twelve, later than Brandon or his middle sister had ever been allowed?

Molly left her husband sitting at the kitchen table, but after turning the corner toward the bedroom, she stopped at the window overlooking the backyard where her own mother's irises stood dormant.

For as long as Molly could remember, her mother had grown long beds full of them outside their stucco bungalow that backed up on a city park in Abilene. Molly kept an album with all the yellowed newspaper clippings, photos of her small mother, hair in a bob even as it grayed, standing in front of the award-winning blue and purple and orange blossoms.

"Mama," she heard Brandon say from the other room, his voice changing. "Molly has Huntington's."

Molly hadn't meant to eavesdrop, but she continued to stand there in the hallway as he added, "What her mother had. Remember? It's what their mother had."

Molly remembered how as her mother became more infirm, she hired young workers to weed the iris beds in the spring and deadhead them in the fall. She would sit in her wheelchair, her body dancing with chorea, slurring orders until, eventually, she lost even that pleasure to the cloud of the disease.

The first time Molly'd invited Brandon home with her to Abilene was to help dig up those irises a few months after her mother's death. They'd only just begun dating and it was autumn, the best time to excavate dormant bulbs for transport to new ground. Dozens of friends and family showed up to help that afternoon and, while the activity was planned as a way for them to take and grow a living reminder of Helen, the flowers themselves were also special: fifty-year-old heritage bulbs, a purer genetic strain than found in irises bought on the general market. Smaller, but more beautiful, she'd explained to Brandon.

It had been hard labor for the group of mostly chubby, middle-aged folks wearing old jeans and baggy T-shirts, going row after row, using their muddy sneakered feet to put weight onto the pitch-forks, unhinging the fist-size white bulbs from the earth.

Molly closed her eyes and thought of how those bulbs had felt like old baseballs in her hand as she listened to Brandon explain the disease to his mother over the phone. That first would come loss of motor control and coordination. Then changes in behavior. Finally, constant shaking, difficulty swallowing, dementia, and death. That was what Molly was looking at, and it could take ten, fifteen years, maybe more, to kill her.

Trudging through the sodden flower beds that day, she and Brandon had taken on the job of grouping piles of the best bulbs and then bagging them such that each contained flowers from all sections of the yard—that way, everyone who took a bag would have a mix of colors when the irises bloomed in the spring. At one point, he'd asked her, "Were you closer to your mother or to your father growing up?"

She told him the truth that day. Her mother was kind but self-pitying and sick. Her father was the family martyr, but he worked a lot and was always preoccupied with her mother's care. "I was closest to my sister. Always. Half of what I know about my parents comes from Flan."

In the next room, there was silence. Molly strained but could not hear Brandon's mother's voice on the other end of the line, her rich accented alto, but she tried to imagine it. *This is horrible news, Brahim*, she might say. Or *How is our poor girl doing, habibi?*

"What about them, Mama?" asked Brandon. "What?!"

What was he responding to? Was his mother asking about medical bills or genetics? Babies? God forbid she was asking about babies. There was a sound, and Molly could have sworn she heard a wail travel through the phone line and down the hall to where she stood. An Arabic wail. But, no. It was not his mother crying through the telephone receiver. It was her husband beginning to sob.

Touching the cool of the window glass, Molly pictured them as they'd been when they walked along that row of irises years ago. Young and in love, she'd had the feeling that, while her mother was gone, she was finding, not a replacement in Brandon exactly, but someone to be the witness her father had spoken of when she and Flannery were children. As they worked side by side, Brandon had told her about his own family, about getting up at three in the morning and going to work with his father, who was a baker for a large supermarket chain. During high school, his father got him summer jobs at the store, so he would sleep on bags of flour until his own shift at the deli began at six. Every once in a while, he said, despite the fact that they worked too hard for little pay, he felt nostalgic for it—awakening on the hard, gentle hills of those bags surrounded by the smell of rising dough.

In second grade he'd started going by the Americanized name Brandon instead of the Arabic Brahim. His mother cried when she called to get him out of class for a dentist's appointment and his teacher didn't know who she was talking about. She said to him later, "How could you do this to me?" Brandon had comforted her then but didn't stop using his chosen moniker, and he said she never brought it up again. He said he imagined that somewhere deep down she understood he was only trying to survive. His parents emigrated from Iraq when they were barely twenty, and they pushed him and his younger sisters to do well in school but after third grade were never able to help them with homework.

As they'd talked that day while her mother's garden was being uprooted, Molly hadn't thought about needing Brandon to watch over her; it was she who had wanted to protect this sensitive, brooding, beautiful man, to marry him. To take care of him.

As Molly listened to Brandon cry, she tried to make herself go to him in the kitchen and drape her body over him like a shroud, to rock him to sleep and have him wake on rolling bags of flour to the smell of rising dough. But she couldn't.

Two weeks later, at Steven and Lou's wedding reception, there was no bouquet or garter toss, no cake-cutting or glass-clinking toasts. Just a big party. There was Thai food from Madame Mam's laid out in big foil containers that people ate on the foldout tables set up ad hoc around a barn on the outskirts of town; there was a dance floor in the middle covered in sawdust donated by Santiago from his fire station renovations; somebody's unwieldy, cone-headed dog sniffed at ankles and begged for food.

Molly sensed a vaguely subdued atmosphere among her friends, despite all their superficial efforts to be festive, maybe stemming in part from the fact they were older now and mostly living in the same city, a wedding no longer the occasion for a group reunion and drunken antics. And Molly was sick and would be for a long time; everyone else, she imagined, was trying to figure out how to apportion his or her grief and concern over the long haul. Not wanting to use it all up at the beginning of the race.

At some point, the music that had been pumping from speakers in the corner of the barn stopped. There was a muffled pitter-patter as three children dressed in matching plaid outfits and black patent leather shoes scampered onto the dance floor holding pieces of white cardboard. There was a drumroll, and the kids held up signs, chanting the words written on them in purple marker: WE-LOVE-STEVEN. We love Steven! We love Steven! And then they flipped them over so that the cards now read: WEL-COME-STEVEN. Welcome, Steven! Welcome, Steven! Welcome to the family, Steven! The sun streamed through the slates of the barn's roof, lighting up twirling dust particles as they spun through the air.

"Who are those little hobgoblins?" asked Flannery, reaching across Molly for the water jug.

"Lou's brother's kids, I think," said Brandon.

"Waste not, want not." Santiago poured everyone more wine-from-the-box. Molly smiled and left hers sitting on the table. No reason to bring attention to her sobriety.

"This stuff is terrible." Brandon took another big swallow.

"We're being shown up by a crew of munchkins," said Harry, faking energy, the only one of them wearing a full suit and tie. "Should we get up there and fuck with some Slayer? Is there a guitar around here we can smash?"

But nobody did anything, and soon the kids requested "The Hokey Pokey" and went around pulling adults who they'd never met before out onto the dance floor. Molly noticed two people whom she assumed were the children's parents, tall and well dressed, standing off to the side, proud smiles on their attractive, bland faces.

"I'm coming," said Flannery, being dragged off by a boy whose hair was slicked back like Buddy Holly. "Hold your horses, kiddo."

Soon, most of the guests were standing in a loose circle, putting their right foot in and their right foot out, shaking it all about, albeit halfheartedly. Molly and Brandon begged off and were left alone at the table.

Molly took a deep breath and let it out. It was a difficult thing to say. "I need to leave."

"I'll drive us home. They'll understand." Brandon sucked down the last of his wine.

"That's not what I mean." She kept her voice gentle, as if she were talking to a child.

"Okay." He stopped. He squinted at her. "Let's quit our jobs and travel. Let's go to Italy. Alaska, maybe. Australia. We could do it." He took her face between his warm palms, but she twisted away.

"I don't think so."

"You're scaring me."

"I'm leaving. I've packed for Abilene, and Papa's expecting me."

"No," he said, but weakly.

"For a while anyway."

They sat there in silence for a minute, both stunned. Finally, Brandon set his glass on the table and sighed. "It was in Abilene where I learned about your Huntington's gene."

Not at all certain she was ready to hear this, she said, "Go on."

Brandon let the story spill from his mouth as if it had been choking him. "I just don't want you to get yourself into something without understanding what it is," he claimed her father had said to him in a man-to-man chat over a bottle of rotgut whiskey in her father's study, papered in blue-and-gold faded wallpaper, his desk shoved up against the window. Brandon said it was not what he was expecting to hear when her father invited him in the day after Christmas, just a year after Molly's mother had died, flashing the bottle of liquor from behind his back while Molly and Flannery remained sprawled on the living room sofa, giving each other foot rubs and watching Fred and Ginger dance in an old black-and-white.

"A horrible disease and a hardship to take care of someone suffering it. Believe me," her father had said, glancing out the window. "I'm not saying I would have done things differently, but I wish somebody'd told me Helen was at risk. I wish Helen's family had told me."

It took a moment for the information to push through the syrupy air of the room and into Brandon's ears before piecing itself back together again in his brain, as if he were an observer watching himself sit there dumbly, blankly, gripping his glass tumbler in both hands.

"I don't understand. Why hasn't Molly said anything?"

"Molly doesn't want to know. She doesn't want to have these years ruined by the foreshadowing, so to speak. Trust me on this, kiddo."

Brandon recalled looking at Molly's father: deep-set blue eyes and leathery jowls obscuring what had once probably been a sharp-cut jawline. Brandon said he'd wondered if it wasn't a trick, a way for her father to get rid of him, to scare him away from becoming too serious with the youngest daughter. But it was true Molly's mother had died from Huntington's. It was true the disease was genetic. What kind of asshole would make something like that up?

"And don't worry," her father continued when Brandon said nothing. "When she finds out, I won't tell anyone you were in on it."

Brandon said he hated the way her father used the words *in on it*, like Huntington's was a practical joke to be played on someone. And yet, Brandon had trusted the man at first, the man who was so much more educated, who seemed so much wiser than his own parents. He somehow managed to hear the words *Molly doesn't want to know* as the equivalent of *Molly told us explicitly she doesn't want to know*, which were, of course, not the same thing at all. They were young and any onset of the disease seemed a long way off, and so in a sense he was also in denial, convincing himself a cure would easily be found in time. Since the gene responsible for the disease had been pinpointed, how much longer could it be before therapies were developed to splice it out or counteract its effects with drugs? Brandon was going to be a scientist. He believed in progress. And most of all, he was in love and too cowardly to be the bearer of such devastating news rather than the savior from it.

Molly listened to the story Brandon confessed into her ear, music booming all around them, the dance floor twinkling with the reflected light from miniature disco balls strung from the rafters of the barn, the faint smell of hay. Then, she stood from the table, a little shaky at first, and walked away. Her husband had known she would get HD from the beginning. He'd known from the very beginning.

She needed her sister, her older sister, who was so tall she could always be found in a crowd, long neck like a homing beacon. Molly moved through the dancers toward Flannery, who was wearing a loud, crazy dress and dancing wildly, maybe drunkenly. Molly touched her shoulder. *I need to talk to you*, she mouthed. Flannery nodded and yelled, "After this song. I love this song!"

Molly felt suddenly ill, a flash of nausea, her skin hot and clammy as she beelined for the door, rushing through the crowd, slipping through without jarring anyone, hoping she could make it. *Please, God*, she thought, *help me make it out of here in time.*

ALYCE

Earlier in the evening, under a sprawling live oak, when her husband, Harry (who'd paid twenty-five dollars to be ordained online at the Universal Life Church), had pronounced Steven and Lou married, Alyce clapped and smiled along with the rest. Seated in the middle of the audience, she was surrounded by a checkerboard of foldout chairs like a maze meant to trap her. Steven and Lou looked happy as they kissed and turned to face the crowd, a vaguely smug, satisfied look on their faces, thought Alyce, who knew from three professional photo albums that her own wedding-day expression had been similar, difficult as that was to believe now.

After the ceremony, Steven's parents began walking toward her, so she smiled and fluttered them a wave before turning in the opposite direction, weaving through the chairs with a faux expression of purpose. She walked until she found herself in front of a white clapboard cottage a dozen yards away, then climbed onto its wraparound porch that was badly in need of a coat of paint. The wedding reception was in the barn, but Alyce needed someplace private where she could push down her feelings of panic.

The front door to the cottage was unlocked, and she inched along a short entryway and into the living room. The interior was furnished but in that way of vacation homes, everything matching and perfectly in place, from the green sofa cushions to the amber lamp to the framed prints of swaying wheat hanging on the wall. No shoes tossed into corners or bills stacked on the counter, no postcards or finger-painted drawings tacked to the fridge.

Taking deep breaths, trying to focus on the physical world outside her own body, Alyce slid alongside the dark wooden bookshelves built into one side of the room, running her hand along the spines of aging clothbound hardbacks. She wondered if they were bought as a set from an antiques shop just to make the place look serious. One volume caught her eye: *The Robin*. She pulled it out and flipped it open to the title page. How interesting. An entire book about the bird. Written in 1970, it was not nearly as old as the emerald-and-gold-embossed cover made it appear.

Alyce heard noises from upstairs, muffled voices and the clicking of a door. Did someone, in fact, live here? Or more likely, members of the bride's or groom's family had rented the house to stay in during the wedding. Why hadn't she thought of that before? Alyce pushed the book down into her purse and walked back outside, down the porch steps to the grass lawn where people mingled, teetering in heels and swilling booze, waiting for the dancing to begin.

The reception inside the barn was loud and crowded, and after enduring it for as long as she could, Alyce wandered outside to the line of Porta-Potties set up next to a restaurant-size sink, maybe built for washing farm eggs or vegetables. Or some more lurid purpose Alyce didn't want to imagine, involving entrails and slaughter and afterbirth.

It was dark now, and as she looked up at the stars, she had the feeling they were pinholes punched in the top of a jar, just enough air seeping in to keep her alive. Inside the portable stall, she stared at herself in the metal mirror attached to the door. Her face was physically coming apart, Picasso-like, separating into pieces until her gaze couldn't put them back together again. Her breath stank. Her skin looked gray. She was not doing well. She was not getting better. She dug into her purse and came up with the bottle of Xanax—she didn't count how many she swallowed before lifting up her dress and sitting down, listening as her stream of urine hit the black pile of shit and piss below.

Wiggling back into her clothes, arms checkered by bits of moon-light filtering through the fiberglass of the outhouse, Alyce heard what sounded like someone retching in the Porta-Potty adjacent to hers.

"Okay in there?" called Alyce.

"Aces." The voice belonged to Molly.

"Drunk already . . . or did you eat the shrimp?"

Molly opened the door, dabbing a wad of toilet paper to her mouth. "I'm not sure if I went into the Porta-Potty because I had to puke or if I puked because I went into the Porta-Potty." Molly smoothed down her navy dress with white piping lining the straps. Her eyes were red and puffy. But even so, Alyce could still sense the pulsing magnetic glow beneath her skin.

"Want to get out of here?" Alyce's heart beat louder through her chest.

"You have no idea," said Molly in a half whisper. She told Alyce she wanted out, out. To disappear for a while. "I was planning to go to Abilene . . . but I'm not now."

Alyce didn't hesitate. "Come live with me at the ranch."

Molly smiled. "That's sweet, but I can't handle being around a family right now."

"Yes." Alyce knew exactly what she meant. "Harry and the boys are moving back into town. To be closer to school. And so I can get more work done." As soon as she said the words, they no longer sounded like a lie.

The two women stared at each other. Alyce reached out a hand to touch Molly's hard, beautiful shoulder. "Come live with me. I mean it."

An hour later, after maneuvering bleak rural roads back to the ranch, having abandoned her husband to represent them at the reception, Alyce stripped off her clothes before going into the studio. She laid the stolen book on top of a stack of unsent letters addressed to her parents in Mexico. (The letters were long and full of rambling recriminations. In them, she blamed her parents for how her life had turned out. She blamed them for being so damn happy and free. She blamed them for the mole on her left shoulder.)

The boys were in Houston for the weekend with their grandparents, so the house was quiet as she returned to the drawings she'd been working on obsessively since the night of the homecoming party. She moved them around on her table, looking at them from different angles, the mouths and eyes and cheekbones of her friends. She had dozens of strong drafts, but something kept her from proceeding to the next stage of the project.

Alyce always did close studies before finalizing a design. She used drawing to investigate images she found aesthetically intriguing: a blue door, a wooden lattice, the spokes of a bike. She tried to find a way to distill the whole into a fragment that carried the feeling of whatever had touched her about the image in the first place. She then moved the elements around, redrawing and redrawing until satisfied with every inch. The process was like sending out a bird from a ship, over and over, until one day it didn't come back and you knew land was near.

But how to distill her new project into something that could represent a complex web of human beings? Alyce knew Molly was the entry point. That something inside her was pivotal to unlocking the rest of the group, the rest of the tapestry. Alyce needed to study Molly more closely.

"Molly," she said out loud to the room. Nothing. Alyce put aside the charcoal drawings and grabbed the stolen book from her desk.

She read. From the book she learned robins were almost never seen in large groups as late in the season as they'd seen them here two months ago—it was earlier in the spring when flocks usually migrated through the Texas Hill Country from Mexico on their way to breeding grounds farther north. There were always rogue birds who got turned around, their migratory wiring twisted by strange weather or faulty genetics, but it was rare for an entire group to be months behind schedule.

For the next several hours, Alyce pored over *The Robin*, far away from the dancing and drinking at Lou and Steven's big event. She read about a myth from a tribe in Canada who believed the Big Dipper was made up of Bear being chased across the sky by three hunters: Robin, Chickadee, and Moose Bird, represented by the three stars of the handle. Bear comes out of his den each spring and is pursued across the sky all summer until in October the constellation is swallowed by the hills, Robin finally managing to kill Bear with an arrow. Jumping on top of Bear's body, Robin becomes covered with blood and so he flies up again, shaking bright crimson onto the autumn maple trees, his breast still, and always, retaining the rust-red color of dried blood. Out the window Alyce thought she could still see flecks of it on the grass of the lawn, left behind by the hundreds of blood-drenched little bodies of her errant, dilatory flock. She could re-create the color in wool dye by mixing sumac and rose hips.

Her thoughts returned to the faces of her husband and sons watching the flock. How they'd been so moved. As if seeing such a sheer number of bodies in one place changed anything fundamental about life. As if it could change what bodies did, which was fumble through the sky, migrate to different places, breed, then break down and die.

Acquaintances often cooed to the effect of how wonderful it must be to have a husband who also worked in the visual arts, picturing a charmed, bohemian life of collaboration and discussion about each other's work. But while Alyce and Harry had always been terribly supportive of each other—he throwing parties after her two gallery openings, she always there, smiling, for his open houses—in reality they gave only superficial attention to the other's works-in-progress. Harry might help her decide between two color charts. She might help him tweak a floor plan so the air-conditioning duct fit. But that was the extent of it.

Alyce thought this was because they'd met so young and had already established a way of being together before either became an independent designer. The early years were filled with rejection and insecurity, so maybe they both intuited that a deep engagement with each other's work would naturally include a level of criticism and hurt feelings the relationship might not survive.

They were both commercial designers, working not for some lofty higher calling, but for other people. Alyce did everything from blankets to wall tapestries, while Harry worked on homes and offices and garage renovations. But still, they managed to insinuate a bit of their own aesthetic into every project. The couple now living in a triangle of steel and glass had come to Harry and Santiago's firm holding sketches for a Spanish colonial. Her Coptic-style tapestry depicting a school of fish that hung in the foyer of the mayor's ex-wife's house was originally commissioned to be an explosion of peonies. But Alyce liked working directly for clients because, no matter how much she persuaded them to tweak their vision in line with her own tastes, there were still parameters, context. She considered the size of the space where the piece would hang, the lighting, the tone of decoration. Now she was learning how much harder it was to do something for herself.

Alyce stared at the sketches of her friends, their faces so alive. So full and in the midst. She tried to reconnect with her purpose: to show her boys what it had been like when she was most happy, when she was lifted up on currents of air, not because she did anything deserving, but just because. She thought of a video she'd watched once in which scientists (using a camera invented to track ballistics) filmed a hummingbird flying through an air tunnel misted with vaporized olive oil. The fog of tiny droplets captured the movements the bird used to create lift and drag, a brief impression of an event left behind after everything was over, like a ripple on the water undulating with residual energy. That's what Alyce wanted to do—capture something transient in the stillness of tapestry. Leave behind a footprint of the best parts of herself, the parts she was no longer able to give her sons in real life.

Alyce began drawing birds around the faces of her friends and above them and on top of them. Robins, robins, everywhere. Arrested. Frozen there on the page. In those days at Marsh, they were flying through the air using instinct, creating their own lift and drag as if by magic.

As she drew, she continued with the stories lodged inside her, fading droplets of olive oil. She told them to her sons as she worked.

There was a game we invented one spring during those lazy afternoons of intramural softball. Our team, Campus Crusade for Christ, didn't win very often, but there was beer in the cooler and time to sit on the grass looking up at the sky, treacly and barely blue.

The game we invented worked like this: We took turns acting as the Inquisitor, whose job was to come up with a question about our futures, and then everyone else had to guess who in the group the Inquisitor had foreseen. Who, according to Brandon, would be most likely to get plastic surgery? Who, according to Steven, the first to have kids? Who, according to Flannery, might lose a limb in war? The game was endless and endlessly permutating.

But, though it wasn't a rule, nobody, in all the years we played the Inquisitor game—at New Year's Eve parties, barbecues, even on the drive back from the funeral for Santiago's father—ever asked who would be the first to get divorced. Harry and I were the first to marry. The first to have kids. Who, according to me, Alyce, will be the first couple to part ways? One day you're drinking a cup of coffee with your son, and the next . . .

The only subject technically off-limits was death. You couldn't ask who would be the first or last or third or fourth to die. Everyone agreed on this. But now it's becoming clearer that Molly and I are in a dead heat to win that one . . .

She heard Harry's key in the door, his footsteps down the hallway. The interruption annoyed her. She couldn't have her family lurking while she prepared this final project. She needed space and quiet.

Alyce waited until Harry had brushed his teeth and settled into the bedroom. Then, she went to him. The spider plant on the dresser, the tall glass of water on the bedside table, even the tiny painting of a ruby-throated hummingbird hanging askew on the wall suddenly seemed filled with foreboding. She looked at Harry in bed with his book, the reading lamp glancing off gray hairs. She felt nothing.

Growing up as an only child, Alyce had watched her friends with siblings fight, sometimes even torture one another. But once, when she threw a water balloon too hard at her best friend Jessica's kid brother, Jessica turned on her. Alyce learned an important lesson: sisters could be mean to their brothers, outsiders could not. She'd admired this brand of familial loyalty and desired it for herself. On nights like tonight, when she tried to remember why she'd chosen

Harry fifteen long years ago, she thought of his stability and kindness and loyalty. She hoped these weren't the only reasons. She hoped there'd once been more to it than that.

Ignoring the tremble of her voice, she glided up to the bed and told Harry she needed him to move out. She needed him to take the boys and go live with Santiago at the fire station.

Harry stared at her in disbelief. The air felt suddenly humid, suffocating.

"Not long," she added. "A few weeks."

"The boys love it out here." He sat up and took off his glasses. "Alyce, sweetheart, why don't you leave. Go on a trip by yourself, if you need it. Go crazy."

She let the double entendre pass. "But this is my artistic fellowship. I have to be here. I need to . . ." She couldn't tell him that she didn't want the boys to see her like this, to become like her, to find her if the worst happened.

"You need help. You need . . . you need to go back to therapy," he stuttered. His voice was quiet, as if he were talking to himself under his breath.

"That's not it." She was speaking automatically now. "It's Molly. I told her she could come here for a while. To the ranch. She needs to think things over. She's the one who needs help." And it was all true. All of it. She felt her body straightening with the confidence of her words.

"She has Huntington's, A. What is there to think over?" His voice grew louder. "How are you going to help her? What are you going to do?"

The more upset Harry became, the calmer Alyce felt. She knew exactly what she was going to do.

FLANNERY

Flannery picked at the blue icing from a half-eaten piece of cake that may or may not have originally been hers. She noticed a shoe poking up from behind a plate of noodles, and after some investigation—ducking under the table and closing an eye—confirmed it belonged to one of the two children asleep on a row of chairs. Maybe it was because Flannery had spent so many hours secretly trying to imagine the color and shape of her and Kunle's babies—ochre, fawn, hazel, café au lait—but since moving back to the States, she felt slightly repelled by the sight of white children. She couldn't help think they looked like unformed globs of dough. Or wisps of smoke that might disappear if you tried to grab hold. On a really bad day, when she missed Nigeria horribly, Flannery walked around thinking all white people, including herself, were nothing more than floating mobiles of bleached bone.

These particular kids, sleeping in their grown-up outfits, made Flan think of the girl in Ojo market standing between two stalls selling brightly colored plastics—plastic buckets, plastic pitchers, plastic spoons and spatulas and cups—wearing nothing but panties, her body coated in dirt as she held a small puffed-out yellow lace dress scrunched in her fists, dunking it into a pail of soapy water with vigor and confidence. It was a Sunday afternoon, and Flannery imagined the girl had only just returned from church and could not bear to wear that hot, itchy dress one moment longer.

Through her champagne haze, Flannery vaguely remembered that Molly had wanted to speak with her about something. She felt a pang of guilt, but it was too late. Brandon and Molly had gone home. Alyce had disappeared. At the edge of the dance floor, Santiago laughed and flirted with a couple of Lou's cousins. She noticed Steven, in his white guayabera and linen pants, finally by himself, drinking a beer and squinting as though working out complex mathematical proofs on the slate of his brain. Flannery drifted across the barn to the groom and gave him a quick hug.

"So you arrived with Santi?"

"We carpooled."

Steven gave her a look.

"I don't have a car, remember?"

"Be careful."

"Yeah, well." Flan had enough problems right now, his petty judgment of her being the least of them.

"Sorry. Forget it." He shrugged. Steven didn't have to say that what he was sorry about was her sister. "Huntington's was what Woody Guthrie had. I didn't know that."

She raised her eyebrows.

"Lou and I have been reading up."

"Congratulations." Flannery needed to stop drinking so much. "I didn't mean that." She remembered the time, in the first stage of the sickness, when her mother threw a party in the garden to show off her bed of blooming irises. She filled a piñata full of airplane-size liquor bottles, not realizing how they'd shatter, spraying guests with booze and shards of glass.

"It took you forever to convince Lou to go out with you. Yet here we are."

"I asked her once, why she'd been so resistant to my . . . charms." He told Flannery that they were in bed, Lou's curly hair wound

around a pencil ("part of her naughty librarian shtick, but that's another story . . ."), and she said she'd thought his dilettante farming
project was a little too precious. She thought he was one of those
self-righteous back-to-the-land romantics who had no idea what
they were getting themselves into.

"So what does she think now?"

"The same," he said, laughing. "It just doesn't bother her as much
anymore."

"She looked beautiful. It was a beautiful wedding."

"An economical, recession wedding, but thanks."

Flannery thought about how Steven and Lou still lived in the
trailer they'd moved into "temporarily" four years ago on the edge
of the farm. "Oh, discretionary income. Who knew graduate school
would be the height of my profit margin?"

"Sushi." Steven smacked his lips. "The way you sluice the wasabi
around in soy sauce before dipping unagi in it with those slick chopsticks. I used to love that."

"Or a professional massage? All that chanty music and lavender
candles . . ."

". . . and the 'happy ending.'" He gyrated his hips.

Flannery felt petty and selfish admitting she yearned for lost luxu-
ries Kunle and most of their Nigerian friends had never experienced.
But Steven was on a roll now, confessing that what he really missed
from his consulting days were adventure vacations. Scuba diving in
Belize. Backpacking through Thailand. "Now, I'm lucky if we make
it to Krause Springs once a year with the gang," he said, referring
to a campground thirty miles north of town that sold cheesy bric-a-
brac at the gate and was often crowded with drunk frat boys slipping
around on the rocks that led to a natural green pool and grotto, lush
with fronds. Flannery could imagine it: Molly videotaping beetles
with her phone; Brandon doing tricks on the rope swing; Maya pick-

ing up shells as Lou read on the rock bank and Steven dove into the frigid water, green and musky in the sun, only to discover how much harder it was to swim beneath the pelting water of a grotto than it looked in the movies.

"We went once in college," said Flannery.

"The time you and Santiago made your tent collapse from whatever robust exercise y'all were performing inside."

"I don't remember that."

"It's okay. Everybody else does."

With the reception winding down and the boxed wine running out, the deejay (Steven's uncle Gabriel, in a baby blue polyester leisure suit) said it was time for the last song before the bride and groom would wave good-bye from their yellow Honda Prelude parked outside, decorated with a full-spectrum rainbow of condoms, red to violet. Santiago appeared, motioning for Flannery to dance with him, and so she did. It was Willie Nelson's "The Party's Over"; they two-stepped. Flannery pulled at her long Nigerian dress.

In part because labor was so cheap in Nigeria, Flannery returned to the States with a duffel bag full of outfits made from wildly patterned cloth. She'd scoured the open-air markets, leaving a wake of delighted cries ("White! Mrs. White!"), before schlepping her purchases to the barely lit wooden shack where a tailor sewed the cloth to fit snug on Flannery's long-legged, flat-chested frame. Her dark blue on light blue adire cloth dress with crisscrossing straps and swirling wavelike patterns was distinctly African and, it turned out, glaringly ethnic when worn by a white woman in the more sanitized and staid surroundings of a Texas wedding. For some reason this didn't hit home for Flannery until she arrived at the wedding itself, looking around at the plain Western clothes in bewilderment as though they were what was foreign.

"Don't you beat all," Santiago had said before the ceremony as the two of them rushed around helping to decorate the dank, smelly barn, tossing flower petals and silver foil stars over everything. "The white princess from the dark continent." Flannery had given him the finger.

"I can't believe he asked you to sing effing Celine Dion for his wedding," said Santiago now, his breath warm in her ear as they danced sloppily to the country music.

At the ceremony earlier, she'd stood in front of the small crowd, holding a scratchy mike and singing "My Heart Will Go On." At Dryden House, Flannery and Alyce had devised a drinking game for the film *Titanic*, which had just come out, and forced everyone to play it over and over, Celine Dion belting out the cheesy song in a continuous loop on the sound track. The game was mostly based around character names, which the actors repeated ad nauseam in every piece of dialogue.

"Jack," mimicked Flannery in a high-pitched voice of faux desperation, trying not to trip over Santi's feet.

"Rose," said Santiago in a low-pitched voice of the same.

"Jack!"

"Rose!"

Flannery was trying to have fun. As she danced, she told herself she wanted to fit in with her old friends again, though Alyce was more and more a stranger and her sister sick. Santiago was the only person who didn't seem to have changed, and an appreciation for that welled up in her. Even when they were all nineteen and took a bus downtown to the tattoo parlor called Forbidden Fruit on Sixth Street, Santiago was the only other one who didn't chicken out, getting a fleur-de-lis tattooed on his forearm. Santiago was always game.

"We're friends, aren't we?" They continued to dance. Flannery immediately wished she hadn't asked. The booze talking again.

"Is that what you call it?" He sent her into a twirl.

Flannery knew her desire to be adored by ex-boyfriends wasn't admirable. She remembered with shame harassing a sad-eyed Australian conservation volunteer whom she'd ceremoniously dumped after only a few weeks of dating, later inviting him to events, showing up unannounced at his door, constantly calling to check up on him. One day he'd finally said, "Look, it's not just a figure of speech when I say I don't want to see you again."

With Santiago, she really thought living in Nigeria would give the grout of friendship time to set, slowly filling in the cracks and gaps left between them. As they stepped and twirled on the sawdust— drunkenly, neither of them particularly good in the first place—she thought about those summers in grad school when they would shack up together, spending nights on booze or cocaine or ecstasy, turning his apartment into a two-person rave, filling it with dozens of plants they didn't know how to take care of, bought impulsively from the greenhouse at the twenty-four-hour big box store. Santiago would drill holes in the ceiling, and they'd hang plastic potted ivies and peonies and begonia, which they'd drape with white Christmas lights, dancing wildly beneath them, shouting out the windows at people walking down below.

"I don't even have a fingerprint," she remembered saying dreamily once as they came down, chain-smoking on the bed, listening to the Smiths over and over on the CD player. She was referring to the background check for her teaching assistantship when the DPS told Flannery her prints were incomplete—not enough curling grooves to distinguish her identity from all the others in the system. "I'm a ghost. I'm not even here." She'd liked the idea of being between spheres, a free agent.

"Oh, you're here all right," Santiago had replied, putting his hand up her skirt, along the inside of her legs that she propped on the bed frame, her legs that went on forever. She'd laughed and kissed him then, saying, "Wherever we are, it's amazing."

As they danced, Flannery gripped Santiago more tightly.

Flannery pressed her cheek against the cool glass of the passenger-side window. Clouds covered the moon and, at the edge of town, the streetlights barely gave off enough light to drive by. As dark trees moved against dark sky, they looked like shadow puppets acting out a tale of horror, screeching and clawing at the air.

When Santiago dropped Flannery at her apartment, he nodded but his gaze remained on the steering wheel, punishing her for not inviting him inside. She knew better—Santiago was an enabler. She squeezed his shoulder before getting out, leaving another trace of her half-formed fingerprints.

The neighborhood was still, and the air carried the echo of an accordion from the cinder-block Tejano bar behind her apartment building. Closing the particleboard door behind her, Flan tossed her dress into the hamper and turned on the shower. Showers wasted water compared to bucket baths, but she loved them. She remembered when she became old enough to take one by herself, how the light shot horizontally through the tiny window near the ceiling, illuminating the steam. The beads of water looked like dust but moved differently when she blew on them, somersaulting more slowly, with a delayed reaction, or what she would later learn to call viscosity. Back then, it was also how she imagined her mother's brain: clouding up with steam, becoming obscured and slow.

Funny to think that she might have become a scientist because of the curiosity that began in her parents' beige-and-pink shower stall. When Flannery had focused on atmospheric dynamics in graduate school—her dissertation was on how Arctic snow melt affected atmospheric patterns of humidity—and began to study snowflakes, her family raised eyebrows. A snow scientist from Abilene, Texas? Where a white Christmas was only an Elvis song on the radio? But maybe that was why she loved it so much. All precipitation was magical to her, extraordinary. On the rare afternoon it rained in Abilene, it was a holiday; the dust settled and everything smelled clean. This experience was something Flannery had in common with Kunle, with all Nigerians who lived in the hot and dry northern half of the country.

During graduate school in Madison, Wisconsin, in the Department of Climate System Sciences (they called students in the more traditional meteorology program "weather wankers"), Flannery joined a lab run by a scientist doing work on the North Pole. She liked the idea of working with ice, with the process of freezing and the idea of stasis, however brief—life suspended.

Flannery turned out to be pretty good at her job, but after six months on an isolated Arctic research outpost gathering data for her dissertation, she wanted to travel somewhere warm before applying for the postdoctoral fellowships that were the natural next step for her research—and that would probably send her back to the North Pole or the Klondike or Siberia. When a grad school friend invited her to join the team of the current international EOP, intended to study changes in monsoon activity in West Africa as a result of climate change, she thought it would be a nice working vacation, a chance to get a tan.

EOP stood for "enhanced observing period," when scientists interested in a similar phenomenon pooled their expertise and descended upon a particular area with ships and planes and satellites and land-roving equipment to spend a year measuring and recording an enormous amount of data at once. An EOP required an army of workers, hiring gobs of recent PhDs like Flannery as well as local scientists.

Flannery was assigned to lead a team performing measurements of air and soil in the Sahel region of Nigeria, stationed at the university in Adamanta. One afternoon, Flannery and a colleague were scheduled to teach three local scientists, including Kunle, how to interpret readouts from the machines before they buried them in the sand to protect the delicate processing chips from intense afternoon sun. Kunle was a no-show.

After the session, Flannery volunteered to follow up and was given vague directions to his room on the outskirts of the university campus, a long, winding walk through dilapidated concrete academic buildings surrounded by the red and yellow blossoming Pride of Barbados, which did its best to camouflage the university's decline.

Arriving at an area of wild vegetation dotted with houses and residence halls, Flannery eventually stumbled into the ramshackle, overgrown yard strung with crisscrossing clotheslines. Kunle's room was in a BQ, or "Boys' Quarters," a term for the small building adjacent to a residence that, during colonial times, had been used to house servants or "houseboys." BQs—and his was no different— were usually a row of three or four rooms connected by a slab porch, which, since there wasn't a proper kitchen, was where inhabitants set up hot plates and buckets of water.

When Kunle pulled open the door, Flannery held out a small bag of oranges, saying, "*Ekaaro.*" To her surprise, standing in front of her was the same preppy man she'd met at the canteen a few days before. Kunle smiled and invited her inside the tiny room he shared with three other graduate students, all from his home state directly to the east. There was one mattress on the floor (they took turns sleeping at different times), one desk, and above it a shelf stacked to the ceiling with photocopied textbooks. There was a small, fuzzy television set and a wardrobe piled with suitcases, which the men lived out of since there wasn't space to truly unpack.

He offered her a corner of the mattress, and she sat down primly, while he lay back against the wall, sighing with his whole body. He was covered in sweat and his face looked hollowed out, which, along with his close-cropped hair, accentuated his prominent cheekbones.

"Malaria?" she asked.

He nodded.

"In Adamanta?" The unique plateau elevation of the city meant most mosquitoes couldn't survive there.

"I went home last week." He smiled. "To my village."

Despite his looking weak with sickness, Flannery could still feel the strong pull of attraction. His pleated slacks and soccer jersey were endearingly mismatched, and she had a strange and embarrassing urge to take them off and wash his feverish body with a cool, wet cloth. She wanted him, not sexually yet, but in some generalized feeling of possessiveness.

"I'm sorry I'm not in a better state. It's not often I get house calls from Americans. How do you find Nigeria?" This was a question everyone asked Flannery and the two other Americans working with her.

"I like it. I'm still here." She flipped through the stack of photographs he offered as entertainment: Kunle as an undergrad lined up with friends and girlfriends; Kunle in the northwest during his Youth Service years.

"You try. You try small, small. But for how much longer?" he asked. The implication: foreigners always swooping down, rearranging things, then leaving.

They lounged together in easy silence, her original mission forgotten. One of Kunle's neighbors from Cross River State stuck her head in to ask if they'd eaten—"Done chop?" They spooned up her Calabar stew, sucking the periwinkle snails from the shells and scooping big chunks of leafy greens with balls of soft fufu made from boiled cassava.

She remembered watching through the doorway the brassy light of dusk slice through the branches of a mango tree and thinking: *What sort of horrible, beautiful place is this?* She remembered touching Kunle's forehead, burning with fever, and closing her eyes. Had she thought of her mother then? Of her mother's worst days and her own many nights waiting for fevers to break and medicines to kick in? Of discovering her mother standing in the middle of the street without pants on, delirious, and leading her back inside? Maybe she did. But she had not yet realized that sickness follows you to the ends of the earth.

Running a bar of oatmeal soap across her chest, Flannery was still surprised how easy it was to once again take for granted all the normal amenities found even in a low-income housing block in the States. Showers and dependable electricity, running potable water, paint on the walls—not that some people didn't live that way in Nigeria, like the wealthy who could afford their own generators.

On the other hand, it really hadn't been difficult to adjust to daily life in Nigeria, either. She'd come to enjoy the tiny frogs that emerged from the drain in her kitchen sink, reading by candlelight or headlamp, the act of bathing by scooping bowls of water from a plastic bucket and pouring them over her head, even the daily trips to the market on a public transportation system that consisted of a fleet of rusting vans, their doors askew, women leaping on and off with babies tied securely to their backs in sheaths of vibrant-colored cloth.

After her shower, Flannery climbed into bed and cracked the sheet so it ballooned up and then floated back down, settling over her. There was the sound of police sirens a few blocks away. She searched the nightstand for her cell phone. It was eight hours later in Nigeria. Kunle would probably be reading in his lab, waiting for the electricity to flicker back on so he could work. She dialed his number, sixteen digits long.

"How body?" were the first words from his mouth. His voice was a space heater radiating warmth that flushed through her body, and she tried to picture him, graceful and solid, on the other side of the phone, eyes shining like mica.

"Body fine-o," she said.

Flannery rehashed the wedding for him. How the ceremony itself had taken place outside the barn beneath an old live oak strung with bits of mirror to catch the sunlight. How the processional was played on a harmonica, and the whole event started late and was poorly organized, which surprised no one who knew Steven and Lou. The booze was free.

"Why didn't she wear white? I mean, except for the obvious reason, oh." His voice didn't sound normal. He sounded exhausted. Sad.

"She'd tell you it was because she prefers the color green, but the real reason is that Lou and Steven sneer at convention."

In Kunle's culture, it was common to have two weddings—one following the Yoruba tradition of dancing, throwing money, and gifting yam, and another, the "church wedding," observing Christian tradition. When they first became lovers, Kunle had been surprised that none of her close friends back home were religious. Technically, Santiago and Harry were Catholic and Brandon was Muslim, but they weren't practicing. In Nigeria, Western religion had become ubiquitous, and even most academics were ardent churchgoers. Flannery tagged along with Kunle sometimes because she liked the singing, but otherwise it was an issue upon which they agreed to disagree. To Flannery the whole thing seemed like a strange imperialistic holdover, but to Kunle it was the only good thing they'd gotten from their colonial years under the British.

"I've been thinking about places we could get married when you come," she said. "There's a city park near the air force base where the trees are full of wild peacocks."

"I was denied the visa."

She closed her eyes. How many disappointments could one month bring?

Kunle told her he had waited in line for two days at the U.S. Consulate in Lagos only to have an American in a suit look at his application for two minutes and shake his head, pointing at the insufficient balance in his bank account. Kunle felt humiliated, the man implying Flannery's letter of invitation meant nothing, that he couldn't be trusted to come home. As though he wanted so badly to live in America he'd do it by subterfuge. "I wish I could be there for you and your sister." To Kunle, family was family, it didn't matter that he'd never met Molly in person.

They were silent for a while. Along with the disappointment, Flannery had to admit that she also felt a little relief. Now she wouldn't have to merge her two worlds. Now she couldn't be blamed for choosing just one: the one that lit every fiber of her being on fire, not the one that dragged her through a mire of sickness and guilt.

"I won't be in the States much longer anyway," she said, willing it to be true. Technically, she could return to Nigeria without funding, but her savings were almost gone. What would they live on?

"You've had a breakthrough." Hope crept into his voice.

"Sort of." Lying in bed, Flannery wished love wasn't so hard on a person. She wished it didn't make everything else so unimportant by comparison. "I might be able to do more of the work from Nigeria than we thought."

"Light will be a problem."

"We'll have to get a good generator." She wrapped the sheet tightly around her, pretending he was holding her the way he liked to, one arm woven through hers.

They spent the next hour doing this—fixing hypothetical problems associated with transferring her project back to Nigeria. Whether she could afford the new malaria meds that didn't give one nightmares or panic attacks. How to go about shipping special equipment for the lab and dashing—bribing—it through the port.

Eventually Flannery became tired, struggling to keep her eyes open. She needed rest to attack her work in the lab tomorrow. To find answers. Plus, she was supposed to help Brandon photograph the snowflakes he was growing via electricity, which was the least she could do after how he'd set her up in his institute, giving her this chance to use the machines that would eventually—they had to!—arrive at something useful.

"Tell me about the palm-wine drunkard," demanded Flannery playfully, yawning, hovering on the verge of sleep. International phone cards were so cheap that Kunle liked to stay on the phone while she fell asleep; he said he listened to the rocking of her breath for long minutes before hanging up.

"You know it better than I do now."

"Pretty please."

And so he began: "One day the palm-wine drunkard was drinking a jug of wine, when someone came running to tell him his tapper had fallen to his death from the top of a palm tree. The palm-wine drunkard decided he must travel to Dead Town in order to bring him back home. . . ."

SANTIAGO

I can crush some pancakes," said Harry, "but that's it."

"Which is exactly why I invited you." Santiago punched a button on his keychain to unlock the car. They were on their way to a cooking class at the organic fortress known as Foodie Farm. "To make me look good by comparison."

Distracted, Santiago narrowly missed running over the heap of construction tools in the corner of the garage as they pulled out of the driveway. Santi was still in the process of renovating the fire station, but money was becoming a serious problem—one of the many reasons he couldn't refuse Harry when he'd called a month earlier to say, "You know how we just gave up our downtown office and decided to work out of the fire station even though it isn't exactly done yet? Well, how would you feel if the boys and I crashed there with you for a few, I don't know . . . let's say weeks?" Harry and Alyce's house in town was rented until next June, and anyway, he said he wanted the boys to think of this as a vacation. Boys' camp at Uncle Santi's.

Santiago was still stunned by Harry and Alyce's separation. (Harry called it "a break," but Santi could hear the fear in his voice.) Harry had been the first person Santi met during freshman orientation back in college, and over the years he'd come to think of Alyce as a charming extension of his old friend. Santi loved Alyce, but when Harry called that day, it felt more like getting the news that your best friend has become paralyzed from the waist down. He would never admit this to Alyce, of course, that she'd never truly existed for him as a separate entity.

Santiago had wondered why Harry wanted to stay at the fire station rather than with Brandon who, because of Molly's defection to the ranch, had a house all to himself that wasn't in the midst of renovations. But it soon became clear: Brandon was a wreck. He moped and cried and occasionally went on a rage. Santiago wasn't sure how much of Brandon's behavior could be attributed to his wife's diagnosis and how much to her absence. The last time Santi had gone over to keep his friend company, a pleasant evening with a couple of beers on the back porch talking local politics turned into Brandon, veins popping from his neck, pretending the fence was Molly's father.

"Can't believe I listened to him!" Brandon chucked two beer bottles, one after the other, at the wooden pickets, shattering brown glass in an unimpressive blast radius. Santiago stood, mouth open.

Just as quickly as the anger appeared, though, it subsided, Brandon shaking his head sadly and saying, "Shit, man. I'll clean this up. Go on home." Everywhere Santi looked, things were falling apart.

He would have agreed to take Harry in anyway, of course, but a roommate helping with the monthly mortgage payment didn't hurt. The firm was technically already paying for half the renovations since the first floor would eventually become the office, but the firm's account was no longer in the black, unbeknownst to Harry. Santiago had cleaned it out fixing the water-damaged copper in Kit Hobbes's lake house, and then in secret, he'd applied for a small-business loan to keep things afloat. The fact that money for the Marfa project, which Harry had been working on for months, was not going to materialize meant no foreseeable injections of cash.

"Steven and Brandon are meeting us here?" Harry asked as they parked outside Austin's Foodie Farm, a wonder emporium of pro-

sciutto, persimmons, red seedless grapes, knuckled heirloom tomatoes, Brussels sprouts on the stalk, microbrews, ornamental gourds,
free-range lamb—a veritable smorgasbord of all things haute and
edible.

"Just Brandon. Steven's boycotting because they won't buy his
beets." Santiago zipped up a black hoodie over his tight-fitting Iggy
Pop T-shirt.

He had charged to his credit card the expensive tickets for this
afternoon cooking class put on by Sarah Bird, one of his favorite celebrity chefs, because he thought it would be a good bonding experience for his best friends, both suddenly cut loose from their domestic
units and looking desperately to him. A role reversal that made him
very uncomfortable.

"I'm trolling for free samples first," said Harry, hands tucked in
the pockets of his khakis as they stepped out from under the misty,
slate-gray October sky and into the warm artificial light flooding
giant crates of mushrooms with exotic Japanese-sounding names.

Santiago followed him to a transparent plastic pod holding cubes
of cantaloupe. "No time for handouts, gypsy. We need to nab spots
up close to Ms. Bird."

"Ah, yes," replied Harry in an exaggerated tone, stroking his
chin. "So we can more clearly view the subtleties of her technique."

"The subtleties of that ass, playboy." Santiago took the toothpick
stabbed with cantaloupe from Harry's outstretched hand and put it
in his mouth.

As they made their way up the stairs to the demo kitchens, Santiago stopped two steps above Harry, took a deep breath, and looked
back at his friend. "I've been meaning to talk to you. About the
Marfa house."

Harry held out a hand to stop his words. "I know." Harry stepped
up so that they stood on the same level. "I'm sorry I've been so slow

finishing it. Thanks for understanding." Harry slid past him and continued up the stairs. Santiago bit his tongue and followed.

"You're going to cut your fingers off chopping like that," said Brandon, as Harry fumbled awkwardly with the fennel bulb they were instructed to dice and caramelize as a crust for the pork tenderloin.

"Leave me alone," said Harry, frustrated, "or I'm going to chop your fingers off."

The cooking studio was arranged like a high school chemistry lab, each oblong station accommodating four students. Brandon, Santi, and Harry had been assigned a station with Ben, a chubby man of about fifty wearing a sweater embroidered with an outlandish winter scene featuring a reindeer sticking out its tongue to catch falling snowflakes and a clumsy snowman fumbling with a corncob pipe that looked more like an amorphous turd.

"Look here, Harry," whispered Santiago, "if you just chop the whole thing in half and put it cut side down, it won't slide all over the place. And maybe tuck your fingertips under so the knuckles face the knife."

Harry stared at Santiago blankly.

"What I like about cooking," said Ben, insinuating himself into the conversation, "is that it's an art. Gotta find your own way of doing things, man."

Across the station, Brandon rolled his eyes.

"Always start with whole spices," said Sarah Bird at the front of the room. Looking at the tilted ceiling mirror, they could see the inside of Bird's frying pan filled with whole coriander, cumin, peppercorns, and star anise. "When you toast them, you're not looking for a color change but for the aroma to open up. If you overcook, they become bitter."

As they worked, Brandon leaned into Harry and Santiago. "The irises are gone. Molly dug them up and took them away." Molly had become a ghost about whom they spoke in whispers.

"Why'd she do that?" asked Santiago, her name like a tender spot on his body.

But instead of answering, Brandon turned to Harry. "Have you talked to Alyce? What are they doing out at the ranch?"

Harry didn't say anything right away, still mutilating his fennel. "I honestly don't know."

Santiago tried to tune out their pain as he julienned a Belgian endive into strips for what the chef was calling "salad nests." Working with food was one of Santiago's few respites. The beautiful alchemy of collecting items that were nothing special on their own, then combining them in a measured and intricate dance to create something magical, or at least edible, was similar to what he did as a designer, except that the result of cooking was immediate. Food didn't take years to come to fruition. Food wasn't expected to last. Santiago recalled the summer when Flannery convinced him to give her cooking lessons, and they made pans of enchiladas or whole baked fish every weekend, inviting friends over like a normal couple who hosted dinner parties for other normal couples. Food was a great domesticator.

Brandon's cell phone vibrated its way across the metal counter toward Santiago, who couldn't help but see the caller: Flannery. As though she knew his thoughts. It took all his willpower not to snatch it up and answer himself. He turned toward his cutting board so that Brandon wouldn't realize he was eavesdropping.

After a long silence, Brandon whispered, "Flan, forget about that. . . . Even if you could make it work, it's just stealing moisture from one region and giving to another. I'm not sure it's even ethical." After a moment he continued, saying, "I don't have time right now. Come to my office on Thursday."

After Brandon hung up, Santiago forced himself to wait a whole thirty seconds before he began probing. It was a delicate skill: investigating and gathering evidence without seeming to do so. Like taking photos with the antique Yashica Mat-124 G that he used to check out from the photography lab at Marsh. He shot Flannery unaware, which was easy with the Yashica because one looked down into the top of the rectangular camera and out of several lenses that opened on the sides. It was impossible for anyone other than the photographer to know at what, or whom, the camera was aimed. Flannery eating cereal. Flannery washing dishes. Flannery walking by a parking garage. Flannery's freckles, emerging like blurs, like raindrops on the lens.

"How are things at the lab?"

"Well. I have an article on ionic snowflakes that's almost ready to submit."

"Ionic snowflakes. That's right. Why again?"

"You don't care."

"I care!"

"If you look at snow under lab controls, you can understand the conditions that make different types of snow and ice in the wild."

"Right. Excellent," Santiago said, nodding, feigning interest. "And why is that useful?"

"There's no clear practical application yet." Brandon leaned over the blue fire of his pan. They were supposed to flambé the last of the sherry liquid because "it wasn't the flavor profile they wanted to emphasize."

"I see."

"Santi, as has become painfully clear to me, science is fucking slow. Progress is never linear, and there are more setbacks than breakthroughs."

Santiago ignored this comment for now—certainly they'd all been disappointed with how their ambitions had played out—and, instead, went in for the kill: "See Flannery much in the lab?"

"Yes." Brandon was not making this easy.

"Think she's serious about the Nigerian? About going back there?"

"I'm not going to encourage this line of inquiry."

Santiago cocked his head. "It's great to get unsolicited advice from someone who spends all day growing snowflakes with no clear practical application."

Brandon shrugged.

"We use kosher salt," said the chef, dumping some into a pot for the braised red cabbage while simultaneously using her other hand to lay out seared pork medallions onto a tray, "because the crystals dissolve more rapidly. If you raise your hand high as you do it, you make a bigger mess but you also get a more uniform seasoning."

Their station partner Ben, waving his hand like an imbecile, interrupted the chef to ask if at home one could substitute sour cream for the crème fraîche. The chef said it would be like substituting Cheez Whiz for Gruyère. A minute later, he piped up again, asking where they were supposed to find duck fat. "Well, expensive places," said the chef patiently.

Santiago could see Brandon's growing impatience, so he motioned for the assistant, a very thin Asian man, who was pouring red wine into glasses off to the side.

"Whatever you're going to do, please don't," said Harry, already embarrassed over an episode yet to occur. Santiago ignored him.

"I know this is unorthodox," Santiago said to the man, stone-faced and wearing a long black apron, "but could I go ahead and get my complimentary glass now? I need the waft of wine while I cook. And so do my friends here."

"I like the way you think," said Ben, assuming Santiago had

meant to include him in this illicit happy hour. "My ex's father was a big alcoholic, so she didn't want us to have anything in the house, you know. She thought it was genetic. But I always kept a bottle hidden in my toolbox—you can bet she never looked in there. Now I can stock a whole bar if I want to. . . ."

"You know what, sir." Brandon carefully put down his chef's knife. "That winter sweater you're rocking, that looks like it was knit by a blind person—well, those snowflakes have eight points, which is impossible. Ice crystals are hexagonal prisms. That means six sides. Your sweater is a fraud."

There was a moment of silence.

"You're probably right." Ben brushed the shaggy gray hair out of his eyes with the inside of his elbow. "My ex-wife always said I had no taste. I bought this at the secondhand store because I thought it looked sharp."

"Just ignore the sweater Gestapo, Ben," said Santiago. "My friend here has no sense of style, but me, I'm an architect. And I think it's charming and recherché."

"It's perpetrating a lie," said Brandon.

Harry looked up for the first time. "You act like you're the only person getting fucked around here, terrorizing old Ben about his sweater." Harry snatched a bottle of wine from the steward and poured himself an absurdly large glass of red. "Well, you're not. I get kicked out of the ranch so that your wife—who should be with you, am I right?—could live there in my place. I fucking love that, B. I fucking love that, you spoiled shit."

"I'm the spoiled shit?" Brandon reached for the wine bottle and snatched it using too much force, pinot splashing wildly, covering himself and his fellows in piebald purple. He tilted the bottle to his mouth and drank, and he didn't stop until the wine was exhausted and a steady dribble ran down his chin.

Harry looked stunned for a moment, and then, to Santiago's surprise, picked up Brandon's bowl of discards—eggshells, peels, the detritus of cooking for a crowd—and dumped them into the pot of braised cabbage. Brandon smiled, as if that were the easiest move in the world to counter, before he swept the resting pork medallions onto the floor, knocking Harry's wineglass off the counter in the process, shards of glass spraying their ankles and feet.

Santiago looked down to see his Iggy Pop T-shirt now stained a timeless plum. Bastards. So much for his thoughtful—and expensive—gift of a bro-down cooking class. As he reached to grab each of his friends by their shirt collars, he thought: What was in store for them if he, Santiago, the perennial wreck, was the one coping best? If he was the one acting most maturely and responsibly? The world must be divinely fucked.

The rest of the room was silent, fedora-wearing hipsters and blue-haired old ladies all staring at them as Santiago led his friends to the back stairwell, his familiarity with Foodie Farm's labyrinthine layout finally coming in handy. "Wait for me out there," he told them, swinging open the door.

Santiago helped a begrudging Foodie Farm employee clean up the glass shards and spilled wine before returning to his place at the station. Alongside Ben, Santiago cracked egg after egg into a silver bowl, trying to imagine the rosemary custard it would become.

Whipping the heavy cream reminded him of the shaving cream with which they covered their naked bodies in college, running through the academic quad, high as kites, making ass prints on the first-story windows of the university library—back when Santiago was the one who had to be reined in, Harry and Brandon always ensuring that things only went so far, never allowing Santiago to get into all the trouble he was revving for. Now, he supposed, it was his turn to protect his friends from themselves.

Eventually, Santiago carried the plates along his arm, as he'd learned waiting tables, out to the back stairwell, where Brandon and Harry sat on different steps.

"Where did you get the pork medallions?" asked Brandon.

"Sarah Bird gave me hers and a man in a golf cart told us to leave."

"We don't want to eat all your food . . ." said Harry, contritely.

Santi shrugged. "There's enough. We'll survive," he said.

When they got to the caramelized custard, he told them what the Dutch say about something delicious: it was like an angel pissing on your tongue.

"An angel?" said Harry. "I like that."

They all nodded thoughtfully. They licked their lips and were momentarily satisfied.

FLANNERY

Snow wasn't white; the ice crystals that made up what was called snow were actually clear as cut glass. When light traveled through a snowbank, for instance, some of it reflected back, which made snow only appear white and fluffy as a cloud (not technically white, either, but the result of more scattered light from millions of droplets of water suspended in the air).

On the day two weeks before, when she had helped photograph snowflakes in Brandon's laboratory chamber, Flannery knew that this colorless, transparent nature of ice crystals made good lighting particularly important. She incorporated colored filters into the microscope in order for the hundreds of intricate shapes and structures to show up on the film in all their three-dimensional glory.

Flannery manned the custom-built machine, essentially a special microscope attached to a camera encased in a temperature-regulated box, while Brandon tweaked the chamber's settings to grow a series of his designer snowflakes. He started with minuscule frost crystals on the end of a wire. Then, he ran two thousand volts through the wire, the electric field attracting water molecules from the air to produce ice needles. Once the electrical current was removed, snowflakes began to grow on the tips of the ice needles, variously shaped depending on exact temperature and level of humidity in the chamber. Flannery and Brandon went through the process more than fifty times using different variations. As they worked, Flannery had no idea that what they were doing would change her entire project. That realization came later.

"Just call me the Iceman," Brandon boasted during hour six of the process, rolling up his sleeves.

"Just call you the obsessive-compulsive."

Flannery's job was to use a small feather brush to move the best-looking specimens under the microscope-camera and capture them before their patterns smudged or evaporated. She'd done something similar in graduate school, but only with real snow coming down in real snowfalls. These electric snowflakes were a little different. They grew like perfect crystal flowers on the tips of ramrod-straight stalks. A bouquet of diamonds. In the microscope each one was a civilization of hexagonal plates and branching dendrites. So much useless beauty.

As they worked, Flannery couldn't ignore the change in Brandon: in place of his usual goofy warmth was the cold precision of a machine. He was doing what he could to hold it together.

"It's normal, you know." She said it as they took a coffee break, waiting for the machine to spit sugared chemicals into their Styrofoam cups. "A lot of HD patients are in denial at first. It can take them a while to break through that. She'll be back."

Brandon picked up his cup of steaming coffee and walked back to the lab without responding.

Later, Flannery noticed Brandon using a dropper to lightly coat the starting wire in a solution from a petri dish labeled I.C.E.9. When she asked what it was, he pushed the petri dish toward her.

"Take a look."

She adjusted the microscope eyepiece until the blurry grayness sharpened into a handful of rod-shaped cells with messy flagellum sprouting from the poles. "Just what I've always wanted," she said dryly.

It was *Pseudomonas syringae*, he told her, a bacteria plant pathologists had been studying for years; it showed up all over the world on trees, grasses, and domestic and wild animals. As it turned out, *P. syringae* caused water-based life-forms to freeze in above-freezing weather. "Gives me a wider range of temperatures to work with in the chamber."

It made evolutionary sense that something had developed this kind of ability, thought Flannery. Freeze damaged a plant, breaking open membranes, making it easier for the bacteria to feast on the nutrients inside.

Brandon had asked her to photograph his snow crystal project because Flan owed him for helping her get set up at the Climate Institute and because he still thought of her as a snow specialist. An Iceman. At Marsh, she and Brandon had both taken a class from a visiting atmosphere specialist who first introduced them to the hidden world overhead.

Flannery had always planned to return to the States and go on the job market as an ice specialist, like Brandon had, after the yearlong EOP in Nigeria was over. Then, Kunle told her how, growing up, full-moon nights were an opportunity to venture through the bush to nearby compounds and chase girls. He also told her a proverb from his village: when the moon is bright, even the lame wish to get up and dance. Falling in love with him was a lot like a full moon: everything suddenly looked different.

At the time, Kunle was still working on his PhD because it took so long to finish school in Nigeria. After decades of harsh dictatorships, even the best Nigerian universities no longer had adequate funding or laboratories for educating PhD candidates in much more than the abstractions of book science, and even the professors they had always seemed to be on strike. To make money for room and board, Kunle worked as a campus *okada* driver, wearing a bright orange vest and oversized helmet, ferrying students from the front gate to dorms and academic buildings on the back of a motorbike for thirty naira. Sometimes, Flannery showed up at the end of his shift; he'd free himself from the orange vest and they'd buzz outside the campus and into Adamanta for a beer before it was time for him to return the *okada*.

On the nights Kunle studied for exams at the building they called the Faculty, reading by the light of a rechargeable lantern, Flannery brought him suya grilled by vendors on the side of the road. They would sit on a concrete bench in the breezeway, devouring the thinly sliced peppered meat from its newspaper wrapping.

"I'm surprised an *oyinbo* can take the spice."

"I'm from Texas. We have a thing called salsa."

They talked about their childhood. How when she didn't know the words in school choir, she'd mouth *watermelon, watermelon, watermelon*. How, as a boy, he had to hide in the yam fields to find a quiet spot to read.

Because they worked together on the EOP project, Flannery and Kunle kept their growing intimacy a secret at first. When Kunle stayed overnight at her place, he woke at dawn so he could sneak out before the campus roads filled with people.

Still lying in bed beneath the mosquito net, half awake, she watched him bathe in the tub across the room. Coated in suds, he scrubbed his body, hair lathered white like an old man's before he dipped the plastic bowl into the bucket and poured water over himself in little sips. Toweling dry, he would turn to her, naked, and ask, "What do you like least about me?" He placed one leg and then the other up on the side of the tub, rubbing Vaseline into his feet and the crevices between each toe until the skin glistened. Before leaving, he would turn his head to the small mirror, making sure there were no stray straight hairs caught on his shirt. Nothing to give them away.

Another time, they sat, hands grazing, on a wooden bench inhaling the smell of toner, trying to be discreet in the chaotic midst of the student center's dozen running photocopy machines, when he turned to her and said, "Everything has changed."

So instead of going on the job market in the States, Flannery found a low-paying position at a small, underfunded research outpost run by a middle-aged, burned-out British scientist, who immediately began grooming Flannery to take over the project. She was no longer an Iceman. She was now a woman of the desert.

Adamanta was in many ways the perfect place for this kind of research. Despite the dangers of sectarian violence (which were significant, the city being located on the fault line between Christian south and Muslim north), they were surrounded by Sahel, the thin zone of transition between the Sahara Desert and the tropics. Desertification was causing the Sahara to move south, overtaking the Sahel. Plants died, and the soil was sucked of its nutrients before blowing away with the wind. This, in turn, meant less evaporation and more reflected sunlight from the land, further weakening the monsoon, causing even less rainfall. When African droughts first became severe in the 1960s, most Western scientists dismissed the cause as overgrazing by the natives. Africans weren't taking care of their land, they said. With climate change now a global problem, nobody dared say that anymore.

Flannery and her colleagues measured the speed of this process. How fast were the tropics becoming Sahel? How fast was Sahel becoming dirt? Could the process be reversed or was it already too late? Her boss, always in khakis and a stained T-shirt, would crouch over topographical maps and say, "It's not like we have the resources to change anything, but at least we can bear witness."

Kunle eventually finished his PhD and began working part-time in her lab and as a lecturer at a small, local university. It was around this time that, through her boss, they first met Mrs. Tonukari, the Welsh woman and forty-year veteran of Nigeria who became Flannery's only model of a Western woman who'd actually built a life here and stuck it out over the long haul.

When Mrs. T came calling, it was without warning and often at the crack of dawn, revving the engine of her ancient Peugeot in the driveway or rapping loudly on the front door. Flannery would ride back with her, sometimes still wearing pajamas, sitting in the passenger seat and holding on her lap the woman's shopping basket full of red bananas, white bread, potatoes.

"If you don't do it first thing in the morning, around here it doesn't get done," Mrs. T liked to say.

Once their car was stopped at a ramshackle roadblock. The young men wearing threadbare T-shirts and sunglasses went on and on about how some bullshit sticker on her car was expired. "Pay up," they said, "or we won't let you through. Pay up or we'll tow your car to police headquarters."

"Oh my," said Mrs. Tonukari. "Oh no."

They spent half an hour in the wilting heat while Mrs. T halfheartedly tried to talk the dubious security detail out of the fine, halfheartedly searched for naira in her purse, which contained multitudes of crap. Flannery looked straight ahead at the road strewn with orange peels and empty plastic sachets labeled "Pure Water." Anyone could see the men weren't police, and they had no plausible equipment to tow a vehicle. *Bargain it down*, Flannery kept thinking, *and let's get the hell out of here*. But Mrs. T was the forty-year veteran of the country, and so they dealt with the situation her way: using flailing, panicky white fear.

Her house on the university campus—Mrs. T's husband had been a professor of engineering until his retirement—had the look of an old farmhouse, out back a clothesline and an overgrown garden, inside lots of books and knickknacks, candles in empty wine bottles, a wooden staircase leading to the bedrooms. She would make Flannery tea while telling stories and pulling books from her shelves, splaying them open to point to things. Books were not easy to come by in Nigeria any longer, and Mrs. T refused to loan any of hers out. Too many of them had walked off over the years, she said.

She told Flannery about when Nigeria was the center of the West African publishing world, when Magazine Road in Ibadan was lined with presses and everything was "more lively." Flannery remembered thinking how it always felt she'd arrived too early or too late to the party in this world. But Mrs. T's nostalgia wasn't based on illusions, and Flannery saw it on the faces of Kunle and other Nigerians, too: so much promised, so much squandered.

Mrs. T had a number of Nigerian friends, but she latched onto Flannery because she was lonely for someone to talk to about her life before coming to Adamanta. She claimed that, to her Nigerian friends, "It's as if I was born the day I moved here."

Mrs. T would pause, squeezing the tea bag between her fingers, before saying, "One starts to believe it, too. Everything begins to revolve around this crazy place and what's going on here, as if Nigeria were the whole world. And for all I know anymore, it is."

Flannery turned over those words as she sat in front of her computer in the middle of the night a few days after finishing Brandon's photo project. The numbers on the screen weren't making sense. Nothing made sense. Everyone else in the lab had gone home, but Flannery couldn't bring herself to leave. If she sat there long enough, something would begin to work. It had to.

When she blinked, she saw images of snow crystals, shimmering with the pink and blue light from the color filters, turning like stars. She saw the drip, drip of the dropper as Brandon coated the ice wires. To distract herself, she opened up the university database and searched for Brandon's new bacteria. *Pseudomonas syringae*. The first article she found claimed it could raise the freezing temperature by up to five degrees, which was really astounding.

People often had the misconception that snow was frozen rain, but, in fact, sleet was frozen rain. As a section of the atmosphere cooled, relative humidity increased until the point of supersaturation. Snow was created from this supersaturated vapor without going through a liquid stage. Flannery wondered what might happen if one scattered Brandon's bacteria as an aerosol into the sky where, in enough numbers, it might also be able to stimulate the creation of snow at above-freezing temperatures in clouds. She clicked through more articles but could find no evidence that this had ever been attempted.

Once ice crystals or snowflakes began to form, they grew in size by sucking humidity out of the air nearby, causing more water droplets in the cloud to evaporate and fill that space. Snowflakes then continued to attract this vapor until becoming too heavy to remain in the cloud, falling to earth. Snowflakes, like raindrops, needed a nucleus around which to form. It was usually dust or soot, but it didn't have to be. It could also be bacteria. It could even be bacteria that happened to make water freeze in above-freezing temperatures. And this is when it struck her: Snow was heavier than water. Snow took longer to evaporate back into the atmosphere than did liquid rain and was more likely to make it to the ground.

Flannery thought about the virga in West Texas, streaks of rain appearing to hang beneath a cloud but evaporating before hitting the land. It was phantom rain that did nothing to help the crops or pastures. Their whole family would sit out on the porch to watch, her mother's wheelchair creaking from her flickering movements: Phantom rain. Phantom mother. Phantom rain.

The virga phenomenon occurred in the Sahel, too. She'd seen it in Kunle's home village in Bauchi State at the end of the dry season because, in the village, everyone was up with the dawn in line with an agricultural tradition that hadn't been much affected by electricity. (Power was even more sporadic here than in the cities, averaging less than an hour per day. Occasionally, someone would yell, "Up NEPA," and everyone would rush to plug something in, to charge whatever they had.) Flannery and Kunle were in town for Easter that year. A wrap draped around her shoulders for warmth, Flannery walked with Kunle at dawn up the main dirt road, rough and rocky, as it wound from the village into dusty farmland, which was where they saw virga in the distance, like the mirage of water in the desert. It made her thirsty.

Kunle's village was beautiful in its way—a pastoral answer to the maddening crowds and jammed roads of the major Nigerian cities. Women carried water on their heads, to and fro from the wells. Cocks fought and chased each other while the occasional teenager kicked up dust on a motorbike, probably going nowhere, killing time. They passed bundles of finch-red sugarcane, a mud hut with a chalkboard outside advertising Arsenal versus Manchester United, an empty schoolroom with the letters of the English alphabet painted on the wall. "F" was for Flower; "G" was for Gun. There was a sign, showing a young woman wearing a headwrap, that said EARN RESPECT. DRESS DECENTLY.

Back at the compound, Kunle's mother would shake her head at Flannery and say, "*Waka waka.*" Although not fluent in English,

Kunle's mother had learned pidgin in the years she and her husband lived in Lagos during his military service. *Waka waka* referred to a person who was always walking from place to place. Their morning walks, without purpose or destination, were inexplicable to a woman who worked so hard that all she wanted in her spare time was to rest.

Kunle's mother was not exactly a warm woman—she'd lived a hard life and showed her love through backbreaking labor: in the field with the yams or preparing huge meals in the kitchen, which was just a fire pit covered with a thatch roof to protect the caldrons and mortars from the rain. There wasn't a single indoor common space in the entire compound. In the mornings, Flannery watched family members emerge from their various rooms, which opened directly to the outside, squatting in doorways to brush their teeth or wash their clothes in a soapy bucket. Then, if they weren't going out to the field, they might set up stools and chairs in the shade around the cooking hut to chat and relax. Someone might catch a chicken to pluck and cook for lunch, the men cracking bones afterward with their teeth, sucking out marrow.

At night, after dinner dishes had been washed and total darkness fallen on the compound, Kunle led her inside his mother's quarters where they would sit on a low bench along the wall. His mother would be curled in motionless exhaustion on a chaise-longue-shaped wooden chair, the shadow of her sharp profile cast by the low light of the kerosene lamp perched beside her on the swept concrete floor. There he and his mother would talk, the two of them, in their own language.

And later, on a mattress in the privacy of Kunle's room, Flannery's head on his chest, he would tell her what she already knew about the slow, creeping death of this village and his mother's way of life. "Our field is three times bigger than it was when I was a boy, but the harvest is one-seventh of what it was then." He stroked the inside of her arm with rough fingertips. "A well is there one day, and the next is buried in sand."

"And it's probably too late."

"Never too late."

Flannery's eyes were closed, but she smiled into the dark. This sort of magical thinking was one of the things she loved about him. Her hand felt for his face, and she traced the lines of scars that ran along his cheeks like a terrace, like a shoreline, a place where the map ends. They were the mark of his people, done through ritual scarification when he was a boy, but she imagined they were the scars of the land, of West Africa itself. She thought briefly of her own family and other kinds of marks and scars, unchosen, that separated them in a different way.

She could feel his breath on her neck when he asked, "Could you live here? Could you make your home here with me? In this fading place?"

"Yes." She said it without hesitation. In this place, she was free. In this place, she was special. "Oh, yes." And the grand idea, the expectation of making their lives together in Nigeria, never altered over the next three years, though there were moments when she wondered if she'd eventually end up like Mrs. Tonukari: bitter and afraid.

Once, Kunle took Flan to swim near a beautiful waterfall on the Gontola River, which otherwise wound wide through lazy side channels and eddies. It had rained the night before and the water ran the color of cappuccino from all the topsoil washing away. They swam, only slightly afraid of the freshwater parasites with their long names and longer lists of symptoms, in a calm spot where the water pooled. An old man stopped to sell them palm wine and later told Flan he'd once been to Texas.

"Where in Texas?"

"You know," he replied, "Texas."

After Kunle left to find lunch, a group of women and children from a nearby village arrived at the river, circling Flannery, coming forward, then retreating, not knowing what to make of her invasion. Eventually they settled nearby and stripped down to their underwear, washing themselves and their clothes at the same time. She felt her whiteness but wanted to believe it didn't fully represent her. She wanted to plead with them: *I am not the place I come from.* Instead, Flannery climbed out, shaking off the water like a dog.

In the lab, these images and memories of Nigeria played over and over in Flannery's head as she worked, day after day, on her new idea based on Brandon's bacteria. She was determined not to forget who she was doing all this for. Not to forget her promise.

A few weeks later, when Flannery finally met with Brandon in his office, she was ready. She explained to him about the prevalence of virga, the rain in Nigeria that never made it all the way down to the fields. But, she told him, pointing to her calculations, if she could seed clouds with his special bacteria to make it snow instead of rain, the precipitation would be heavier and colder, less likely to evaporate. The ice crystals could be grown in clouds over specific areas, and as they fell to the ground they would melt, causing precipitation that had a chance of hitting the soil.

"This bacteria causes things to freeze in above-freezing temperature—but not by much. Enough to do this in West Africa?" Brandon looked like he hadn't slept in days.

"I don't know yet," Flannery said, truthfully. "Depends on how high up in the atmosphere we can make the process viable. Will you help me? Let me use your ice chamber?"

"You'll need a certain level of moisture in the air to form around the bacteria." He rubbed his eyes. "Will there be enough?"

"Yes." Flannery was aware her voice sounded more stubborn than reassuring—not just hopeful, faithful, like Kunle's magical thinking. "I think so."

"You can't use the ice chamber." Brandon sighed, taking the pencil out from behind his ear and making marks on a blank sheet of paper. Flannery's heart seized.

After a minute of ignoring her as he scribbled, Brandon looked up and said, "We'll need something bigger than my ice chamber. Much, much bigger."

Flannery stayed up the rest of the night, fiddling with Brandon's numbers, experimenting with computer models. She wasn't sure at what point she put her head down on the desk and began to day-dream. Or was she falling asleep?

"You know that whatever it is I'm developing won't save your mother's farm." She said this in her head, in the mush and muddle of dreamscape. "It takes years for advances to make an impact." Kunle was not there to hear her speak and yet he was.

"So what are you going to do?" he asked, his voice like a caress along her neck. "Make it snow in the desert?"

She tried to keep her eyelids open but their tiny veins filled with liquid metal, weighing them down. "That's exactly what we're going to do," she said, or maybe did not really say, becoming lost in the thicket of sleep. And in her dreams, snowflakes and tiny grains of sand were harmlessly swirling together through the atmosphere, a sandstorm of snow. And in her dream she reached out a hand to touch them, and they were warm. And they were cold.

And in this place where snow and sand mixed together, her sister was not dying. And in this place she had no sister at all.

ALYCE

olly's arrival at the ranch, holding a suitcase and two burlap sacks filled with iris bulbs, was more or less having its desired effect: Alyce was working on her tapestry.

Still not sleeping in any traditional sense, Alyce spent the daylight hours dozing on the sofa, in and out of strange dreams filled with dirty-winged birds and nests made from her own things, tapestries and dish cloths and cheap jewelry passed down from her grandmother. She oozed through the kitchen nibbling on stale crackers, absentmindedly watched reruns. She pitched back and forth in the rocking chair on the porch as mohawked roadrunners hopped their way through the yard; as quick as the insects they hunted, they barely noticed her, occasionally flipping up their long tail feathers in a show of indifference. During the day Alyce seemed to float in a vat of molasses.

But her torpor lifted as night fell. She walked the perimeter of the ranch house locking doors and turning on lamps; they ate a late dinner standing in the kitchen, Alyce picking at a turkey sandwich on rye, Molly devouring the same along with sides of collards or pasta salad or beets plus whatever Alyce couldn't finish. Alyce was amazed by all that Molly could consume. Alyce used to carry a piece of paper in her pocket with quotations given to her by her first therapist: Believe your family is worth living for even when you don't.

Hold on to the memories depression tries to steal and project them into the future. Eat when food revolts you. *One out of three ain't bad*, Alyce thought, shoving another bite of sandwich into her mouth, forcing herself to chew.

Before Molly trundled off to bed, Alyce would wrap her arms around her friend's shoulders, elbows squeezing in tight, and allow whatever dark energies pooled inside this woman to flow into Alyce's own hands, her knotty-knuckled weaver's fingers. Then she went into her studio and worked.

On this particular night Alyce stood taut in front of the loom, hands quivering along the warp. Tonight she was unspooling Flannery onto the frame, blowing tangy, hot breath into the emerging form, animating it like a puppet, trying to channel the pressure from Molly's sharp edge of life pulling adjacent to death, a convergent boundary.

As she worked, Alyce daydreamed about the myth of the goddess weaver, daughter of the jade emperor, who wove the light of stars into what the Chinese named the Silver River, which ran, spangled, down the night sky outside Alyce's casement window. She looked up at that splash of galaxy, sugar falling into a pool of ink, and felt a grandiose affinity with this celestial weaver, her fingers working one butterfly of thread over, under. Over and under. One row of contrast color made a dotted line; two rows a solid one.

The purpose of the loom was to keep the warp, the threads running front to back, rigid so Alyce could weave the weft, or side-to-side threads, through and then pull the beater forward to press the material tightly into place. The pads of her bare feet pedaled the treadles, which were harnessed to shafts separating various strands of the warp, opening what were called sheds. Unlike the big vertical looms used to weave medieval tapestry, this production-style loom revealed only one small section at a time laid out under Alyce's hands, the unwoven warp rolled up on the back beam, the already woven cloth on the front. The piece of tapestry that she worked in was eight feet by one foot, but she really only had a four-inch-wide strip where she could freely maneuver the butterfly into the intricate patterns required. Once a section was finished— many hours of work—she ratcheted the loom forward to begin on the next part.

Learning to weave was one of the few things she remembered fondly from her childhood. Her eccentric father had given Alyce her first handheld frame loom when she was five. He'd learned to set one up in the art education classes he'd had to take so he could substitute teach between the Renaissance Fairs where he and Alyce's mother dressed up like knights and wenches. Later, after watching Alyce spend hours working cloth after school and on the weekends, her parents called a company that made big floor looms and pretended to be textile dealers setting up a new business. The company let them borrow a horizontal loom for their "showroom," and it barely fit shoved up next to Alyce's single bed. She considered it the nicest thing her parents ever did for her.

Mostly, when she thought back on growing up, Alyce remembered feeling like the third wheel to her parents' full life: long hours of tagging along. And what stuck out in particular was the winter when she was thirteen and her jaw had to be wired shut after a collision in a volleyball game left it broken in two places, and how she lived through those weeks in a liminal state, a drug-addled witness responding to outside stimuli with grunts and shakes of the head. Looking back, she recognized this as her first depressive episode.

Alyce's family traveled to Texas that February—her parents were working a Renaissance Fair in the Hill Country, demonstrating candle making and blacksmithing in open-air booths while Alyce sat sullenly on a bench watching the sword swallowers open their gullets and slide thin sheaves of metal all the way down. Her wired jaw gave her an excuse not to talk to anyone.

"Watch as I stretch out its tail," her mother told a group of children, shaping a black-and-green strand of hot wax into a miniature dragon with puffed-out cheeks. Her mother managed to look glamorous even wearing the flouncy skirt and purple felt vest of her costume.

During that trip, they camped in the yard of another Ren Fair enthusiast her parents had met through the circuit, a hippie who grew marijuana plants in his closet and played the mandolin on his porch every morning.

On Alyce's birthday, her parents and the hippie took her out to a seafood place—despite the fact she disliked fish and couldn't open her mouth—and her mother asked the waiter, "What do you have that can fit through the space between her teeth?" She was given lobster bisque and a straw. Every time she sucked in through the plastic tube if felt as though Alyce were filling herself with hot air like a balloon until she floated upward, her parents flirting down below, eating off each other's plates and holding hands beneath the table. The hippie smiled at her, but it was a probing, curious smile, and she looked away.

February in the Texas Hill Country was also when the purple martins arrived from South America, and so, one afternoon, her father drove the three of them to an open field with tall poles topped with martin houses strung from one end to the other like a necklace. Martins were odd migrants because they leapfrogged their way up North America: the first group traveled in February to Texas and parts of Florida, where they spent the entire breeding season; the next group came in March, ending up in the Midwest; the final flocks arrived in Canada in May.

That particular winter was unusually cold for the Hill Country, though, so when the purple martins arrived in Texas, there was little insect life on which to feed. Having lost most of their stored fat during migration, the birds Alyce and her parents saw near the martin houses looked thin and sickly. The purple sheen of their feathers was dulled, their bellies were shrunken; one bird even fell from his perch while they watched and never got back up. Her mother's face was grim as they returned to their puke-green Plymouth, binoculars in hand, but neither of her parents said anything, perhaps aware that suffering was a fact of life they could neither protect her from nor adequately explain.

As she stooped over Flannery's form on the loom, working the thread, Alyce decided her adult depression was actually not so much like the winter when her jaw was wired shut and she went to look at purple martins in the Hill Country. Rather, her adult life was more like being a purple martin that winter: losing the desire to go on.

But when night weaving, Alyce was invincible; she was in control; the tapestry was an all-knowing projection of her own migration across the Silver River, moving at night like a criminal on the lam, like a flock of robins or purple martins taking advantage of the still and silent nighttime atmosphere to migrate long distances. Somewhere in the vast inner sky where her subconscious floated like pretty little storm clouds, Alyce knew this tapestry couldn't save her. But maybe her sons could look at it, touch it, and be satisfied. The tapestry would be full of the friends who had known her boys since they were born, and Alyce was convinced, when the time came, that these people would circle to protect Jake and Ian from the worst.

Flannery emerged slowly. Little by little. In oranges, for the long tunic and iridescent scarf she wore in college, and metallic browns, for her hair and freckles and eyes. Autumn colors. Earth tones. With fabrics that grew from the earth, cotton and linen. Wool shorn from the backs of sheep or llamas or sometimes goats, and silk stolen from the silkworm, spun into yarn, all of which Alyce now wove together.

Alyce used to draw her final designs on vellum, a heavyweight tracing paper, using a grid and protractor for precision, and then place them behind the warp as a pattern. But over the past few years she'd developed a technique whereby she dyed the warp itself to approximate the design, and then elaborated from there, freestyle.

Most tapestry weavers used a plain, cheap material for the warp because it was only a backbone for the real design. But Alyce used hand-dyed wools and silks because she liked to leave stretches of the warp exposed and brocade on top to give the material an almost sculptural quality. For the weft, Alyce chose a fiber that was airy and malleable so she could pack and shape it, and the delicacy of her materials meant it was not uncommon for threads to break when she initially cranked the warp onto the loom. When this happened, she would tie off the break and deal with it when it came up in the weaving by weaving weft over the break until it was unnoticeable to the naked eye. And the finer the warp threads, the closer together they could be, the more detail was possible, and the longer the weaving time. One of her teachers used this rule of thumb: an hour a yard to weave plain cloth, an hour an inch to weave tapestry. Alyce didn't rush, but neither did she rest.

Early in the night, as the whip-poor-will called back and forth across the yard, she put on an album—ambient trance for its repetitiveness—on low volume, so as not to wake Molly in the adjacent room, but by halfway through the first track she'd tuned it out, hadn't noticed when the album finished and the noises of the night took over. For the ranch was never silent, always creaking and groaning, animals making their contributions of howls and scrapes and high steps through the fallen mounds of leaves covering the ground in dunes. Autumn colors. Earth tones.

But then Alyce heard something that did grab her attention, causing her to stop short, head perking up like an antenna: a shrill cry tore through the night. She tried to place it. Screech owls? A howler monkey from the rescue zoo down the road? Then, the scream came again, sounding much closer. Actually, it seemed to be coming from directly down the hall.

The door to her studio burst open and, for a moment, Alyce thought it was her oldest son, Jake, running from a nightmare. But, no. Her sons were gone, and Molly stood there in a nightgown, panting, eyes wide, yelling, "Bat out of hell!"

"What?" Alyce stood, using her body to block Molly's view of the loom behind her. "Are you hurt?"

Molly fell quiet, then smiled sheepishly. "I'm not hurt. I woke up to pee, and then I was attacked . . ."

". . . by a poor bat that somehow got stuck in the house. Show me." Alyce closed the door behind them, relieved once Molly was outside the studio.

In the bedroom that had once been her sons', bunks still stacked in place, Alyce took a broom from the corner. The frightened bat swooped erratically back and forth, throwing itself off the walls as if stuck in a crazed pinball machine. Alyce had the sense the animal was trying to shake the house off like a hat. Molly screamed again when it dove toward their heads.

Patiently, Alyce used the broad lunging motions of the broom to herd it out of the room and down the hall. The bat dodged and squeaked and darted, but eventually complied. When they got near the front door, she kicked it open and, with one large swat, guided the bat outside.

"Nothing to it."

The house quiet again, Alyce wanted to return to her loom, the weaving rush still coursing through her. She felt antsy as Molly followed her to the kitchen, chattering away: "Thanks. Now I feel silly. I have to pee like three times during the night, and when I saw that thing's beady little eyes staring at me from the ceiling, it freaked the shit out of me. No way I'll get back to sleep now. . . ." Molly began making a pot of coffee.

"Sometimes they get in through the fireplace." Alyce stuffed the broom into a closet. "Not often, though." She inched her way awkwardly toward the kitchen door.

"Alyce," said Molly, holding her gaze. "Have a cup of coffee with me. Please."

Alyce nodded. Leaning against the counter, she thought back to her loom, still mentally weaving, under and over. Then, suddenly, she felt desperate for water—she often forgot to drink while she was working—and took a glass down from the cupboard only after catching with the palms of her hands those first deep sips from the tap. As she looked out the window, something moved in the yard, skirting the edge of the porch just past where the moonlight stopped. Four creatures, like dogs, but more muscular. She'd heard coyotes most nights howling back and forth across the 250-acre property, but this was the first time she'd caught sight of them.

Alyce motioned for Molly to follow her into the living room for a better view. The darkness blurred the beasts' edges, causing their movements to seem stealthier, more menacing. The smallest one shifted from leg to leg as though waiting for something. There was a firefly, and the small coyote jumped after it into the air, playful but ungraceful, crashing back down to the ground.

"Holy cow," said Molly.

The coyotes must have been together, a pack. And yet Alyce thought they took almost no notice of one another, like it was only an accident that they'd each found themselves here in the yard of this particular ranch on this particular night, an apathetic partnership of utility.

Everything is so strange, thought Alyce. There was an old wives' tale that a bird in the house foretold a death in the house; she wondered if it was the same for bats. She thought of the baby birds, knocked from their nest on the porch, squirming and naked in the grass. All signs pointed in one direction.

The coffeemaker dinged at the same time that the coyotes disappeared out the gate. In the kitchen, Alyce watched Molly, now wearing a wool sweater, pour steaming black liquid into two cups resting on round saucers, the discreet movements of her body like yarn coming together on the loom. There was something different about Molly.

"Why do you have to pee three times a night? Is that one of your symptoms?"

"Yes." Molly sat at the small square country table. "But not of HD."

The two women looked at each other. Nothing shocked Alyce anymore. She sipped and then nodded. "How many weeks are you?"

"It doesn't matter." Molly blew gently on her cup. "It won't be here much longer."

Alyce wanted to say, well, in that case, it fits right in. But she didn't. "I'll go with you to the clinic."

"Soon."

They drank their coffee out of cups covered in geometric designs that Alyce didn't remember buying at a table that felt like someone else's. Where did all this stuff come from?

"Don't you miss Harry?" asked Molly. "And the boys?"

Alyce shrugged. "I have you." She didn't notice the curious look Molly gave her.

The truth was Alyce did not feel the absence of Harry and her sons so much as she felt the absence of their needs. The absence of the need to check on them in their sleep. To see if they were still breathing. The absence of the need to make breakfast in a few hours. Of the need to smile and respond to questions and entertain them and listen to incoherent children's stories.

"You didn't have to kick them out," said Molly. "I still feel horrible."

"Not this again." Alyce was unable to keep the sharpness from her voice. "It was inevitable."

"Okay. Then why be so weird and secretive about it?"

"People separate. It's sad; it's not weird. Harry needs to learn to be on his own. And so do I." Alyce got up and placed her cup in the sink. "Get some rest, babe. I have work to do."

"Another mystery," said Molly.

Inside the cluttered studio, warmly aglow with three green lamps craned directly on the loom, Alyce slumped onto her stool. Any mention of Harry and her children felt like a distraction from the cause.

She looked down at her embedded wedding band, impossible to get off her finger without petroleum jelly. She and Harry had been married at a Houston society event—in a chandeliered ballroom with turtle soup and a ten-piece zoot suit band—that she truly thought lovely even if it was far from the wedding she would have planned in the absence of Harry's parents. The wedding itself was mostly a blur. She remembered much of her and Harry's excitement stemming from the distinction of being the first in the group to get hitched—not because their friends mooned over getting paired up, but because a wedding seemed to signal that they were all entering a new, possibly exciting stage of life. It was the same when Jake was born. The novelty of babies. Nobody else had any yet, which meant they still had extra time and money and attention to lavish on the new, little family.

Flannery brought baby Jake carved wooden animals from Nigeria when she came home for Christmas that year, and she cooed over him as if he were the most miraculous thing. Then her best friend returned to Africa and left Alyce pressing the mysterious new baby to her chest, the wooden animals staring at her from a shelf. She hadn't necessarily wished she were Flannery, living and traveling in far-flung places, but she hadn't wanted to be herself, either, all alone with an incomprehensible being for whose very life she was entirely responsible. It began feeling less like a choice and more like a game of musical chairs—the music stopped and she was surprised to find herself sitting next to Harry holding this baby.

It was around this time Alyce and Flannery began trading books, one of the ways they kept in touch across continents—through marginalia scribbled in the paperback novels they loaned back and forth. The things you didn't necessarily say out loud over the phone.

It was to Nigeria Alyce sent *Anna Karenina*, the ending highlighted by a heart with an arrow through it. She'd sent that book right after learning Flannery planned to stay in West Africa once the EOP was finished.

"How are you living?" Alyce had asked when Flannery told her she wasn't ready to move back.

"I'm living with that guy I told you about. We're okay. I spend my free time reading paperbacks from the book trade library they keep at the university here. I'm down to the French detective novels."

"You don't speak French."

"Right now I'm reading about a rabbit who steals diamond necklaces. Although it might actually be about a woman in a hat who likes spaghetti."

"Or a butcher who keeps hundreds of parakeets in the basement."

"So you've read it."

Later, Flannery responded to *Anna Karenina* by sending Ben Okri's *The Famished Road*, underlining this on the first page: "And we sorrowed much because there were always those of us who had just returned from the world of the Living. They had returned inconsolable for all the love they had left behind, all the suffering they hadn't redeemed, all that they hadn't understood, and for all that they had barely begun to learn before they were drawn back to the land of origins."

When Harry started thinking about opening his architecture firm somewhere outside his hometown of Houston, Alyce had said, "Well, we could go back to Austin, if you really want to," as if she had no particular stake. Only please, Brer Fox, please don't throw me into the briar patch. But she was wrong if she'd thought returning to where they'd met and fallen in love would change things. One morning, two years after the move, lying in bed as the alarm went off, two children watching cartoons in the living room, Alyce realized she was more than just bored, more than just depressed. She was no longer in love with her husband. Where they had once both been birds, coasting along as part of the same flock, over time he'd become the hunter who stalked her, trying not to cling, remaining perfectly still in the blind, waiting for her to get close to him again. She was spooked; he was paralyzed.

Alyce picked up the butterfly filled with fine, gold metallic yarn and pulled it along where the shed separated every other vertical warp thread. Working the yarn more slowly, she made a curve by stepping the weft, finishing the shape of Flannery's shoulder. Then, to fill in the core, she began crosshatching gold thread with orange; when the yarn turned to go the opposite direction, she used the interlocking technique to avoid creating a slit in the fabric. For this to work the two weft colors had to be woven toward each other in one shed and away from each other in the opposite. This was the only rule of tapestry that couldn't be ignored.

Weaving two similar colors together created shading. It imbued that area of the cloth with a richness and, in this case, made Flannery's neck appear to reflect light. Sometimes Alyce used up to five hues to shade one object, still giving the illusion of a single blended surface.

As she wove, Alyce's thoughts returned to Harry, trying to piece together where things first went wrong between them. Because that was something else her sons had a right to know. She was weaving them a tapestry about her greatest happiness—wouldn't they eventually wonder why it hadn't lasted? And if she said the words out loud, was it not possible the syllables might wrap themselves around the threads, becoming part of the wisdom of the tapestry itself?

When you're older, you'll start to wonder why your father and I split up. You might even be angry. Kids worry it's their fault; it isn't your fault.

Which is not to say things didn't change when you showed up. You see, parenthood expanded your father: he became warm and doting, attentive to the slightest shift in your moods as if connected to you through shock sensors. He goofed around the house, play-wrestling and singing lyrics to the dumb songs you learned at daycare.

Do you remember how when we moved to the ranch y'all were frightened by the moans coming from the lions at the rescue zoo a few miles away? Your father made a pen in the living room out of chairs and got inside to show you how sad the caged lions were, not scary. "Roar," he said pitifully, crawling and hanging his head. "Roar."

Well, I didn't transform into a natural parent like your father. I suppose I'm not particularly wired for nuclear family contentment in the first place. Here's the only way I can think to explain it: Before either of you were born, your father and I used to make trips to wherever our closest friends were living at the time—your uncle Steven consulting in Dallas,

Aunt Flannery in grad school in Wisconsin, Santiago in Boston, even Brandon and Molly that year they lived in Ann Arbor. We would arrive and buy an unlimited bus pass and a map to the museums; but these plans usually turned into spending all day making fall soups in the apartment, reading next to windows that were open to counteract the first week of heat from angry, spewing radiators. Butternut and acorn squash, leeks and celery. We drank cheap wine from the corner store and dipped bread into the soup, getting full until we no longer felt up for dancing at the one club that wasn't too posh or too ghetto or too hipster or too fratty, and would instead play Trivial Pursuit or Scrabble until drink made us sleepy, snuggling into the hard mattress of the pullout sofa and drifting off to the sound of sirens and passing car stereos.

What am I trying to say here? Maybe that part of the initial glow between your father and me had something to do with our place in the larger group living at Dryden House, that special web of chemistry and exclusivity, which after graduation scattered and weakened. It sounds awful, but on our own, maybe Harry and I just weren't enough.

Of course, one of my therapists suggested the problems began earlier. Not with Harry but with me. Did you boys know I was a mechanical engineer once? Growing up, I'd wanted so much to fly like a bird, then to at least make planes that flew like one, effortlessly—so I went to an engineering college. We were nerds, immersing ourselves in propulsion and aerodynamics, navigation systems and, my favorite, celestial mechanics. What a name—celestial mechanics. The tools of creation itself.

During one of these all-nighters—have I told you this story already?—I joined a group of engineers angry about the raise in tuition announced that day in the student newspaper. With pulleys, winches, ropes, and two twenty-foot wooden A-frames, we managed to lift and turn a full 180 degrees the, I don't know, two-thousand-pound statue of founder William Marsh that sat in the middle of the academic quad. We turned its back to the administration building. The university paid some-

thing like two thousand bucks for a construction firm to turn the statue back around. It took them a week, and they broke it in the process.

After graduation, I was miserable. I worked for an airplane manufacturer outside Houston for one year and learned that the chance to do a new plane design was remote; mostly what aeronautical engineers do is confirm calculations, make minor adjustments. So I quit and began making my living halfheartedly as a commercial fiber artist, convincing myself it really wasn't so different from what I'd done as an engineer— taking materials and testing them, contorting them—just on a smaller scale, without lives riding on it. Weaving was satisfying, nothing more, nothing less. I did a little each day and eventually a concrete object was the result. For a while it was enough.

I had hoped the buoyancy that surfaced at Marsh might become the fact of who I was as a person: an easy, lighthearted floater. Helium. Back then, it was the way I draped my pale limbs over Harry in the library and at the campus pub that made up for his rigidness, my airy affection that emanated outward and surrounded our friends. I had thought that was the beginning of something bigger. A marriage, a family. But it wasn't the beginning. It was the thing itself, and it was almost over.

After tying off the threads to Flannery's torso, a flush of luminescence already visible on the horizon outside, Alyce felt like a washcloth all wrung out. She went into the bathroom, splashed water on her face. As she hung the towel back on the rack, she noticed something strange sticking out of Molly's bathroom case: prenatal vitamins. Alyce wondered what a soon-to-be-terminated fetus needed with those.

MOLLY

The two women sat on the low-water crossing, feet dangling into the creek. The day was overcast, and occasional sharp gusts of wind whipped through.

"Can't a dying woman get any sunshine around here?" Molly's hands were wrapped around the plastic cup of watermelon agua fresca she'd taken to blending for herself each morning.

"Oh, no," said Alyce, although there was no bite to her words. "You cannot start saying shit like that."

When Molly looked at Alyce, it was like looking at an old photograph where the colors had become washed out. "I bet Jake and Ian had a ball swimming here in the summer." Below them, minnows circled and dispersed, circled and dispersed. "Is that a rope swing down there?"

"Um-hm," said Alyce groggily. "Ian's too young to use it, though."

It was early November, and the creek running through the ranch had come back from the summer drought and was gurgling along, water flowing over the limestone bottom in a blue-green translucence. It was deeper than it looked.

Even abbreviated conversations with Alyce, like this one— about something in particular, out in the daylight—were rare. In the weeks since she'd arrived at the ranch, Molly felt like an ocean lapping against Alyce's rocky shoreline. They crossed paths in the early morning and late at night—she'd watched Alyce stand in front of the open fridge for long minutes, as if pulling free a carton of pulpy orange juice took the mustering of unfathomable strength—but the rest of the time they existed in parallel planes. Molly spent most of her days walking: from room to room in the ranch house and over the wild acreage outside, one hand placed on her belly as if she might fold over and be sick, fighting imaginary arguments with her husband and her father. Why did you collude to keep this from me? How could you turn out to be such bastards? Molly must have walked a hundred miles.

"It's been more than a month." Molly consciously kept her voice easy, as if she were talking about what to cook for dinner. She'd hoped her friend would reach this realization on her own, but it had become obvious Alyce needed a push. "That's a long time in kid years. You've got to invite them out, Snow White. Whatever's going on between you and Harry, you're still their mother."

Alyce skipped a stone across the surface of the water. "Being a mother is hard. In the best of circumstances. I just want to make that clear."

Molly swallowed and returned her attention to the creek. She wondered if that might be a water moccasin periscoping its head just before the bend. "I'll help you. I know you're not feeling well, but we can entertain them for one afternoon."

They sat in silence for a moment, but Molly just couldn't help herself: "Alyce, I don't know a single person who regrets their children after they're born."

"I don't regret them," said Alyce quickly. "They're good boys. But don't kid yourself, Moll. People don't allow themselves to regret their children—it's a physiological defense mechanism—but that doesn't mean they were all meant to be parents. That doesn't mean the decision should be made lightly."

"Christ." Molly stood, not sure if she was still angry about Al-

yce's abandonment of Jake and Ian or at what her friend was implying. "Just invite them out here. Or go to the city to see them. You
have to. It's your job."

Alyce shrugged. "Fine. When are you going to invite your family
out?"

Molly watched a blue heron dive-bomb a fish jumping from the
creek. Alyce must have known that Molly couldn't see those people
because then it would become real, the small swell of her stomach
growing in prominence each day, refusing to be ignored. When
she thought of what was inside, which she tried to avoid doing, she
imagined a cold pinprick of light. "I'm going for a walk."

"Okay." The dark circles under Alyce's eyes made it clear she'd
been up most of the night in her studio, as per usual. Molly watched
her petite friend rise to her feet in baggy flannel pajamas, house
shoes coated in dirt, holding a stretched cardigan closed with one
hand; she tried to tease out the contradiction between Alyce's obvious frailty and the growing sense that this broken woman was the
only thing protecting Molly . . . from what?

The two women walked separate ways.

As Molly moved along the trail winding between thickets of dense
cedar, her thoughts returned to what she'd read in the newspaper that
morning: the city's budget shortfalls meant all public pools would
remain closed next year, their gaping concrete mouths empty. The
article made her think of Brandon. Though it was months away, her
husband always looked forward to March, because that was when
the swimming pool in their neighborhood usually opened—spring
being just a milder form of summer in central Texas. He swam laps
there on his way home from work, and Molly liked to imagine him:
pausing every few lengths to clear the fog from leaky goggles, the
reddish evening sun fanning through the struggling magnolia tree
that shaded the north corner. The pool was small and surrounded

by a thin perimeter of sandy ground that refused to grow grass, but Brandon wouldn't notice that once he was in the water, following the black lane marker painted on the bottom of the pool. As he crawled toward the deep end, the bottom receding beneath him, he told her he liked to imagine his body was an airplane taking off until he flew miles above the ground, the settled leaves on the pool floor little towns in the distance below. On the return length, his body seemed to float back down, landing softly in the shallow end.

Molly understood that the swimming pool served as a cushion between his two worlds. Between science and home. It pained her that he would lose that next year. It pained her that everything about his life would be different now.

As she walked, she also obsessed about the book still ensconced in her suitcase. Her mother's journal. Molly's father had given it to her years ago—at the time, she'd thought because Flan was always moving. She could now almost laugh at her naïveté, at her father's blunt hints. But still Molly had not read the journal, not a word of it, afraid of what she might find in the thoughts of a woman dying from a horrible disease, knowing she'd likely passed it on to at least one of her children. Occasionally, Molly took out the book and flipped the pages with her thumb, letting the handwritten scrawls pass too fast for any one word to catch. Was a short life better than none at all? Was that a stupid question? How selfish was it to have a child when you knew your blood was a vector for poison?

That afternoon, Molly stood at the door to Alyce's studio under the pretense of borrowing packing tape and scissors from the dented metal supply cabinet for a package she was planning to mail. Alyce was creepily protective of her studio space, but for once she was fast asleep in her bedroom, and so Molly decided it was best to act now and apologize later.

Swinging open the creaky door, Molly was confronted by what Alyce had been working on so intensely, so secretly, all these weeks. The ends of the tapestry were rolled up on the loom like two ends of a scroll; Molly could see that the entire work would be enormous. The section splayed out flat was unfinished and reminded her of the diagrams of human bodies found in biology classrooms, each successive layer revealed: skin, then muscle, then bone. At the right end of the loom the picture unraveled into nothing but rows of taut threads. A skeleton. But on the left, the image was almost fully wrought.

Molly remembered learning about the famous unicorn tapestries from medieval times, the white-horned colts prancing among lush spring gardens on blue backgrounds, shimmering and grand, nothing like what was displayed on Alyce's loom. What Molly saw spooked her. The image appeared to be moving across the cloth. And yet something about it was familiar, like a scene from a dream Molly barely remembered. A fluttering at the periphery, a rising up. Molly put her hands in front of her face, looking at the tapestry through the lattice of her fingers. It felt like when she'd awoken to the bat in her bedroom, the screech and wing beat as it flew past her.

The image made Molly think of her sister, something in the expression, in the tilt of the head. It wasn't even a human figure and yet, if she squinted, she could almost believe her sister was standing at the corner of her vision. Almost. If like Ovid's Philomela—raped and her tongue ripped out, with no other means to speak—Alyce was trying to tell her something by weaving this tapestry, Molly did not yet understand what it was.

She grabbed the packing tape from the cabinet and quickly walked out of the room.

Molly left the ranch, driving out of the gate and down the country road toward a forked Y where the blue post office drop box sat exposed in the sun. It was the farthest she'd been from the ranch in weeks. The rural isolation felt protective but also like a strange purgatory, an anteroom before the end.

From years spent around scientists, Molly knew there were two theories about how the universe itself might culminate: expansion or contraction. In the expansion scenario, the universe would just continue unfurling from the Big Bang until the pull of gravity that held galaxies and solar systems together weakened and the energy in stars dimmed. Everything would get farther and farther apart, growing colder, snuffing out.

Proponents of the second theory thought the outward-thrusting universe would achieve a final point of tension, like a balloon reaching its limit, at which point everything in the universe would begin to reverse course, contracting back into the single point of origin, a pebble of fire.

Molly didn't have feelings one way or the other about what might happen to the universe—frankly, she didn't really care, seeing as how humans wouldn't be around for the big reveal—but nevertheless, as she'd sat at the kitchen table earlier wrapping her mother's journal in bubble wrap, this thought crossed her mind: most people's lives are like the second theory. We contract back in on ourselves. We slowly lose the ability to work, to remember, to function. We lose friends and know fewer and fewer people in the world. Mostly this happened later, in old age. But not always.

From watching her mother, Molly knew this cycle sped up when a person became terminally ill, the heavier burden shared between fewer people, the seraphim who tacitly agreed to take on the difficult emotional and physical work of transporting you to the other side. In the middle stage, when the chorea had worsened but her mental faculties were still mostly intact, Molly's mother sometimes cried as she took pill after pill, each swallow more difficult than the one before.

As Molly rolled down her window to drop the package into the mail, Flannery's address staring back in bold, black ink, she almost began to cry herself. Dropping her mother's journal into the yawning hole of the postal system seemed like a betrayal. But her mother had been gone a long time. Her mother's story was not necessarily Molly's, though they would die the same way. Molly wanted to remember her mother for other things: For turning suddenly to spray them with the hose as she worked in her garden, tiny hands in oversized work gloves. For practicing her cockney accent, in preparation for *Pygmalion* auditions, during their Friday-night spaghetti dinner.

Molly forced herself to wonder why she felt compelled to send the journal on to Flannery, as if her sister would know what to do with its unholy heft. As if by being free of the disease, her sister deserved some role in Molly's disintegration. But the real reason was that Molly wasn't sure she remembered her mother spraying them with water or speaking in a bad cockney at the dinner table. Those were stories Flannery told; it was Flannery who translated their mother's life for Molly.

As she drove back to the ranch, Molly felt like a leech. A bloodsucker. Flannery had her faults, to be sure, but Molly was only beginning to understand how much and for how long she'd used her sister, too.

Growing up, Molly believed Flannery understood things about the world she herself did not. And this was probably true at first. In a house full of secrets and illness, Flannery was older and grew more quickly attuned to the subtle gambits living there required. Flannery knew when to turn up the pink jam box to drown out sobs from the other room. When to nudge their parents out of silence by catapulting canned spinach or mashed potatoes onto the pink antique wallpaper. And when to just disappear from the house altogether, sitting one-behind-the-other on the Nash "Executioner" skateboard and rolling down the bumpy asphalt hill.

Molly got through by following directly in Flannery's footprints: keep your head down, put one foot in front of the other, don't look up or around because vultures might be circling. She followed Flannery to Marsh and co-opted Flannery's friends—it was what she'd always done. She also fell in love with them, like she fell in love with worlds in her illustrated books as a child, thinking if she managed to pry her way inside, the characters there would protect her from whatever lurked in the dark water below the ocean surface, so deep she couldn't begin to fathom what it might be.

Flannery moved to Nigeria the same year Molly and Brandon lived in Ann Arbor for Brandon's postdoc, and it was the first time Molly had been entirely separated from her father and sister and sister's friends. She remembered it as a time of waiting. Waiting for Brandon to meet her at a fancy hotel bar, for example, an Asian woman with an enormous diamond ring sitting a few stools down talking to the bartender about her husband's organization: something that involved repairing limbs. The bartender made an amaretto sour for the woman and a martini for her husband, just arrived with their twentysomething daughter who whispered "Make it neat" to the bartender; they all laughed. The woman handed the drink to her daughter and said to the bartender, "They're really the drinkers." Molly eavesdropped as the father told his daughter, who must have been a University of Michigan student, that he was proud of her but that she had to be—he pointed upward—"top, top, top to get into PhD." Molly felt alone. She thought of the volunteer group that stood on the corner of a major downtown intersection during the dark, brutal Ann Arbor winter with a sign reading FREE HUGS.

When she finally saw Brandon walking across the room toward her, smiling—they were meeting to celebrate his first publication—

everything was suddenly all right again. He was her most precious representative of the magical, safe environment her sister and her sister's friends created for Molly, like a tortoiseshell. She remembered thinking in that bar in Ann Arbor that the fact was, in the real world, you couldn't be with everyone you loved. You had to pick one person, follow him, and hope he followed you.

But now, as Molly pulled her car in behind the ranch house and turned off the ignition, watching Alyce emerge from the door and sit heavy on the porch swing, she thought: What if your life turned out to be more than one person could handle? Molly wanted to pick up the phone and call her husband, dial the only number she knew anymore by heart. She imagined what he might be doing at that very moment: walking down a bland, institutional corridor, his heavy bag hanging crosswise on his shoulder, but also feeling burdened by all the things lost: the loss of his youth, of his parents' language, of the security of a social fabric where one could count on raises and tenure and stocks going up over the long haul, of his wife.

Molly knew Brandon would try to comfort her, but in that moment she could not bear the thought of his confused, wary, frightened form of comfort. If a woman cries and nobody is there to see it . . . ? She didn't make the call.

FLANNERY

lannery's life was now pushed along by an all-consuming current: lab, sleep, Kunle; lab, sleep, Kunle. She was focused. She was an arrow on the way to its mark. Her sister's disease was the air around her, impossible not to breathe in with every breath, but possible to ignore in that way one always ignores the unconscious workings of the body.

Brandon helped her begin new calculations, and Flannery existed to make them work, returning to her apartment only to sack out, shower, and have long, meandering conversations with Kunle on the telephone as she trolled the Internet looking for nearby silos to house the custom ice chamber that was their next big move. Every step forward in the project felt like a step closer to Nigeria.

As weeks passed, her love for Kunle became like light through a prism, each beam emerging as a different color. Some days it was a love that made her sick to her stomach, an anxious and jealous love, an insecure love of long violet days. Some days she loved him to obsession, to distraction, almost to the exclusion of all other thoughts, a bright red pulse. The timbre of his voice became home.

Their relationship reverted to its earliest phase. They talked on the phone like teenagers, flirting and teasing each other, revealing old secrets from childhood. They talked about what they were wearing and eating, what they dreamed about at night, what they overheard on the bus. They played each other new favorite songs, holding a cell phone up to computer speakers. When she didn't think about Molly, when she was able to keep everything compartmentalized, Flannery would even have said she was happy.

But though they talked every day, stories and anecdotes spilling out of them, and though Flannery was pursuing the cloud-seeding project for Nigerians like Kunle and his family, they rarely spoke of work or her progress in the lab. He asked, but she put him off. She told herself it was because he wasn't a snow scientist, an Iceman, and wouldn't understand the intricacies of what she was up to.

But one morning he brought it up again, more forcefully, wanting to know why she'd changed projects. "Flan, explain it to me again. Why is this taking so long?"

"Because it will work." Flannery was at her apartment eating breakfast, mopping up the last bits of egg yolk with a slice of charred toast.

"But if you just keep starting over . . ."

"What I'm doing could save the Sahel. Maybe. Eventually."

"But when will you be back?"

"You're not hearing me," she said between bites, spearing triangles of grapefruit, slipping them onto her tongue and pressing out the sour juice with the roof of her mouth.

"I hear another white person convinced they're going to save Africa from itself."

"Don't."

"Send along your data," he said. "I have to go now if I'm going to make it to evening service, but e-mail me what you've got so far." Kunle's church was called Redeemed and consisted of a small congregation in a concrete strip mall. Back in Nigeria, Flannery's favorite part of Sunday was watching Kunle press slacks and a white button-down oxford, standing next to the ironing board in his boxers, stroking hot metal over cloth with a gentle precision.

"I'll e-mail it to you."

After breakfast, Flannery didn't feel like going directly to the lab. The conversation with Kunle had left her feeling at loose ends. On a whim, and perhaps also putting off the task of organizing and sending her work-in-progress to Kunle, Flannery decided to attend church herself. It was Sunday morning on her side of the world, and there were several churches nearby. Surely one of them would have a service. While Flannery didn't believe in God per se, she liked the idea of a solemn space where she could sit and think, of being in church at the same time as Kunle, mirroring him across an ocean.

Wearing a floral consignment-store dress with a high waist, she walked ten minutes to the orange-brick Methodist church that she'd passed so many times without thinking and settled down into a pew beneath a stained-glass window depicting Jonah being swallowed by the whale. As she waited, Kunle's accusations came back to her. Was she doing the wrong thing? Just another white person trying to save Africa from itself? She remembered when two men were digging a ditch for a sewer pipeline behind her house in Nigeria, and she watched them from her kitchen window. They were waist-deep in the hole, scooping out black dirt with shovels. Not wearing shirts, their torsos glistened with sweat, smooth and hairless as newborns; wiry and chiseled; darkest, shiniest obsidian she'd ever laid eyes on. At that moment Flannery was a redneck who whistled obscenely from a truck. Or she was Lorca writing Spanish poems about gypsy women.

After a short processional, the entire church stood and sang "Glory Hallelujah," gospel style, hymnals yawning open.

"Church in the morning, science in the afternoon," she used to say to Kunle as they walked back to campus, linked arms swinging alongside their bodies.

"Whatever you do, just don't call me a 'freethinker,'" he would joke, mocking the fact that this was a derogatory term in Nigeria for atheists or agnostics.

The sermon that morning in the small church in East Austin was on the parable of the talents. The landlord goes away and leaves his "talents," or money, with three servants; the first two invest what they were given and double it while the third simply buries his in the ground for safekeeping. Upon the landlord's return, he praises the first two for their enterprise and castigates the third for laziness. The minister at the pulpit, swaddled in billowing, wine-colored robes, told Flannery and the rest of the congregation that this parable had very little to do with money or the stock market "as some capitalists would have it." He claimed it was about not wasting what the Holy Spirit had given you. Do something real with your personal talents; take risks out in the world.

As she listened to the call-and-response between the preacher and congregation, Flannery's hands became fists. She wished Kunle were sitting beside her on the pew, listening to her vindication. Do something real with your personal talents, the pastor had said. Take risks, he'd said. Change the world, was what she heard. She needed Kunle to understand that this was what her cloud-seeding project could do. Where was his magical thinking now?

At the Climate Institute in the middle of the night, the only noise was the squeak of the janitor mopping the floor with long, mechanical strokes. Some nights one or two graduate students roamed the halls, having started an experiment too late in the day, held hostage by the unhurried pace of biological or chemical processes. But not tonight. Tonight it was just Flannery and the janitor and Kepler.

It was common to hear ice specialists tell students the earliest scientific account of snow came from Descartes, whose "Les Météores" described the product of winter storms as "little roses or wheels with six rounded semicircular teeth. . . ." But, decades before, Johannes Kepler, the astronomer who discovered the laws of planetary motion, wrote a small, little-known book, a New Year's gift to his patron in 1611, called *The Six-Cornered Snowflake*. Flannery's copy, dog-eared and worn, had the original Latin on the left, the English translation on the right.

In the background, Flan was running numbers through her computer model as she had every night this week, and as she sat at the long white table in front of the big white screen, she reread Kepler's little tract of intellectual curiosity, following along as he attempted to puzzle out the question of *why snowflakes, when they first fall . . . always come down with six corners and six radii tufted like feathers.*

The computer modeling for something like cloud seeding was slow and arduous. She played with humidity percentages and temperature; she adjusted the software's equations and started over. It would work eventually. It had to. Flannery waited.

She'd heard nothing from Alyce or her sister in weeks, and their disappearances from her life made her feel both excluded and relieved. But mostly she didn't think about them at all. She thought about her project, about Kunle and Nigeria and snow falling in the desert.

Flannery took comfort in Kepler, imagining the young astronomer during a dark Prague winter, crossing a bridge over the Moldau under moonlight, watching flakes from a snowstorm *bearing a likeness to the stars* alight on his coat before evaporating into shapelessness. Even the earliest known scientific drawings of snowflakes were done fifty years after Kepler's book, in the 1665 *Micrographia* where Robert Hooke used a crude microscope to first view the intricacies of snow crystals up close. Even he had to draw them from memory, though; they melted too fast.

Kepler had nothing but his eyes and his mind to ask *who shaped the little head before it fell, giving it six frozen horns.* It was not really less magical to Flannery now than it was to Kepler then. She knew snow-flakes were six-cornered because of the crystalline geometry of ice molecules—something that took three hundred more years and the x-ray machine for scientists to discover—but they still used the word *morphogenesis* to describe the process of water vapor condensing into snow. A self-assembly. A spontaneous creation of form. As though snowflakes were indeed motivated by a kind of soul, or what Kepler hypothesized to originate from the facultas formatrix, an enigmatic, shape-giving force that radiated from the bowels of the earth *and its vehicle is vapor, just as breath is the vehicle of the human soul.*

On this nighttime wandering with Kepler's book, Flannery fancied she was the astronomer and Kunle her patron, to whom she tried to explain snow crystals. Psalm 147:16 reads, "He giveth snow like wool; he scattereth the hoarfrost like ashes." Flannery imagined holding a handful of beautiful six-cornered stars out to Kunle, who had never touched snow before, as a gift. Like the gift of this small book that Kepler presented to his friend, except Flannery's gift would be better. Flannery's gift might transform the small, shriveling yam farm Kunle's mother slaved over into something green and vibrant again.

Dressed in Kepler's coat, she would tell Kunle to look closely and ask if he thought it formed such a shape *according to the dictates of the material, or rather out of its own nature, to which would be innate either the archetype of beauty that is present in the hexagon or an understanding of the purpose which that figure serves.*

She would walk him inside a stone house to find a jar of honey-comb on the shelf, and she would lift the waxy cells out of the container and press it into his hand, dripping with sticky honey that he would lick from the tips of his fingers. Look, she would say, how the honeycomb has a similar structure. *If you should ask the geometers on what plan the cells of bees are built, they will reply, on a hexagonal plan. The answer is clear from a simple look at the openings or entrances, and the sides that form the cells.*

And that is not the only thing in nature. From a bowl of fruit on the wooden table she would grasp a pink pomegranate and cut it open, letting the seeds spill out. They would stare at the pulpy hexagonal caves where the rest of the seeds remained trapped. *The material is certainly not a factor because the bees do not find rhombic plates of this kind already in existence anywhere. And the cause of the shape of the pomegranate seed is thus in the soul of the plant, which is responsible for the growth of the fruit.*

Kunle would look at her and nod but say that snowflakes were not bees nor were they pomegranates. Snowflakes were not alive. *No such purpose can be observed in the shaping of the snowflake, since the six-cornered arrangement does not make it last longer, or produce a fixed, natural body of definite and lasting shape. My response is that the formative principle does not act only for the sake of ends, but also for the sake of adornment.*

Flannery would nod and lead Kunle back outside to look at crystals from inside the earth. They were also made from self-organizing molecules, which was why diamonds and rubies and emeralds each have a particular pattern of facets. Pliny the Elder thought quartz was ice frozen so hard it could not melt.

At this point Kunle would take her hand and bring her into the winter bathroom, where they would slowly strip off their coats and clothes to stand naked, staring at each other's needy bodies. He would point to the snowflake-like frost on the window from where the glass came into contact with the steam of the hot bath *when the*

rigor of winter comes up against broken windows. . . . For what entrance,
what exit, what narrow openings, what struggle can there be in the wide
fields of the air?

Kunle would hold Flannery to his chest as they stood surrounded
by the steam and frost of seventeenth-century Prague. They were
together. Flannery would feel her own body slowly become the
shape of a snowflake, beginning with the hard, brilliant crystal
center and expanding out to the delicate branches made of hair and
fingernails. She would begin to fall through the night sky; *all the*
tufts point outward from the center of the star or double cross, almost like
the needles on the branches of firs—which is proof that the formative force
builds its nest in the center and from there distributes itself equally in all
directions.

Two days later, Kunle called. Flannery had just arrived home after
another long night at the lab and was picking up her mail at the
apartment complex office, a small brown package from Molly.

Kunle had read through her data, he said on the phone, and was
not impressed. He could hardly believe she was extending her stay
in the States to work on something as ridiculous as cloud seeding.

She felt her body turn red, a rising warmth. His voice was a stone
being thrown at her. "Did you even look at the proposal? The numbers are showing it could work if we seed in the troughs of high-
pressure cells."

"With potentially disastrous results for neighboring regions . . ."

"We don't know. . . ."

"Let me land. What you're doing," Kunle told her—accused
her, "is for yourself. It's no longer about my country. It's not about
anyone but you."

He sounded so far away. Flannery panicked. If only Kunle were
right here, with her. Then she could explain things properly. She

closed her eyes. She silently, reflexively began reciting the types of snow crystals she'd learned in graduate school: diamond dust, stellar dendrite, sectored plate, split star, needle, chandelier crystal . . .

"If you cared about me and my family, you'd be here. You'd be with me in Adamanta."

Diamond dust, stellar dendrite, sectored plate, split star, needle, chandelier crystal . . . on the other end of the line, Kunle went on talking and talking, his voice rising and falling, but the words blended together until it sounded as if he were speaking a different language, his real language that she did not understand. Flannery hung up the phone. Just another dropped international call, she would tell him later. So sorry. So, so sorry.

She looked down at the package in her hands, her sister's name scribbled in the return address box, and felt confused and numb. Kunle was wrong about her project. Flannery was determined to show him just how wrong.

SANTIAGO

*I*f he were asked, which he never was, Santiago would say he was hanging in there.

One cold Saturday in early November Harry's two boys played video games with lots of explosions and hung from the exposed beams of the upstairs, screeching like howler monkeys, forcing Santiago to escape into the relative quiet of the fire station's still-unfinished downstairs bathroom. He placed a sheet of particleboard over the bathtub to create a makeshift desk for his laptop, sitting cross-legged on the floor strewn with jagged bits of tile samples.

Santiago could feel Harry's presence in the other room, still working on the Marfa cube, rotating the images with his mouse, scrolling through specs. Sometimes Harry said things under his breath to which Santiago didn't know how to respond, things like, "This is what it must feel like to design a piece of sky." And, "The problem with the desert is that it's not square."

Santiago was trying to earn extra cash and exposure for the firm by entering design contests like the one he was working on now in the bathroom. The City of Houston wanted images for a campaign to advertise its sprawling, polluted metropolis as a still-thriving business hub, claiming to be in search of something edgy and innovative, not just the regular Tourism Board claptrap. Santiago doubted that, but figured it was worth a shot.

Contemplating which images to submit, he clicked through digital photographs taken recently on a cloudy day at the Houston Ship Channel—before his camera was almost confiscated by security guards suspicious he might be scouting the dredged waterway for a future terrorist attack. The photographs were close-ups of the stacks and stacks of shipping crates assembled on the docks like enormous Legos. Square after square of ribbed color—blue, red, yellow, orange. A series of industrial Mondrians.

Santiago ignored his phone vibrating against the particleboard, a call from one of his two tías who were fighting over him, each trying to convince the orphan nephew to visit her for Christmas next month. One lived in Brownsville, the other in El Paso. One would drag him to spend the evening at the candle-lighting ceremony at Our Lady of Guadalupe; the other would get drunk on wine coolers and talk about her childhood until she went to bed weeping. His current plan was to open another credit card account, buy them both fancy smartphones as Christmas gifts and not make an actual appearance at either place. Though Flannery was still playing the distant workaholic, Santiago secretly held out hope of securing an invitation to Abilene for the holidays.

Like most children, Santiago had loved Christmas growing up. His mother ran off before Santiago turned a year old—she was a *güera* who'd worked as a waitress in the restaurant where his father was a line cook. They were young and the pregnancy unexpected. After she left, they didn't hear from her again until a letter arrived ten years later informing them she'd died in a motorcycle crash outside Albuquerque, leaving Santiago $478.60.

So Christmas had always been just him and his father, who worked most of Santi's life as a Brownsville city bus driver, eventually moving up into middle management a few years before retirement. Whenever his father had to drive on Christmas Eve, Santiago would ride the bus with him all day long, sitting proudly in the jump seat, and after the shift was over, his father would drive them to look at Christmas lights in the wealthy, historic neighborhoods. The houses, with circle drives and big picture windows, put on elaborate displays of fake snow and tacky plastic nativities and mechanical elves moving hammers up and down in Santa's workshop.

It never really snowed in South Texas (or what locals called the Valley), but to Santiago, these displays of bedazzled trees and fake wintry scenes were better—more magical somehow—than the real thing. Even as a small boy, he understood that reality rarely lived up to fantasy. His father had known this, too, and ultimately that truth weighed him down until he could no longer wriggle out from under it. Santiago preferred to say old age and the boredom of retirement were what precipitated his father's car accident, but he knew it was probably more than that. He knew it was bigger than the word *loneliness* made it sound.

Santiago was learning that it was almost lonelier having Flannery back in town, physically nearby and yet not within easy grasp. He was afraid to spook her and restrained himself from picking up the phone each night before bed. But in another sense, Santiago was technically less alone now than he'd been since living at Dryden fifteen years ago—Harry and the boys staying at the fire station meant voices and scampering feet followed him everywhere—which was why he wasn't particularly surprised by the loud thump that suddenly reverberated against his office/bathroom door. Santiago leaned forward to turn the door handle, and Jake and Ian fell forward into the cramped room, their matching bowl haircuts making them unequivocal brothers. They smelled slightly sour.

"What's up?"

"Dad sent us to find you," said Jake, smiling goofily. "The washing machine's not working."

"Yeah, I forgot to tell him, it's on the fritz again." He sighed and closed his laptop. Everything was on the fritz again. Life was on the fritz.

Before leaving the small, square yard, Santiago knocked ice from the branches of his nandina bushes so they wouldn't bow permanently beneath the weight of the freak November storm. A rusted metal walker nestled beneath the withered tomato plants in his neighbor's hibernating vegetable garden.

"Do we have to walk?" asked Jake, swallowed in a puffy coat.

"You need to burn off some energy." Harry arranged the mesh bags of dirty clothes into a pair of backpacks. "Think of it as an adventure."

Across the street, a man sat on his porch's blue recycling bin, playing the guitar. Three women, plump and pretty and wrapped in scarves of peach and lace, ears sporting large bangles and mouths filled with gold teeth, pushed baby strollers down the street, speaking to one another in a lilting Arabic.

As Santiago, Harry, and the boys turned the corner, making their way toward the Laundromat on the less savory edge of downtown where gentrification had yet to reach, they passed a group of toddlers from the preschool down the block. A middle-aged woman held a red rope attached to each of their little wrists—she had them leashed together like a dog walker out with her mutts and was trying to steer the kids in a direction, any direction.

Jake and Ian walked gingerly along the curb as though it were a balance beam, one foot in front of the other. "Look at me, look at me," said Ian.

"All little kids can do that," said Jake, disdainfully.

A bell chimed the top of the hour as they passed a man so fat his elbow bones were barely dots standing at the bus stop holding a take-out sack from a place that served Chicken and Waffles. A button on his coat read WHY, YES, I AM A ROCKET SCIENTIST.

The Laundromat was crowded, but Santiago and Harry managed to find two washers next to each other, one for darks, one for whites.

"How do these things work exactly?" Harry was only partly joking.

Shaking his head, Santiago grabbed the Ziploc full of quarters from Harry's hand and put them in the machine, punching buttons for temperature and cycle time.

"Let me tell you a secret, boys." Santiago leaned down. "Your father is what we call a sheltered, high-society pansy ass. Repeat after me."

"Uncle Santi said ASS."

"*No mames, güey*," replied Harry, grabbing his youngest and covering his ears with his hands too late for it to matter.

"*Cállate, gringo.*"

"Quite right," said Harry, in a smug way that annoyed Santiago.

While Santiago made fun of Harry's privileged upbringing, it was part of what made them good business partners: Harry could slide into that languid sense of entitlement that put wealthy clients at ease while Santiago, with his androgynous appearance and posture of cocky indifference, contributed their firm's edgy aesthetic.

As much as the two friends were alike in their taste for clean, modern (expensive) design, Santiago knew what it was like for those things to be out of reach, which was why he'd always felt a little closer to Brandon back in college. Once, when Brandon's mother called Dryden House to speak with him, Santiago had attempted to say an Arabic greeting Brandon had taught him, but there was only a stunned and awkward silence from the other end. Santiago realized then that he and Brandon were the same—they'd made it to where they were not through financial resources or family background but through hard-won cultural fluency and personal reinvention.

They all liked to joke about how the ethnics and the honkies had automatically gravitated toward each other that first day as the four of them moved luggage into their assigned dorm suite freshman year; Santiago and Brandon choosing one cramped bedroom with beds bunked above desks, Harry and Steven the other, the two rooms connected by a small living space with a bathroom off to the side. In less than a week, the four of them were sneaking into the college basement where endless switch boxes lined the wall, egging on Brandon until he figured out a way to remove the filters on the cable system so that the entire dorm received the Playboy channel. Their biggest problem in those days was having a lighter but no cigarette, a cigarette but no lighter.

This serendipitous assignation of the fates, this random administrative decision to place the four of them together, was probably the only reason they'd become close friends. They were different in so many ways, and yet the accrual of those days and years gave them the intimacy of brothers, an intimacy Santiago only afterward realized was almost impossible to develop later in the surface world of adult friendships.

As he and Harry and Harry's sons sat on the row of sticky, blue plastic chairs lined up against the glass storefront, they watched the clothes spinning in the front-loading washers, transfixed. Santiago imagined himself sitting there with Flannery, who in college used to put underwear on her head and imitate Carmen Miranda while they waited in the basement laundry room for their clothes to dry, and escaping this strange new bachelor family, which reminded him too much of the hours spent growing up in a place just like this, his father barking at the owner of the Laundromat to turn down the television so Santiago could concentrate on his homework.

A rangy man stood directly in front of them folding his T-shirts. He wore a belt of spikes, his right arm sleeved in pentagram tattoos and a Harry Potter paperback sticking from his back pocket. On the television hanging from the ceiling, Maury Povich was doing a show on women who had lost lots of weight. Everyone in the Laundromat seemed to be yawning, one after the other, like the wave at a baseball game.

The boys squirmed around but seemed mostly content coloring in the picture books Harry had brought for them. At one point, Santiago took some cheese and crackers out of his messenger bag and put them out on the folding table, next to the crayons.

As Ian tried to put a slice of cheddar onto his cracker, the cheese broke into two pieces. He said he didn't want it anymore, pushing the yellow bits onto his father.

"Eat the cheese, son," said Harry, who in the weeks they'd been at the fire station hadn't once complained about having to take care of the kids by himself. "It tastes the same."

The boy refused. Santiago tried to imagine what the kid thought had changed about the piece of cheddar. It was broken.

"Man up," said Harry.

Ian looked down at his feet. Joy and despair seemed to rain down on him so quickly, thought Santiago, changing every feature of his puttylike face into the expression of his innermost emotions. Children were annoying, but by God, they were transparent. Looking at Harry's youngest boy, Santiago remembered how proud and self-important he'd felt, how respected, when his father would say, "*Dueño. Señor.* My boy is smart, an intellectual. He needs to read his textbooks in quiet. *Por favor*, turn the sound down."

"Little man understands the importance of structure and aesthetics," said Santiago, intervening, trading his own cracker/cheese construction for Ian's marred one. "Perfectionism is undervalued in this world."

Ian's face transformed back into a grin and, for the first time, Santiago saw the glimmer of a person existing inside the child. A real human being shaped by those nearby. The thought warmed him.

Later that afternoon, Alyce arrived to pick up the boys at the fire station. Harry had told Santi that morning she was going to take them back to the ranch for the weekend, his voice flat and eerily neutral.

She arrived fifteen minutes late in baggy blue jeans and a floppy hat. Santiago watched the boys hug her excitedly, Ian vining his entire body through her legs, and he was struck by the way they both looked up at their mother with a certain wide-eyed reticence, like they were in the presence of a beautiful specimen of a different species.

"How's Harry?" She waited by the front door while the boys went to the bathroom once more before the drive.

"I can get him."

"Can't you tell me?"

"He's managing. He misses you."

"Think so?"

"What do you care? Ask him yourself." Santiago felt sorry for her, but why should he make it easy? Harry deserved better. Alyce smiled sadly and reached out to touch the back of Santiago's hand before ushering her boys out the door. Santiago felt a small pain in the wake of their leaving.

The couple had decided to give each other space, so Harry remained upstairs in the kitchen during the handoff. Santiago imagined him standing there, his hands on the smooth metal counter, suspended in a web of silence and hurt. Giving Harry that moment without witness, Santiago stayed where he was, thoughts returning to what had happened at the park earlier in the week. They'd taken the boys to play on the swings, but Harry's attention was immediately drawn to the adjacent skate park, saying how it had been years since he'd skated but that he used to be pretty good, spending hours doing aerials on the wooden ramp he and his childhood buddies constructed off to one side of the driveway.

Inside the skate park, a land of swirling concrete curlicues, there were three boys no older than fifteen, skating down into the bowl to gain momentum and then ascending up the transition, then the vert, performing tentative grinds and unremarkable 50/50s. They wore helmets and knee pads in color-coordinated patterns, which would have been unthinkably uncool back in Harry and Santi's day. Suddenly Harry was hopping the fence and borrowing one of the boards.

Santiago watched as his friend began rolling forward, one Converse sneaker balancing on the gritty, gray board; the look on his face said that he intended to teach these young punks a thing or two. Harry rolled faster and then tried to catch an aerial over the lip of the bowl, a simple backside air, before the board began to slide out from under him, abandoning his feet. Harry went flying through the air, tumbling down the side of the bowl into the bottom, an audible crunch as his shoulder landed first. One of the kids behind him said, "You know, mister, you should really wear a helmet," and it was all Santiago could do to keep from laughing. But it was sad, too, to be confronted with the fact that there was no going back.

Eventually, Harry came downstairs, meandering around the open space stacked with saws and planks. Santiago watched him, trying to decipher how a man lives without his limbs. How a person keeps walking when so much of what he must have thought integral to the function of his body, to his life, suddenly disappears.

"Harry, there's something I've been meaning to tell you." Santiago swallowed, gearing himself up to confess about the Marfa project. "It's about the firm."

"Do you think Alyce will get better?" Harry stared into space. "Do you think she'll let me move back in soon?"

"Harry, listen to me."

"I really don't want to talk about work right now."

Santiago stood still, staring at his best friend, unsure of how to proceed.

"Let's order a giant pizza," said Harry suddenly, as if it was the greatest idea of all time. "On me."

Santiago sighed and wished he could say yes.

"I'm going out. I have a date." Santiago saw the look of naked panic on his friend's face and knew he should cancel, knew Harry needed company tonight. But it was Flannery. She was always so busy; it was increasingly rare that she agreed to see him, much less asked to see him. "You'll be okay?"

"Of course," said Harry, halfheartedly. "Who's the unlucky lady?"

"Someone I met at the coffee shop. She's old enough to vote but not to drink at bars."

"You are such a prick."

Santiago looked Harry in the eyes. "I know."

Flannery smiled and kissed him sweetly on the cheek, standing over him at one of the picnic tables in front of an Airstream trailer called Pig Vicious, her hands swallowed by the sleeves of a yellow sweater, baggy and too long for the current fashion, her braid caught up in the collar.

Though she didn't nudge him or put her hand on his thigh, she did slide in close beside him on the bench. People might assume they were together. It was possible.

The place was BYOB and he poured Vinho Verde into plastic cups.

"Order me the pork belly slider, will you?" Her dimples hollowed.

It was already getting dark, the place illuminated by colored lights strung over the small field of tables. As he stood in line to order at the trailer, he looked back at Flannery and her face was a carnival of red-and-blue-lit freckles.

They talked about the news, about nothing. She asked him how business was going, and he shook his hand to indicate so-so.

"Wallpaper design." He took a bite of cheese grits. "I'm working on this whole gnarly retro thing to sell to those idiots in charge of the Governor's Mansion restoration."

"You qualified for that?"

"Like, am I board certified in wallpaper? Architects are the top of the design food chain. We do it all, baby." Architects were notorious for this kind of ego—claiming the ability to landscape, decorate interiors, anything—and sometimes Santiago liked to perform to type.

"Have they showed any interest?"

"Kind of," he said. There was no way he was going to confess the real state of affairs, which was that the Governor's Mansion people never even called him back. Women were not attracted to failure.

"Has Brandon told you?" she asked.

"Told me what?"

"About the silo? My project has veered off in an entirely different direction. It's crazy. He and I are collaborating now." From her bag, she took a thin scroll of paper, which she unrolled, smoothing it along the table. It was a blueprint of sorts, a long sheet of graph paper covered in a pencil drawing of some sort of medieval tower, the top of which was filled with sharp-toothed circular gears and what looked like a system of pulleys.

"Oh."

She told him about how they had come up with a model whereby rain clouds in West Africa could be stimulated to create rainfall via the injection of ice crystals. She said that in order to get funding and permission to test this theory under real conditions, they would need to demonstrate a sound "proof of principle." They'd found a silo outside of town tall enough to conduct the experiments in, but they needed to get it temperature fitted and pimped out with a snow machine. She had an appointment to look at a used machine from a ski resort in Utah.

"Sounds complicated." Santiago was becoming suspicious. Neither Flannery nor Brandon ever explained what they were working on in lab in so much detail to Santiago, whose only science credit in college was a course for nonmajors called Natural Disasters.

"And expensive," she said.

Ah, he thought, steeling himself. Here came the rub.

"I need a loan."

"A loan." He sighed.

"Not a personal loan, but from your firm. I'll pay you guys back with interest once the NSF picks up our grant."

They were blinded for a moment by a pair of headlights, a car pulling out of the adjacent parking lot. "Where did you say you're going to buy the snow machine?"

"Utah. Park City. They just updated their equipment and are looking to sell some of their old snow machines."

They'd finished the wine, and Santiago rolled the empty bottle back and forth across the picnic table, coalescing a plan. "I'll loan you the money if you let me go with you to Utah."

She looked at him for a minute, and he could see a struggle. Why was she being so difficult? Why wouldn't she let him back inside? Years ago he remembered her saying—or had he been the one to say it to her?—that if true love came knocking on your door after ten years asking you to move to Peru and start a llama farm, you said yes. No questions asked.

"It'll be fun. A vacation." Santiago thought about his plastic Jesus. He thought about how prayers were so selfish and yet everyone prayed them anyway.

Flannery's smile was tight and her eyes a little desperate. "Deal."

She began talking distractedly, and Santi only half listened, pulled between worry and excitement. ". . . Hopefully I can convince these guys to give us the machine for cheap. It's just a short-term solution, obviously. Most of the real work will come later, when we get permission to buy time on the NCAR's lab plane and actually take the project to West Africa. . . ."

Santiago had come to despise the word *Africa*; it made his stomach clench. But Santiago was resourceful, and he seized his chance. He knew he was using Molly, but she of all people would understand.

"West Africa?" he interrupted. "Really, Flan? You don't actually plan to leave your sister anytime soon?"

Flannery's face froze.

"I know what it's like." He set his trap gently. "You don't get that time back."

He leaned forward and touched her hand, only vaguely aware that he was twisting the truth. Because it hadn't been the same for him. He hadn't seen it coming at all.

Two years ago, his father was returning from a gun show in Dallas— one of his few hobbies was old shooters—and he'd stopped in Austin on the way back to spend the night with Santi. They watched a baseball game on TV and fell asleep early, nodding at each other before turning in. The next morning he and his father sat around drinking the strong coffee Santiago made in his French press.

"*M'ijito*," said his father, thinner than he used to be, in Wranglers and work boots. "I can't believe the Rangers choked again. *Están muertos.*"

"What else is new?"

What else is new? Those last moments with someone. An insignificant phrase that might otherwise immediately fade into memory. What else was new? Had Santiago inadvertently echoed his father's own fears and feelings? What else is there to live for? Who else is there to live for? What else is new?

His father asked for directions to someplace nearby where he could get the oil changed in his old beater. He hugged Santiago, one hand cupping his son's skull. Then, he left.

Santiago's father's car had shot off the side of a bridge on a small back highway on the way to Brownsville. It could have been an accident except that a rancher who witnessed it had seen him gun the car before it swerved at just the right angle to make it over the barrier.

The tías took care of the details. Everyone descended upon Tía Eugenia's house because it was the largest, bringing along with them enough food to feed the small army of mourners: enchiladas, beans and rice, fruit salad, thumbprint cookies, menudo, iceberg lettuce and tomatoes, chips and salsa, miniature burgers, tres leches, a cheese plate.

And after the Requiem Mass, sitting on a sofa in the living room, Tío Mike brought Santiago a plate, which he accepted passively, though he wasn't hungry.

"Isn't it nice your father left his affairs in such order?" Tío Mike, Eugenia's husband, was almost seventy, but his thick hair was only beginning to silver. "Not much inheritance maybe, but no outstanding payments, no back taxes. You might even make a little off the house when you sell it . . . pay off some of that school debt of yours."

"I'm going to buy a fire station."

"Your father was a responsible man. Without being given a lot of opportunities like you, he still managed to keep everything together. That's a rare quality."

Santiago remembered being shocked at how a man who'd spent years berating Santiago's father for not being more involved in "la familia" could now claim his feelings were no more complicated than respect for his brother-in-law's frugality.

"Dad killed himself. I'd say the one thing he didn't do was keep everything together."

Santiago's father had kept a little notebook in the glove compartment of every car he ever drove, logging gas mileage and pump prices. Long lists that gave the illusion of control. He made his son do it, too, when he got old enough to drive, and Santiago wanted to know: What did it get him? What did all that get him in the end?

In the summer, on his father's days off, they would slip into the nice lagoon-shaped pool in the gated community rather than go to the public pool downtown where his cousins went, his father saying, "What will they do? Throw us out? We could live in this neighborhood for all they know." His father, trying to blend in, would lie on his back beside the water, though it wasn't like he needed a tan, while Santiago swam and dove off the high board, and by the time they left, his father's back would be pocked and indented from the pebbled patio. Like the moon. His father was a kind of moon. Steady, bright, swollen with all the answers if you just asked the right questions.

As Santiago drove Flannery home from Pig Vicious, her bike sticking awkwardly out of the trunk of his MINI Cooper, he wondered if his father would be proud of him.

Maybe it didn't matter, he thought. Maybe that wasn't the most important thing after all.

FLANNERY

*F*lannery sat on a small balcony outside a ski resort hotel room reading her mother's journal, which had arrived two weeks before without even a note from Molly. As Flannery read, hoping to decipher her sister's message in their mother's words, she glanced occasionally at the smattering of people going by on the ski lift framed by quaking white aspen trees on the opposite hillside. Many of the trees were bare already; others still held the fading sunshine-yellow leaves of late autumn, tinkling in the wind like earrings.

It was still technically the off-season. Skiing didn't start for another couple of weeks, and so the ski runs looked like shaved streaks in a full beard of grass. Lifts ran for scenic purposes and to transport people to trailheads for hiking, and some of the passengers noticed Flannery sitting below them and waved. One boy rode in a lift car by himself, lying facedown on his stomach, jacketed arms hanging and flopping as though they belonged to a dead body. Flannery smiled at him and pulled the thick white robe further around herself, sipping hot cocoa made from water mixed with a packet of brown powder. She wished she could live her entire life in a robe like this one—regular clothing was annoying, always a pinch from the waistband or the elastic of underwear. In Nigeria, she wore a colorful wrap around the house, tied in a knot above her breasts. During the season of harmattan—brutally hot, brutally dry—even Kunle stripped off his sweat-soaked clothes when he came home, replacing them with a wrapper tied at the waist before taking a nap on the cheap foam mattress beneath the shroud of mosquito net.

Flannery had spent much of the last three days in the dark bowels of a warehouse next to the ski resort, learning how to work an aging, out-of-commission snow machine. The resort's "snowmaker," a fifty-year-old man in starched overalls, showed her how to hook up the gun, shaped like a spotlight, to a water source and air compressor before programming the computer based on the temperature and humidity outside. The machine was getting too old to absorb the vast amounts of water and air pressure needed to "snow a slope," as the man said. But Flannery didn't need a lot of snow. Flannery needed the right snow.

As she got more comfortable with the rickety, metal contraption, Flannery named it "the Super Eagle," after Nigeria's soccer team. Seven thousand dollars was a lot of money, she knew, but worth it—more than worth it if it could demonstrate the viability of her project. She would take the machine home, and it would perch in the top of an empty silo in the Hill Country and make snow that fell at above-freezing temperatures.

Santiago was taking her out to dinner that night to celebrate the purchase of the snow machine, but it was still midafternoon and he was off on a hike along one of the trails, leaving Flannery alone in the hotel room to read: he'd always understood that she was a person who needed space. Sitting there skimming her mother's journal, she discovered that most of the entries were not about living with Huntington's at all—they were from before that.

Her mother wrote that she'd fallen for Flan's father in part because he was the only college student she knew in Denton, Texas, with a piano inside his apartment. The piano was black and waxed to a shine. When Flannery's mother first noticed the instrument, on a visit to return a Graham Greene novel borrowed in class, she had imagined the handsome young man playing mournful sonatas late at night, brimming with otherwise unseen emotional depth and complexity.

Flannery found this striking because she never knew her father to own or even play the piano. Was it one of those things you sell and give up after having a family? Did he think one quixotic dream was enough? Or had her mother made the piano's presence in the apartment into more than it was?

Suspended there on the ski resort balcony, Flannery read the words of someone she barely knew. She learned that what her mother considered the triumph of her honeymoon was standing in front of Rembrandt's painting *The Night Watch* without anybody else in the room. She and Papa woke before dawn to be first in line at the Rijksmuseum when it opened, and they promptly bypassed the first floor, racing upstairs to the room where this gargantuan work of art hung, the masterpiece to which the rest of the collection surged, filling an entire wall with its ambition, or as her mother described the artist's use of movement and contrast: "light in the darkness, light in the darkness, light, light, light."

Having used up most of their honeymoon money on the airline tickets to Holland, they spent their days walking, weaving through streets and canals. She didn't write "holding hands," but that's how Flannery imagined them. They went on a canal ride one afternoon, and the wind bit through her mother's light jacket. The prostitutes standing in the windows of the Red Light District weren't afraid to look her in the eye.

Parts of these Holland entries contained only words or phrases: "almost mowed down by a bicycle," "everywhere men with small children," "gray skies again," "flowers are cheaper than breakfast in Amsterdam." And this was when the real reason for choosing

Holland came out: they went for the flowers, a gift from her father to her mother for tulip season. They took buses out of the city to visit farms where it looked as if the fields had been dipped in colored paint. There was a restrained relish in her mother's descriptions of these places, the flowers blossoming in perfect rows, "orderly as West Point cadets."

Her father was self-conscious of their Texas drawl, of being seen as country bumpkins, and his attempts at blending in or appearing cosmopolitan in Amsterdam failed at least in one instance when a cheesemonger said sternly to Papa, "Maybe I will touch the cheese." Her mother tried to recover by telling the man they'd like to buy 100 grams of the blue next to it labeled "Stinking Bishop." The cheesemonger told them it was not a blue cheese—"Does it look blue?" It did not, but the only "stinky" cheeses she'd ever encountered were blue, and so her mother just assumed that beneath the rind somewhere ran hidden veins of cobalt, streaks and streaks of them.

Flannery found it interesting how little about her father was revealed through her mother's account of that trip. There were oblique references to his famous know-it-all chatter ("Ned reminded me that it was the American army who helped the Dutch stop the Germans at Arnhem . . .") and lots of collective "we"s throughout, but the only real insight into their newlywed relationship came when she described the place where they stayed. Draped in red and smelling of cat piss, it was a cheap rented room, the owner of which offered them a shot of corn liquor upon their arrival. The tram ran loudly right outside their window at all hours. Her mother hated the room, and trying to fall asleep in it made her homesick. But she wrote about how eventually she decided to curl into her husband's chest and close her eyes, imagining the life and home they would build together. She forgot the existence of the lumpy bed beneath her and made him the shield between herself and the world outside. As far as Flannery had been able to tell growing up, it always remained more or less that way.

As she began to read about life after their honeymoon, Flannery heard a sharp slapping sound from the sliding glass door that led to the hotel balcony, and she looked up to see a naked, almost hairless ass pressed against the glass. Santiago was back from his walk and giving her the moon.

She shook her head before returning her attention to the journal, willing herself to keep reading, to keep moving toward the conclusion, though she knew the ending by heart.

Flannery dressed for dinner in front of the hotel bathroom mirror, putting in opal teardrop earrings and zipping up a black sheath, both on loan from a woman at the Climate Institute because Flannery no longer owned any nice Western clothes. As her spine disappeared, she wondered what her mother would have thought, if she'd lived to see them, of the tattoos that covered most of Flannery's back, red sugarcane and a tall Nigerian palm next to the vine with star jasmine flowers blooming up and down an intricate twisting pattern of green. The star jasmine had taken ten sessions with the tattoo artist over the course of a year and, at the time, back in graduate school, she'd done it in part because she believed tattoos made otherwise plain women look interesting. Some of it spilled over her right shoulder and down her tricep, the vine forcing its way out of the black sleeve of the dress. Looking at herself in the mirror, the contrast of tattoo and formal wear, Flannery tried to imagine herself as an American professional, an establishment scientist who attended faculty meetings and conferences and sat through fund-raising dinners with a suited Nigerian husband. It was hard to imagine foisting such a life onto Kunle or herself.

As she and Santi strolled through the lobby, Flannery ran her hand along a bowl filled with waxy, red apples. She was not one for public affection, but Santiago put his arm around her waist when they walked out of the hotel together; at any moment she could collapse and he would catch her. There was an old comfort in that.

The restaurant on the edge of Park City was inside a converted greenhouse where the tinted fiberglass had been replaced by thick panels of glass. There was no menu, and it was expensive. Flannery, already embarrassed about having to ask for a loan, would never have suggested such a place. It was Santiago's idea—he said he was feeling flush.

They sat across from each other at the slate gray table in an easy silence. She noticed for the first time how the web of small wrinkles around Santiago's mouth had become deeply etched into the skin, as they often were on the faces of smokers. If Flannery was honest with herself, she could see that Santiago looked full of a tender, empathetic affection for her. His face said: *Tell me what to do.* His face said: *I'm trying to help.*

Trout topped with a sweet cabbage and Swiss chard slaw. Roasted golden beets. Pistachio mango pudding. Wine. Flannery watched what appeared to be a mother/daughter pair sitting on cushioned seats in the corner. The mother wore linen, gray hair pinned to the top of her head. Her adult daughter tapped on her phone.

"I hope I'm not cold like that with my children," Flannery whispered, and the images that flashed in her mind were of brown, mocha children. She shook her head.

Santiago reached across the table, running his index finger down the inside of her arm in a gesture that was too intimate. She let him. It started to rain outside; smears of water ran down the high angled ceiling and long glass walls so that the trees became blurred and out of focus.

"Dinner inside a metaphor," he said.

"We shouldn't throw stones, then." She signaled the server for another bottle.

"That's not a metaphor; that's an aphorism."

She shrugged. She had never been inside a glass house before. With each bite, she felt like a traitor to Nigeria and to Kunle, who, even if he could afford it, would never come here because the prices would only make him think of what this money could buy back home.

"How's Molly?" Santiago gave her a sidelong glance when she didn't respond right away. "Did you know that when she moved out, she told Brandon if he tried to contact her before she was ready, she'd never come home? Such a bluff, but he's scared."

"Jesus." She shook her head. "He didn't tell me. He still comes to the lab every day, though, and putters around."

The food kept coming; they ate like gluttons.

"Remember when you came running into the backyard to tell us that Amanda was transferring to Stanford to join the crew team and that if we didn't find a replacement pronto, your annoying younger sister would take over that room?"

"You and Brandon just sat there grinning at me like idiots."

"Your sister was hot. We couldn't see what the problem was."

They laughed. Flannery loved that he remembered those moments. She loved that he loved her sister. "I haven't seen Molly lately, if that's what you're asking me."

Santiago poured more wine. "It's funny how we have a hard time imagining anything ending until it does. I only visited my father once in the year before he died. He'd made sure Brownsville didn't have anything for me . . . but the thing is, it did. It had him." He paused, fork in midair; light from frosted lamps danced along glass walls. "My father may not have been on the best terms with his family, but at the funeral you wouldn't have known it. They were the wet earth taking him back."

He told her that the night before, at the wake, his father's body had been laid out in the open casket for viewing, puffed up by gratuitous folds of white satin. Santiago hadn't understood the need for this, his father's mangled body reconstructed by the mortician to look like a waxy replica of someone he might have been distantly related to. It didn't matter that Santiago was opposed to this pornography of detail. No one asked him.

"At some point, after Communion and all the Ave Marias, I felt a hand press into my back and knew it was Molly. She said, 'You have to forgive yourself for not appreciating it enough,' and I told her that I had appreciated him. She said, 'We all have to forgive ourselves for not appreciating life enough.'"

Flannery hadn't come back from Nigeria for Santiago's father's funeral—it was too short notice, too expensive. She suddenly felt guilty and tried to imagine him there, upright and dry-eyed while long Latin prayers flowed one into the next. In all honesty, she'd only ever visited Santiago for her own reasons, never for his. At the end of spring semester of his first year of graduate school, she'd called from Madison, just having finished her exams, to say, "Send me a ticket." He'd told her he would send her money for bus fare, but he didn't think you could buy a physical ticket in advance anymore.

"Send me a ticket." Why had she insisted?

"How 'bout I draw you a ticket and send it with money for the fare."

Had she used Santiago—for comfort, companionship, support—pretending he hadn't minded, pretending that he was using her, too?

Flannery looked at the last bit of fish on her plate. "Sometimes Molly and I made fun of our mother with our friends. We mimicked her strange way of moving and talking. I hate myself for that now."

"You were just a kid."

"My father was protective, though. He used to carry around a fucking HD fact sheet and hand them out to people who stared at her in public places." As she spoke, Flannery realized these were memories she and her sister had never talked about.

"I could build you something like this, you know," said Santiago, looking around at the glass building. "There's a lot for sale not far from your sister's house."

Something tightened within Flannery. "How do you know?"

He didn't say anything. He smiled sadly out of the corner of his mouth. "Maybe I'll build it for myself."

"What about the fire station?"

He finished chewing and cocked his chin. "Who cares about the fire station? The fire station isn't important. Family is important." His voice was insistent. "We are the lucky generation. We can live anywhere."

Flannery felt despair flow down her throat and flood her belly. When her face flushed, she could tell that Santiago, who reached out a hand, thought she was upset at him. But what she was feeling was the wrenching nausea of ground moving beneath her. She had a home in Nigeria. At that moment all she could think about was how, in a room smelling of cat piss, her father protected her mother from the world. Light in the darkness, light in the darkness, light, light, light.

Back at the hotel, Flannery took a shower, letting the water get so hot she could barely stand it, steam rising, her skin splotching pink. The small hotel bottles of shampoo and conditioner were lined up on the side of the tub so perfectly, so straight; she almost couldn't bring herself to pick one of them up.

The image that had stayed with her from the journal was the one from the honeymoon, her mother in red sheets curled up like a shrimp into her father's torso. But that wasn't really the whole story. Years later, her mother wrote of trouble at the greenhouse where she worked part-time: she was no longer able to do the books with any confidence; she was caught giving the wrong change on multiple occasions. She was having trouble remembering her lines for the plays at the community theater. The diagnosis came as a shock. She knew her own father had been very sick, but nobody had ever said out loud that it was genetic. In the journal, Flannery's mother didn't explicitly mention that Papa had left her after learning she had HD, only his return three months later. Flannery would have been two years old at the time. She could hardly believe it: her father had left and come back, and she'd never known. It was the last entry in the journal, and her mother wrote, matter-of-factly, that, in the first month he was gone, her milk dried up and her youngest daughter, Molly, weaned herself. She wrote that since Papa had decided to come back to her, she would never ask for anything again. She wrote that, while the women in her Jazzercise class were always harping about how surprised they'd been by all that it turned out they could do—divorce that bastard, start their own company—Flannery's mother was more surprised by the opposite, by all the things in the world it turned out she couldn't change.

Flannery racked her brain to connect the dots. Molly had followed her to college, followed her to Dryden House, and gone on to marry her close friend. Like their father, Flannery had a responsibility that didn't end just because they'd grown up, and she'd been shirking it. Flannery who moved abroad. Flannery who couldn't bear to help uproot her mother's irises. Or imagine living without her little sister in the world. All the things one thinks it is impossible to bear and yet. And yet. Who does not have to bear them?

Maybe Flannery could save the Sahel from a laboratory here. That's what most scientists did: made their laboratory into their world. Because Santiago was right; they were family. She closed her eyes and repeated the word over and over, trying to comprehend its full meaning: *Family. Family. Family.*

As she dried off, she heard sounds of Santiago returning from a smoke on her balcony. In the mirror, she watched him walk past the crack in the bathroom door. Santiago, whom she'd known forever, and who'd known her sister forever. Santiago who worshipped her. Santiago who was loyal and never asked her to explain. Santiago who bought her sister silk scarves at yard sales. Santiago who understood what it was like to lose a parent. Santiago who was here.

Without knocking or calling out a warning, he opened the bathroom door wide to her standing in front of the mirror, the chocolate brown towel held tight around her body, hair wet and tangled. She didn't turn around, but he must have been able to see the curve of her buttocks in front of him, the curve of her small breasts reflected in the mirror. She stared at him behind her in the reflection, his body sinewy, what they used to call punk-rock-skinny.

He came toward her and reached out both hands in slow motion, touching Flannery on each shoulder blade with the very tips of his fingers. He moved down her spine, one vertebra at a time, pulling at the towel until she raised her elbows from her side, like a bird flapping its wings, and the towel fell to the floor.

Afterward, Santiago lay motionless, one arm flung around Flan's waist. His breath sounded shallow, and she wondered if he was only feigning sleep. Flannery tried to match her breath to his, tried to keep down the waves of panic that threatened to come up like vomit.

In Nigeria, Flannery for the first time in her adult life had ruminated on the word *home*. There was a man on UniAdamanta's campus who peddled pirated books, and he spread the faded photocopies over his car parked along the inner loop. Once, walking in that warm halo that surrounded her for the hour after she and Kunle made love, she bought a book by Heidegger called *Building Dwelling Thinking*, just because of the title. In it, the philosopher performs artful feats of metaphysical etymology: "The Old English and High German word for building, buan, means to dwell. This signifies: to remain, to stay in a place . . . to preserve and care for, specifically to till the soil, to cultivate the vine. . . . We do not dwell because we have built, but we build and have built because we dwell, that is, because we are dwellers." Flannery learned that the word *habitual* comes from "we inhabit it." Her daily routine, then, was also in a sense the place where she dwelled. A bed within a house. A house within a town. A town within a country. Lying next to Kunle one morning, she babbled to him about the book, wondering out loud whether she was ready to choose one place, to watch the accrual of seasons, to become a caretaker and till the soil. Cultivate the vine. Stay. "I want to dwell," she said, excitedly. Kunle nodded and laughed because he'd never known any other way. Had he believed her? Believed she meant it? Had he realized that Nigeria was the first place for her where home meant a growing of the vine, not a dying of it?

One day Kunle's youngest aunt came to visit them, and she joked, like he did, in that way that wasn't really joking, saying Flannery should only continue visiting the family village if she planned to stay. "It doesn't seem fair for you to go all that way just to make us miss you," she said. "I hope you're not playing dice with our emotion." She went on about someone she knew who married a Korean woman. Apparently, the woman gave them trouble because she refused to eat their food or drink their drink.

"Flan loves our food," Kunle told her.

"Tell Flannery I'll teach her how to cook it properly," she said, as if Flannery were not sitting in the room. "That is, if she's still here the next time I'm in town."

Sweating beneath the mosquito net, plagued by the insomnia that was a side effect of her malaria pills, Flannery sometimes lay awake in Nigeria thinking about how, in college, before they'd leave Dryden House to sashay over to the campus pub looking for beer and boys, Alyce would jokingly recite an incantation: "Spindle, my spindle, haste, haste thee away, and here to my house bring the wooer, I pray." It was from a Brothers Grimm fairy tale wherein the young spinner's magical spindle flew from her hand, unraveling behind it a thread that the prince could follow back to her. And when they arrived at the campus pub, plunging into the roar of music and laughter and pool cues hitting their marks, Flannery would look over the droves of men in baseball caps and hemp necklaces, like her mother in search of the one vein of blue beneath the rind. In Nigeria, when she touched Kunle's skin as he slept, she felt it. Invisible, but there. Home.

But now she wondered if she'd been wrong. Flannery had learned what it meant to appreciate a home, but maybe she had chosen the wrong one. Maybe she would never really belong in Nigeria, and Santiago, sleeping gently across the room, and her sister and all the rest, maybe they were the home she was supposed to return to finally.

Flannery's cell phone vibrated on the dresser across the room. Without looking, she knew it was Kunle calling, and she used the noise as an excuse to slip from bed. She didn't go toward the phone, though, instead retreating to the bathroom, sitting on the lid of the toilet, shivering. If she were to pick up and listen to Kunle's voice, she would feel as though life in Nigeria were still waiting for her with its grilled suya and harmattan winds, with its poverty and fly-covered meat and easy love. His voice had become more desperate, but still full of longing, still waiting.

Flannery was living in mental possession of two worlds, but she would have to choose. It was only a matter of time. Mrs. Tonukari had been right when she dropped off Flan at the airport. This time, it wouldn't be so easy to come back. Nigeria was receding.

Mrs. Tonukari didn't believe in e-mail and was too hard of hearing to carry on a viable conversation over an international phone line, and so the Welsh woman wrote Flannery letters, scribbled in four different colors of pen. Most of these letters had gone unanswered—Flannery didn't know where to begin. She already knew the answer Mrs. Tonukari's life had given. She just didn't know if the answer would be the same for her.

Flannery remembered spending one evening on the old woman's porch in Nigeria, watching the quickening of dusk, until Mrs. Tonukari shooed her away early, saying she and her husband had to leave at dawn the following day for a funeral in Abuja.

"I hate getting old. It's so much harder to get the energy to do things like leave the house."

She asked Flannery if she was familiar with any of the Welsh writers.

"Just Dylan Thomas. 'Rage, rage against the dying of the light.'"

"It's funny," she'd replied. "My husband quoted that line to me recently, telling me I needed to fight harder. But Dylan Thomas died in his thirties in a pile of filth. So what does a young man really know about all this?" She pointed at her hands and feet swollen with arthritis. Flannery thought: *She has not aged gracefully, but she has survived*.

During the years she lived down the road from Mrs. Tonukari, Flannery was young enough to think: *I am not like her*. And she was old enough to doubt whether that was entirely true. The country had taken something out of Mrs. T, like the flesh of an avocado spooned from its skin. How did a young, intrepid Welsh woman, someone who put on avant-garde plays and was willing to turn her life upside down for a handsome Nigerian, manage to live here so long and still be so afraid most of the time?

But now, from the other side of the world, Flannery realized she had been worried about the wrong things. Fear wasn't the biggest danger after all. Believing you really belonged there was.

She remembered one humid, overcast rainy-season afternoon when she tried to catch a bus to downtown and was accosted by beggars. In the States, they would probably be considered black. But, there, the immigrants from the country of Niger or Nigeriens—the second "e" delineating them from Nigerians—were sometimes referred to as "her people" because of their honey-colored skin. "Look, your people are calling to you," Flannery's companions would sometimes say as they walked out of the main gate of the university, out of its comparative placidity and order, its concrete drainage systems and pruned tropical plants, and into the teeming activity of Adamanta with its *danfo*s zigzagging off the road just long enough for a few passengers to slip on, its market stalls selling vegetables and pirated DVDs, and its shopping complex housing dimly lit cybercafés, small Pentecostal churches and pharmacies whose shelves were often bare besides a few boxes of Panadol and stacks of oversized greeting cards the height and width of a billboard.

But that day the Nigeriens, "her people," ragged and dirty children with hair curling into loose locks, grabbed tightly to Flannery's arms and wrists and put fingers to their mouths, speaking without having to say anything: *feed me, give me money, see my need*. They targeted her more vigorously than they did others, and she was pretty sure it wasn't because they thought of her as "their people" but because her pale skin and hair signified something more important.

She shouldn't give them anything. She knew that. It encouraged dependence; it solved nothing; they should be in school; you couldn't just throw money at a problem and expect it to disappear. But.

It was hard to take the individual case—these small children clinging with such ferocity—and judge it impartially on a global scale. They were still children. They were still hungry. She still had naira bills in her bag whose absence she would hardly notice. And, really, that's why they targeted her; why, when she shook them off, they just continued to reattach themselves, multiplying; why their faces contorted into such horrible, such studied, such melodramatic expressions of despair: they sensed her indecision. They smelled her pity, and it gave them hope.

As she sat inside the rapidly filling *danfo*, a man grabbed the door with one hand while tossing crinkled naira to one of the beggars with his other. She looked at him as he squeezed into the last seat. Noticing her gaze, he said in English, "I can't imagine how bad things must be in their country if so many of them come to this god-forsaken place for a better life." He half smiled. And the *danfo* kept moving.

Flannery and Santiago's flight didn't leave Utah until evening, so the next morning Santiago took her fishing on the Provo River. The river was fast and clear and wild. Herons touched down and took off from the surrounding wetland. Canada geese honked at them overhead on their way south for the winter.

Flannery slipped while casting, and her booted foot slid into the water, so frigid she immediately sat down on a rock to recover from the shock. Santi, wearing a wool-lined corduroy jacket, looked at home fly-fishing, swinging the gossamer line beautifully over the water, gently landing the tiny black-and-red fly on the surface of the river before the line hit. Flannery had never been fishing before, so she stuck with a rod and spinner, a green plastic minnow she named Iggy. As they stood on the rocky banks, surrounded by wintry white sunlight reaching through the trees like fingers, she remembered the hand-tied fishing flies Santiago's grandmother used to make, the ones he had in the display case in the fire station.

"This is so much better than fishing in the catfish tanks back home." Santiago grinned.

"Say that again after I catch something." A fish jumping in the rapids taunted her.

A group of serious-looking fishermen with a guide from a sports store in town walked by on the path behind them, crunching the brown grass, going downriver to find their own spot.

Santiago made a cast and then said, "I want you to move in with me. When Harry moves out."

Flannery's body stiffened, unnerved by the statement. She conjured an image of the two of them sitting across from each other at a dining room table. They were eating meat loaf.

But Flan didn't respond because, just then, her line tugged, and her throat loosened, letting out a shriek of surprise. Santiago scrambled over with the net and told her to keep reeling it in, but not too fast—best to tire it out some. The cold steel water roiled about the struggling animal, the line tight and quivering. When the fish emerged from the water, Santiago declared it a fourteen-inch brown trout and scooped the head with the net while grabbing the tail. Her hook had caught the poor fish in one gill, which meant it couldn't be released. Couldn't be saved.

But even as she watched him secure the first fish she'd ever caught—unhooking it and flipping out his pocketknife—in the back of her mind she was still thinking about his offer. To say yes would be the final betrayal of Kunle. To say no would be a betrayal of her sister, her own flesh. Santiago squatted beside her on the river, and she loved him in a different way than she loved Kunle: in that way you love your fumbling past and your brave and careless youth.

Looking at the dying fish, she thought about the graduation trip she and Alyce took during college to watch songbirds during their big migration through Cyprus on their way to breeding grounds in northern Europe. It had been Alyce's idea, of course. They dressed in Windbreakers, carrying binoculars and backpacks filled with beer. When they discovered rampant illegal poaching—long perching sticks covered in sticky lime used to ensnare shrikes, warblers, blackcaps, golden orioles—Alyce insisted on ditching their plans to get drunk and watch birds for volunteering with a group that snuck around disabling traps. They spent the next two days with a gaggle of ex-pat Germans and Brits tramping through private orchards and public parks, trying to save the ones still alive, caught by tail feathers or a beak or the tip of a wing. Some were too far gone by the time they were found and mercy was administered with a quick twist. Flannery never volunteered for this task, but Alyce agreed to do it once. Later she said she had pretended to be opening the lid off a jar of salsa.

As Santiago readied the knife, she stopped him. "Let me," she said. It was not what she wanted to do, but what she should do— Flannery was beginning to understand the difference. "I caught him. I'll kill him."

He showed her where to cut so as to make the end as quick as possible, and she gulped air and squeezed his pocketknife like it might jump or wriggle loose from her hand. As Flannery slid the blade in behind its eyes, she noticed the glint of blue iridescence that ran up each side of the speckled fish. She killed it. A pang went through her chest. Her mother. Molly. One day, her father and Kunle and Santi and Brandon and Alyce and Harry and Steven. One day, herself.

She looked straight ahead as Santiago took her photograph holding the brown trout by the mouth. From now on, she hoped she could do what was right for her sister and her friends. And if she couldn't make her home with Kunle in Nigeria, she could at least spend her life as a distant caretaker of the Sahel. She would bring Kunle and his family snow in the desert; if it could be done, she would do it. Looking at the camera as the shutter clicked, she wondered what to do with Santiago. Set him free or keep him? He was such a painful sweetness. A different kind of home. One way or the other, he might still be saved.

SANTIAGO

*I*n the kitchen, mixing himself a strong drink, Santiago thought about the winter break when he and Flannery took off with Alyce and Harry in Harry's Jeep, like two old married couples, listening to Lightnin' Hopkins cassettes, passing around fists of Twizzlers, rotating drivers each pit stop. Camping in Big Bend National Park, the four of them had been surprised by a freak snowstorm that blew in overnight and made the trails along the ridge icy and dangerous. That red and brown mesa landscape of far west Texas was usually dry and sunny even in cold January, and so they hadn't been prepared with snowshoes or spikes for their boots.

"Find a dead branch to use as a walking stick. Stay close. If you feel yourself slipping, crouch low," said Harry as they finished packing up their gear. "And try not to take anyone else with you if you fall."

"That's comforting," said Flannery. "Isn't there another way back?" Santiago was the only one who knew she was afraid of heights, of standing near the edges of roofs or even balconies.

"Not if we want to get back to where we parked the Jeep," replied Alyce. "Harry's exaggerating. It won't be that bad."

Santiago silently positioned himself behind Flan as they started out on the trail and, when it became a steep drop on their right, he held her exposed shoulder with one hand and placed his right boot to the outside of hers. They stepped forward in sync, like a child dancing with her father by standing on his feet. Desert lizards scurried across the whiteness in search of cover.

"Anybody else want a Leg Opener?" Santiago stepped into the "living room"—an open area on the second floor of the fire station—clinking the ice in his peach-colored glass of brandy and butterscotch Schnapps, the last crepuscular light fading outside the fire station's industrial windowpanes.

"Sure. And then I'll take a reach-around," said Brandon, who'd recently cut his hair so the curls now sat tightly coiled next to his scalp.

"I'm sticking with my martini." Steven didn't look away from the football pregame.

The televised picture was projected onto a white wall. Santiago and Steven sat like bookends on the worn leather sofa, Brandon sprawled in the imitation Eames chair. Santiago held a kitchen timer that went *tick, tick, tick* in the background. He was perfectly buzzed. He was thinking about not thinking about Flannery.

Last week, when he dropped her off at her apartment from the airport, she told him, "I need to take care of some things." Santiago nodded, hoping these "things" had to do with breaking free of her commitments in Nigeria and preparing to make a life here with him. They'd made love, which must have meant something. But as the days passed without a phone call, the more nervous and fucked he became.

The timer went off, and Santiago slid into the kitchen to check on the fish. The red snapper still looked translucent in the middle, so he left it in for another minute while he cut the cornbread into squares, put the roasted asparagus on a serving dish, and tasted the pineapple and habañero sauce to make sure it didn't need more salt. This efficient and well-prepared meal made Santiago feel that everything else in the world could be faked. He and Flan would be fine.

"Come and get it." He slid the filets out of the oven.

The two other men walked into the kitchen and served themselves. Brandon shook his head and said, "No queso or guacamole? Nothing fried?," at which point Santiago made a move to take his plate away. "Not complaining. Just saying."

"How else are we going to keep our figures?" asked Santiago.

As the opening commentary became the first quarter, more mixed drinks made their way around the room, into glasses and through parted lips. Their typical debauch.

"Hey! Illegal formation!" yelled Santiago when the whistle blew.

Steven raised his eyebrows and squinted at the projection.

"That was an intentional grounding if I ever saw one," Santi continued, an asparagus spear hanging from his fork. "What we need now is a good old-fashioned Statue of Liberty. No, a full-court press."

"You said you wanted to watch the game with us." Brandon did not look amused.

"I spent all afternoon googling sports. Can't you tell?" Santiago erupted into giggles. "As a Latino, I'm contractually obligated to prefer fútbol."

"Where are the children? Obviously Jake and Ian need a real adult around here to teach them a true appreciation of the national sport of Texas."

"I would do it," said Santiago, "but my bike is in the basement of the Alamo."

"Where is Harry, though, really?" asked Steven. "Wasn't he supposed to be here?"

"He texted that he was running late. Must have been traffic on his way back from dropping the boys at the ranch." Santiago tried to concentrate on the game, bodies dressed up like marshmallow men rolling around silently on the ground, wrestling for possession.

"This is a travesty." But to prove Brandon wrong, the fortunes on the screen suddenly turned. A roar rose from the speakers. The Cowboys made an interception and scored a touchdown.

"How about dessert," suggested Santi. "Rice pudding with cherry juice and pistachios."

"Of course you did." Steven stood up and slapped his belly.

It was during a commercial break that the inevitable finally happened. Santi was pissing in the bathroom when he heard a noise outside the door, the sound of footsteps coming up the stairs. After flushing his brand-new high-efficiency low-flow toilet and walking back into the living room, Santiago found himself facing the strangely intense gazes of three men: Harry flanked by a worried-looking Brandon and Steven. Harry's face was puffed up, as though from a bad allergic reaction.

"You are a fucking asshole" was the first thing out of Harry's mouth, and suddenly Santi understood. Harry wasn't late because he was dropping off the boys, he was late because he'd been to the bank. Harry had finally learned about the money, or the lack thereof.

Santiago nodded his head, figuring it was probably better not to speak.

The first punch did not feel as expected. It didn't stun or tingle. Things didn't suddenly go mute, nor did his surroundings begin to move in slow motion, the mouths of his friends stretching into grotesque O's. The moment Harry's fist connected to the cheekbone, it just hurt like hell. Santiago's right hand went to the wall behind him for support while his other one automatically shot up, but not in time to block the second blow. Jab, cross, hook. His father had taught him that, too. After the third punch, Santiago fell down to his knees.

By this time Steven and Brandon were shouting and pulling Harry back by the shoulders. Everything became incredibly loud, Brandon and Steven yammering over each other, trying to figure out what was going on. Santiago hoped he looked stoic and apathetic from his position on the floor as Harry stared him down, ignoring the men grabbing and pulling at him from the back, arms loose by his sides. He knew Santiago wouldn't fight back. And he didn't.

"How could you? You screwed us. You totally screwed us," Harry was saying, at which point Steven and Brandon stopped talking, loosened their grips, listening. "Who the fuck do you think you are?"

Santiago had no answer. Would anybody believe that he hadn't allowed himself to imagine this far ahead? Hadn't allowed himself to consider that things might not work out for him, after all his struggles to get out of the Valley? Hadn't he gone to the right schools, met the right people, worked hard? His tongue tasted like copper.

Santiago tried to stand just as another punch was thrown. And finally, things did begin to slow down. Wafts of sound floated above him. Santiago was hurting. Pathways of hurt flowed out from his face, through his head and torso and limbs, to places that hadn't even been touched, a domino effect, the train tracks of his nervous system stinging and crying out for some sort of relief. He had failed.

Amid this embarrassment and defeat and physical humiliation, Santiago remembered: Beating sun. Prickly weeds. Sweat dripping down his neck. He was in high school and his father punished him for coming home drunk and passing out on the kitchen floor by making him mow the yard, hungover in the one-hundred-degree Brownsville heat. Santiago mowed the words LIFE IS PAIN in big letters in the front lawn before slowly erasing them as he pushed the machine over prickly weeds in the beating sun, oblivious to the fact that one day this wouldn't be the worst thing his father did to him. That one day the worst thing would be imagining how the seat belt felt locked in tight around his father's torso as the car plunged into a ravine, no bobble-headed Dashboard Jesus to wink and nod along with him as they flew.

"Somebody around here has to start telling the truth," Harry was saying to the other guys and Santi wanted to respond, *Why in the world does anybody need to do that?* And as he watched his friends, now bickering among themselves—Harry whose wife didn't love him and Brandon whose wife was dying and Steven whose farm was going bankrupt—Santiago had the realization that this wasn't all about him. Some type of pain ran like a thread between all of them.

He closed his eyes, retreating once again into the memory of the winter camping trip. The morning of the snowstorm, burrowed away from the cold in the sleeping bags they'd zipped together, Santiago had sensed sunrise through closed eyelids, floating half suspended in dream matter until Flannery touched the tip of her cold, freckled nose to his.

ALYCE

On the day before Thanksgiving, Molly borrowed Alyce's truck to drive into town. The low-water crossing was covered by six inches of water, enough to make them nervous about splash damage to the engine of Molly's low-riding compact, but there was no indication of the impending flood.

Molly had an appointment at a women's clinic in town. Only visibly pregnant because she was otherwise so thin, she wore a gray hooded sweatshirt, bushy brown hair sticking out from the hood like a lion's mane. Alyce noticed she hadn't bothered to make herself breakfast.

"And you want to go by yourself?" asked Alyce again, fishing for the spare keys in one of Harry's messenger bags.

"No worries."

"Someone's got to pick you up after. They require it, don't they?"

"They want me to stay overnight—in case of any complications with my HD."

Before Molly turned to leave, Alyce reached out and touched Molly's forehead with the tips of her fingers, like a blessing.

Each morning Alyce felt slightly less groggy than the one before, Molly having made progress in coaxing Alyce toward the circadian rhythm of the mainstream world. The tightness in Alyce's chest was loosening, and most of her breaths now arrived without effort. Alyce was wary, though, because she knew the change was temporary. The molasses would be back. Maybe next week. Maybe later today.

The tapestry was making good progress, and Alyce anticipated working through Thanksgiving Day—Harry and the boys would be at his parents' in Houston, and it had been decided she would remain at the ranch. Everyone agreed with the arrangement (except the boys, who, like most children, had no choice). She would see them when they returned, and strangely, she was almost looking forward to the way their voices rang too loudly through the air, the way they stumbled through the house like drunks.

With Molly gone, Alyce sat back down at her loom, placing the soft pads of her bare feet on the wooden pedals, picking up the shuttle with her left hand, rolling her neck and starting where she'd left off, with Harry. He was the last figure before she wove herself. It had been easy to choose the colors for her husband—light blues and dark browns—but she was still experimenting with his form. She took a deep breath and began:

You've probably wondered how your father and I met. What happened the moment we laid eyes on each other.

Well, first I have to tell you that Flannery and I were known freshman year as the "Party Girls." At a nerdy engineering college, it didn't exactly take much partying to get that reputation, but let's just say we tried to live up to our moniker, rushing home from class to study so we could make it to the campus pub by ten. I'd actually prefer if you boys experiment with pot instead—much safer as long as you don't just buy it off the street from some methhead who's cutting it with oven cleaner or whatever. I mean, you still have to be smart.

Anyway, at Marsh it wasn't unusual for there to be a keg somewhere on the weekends. One night, Flan and I were at a party across the quad. It was lame, a bunch of ChemEs sitting around not talking to one another, but we didn't want to leave because then where would we find free beer? So

*Flan came up with the idea for us to steal the beer and take it back to our
dorm. The keg was in the bathroom, only about half full, and so we just
carried it out through the other bedroom suite and down the stairs.*

*Flannery had already met Santiago, I can't remember how, and we de-
cided to take the keg to his suite because it had a window that opened onto
the roof of the cafeteria. I banged on the door, and when Harry opened
it—to be honest I remember him seeming a little stuck-up at first—we
just walked right in. The confidence of youth. The guys heaved the keg
onto the pebbled tar roof, and we sat out there drinking and talking until
the sun came up. Maybe I should remember something more specific about
Harry, about what eventually drew me to marry him, but I'm telling the
truth here. And the truth is that what I remember most about those years
is that they were fun. We were happy. That's what I remember. When I
married Harry, that's what I was trying to marry, I guess. But as it turns
out, you can't marry a time in your life.*

Alyce stopped weaving. Her phone had been beeping on and off
for the last fifteen minutes, and she couldn't take it anymore. She dug
it out of her purse; the screen showed five missed calls and a handful
of texts from Flannery. Alyce sighed. Flannery's texts were becoming increasingly frantic. Saying she'd just returned from some trip
to Utah. That she wanted to help Molly. That she was ready. She
was sorry.

Part of Alyce wanted to reassure Flannery; part of her wanted
Molly all to herself. Alyce texted back: *Remember when we stole that
keg from Baker? Wonder what they thought when they walked into the
bathroom and it was gone.* . . . Then, Alyce turned her phone off.

Alyce looked out the window at the bird feeders swinging as the
wind picked up outside. There were no birds. The migrants were
gone, the year-round dwellers hiding, out of sight. Around midafternoon, just as the rain began flinging juicy droplets sideways
under the overhang of the porch, Alyce heard a loud rumbling and

crunching down the road. It didn't sound like an animal. It sounded like a truck.

Throwing on waders and a poncho, she set off down the caliche road, which was already puddling and slick. The road curved at the end of a patch of oak trees and, ten yards farther, descended into the creek bed. There she saw her truck almost across the creek, which was now flowing at least a foot over the pavement on the low-water crossing, but the rear driver's-side tire had slipped off the road and lodged in a drift of silt. The tires spun. Molly stuck her head out the window and waved.

"What are you doing here?!" yelled Alyce. The rain and the rushing creek made it hard to hear anything.

"I'm Craig Bent!" Molly yelled back, excitedly.

Alyce felt put-upon and confused—who the hell was Craig Bent? The rain seeped into the neck of her poncho as she wheeled around searching for a suitable log to put behind the tire to give it some traction. Water refracted off the tops of leaves, flashing bits of color. She settled on three large limbs of cedar lying beneath a canopy that had kept them mostly dry.

"I'm Craig Bent!" Molly was grinning like a madwoman as Alyce approached the truck with her load, trying to stay balanced as she walked through the foot of fast-spitting water sluicing over the crossing.

"For God's sake, Molly, stop spinning the wheels for one second!"

Alyce crouched under the truck, getting mud caked up to her elbows as she positioned the wood. Then, she shimmied her way along the passenger side and used her arms to pull herself in through the window, butt and torso first, her legs kicking in the air like a pole dancer.

"What is going on?" asked Alyce in the cloister of the cab, catching her breath, feeling dampness soak into her bones.

Molly pressed down on the gas slowly and the truck made it across the creek. "I've been trying to tell you. I'm pregnant."

Alyce looked at Molly's profile. "Still. You mean you're still pregnant."

Back at the house, Molly emphasized that she had not canceled the abortion, only postponed it. She told Alyce she hadn't said the word *baby* out loud even once until sitting in the waiting room at the clinic and the nurse called her name, to which she responded without thinking, "I'm having a baby." She said she wanted to be alone with the idea for a while longer.

Alyce looked at Molly's softly arching belly—really looked this time rather than forcing her eyes to slide over the small protrusion like it wasn't there. She couldn't help but imagine a bird's egg nesting inside. A white shell dappled in splotches of beige. The gooey nutrients of yolk forming a cushion as oxygen was absorbed and expelled through tiny little holes in the delicate shell. A cocoon.

"I feel good." Molly looked out the window. "When the rain lets up, let's go for a hike along the cliffs. There's a place where a group of wild turkeys are roosting for the winter. When they're asleep, it looks like the tree is growing turkeys, just hanging there, plump and delicious." She sat at the kitchen table while Alyce unloaded the groceries Molly had brought back with her in canvas bags. Alyce tried to shake herself out from under the layer of fog that was settling back over her like a veil.

"Thanks for buying food." Alyce looked quizzically at some canned pumpkin.

"I noticed our Old Mother Hubbard cupboard," said Molly. "We're doing Thanksgiving dinner here. I've decided. Then, we'll rent a movie."

"If we can make it out."

"It's just drizzling now."

"What matters is how hard it's raining upstream." Alyce slowly put away the cans of cream of mushroom soup and boxed macaroni and cheese, feeling vaguely disgusted by the sight of so much brightly colored packaged food. "Have you told Brandon?"

Molly looked up, her cheeks still hollow, not yet having taken on the fullness of later pregnancy. "No." She said the clinic told her she'd have to wait until sixteen weeks for the genetic test for Huntington's, when it was safe to perform an amnio. "Then I'll decide."

Alyce did the math: sixteen weeks was only two weeks away. Would Molly leave her? Leave the ranch if she decided to have the baby? Alyce shivered at the thought.

As evening approached, it rained harder and the creek continued to swell, creeping up the road toward the house. What had once been a pleasant whoosh, a sweet and distant gurgle, now roared with a mean pleasure as the two women sat on the porch wrapped in scratchy, pink Mexican blankets and drank hot ginger tea, Alyce's laced with brandy.

Water was ubiquitous, thought Alyce—everyone so accustomed to it: drinking it, bathing in it, throwing it on lawns and plants, all while taking for granted what water was capable of. The way it parted and joined seamlessly and with little effort. The way it breathed in swells and waves. The way it rolled down rocks to form rapids, somersaulting like perfect little gymnasts. Some people—even Alyce when she was weaving in the middle of the night—believed in a life force that moved through the universe. And if such a power existed, surely its closest physical embodiment must be water—not air, not breath. Water could become one with ground or air or body. Alyce envied water its life without circumference; like the robes sewn by the goddess, it had no hemline.

Alyce and Molly watched the hungry creek blanket the shrubs and cedar trees down below like a mantle fattening in front of them. Lord willing and the creek don't rise. They talked about President Obama's health care bill and cedar fever and about a teenage daughter of someone they knew who had been charged with burglarizing her own grandparents' house. Alyce was finding that she had extra words after all. That she was not entirely empty. Part of her wished her sons were there, so she could pick them up by the arms and spin them in circles until they fell down dizzy from the effort.

"Let's play the Inquisitor game," said Molly. "Who will be the last Dryden housemate to kick the bucket? Last man standing?"

Alyce said what Molly wanted to hear. "Brandon."

"Yes. Brandon." Molly shifted her weight and the chair creaked. "When we played Inquisitor back at Marsh, you guys never chose me for anything."

"You were younger, newer to the group. We forgot about you."

"But it's also like you knew somehow. Knew what was going to happen to me."

Night had arrived fast, as it did in early winter, and Alyce was finding it difficult to sit still, to resist the urge to escape into her studio and her tapestry. "Molly." Alyce leaned forward to look her in the eye. "We didn't know. I didn't know."

Molly smiled back at her and nodded. "I'm glad I'm here."

And Alyce didn't know if her friend meant here at a ranch in the middle of nowhere, or here in the world, glad to be born, but she answered anyway. "So am I."

What she didn't say was that one person's will to be here did not always get passed down to another. That the reason Molly felt comfortable at the ranch was because Alyce was the only one unafraid of death. Alyce's concern was only with the superficial, concrete things one could do something about: Are the pillows on your bed too soft?

Did you get enough to eat? Let me put your whites into the washing machine with mine. Yes, you are going to die.

At dawn, Alyce yawned and looked out from a house that was now riverfront property. The creek bed itself was fairly steep and so water had risen steadily but hadn't really flooded until sometime in the early morning when it reached the plain of grass that led up to the house. Like a tick engorged with blood. Luckily, the front yard was spared, the water having crested a few yards before the cattle guard.

"Isn't it gorgeous," said Molly from her seat on the porch, as Alyce swung open the screen door.

"You're up early."

"You're up late."

Molly motioned for Alyce to sit beside her. The hummingbirds were blitzkrieging again, battling for control of the sugar water in two red feeders, whizzing through the airspace of the porch in figure eights, dive-bombing, duck and cover.

"My dad's upset I didn't make it for Thanksgiving," said Molly, lifting her cell phone in one hand. "The great thing is . . . I don't really care."

"Tell him you're flooded in. You, Molly, son of Ned, have been cruelly separated from your family by the forces of nature," said Alyce, dramatically. "Like the goddess weaver separated from her mortal lover, a cow herder, when the Celestial Queen forbade her crossing the Milky Way to visit him."

"He said Flannery is on her way to the ranch."

"Oh."

"Is there any way for her to get in with all this water?"

"Skydive. How long will it take her to get here from Abilene?"

"Four hours, give or take."

There was an old retired couple who lived on the large ranch north of the house. One weekend, after they'd first moved in, Mr. Rose picked Alyce and the boys up for dinner on his off-road 4Runner, which he called "Calamity Jane," weaving through the assemblages of cacti with the gusto of a teenager. But the Roses were out of town for the holidays, so the only way in or out would involve walking miles through their property to where the highway curved, and Alyce didn't know the way.

"It's Thanksgiving," said Molly. "Call your sons."

Alyce didn't protest. Sometimes it was nice to be told exactly what was expected of you.

She dialed her husband's number. Her husband—he seemed part of another life. But no, that wasn't fair. There were small moments when she missed him, when she swore she heard his voice calling from the other room.

"Hello." His voice. There.

"Harry."

She heard him yell into the distant void: "It's your mother."

These phone calls were exquisite torture. As though parenthood wasn't difficult enough without attempting it from a disembodied state, no visual clues to help decode what was really being felt and communicated.

"Jake," said Alyce. "That you, kiddo?" Her body leaned forward, and she cupped the phone, as though the only problem was being able to hear clearly.

"Mom. I killed a cockroach."

"You did?"

"Grandma was afraid but I wasn't."

"My resilient boy."

There was a silence.

"You're very brave," Alyce rephrased. Sitting there in the rocking chair on the porch, her heart grew big until it felt like her body existed inside of it instead of the other way around.

"Ian doesn't want to talk. He doesn't like the phone."

"I know. It's okay."

She heard Harry in the background say, "Tell her you love her."

"I love you, Mom."

"I love you, too." And she did love them. She just wished her love were more useful than it was. She wished her love could make everything better, make her better. She thought again of the tapestry growing wild on her loom in the studio and felt a stitch of hope.

When Alyce got off the phone, Molly was staring at her from across the porch. "You made two new people out of nothing."

"For what it's worth."

"When can they tell you if it's a boy or a girl?"

"Twenty weeks or so," said Alyce, "if you want them to." For most people this might mean: if you don't want it to be a surprise. But here she meant: if you decide to have the baby at all. Then she asked, as gently as she could, "Are you sure you want to do this? Even if the fetus doesn't carry the gene? You have a lot on your plate." She used the word *fetus* purposefully.

"I'm not sure." Molly, her thick hair pulled back in a pink bandanna, tilted her head. "But is it really the worst thing? I'm already showing symptoms, so this will be my only chance. And I'll have help," added Molly.

Alyce raised her eyebrows. "When Jake was born, I spent thirty-six hours in labor, agreed to every drug they offered. He came a week early, so my ob-gyn was out of town and the replacement was this fat, hairy man who didn't explain anything that was happening." She told Molly about how he'd cracked inappropriate jokes

("Did you get that Brazilian for me?") and how the thought of his fingers between her legs made her gag, and once, when Alyce was pushing during a contraction, "I shat right on him and high-fived myself." She told Molly how, when Jake was finally born, the nurses didn't put him in Alyce's arms immediately, but rushed him out of the room to clean him first.

"What did you do?"

"I panicked. I told Harry: 'Follow that baby.'"

"And he did."

"And he did." Alyce remembered feeling a longing for the baby but also a sense of relief as he was carried out.

"Brandon will be an excellent father, too," said Molly.

Alyce heard: Will. Not would.

For Thanksgiving dinner, they laid out food on the table: a dry, overcooked Cornish game hen; chopped celery and carrot sticks; canned cranberry sauce; recently unfrozen dressing; gooey, neon mac-and-not-really-cheese; and a pumpkin pie of premade filling in a premade crust. They heaped their plates and took them outside onto the porch, in full view of the water that surrounded them; it was like they were stranded on a deserted island, removed from civilization altogether, if not denied access to whipped cream in an aerosol can.

Alyce was surprised to find herself starving. She closed her eyes, relishing the feeling of need. It was nothing like the meal Alyce herself would have cooked, and yet she ate with feral abandon, shoving the salty, sugary, dry food into her mouth. Ravenous for the first time in months, her cheeks squirrel-like.

Molly laughed at her. "Who's the pregnant one?"

Alyce asked herself, not for the first time: Why was there a levity to friendship that didn't exist with family?

When Molly and Alyce put their feet up and leaned back, over-turned roly-polies with no intention of moving for several hours, it was afternoon and the creek already receding before their eyes— Alyce could see bits of damp grass left in its wake. And yet the surface of the water gave off the appearance of complete, unwavering permanence, such that she struggled to remember how the land looked without water swallowing the road.

Flannery arrived with a flourish, as always, honking the car horn in the flooded quiet, fast and high-pitched, like a synchronized pack of geese.

Molly and Alyce stood up at the same time and strolled down the wet and muddy road in their rubber wading boots. They didn't rush. Molly grabbed Alyce's hand, and when she did, a surge of emotion rolled through Alyce's body.

They waded through the dirty, churning flotsam until, water up to their thighs, they got to the bend in the road where they could see the other side of the creek, now more of a pond. Where usually it would be easy to throw a stone from one side to the other, even to hold a conversation with someone on the far bank, now the water was so wide that Flannery was a small figure in the distance perched on the hood of Brandon's car, her head in her hands. Was she crying? Or merely bone tired?

When Flannery saw them, she slid from the car and put her hands in the air. She looked as though she were signaling the start of a race. Her hair was tangled, and her clothes hung awkwardly on her body. She yelled something and waved her arms around, but they couldn't hear her. Maybe the word *no* drifted over on the wind. And the word *must*. Alyce felt guilty standing there in the water, holding the hand of her best friend's sister as if she were about to baptize her in the creek. Who had betrayed whom? How was this supposed to go? Red Rover, Red Rover, why don't you come over?

Now Flannery was getting something from inside the car. It was a book, and she held it up in the air. Alyce looked at Molly, facing serenely across the water toward her pleading sister. Molly nodded her head a few times, and then lifted her hands in the air, but this seemed to throw her body off balance and she faltered, splashing Alyce as she regained her footing.

"Let's go. There's no way across."

They waved to Flannery and waited for her to wave back before turning and slowly wading down the drunken road toward the house. Alyce slipped her fingers free from Molly's and pressed her palm against the woman's belly. They stopped walking for a moment. Alyce felt the power of Molly's death behind the little egg of life. She was afraid it might be loosening its grip.

As they climbed the porch, Molly said, "It's not my sister's fault she didn't get the gene." She sat down on the swing.

"No."

A gust of wind swept through, knocking forks and napkins off the small table. They let the items go.

"I was thinking about the kissing contest you and my sister won," said Molly, "and I'm curious."

"Yeah?"

Molly smiled shyly, kicking her feet out in front of her. She didn't say anything. Alyce laughed, maybe the first real laugh in a long time. She turned Molly's face toward her own and kissed her heart-shaped mouth.

MOLLY

At the doctor's office for her amnio, the thickest needle Molly had ever seen pierced her belly and sucked fluid from her uterus, teeming with the genetic material of her unborn child. Molly's eyes watered from the pain. The doctor asked if she wanted to watch on the ultrasound screen but Molly shook her head.

Looking around, she thought: *In a decade, this examination room, with its crinkly white paper and generic posters, will be arena to the hopes and dreams of other mothers-to-be.* Her own child, if she decided to have it, would be nine years old. Molly would likely still be alive then but in an advanced stage of the disease, in a wheelchair wearing diapers, depressed and mostly uncommunicative, language having piled up on the tip of her tongue, lost to the dark recesses of the brain. Afraid? Ready? Both? Even at that point—she remembered how it was with her own mother—when she slept at night the chorea would disappear, and she would look like any other forty-four-year-old woman. Peaceful. Dreaming. Released from the daytime cares of the world.

After half listening to medical specialists slowly list the risks of her pregnancy and delivery, Molly left the medical building and walked into the adjacent park. Branches of dull winter trees, empty of leaves, pointed down at her with displeasure. A group of joggers ran by on the trail wearing sleek suits of spandex, and two dogs wrestled in the pond. The bamboo separating the park from the houses farther up the hill stood brown and jagged like a wall of upright chopsticks. More than anything, Molly wanted to see flowers.

She drove to the nearest grocery store, walked inside, and grabbed the first bunch of color wrapped in green plastic. As she stepped across the street to her car, clutching the daisies in one arm, a woman stopped her and said, "Oh my God. You look like you're out of a movie." Molly could not bring herself to smile back. How does one respond when the outside and the inside are still so incongruous?

Life rushed forward for these people and yet, for Molly, it slowed. This was what it felt like for the end to close in on you. To know more or less how everything would turn out. Molly would never change careers or move to a new house or city. For Molly, it was all done. Except for the little spark of life she carried. This was hers; hers and Brandon's. If she managed to carry it to term, it would be the last new thing she would ever do.

Buttery sunlight fell on Molly and Alyce as they stooped beside the small rock wall that ran along the west border of the yard, a crumbling, knee-high remnant built as a property line by the first ranchers who'd lived there more than a hundred years ago, before the cedar had sucked the land dry like a plague.

Molly had decided it was time to plant her mother's irises. If she waited any longer, it would be too late for the bulbs to settle in before spring. The two women finished preparing the ground by loosening soil and mixing in compost with a pitchfork.

"Don't plant them too deep," said Molly. "The top should be barely covered." But what she was thinking was this: *What a pair we are. I feel guilty for wanting a child. You feel guilty for not wanting the family you already have.*

Alyce nodded and gave a thumbs-up before bending back over the ground, but in her corporeal movements, the strain of her neck and the grip of her hand, Molly imagined her friend was also finally admitting how she'd resisted getting help because being sick was a good excuse for not being happy with the choices she'd made.

Alyce and Molly traded off digging holes and placing the dormant iris bulbs into the ground, patting the damp soil around them like tucking small children into bed.

"Where did I leave the rest?" asked Molly at one point. What she really wanted to know was whether she could leave the ranch. She needed to go home soon, and she wanted to know Alyce would be all right without her.

Alyce grunted. "On the porch."

Molly walked over and picked up another bag. She liked the way the iris bulbs felt in her hand, gritty baseballs, concrete objects inside of which so much pulpy softness lay dormant.

As she neared Alyce again, Molly felt the energy of her friend's secret tapestry. Flapping and fluttering. Rising up. The expanse of sky and night and endless distances to cross. And in that moment, Molly understood the real reason she'd come to this ranch, which was to make an alliance that might one day be absolutely necessary. Because Molly had no intention of living out the last horrible years she'd seen her mother endure. She would not allow those she loved to watch the worst of the horrors.

"Can you hand me the water?" asked Molly. *Will you help me when the time comes?* Asking for something was really more of a statement about what you were ready to give. Will you marry me? just a way of saying, I'm ready to marry you. Molly thought about the baby titmice that had fallen from their nest and how Alyce told her she'd swept them onto the grass so their deaths wouldn't seem quite so brutal. Molly knew that her baby could not save her.

"Here you go," said Alyce, after stopping to slug from the plastic bottle that had been perched near her on the stone wall. *I will see that what needs to be done is done.*

The kiss, thought Molly. The kiss that day on the porch equaled a promise. That kiss meant they were still alive.

An hour later, when Molly and Alyce finished, the sleeping flower bed in front of the wall was six irises deep and ten long, spikes of green leaves sticking just out of the ground, like fingers clawing from a shallow grave.

They sat on the wall surveying their handiwork. It was good.

As Molly heaved her pregnant belly out of the driver's seat, she realized she would miss this feeling after the baby was born. She had never been so physically substantial and fully present in the world.

Molly walked the blue stone path toward her house. A thin layer of morning frost glazed the winter lawn. She looked up at the corrugated tin roof, topped by a rooster weathervane she'd found at a junk store on the way to Abilene, and decided that the roof would likely need replacing in another five years or so. Her child might be four years old. Molly would still be alive then, using a cane, irritable and prone to rages because one of Huntington's myriad effects was to turn the dial of one's personality several notches darker.

Brandon's car was parked beneath the carport; a lamp was on in the kitchen. Molly stopped at the small concrete porch and watched her husband's shadow through the window. Brandon's shoulders were bent, head and neck flopped forward. For a moment she thought he was slumped on the counter and a tremor of fear, a different kind (there were so many), ran through her body. Then there was a pumping movement from his right forearm, a fast tapping. He was crushing something with the granite mortar and pestle they'd received as a wedding gift, crouched over the job. She smiled. Brandon was still here, same as he'd always been, puttering around the kitchen before work.

Molly stared at the doorbell, but her arm did not reach for it. She slipped the house key from her coat pocket and turned it in the lock, swinging open the front door, fast and with her eyes blinking closed.

Brandon, in flannel pajama pants and a bleach-stained sweatshirt, turned slowly, unsure of what to expect from an intruder with a key. His cheeks were streaked wet.

"You're crying," she said.

"The onions." The cutting board next to the mortar was littered with shallots.

Molly stood in the entry to the kitchen with her coat still on— she wasn't ready to take it off. She needed to find her balance. The only time she'd left the ranch in the past months had been for doctor's appointments and grocery trips, Alyce harboring her as if she were a draft dodger, a bank robber. On the porch there she'd spent long hours looking out at the vast acreage of tightly woven oaks and cedars like a normal person might watch waves crash along a craggy beach, rocking herself back and forth, securely tied up. Harbored.

Molly thought it would be difficult to move from all that back into the enclosure of her urban neighborhood just off the highway, back into her small, modest house painted the colors of a lazy winter sky, grays and light blues. Back under the watchful gaze of Brandon. She thought she would feel unmoored. And yet, now, here she was.

"Staying awhile?" His voice was shaky but neutral.

"If that's all right with you."

Down the block a car alarm sounded.

"Your father's been calling and calling."

"What did you tell him?"

"Nothing."

She couldn't resist: "You're so good at keeping secrets."

Brandon's face remained unchanged, but his body lifted as if to brace for something. She didn't feel guilty for saying words that were true, but she did feel a need to ameliorate their harshness. So she took off her coat.

"I'm hungry. What's for breakfast?" She tossed the parka onto the sofa.

He didn't exclaim, or suck in breath, or get saucer eyes. He just stood there, staring at her taut round belly, trying to compute all the things one tries to compute when given life-changing information. Molly understood precisely.

"Omelet?" he asked finally, his mouth almost grinning, though his eyes retained that look of hurt. She knew what that was like, too.

"And tea? Do you have any tea?"

"We do. Of course we do." He went about heating the skillet and boiling water in the kettle. Molly sat at the table and watched him sauté onion and garlic in the small frying pan. She was tired and hungry, almost happy. When the old anger tried to rise up, she pushed it back down.

"Where are your things?" he asked once they were both seated at the table, napkins on laps, eating the fold of moist egg. He was wearing his hair shorter now, close around his head like a sheared sheep. It made him look older.

Molly said her bags were in the car and, when he asked about the irises, as though he doubted she could really be back without them, she told him how she didn't want to be weighed down by those purple and gold sirens any longer. They were her mother's irises, not hers, and they belonged at the ranch now. Molly didn't want to spend the time she had left working in the garden, grieving for skills and mobility that were gone forever. She had better things to do.

Her hand jerked a little as it raised the fork to her mouth—she didn't try to hide it.

"A girl or a boy?" Brandon asked shyly.

"There's a sonogram scheduled for next week. We can go together?" She would wait until later to tell him that she was also seeing a high-risk specialist—her own symptoms made the pregnancy dangerous; she'd likely be put on bed rest soon—and that she'd signed up to join a double-blind cohort study for after her pregnancy.

He nodded. His face tightened. "What about the . . . ?"

"Reduced penetrance." She emptied the diagnosis onto the table like spare change. "Indeterminate conclusion. The child can get tested again when he or she turns eighteen. If they want to. They will be offered all the possibilities."

Molly understood that doing things differently than her own parents didn't guarantee a better outcome. She wouldn't dare express out loud her hope that this honesty would teach their child how to take advantage of life, to notice its passing and appreciate it more than other children possibly could. If the fetus had turned out to have full penetrance, which meant a one hundred percent chance of getting the disease, she would have aborted it and told Brandon nothing. Spared him the knowledge entirely. But reduced penetrance meant life for the child would be something like life was for Molly and her mother, full of uncertainty. Research had shown that HD, while a dominant gene, was not a switch that turned off or on—the mutation was initiated by extra repeats of the codon CAG. If the repeats were less than thirty-five, one would be free of the disease. If forty or more, it was a sure thing. However, there was a gray zone between thirty-five and thirty-nine where some people would get it, some wouldn't. Molly's fetus: thirty-nine. One repeat short of determination. A cosmic joke.

Many people would abort at thirty-nine repeats, though; it was just too close, too chancy. But it was a risk Molly was willing to take. And by making the decision alone, Molly would be the only one to blame if the child grew up to think differently. And that was all right, because Molly would be gone.

Brandon reached out his hand and let his palm touch down on Planet Babe, as she and Alyce had begun calling it. His fingers were gentle. "A gene therapy will be discovered in time." The love of her life, the atheist and rationalist, the man for whom research had, along the way, become just a day job, even he wasn't able to escape the illusion that we can make up for the pain we cause, she thought. That we can fix what is broken in the world.

Molly remembered how, early on, when her mother was first diagnosed, there was real anticipation in the Huntington's community that finding the gene would bring a quick cure. That hadn't been the case, not in the thirty-odd years since, and as with cancer and Parkinson's disease, all Molly hoped for now were minor improvements in treatment that might convey minor improvements in quality of life.

Of course, some things in life could be repaired. Not returned to the way they were before, maybe, but patched up. Made workable again.

"If it's a girl, she could be Helen after your mother," he said, tilting his forehead toward her. They were settling back into their own little world, their snow globe.

"No afters." Molly stacked their empty plates one on top of the other.

"What will we do about your father?" Brandon cracked his knuckles and spun his wedding band. "We can't hide this from him forever."

"My father," she said, wishing she could have a cup of coffee from the carafe that sat on the stovetop. She was so tired these days, and the dining room chair so uncomfortable; her belly prevented her from scooting flush to the table. "I wrote to him that I needed space and time."

She could tell Brandon did not full-heartedly welcome this information—the squint of his face said he thought she was being cruel. She didn't care. To keep looking her father in the eyes after what had happened was to continue unbinding the connections holding her entire childhood together. She couldn't bear it. It may not have been fair, but fair had flown.

When Molly remembered conversations or outings with her father, they were refracted through a new prism of menace. When they had gone to the State Cemetery, for instance, the rolling grounds in East Austin where war heroes like Edward Burleson were interred next to politicians, Rangers, and other famous Texans, like Barbara Jordan and James Michener, Molly was seventeen. They'd driven to the state capital to see the Daughters of the Republic of Texas honor with a cenotaph one of their ancestors, Catherine Overton Jennings, who was known for riding through the Hill Country to tell settlers the Alamo had fallen and warn them to flee for their lives—Santa Anna was on the way. It was called the Runaway Scrape.

At the time, as she and her father walked through the grounds, Molly found it amusing to meet these people, who introduced themselves as "Honeybunch" and "Bluford" and told stories of dead but colorful relatives who had been horse rustlers and bank robbers, while drinking punch in salute of a woman long gone and mostly forgotten. (In Molly's generation it was not so fashionable to be an Alamo defender—after all, it wasn't as if the Texicans hadn't basically stolen the whole place from Mexico.) Her father did not find those people silly and ridiculous, though, and, in fact, had a grand time taking notes and tracing family trees. He even went out of his way to bring a bouquet of wine-colored carnations, the Lockwood family funeral flower because, two generations earlier, they were the only flowers grown in the local greenhouse during winter.

Now, when Molly looked back at this afternoon in the State Cemetery with her father, it seemed like an attempt to get her on his side of family history. To show her the part of the family where strength and heroism originated. To let her know he'd given her nothing but a noble, unadulterated pedigree. His relatives were honored by brass plaques, buried next to the greatest men and women in the state. Molly's father couldn't be held accountable for any bloodborne wrath her mother might have passed down.

Molly lurched up from the table and carried the plates to the sink.

"Why forgive me?" Brandon asked. But she knew, deep down, he'd expected to be forgiven, and what he was really asking was: Why not forgive her father, too?

"I choose my family from now on."

As she looked at the wooden countertop, a few knife nicks and wine stains marring its surface, she thought about when it would need to be replaced. Her child, if Molly was able to carry it through the next few months, would be about seven then. Molly might still be alive but she would be using a walker, grown thin from the chorea that made it increasingly difficult to get enough calories into the body, paranoid and maybe less afraid, maybe more. Unlike people suffering from Alzheimer's, HD patients didn't lose the essential self but retained large chunks of memory and personality. Molly was not yet sure if this was a blessing or a curse.

She couldn't decide which aspect of Huntington's was most devastating: the horrors of the disease itself or the genetic dominion, which forced you to watch its long, pornographic destruction in those close to you, glimpsing your own future before it happened, knowing too well what lay crouched in wait.

But Molly still didn't know whether she would be more or less afraid than she was now. Lately, she'd been wondering if there was a finite amount of fear in a person. If fear could run out, like when you open the fridge and there's no milk. And if fear can run out, what would it mean? Peace? Apathy? Emptiness? The end?

She looked at the face of her husband, whom she loved more than anything in the world. She could admit that now. There was a tightness to his forehead, the emerging lines like a map of small hurts. She kissed him on the cheek, imagining her growing body becoming softer, skin melting onto Brandon's and fusing them together. She tried to breathe in his pain and breathe out a large blue sky.

HARRY

By some unspoken code of friendship, every weekend that Alyce kept the boys out at the ranch, someone invited Harry to dinner so he wouldn't be alone.

Tonight he was at Heavy Metal Farm with Steven and Lou eating tofu stir-fry with brown rice and sitting on the picnic table just outside their trailer as glowing embers from the chiminea took the edge off the still-chill night air. Harry remembered walking these fields with Steven a year after his friend bought the land. The ground had been black and loamy, only just tilled by the gaggle of young, underpaid farming interns, and Steven had picked up a handful of rich soil, turning to Harry and saying, "Good enough to eat."

Their daughter, Maya, picked at her food; her pleading face said she wanted to ask for a grilled cheese sandwich but was too shy to with Harry there. Harry loved his boys fiercely but had secretly always wanted a girl. He used to hope Alyce would eventually be ready for a third.

"Bet you've gotten spoiled eating Santi's cooking." Steven licked soy sauce from the whiskers of his beard. "I am but a humble plowman. Plowperson? How the hell do you say that?"

"No, it's good. Santiago's making me fat," said Harry, though it wasn't true. Over the past months he'd grown wan, the sockets of his eyes probably casting shadows in the light of the fire.

"Speaking of fat," said Lou, laughing. "You should see Molly."

Harry smiled. It had been two months since Molly's return to the city, and they'd all rallied around her news. But every time he saw her or heard her name, the only thing Harry could think about was the ranch. Alyce alone at the ranch.

"I have some Brussels sprouts for you to take home," said Steven. "First of the season." Earlier in the evening his friend had revealed, looking off into the distance as he spoke, that it was also Heavy Metal Farm's last season. The bank had finally come knocking. He said he hoped his daughter would remember these years when her father did something he was proud of all day long.

"Santi will know what to do with them."

"Where is he, anyway?" asked Lou. "When I invited him to dinner, he texted saying he was out of town."

"Interviewing for jobs." Harry shrugged. He and Santiago had made peace since their fight—Santiago was so penitent and Harry eventually able to admit he'd also ignored their problems, which allowed Santiago, in a sense, to go rogue. But even so, the firm was unsalvageable. They couldn't work together anymore, and Harry would be moving out of the fire station at the end of the month. The vacation from his life was almost over.

"I don't think it's going very well," continued Harry. "It's hard for everyone right now, but especially architects. When nobody's building, who needs a designer? I might even take this summer off, go somewhere cold. Alaska. The South Pole." What Harry didn't say was that he didn't know how he'd ever work again. Harry was lost.

"The moon is cold," said Maya, pointing to the slice of it rising on the horizon.

"Or you could just turn up the air-conditioning and rent *Doctor Zhivago*," said Steven. "Santiago has a ushanka hat somewhere. Remember? He wore it with his boxer briefs to Brandon and Molly's wedding?"

Steven's banter felt forced. Even Maya stared glumly into her plate of food. Then, the girl sneezed three times in a row.

"Maya," Harry said, putting down his fork and looking at her, "did I ever tell you my family is from Finland on my mother's side? In Finland, when you sneeze three times in a row . . ."

Two weeks after dinner at Steven's farm, Harry called his wife.

"I want to come over." The digital clock on the wall of Santiago's guest room told Harry it was two in the morning, and he hoped her ringtone hadn't woken Jake or Ian.

"Now?"

"Yes." He didn't allow his voice to become gentle.

"Won't that confuse the boys?" she asked.

"I'll be gone before they wake up."

"I'm not sure what's left to talk about."

"I don't want to talk." He held his breath.

A pause, a caesura. And then the word, "Come."

Harry was already pulling on jeans and a sweatshirt, feeling around for his flip-flops. Harry told himself he was only driving out to the ranch to make love to his wife, and then he would return to this exile without protest. But, secretly, deep down in the part of his mind he didn't like to explore or examine, Harry believed Alyce would ask him to stay.

He would touch her, and she would remember how the copper birds flocked on the ceiling of his room at Dryden House, imperfections blurring into beauty.

ALYCE

After hanging up with Harry, Alyce padded through the ranch house on the way to the front door, kicking aside tangled balls of tinsel and gold Burger King crowns. The boys had invented a new holiday called Castlemas, where they wore crowns and decorated the house with shiny treasures, waving silver serving spoons like scepters and making decrees. Jake decreed the official food of Castlemas to be peanut butter sandwiches and Ian decreed it was okay to pee in the yard and Alyce decreed that you had to move from room to room by leapfrogging. It was the sort of day Harry would have loved. It was the sort of day Alyce pretended to love, forcing her way through it with the invisible muscles of fake joy. The boys also decreed there would be no bedtime, but even so, they were all passed out by eight o'clock, smeared in glitter and melted chocolate. Even Alyce.

As she brushed her teeth and washed her face, Alyce tried to ignore the stacks of boxes everywhere, symbols of impending departure; the fellowship at the ranch was coming to a close next month. It hurt to leave. It felt good to hurt.

The late winter and early spring had been lively: White-tailed does showing up with their wobbly fawns, just as night lifted, to eat the corn Alyce left at the edges of the dewy yard. Wild turkeys mating and on the move, the hens crouching low to scour and peck the ground for worms and seeds, all the while seeming to ignore the gobbling blue-headed males attempting to get their attention by prancing in front of them, displaying enormous fans of feathers, regalia that sprang forth from their bodies like jazz-hands, like the images of turkeys children make at school by tracing their fingers. Alyce had also had her first and only encounter with a diamond-back rattlesnake when, walking back up the gravel path from the swimming hole, she'd been startled by the hiss and rattle of a slithery dee coiled in the road. Her heart beat faster in her chest: *I live. I live. I live.*

The yucca were in bloom, white flowers pluming up into soft cotton clouds, and the prickly pear were opening their paper-thin purple and yellow flowers, probably fruiting soon, although it was unlikely Alyce would get to see one of the sweet juicy bulbs before the raccoons and possums picked them off. In the last week, she'd seen a pair of painted buntings outside her casement window and at least one rose-breasted grosbeak, covered in geometric swaths of red, white, and black. According to the bird book on the shelf, grosbeaks shouldn't have been in the Hill Country yet, but there was no mistaking it. The ranch seemed to attract vagrant birds, those aberrant individuals that, for reasons of strange weather or a reversed compass or simple curiosity, ended up out of the migratory range of their more normal counterparts.

Alyce waited for her husband on the porch in the dark, like a teenager, dying for a cigarette though she hadn't smoked in years. She felt a strange shift in her belly—butterflies—and remembered the fairy-tale rhyme her mother used to chant, whispering it aloud:

Spindle, my spindle,
haste, haste thee away,
and here to my house
bring the wooer, I pray.

For a moment Alyce imagined herself a poor woman in a cottage in the woods, tossing her spindle into the thicket like a fisherman flings his line.

But she didn't believe in spells. She and Harry couldn't go back, though she could pretend for a few hours. Feeling things she knew were ultimately pointless, that changed nothing, and yet were also nice in their way. For just a moment to believe entropy was reversible.

Harry drove up to the house slowly, headlights off. He stepped out of the car wearing blue pajamas and flip-flops and a puffy jacket. His face looked white in the moonlight; two little pockets of shadows rested in his dimples when he smiled. She looked at him, flesh and blood, and felt the aftertaste of desire on her tongue.

As he walked up the steps of the porch, she unbuttoned her shirt. It was chilly, the March air hitting her nipples like a shock. She took a sharp breath in. Then, Harry covered her chest and stomach with his, enveloping her as she walked them backward through the door. Like a film moving in reverse, they glided through the living room, past her studio, past the kitchen, past the boys' room where they stopped and lightly clicked the door shut, the greenish glow of a night-light escaping beneath the crack.

As they reached the master bedroom, goose bumps broke out on Alyce's shoulders and arms, and she remembered what she said after they made up from their first big fight when they were only twenty-one years old: "I discovered I fancy you again." She felt the pricks of hair along the back of Harry's head and neck. The same body. The same touch. The same movements as they found their rhythm. It could have been any of the hundreds of times they'd made love. It was all those times. There was the cadence of the clock on the wall, its bright silver hands moving forward with controlled relish. The blanket sliding off the mattress. The creak of the floor.

And afterward, as they lay on the bed, spent, Alyce could see in Harry's face what he was too afraid to say: *I believed my love would always be enough*.

Alyce stared at him and thought: *Love was never enough*. Not by itself. She felt the presence of the tapestry in the other room as if it were a living being. Listening. Waiting for her.

Voices ricocheted off the walls of the small gallery space. Alyce skimmed her hand along the bar and plopped a lime into her seltzer water so it looked like she was drinking a gin and tonic. Her new therapist encouraged a multipronged approach. Medication but also exercise and vegetables and cutting back on the drinking. Alyce's response, turning her cheek to the cool leather of the therapist's Mission-style recliner, had been to shrug and say, "Sure." Why the hell not.

Alyce looked evenly at the wheeling groups of people chatting and spearing cubes of smoked Gouda and thought: *At least it was a good turnout*. Most of the attendees were friends and weavers, otherwise known as "people without enough money" to buy the biggest tapestry she'd ever made, eight by six feet (the width limited to the width of her loom).

The event was a closing reception for her fellowship at the ranch, and it seemed none of the local newspapers or magazines had decided to cover or review it. Not a single art critic in the house. Her masterpiece, her personal apex, greeted not with applause, not with jeers, but with a distracted silence.

She watched as Flannery, Steven, and Lou huddled in one corner, Flan's hands behind her back, fingers brushing the wall. They were drinking and probably talking politics, guessed Alyce, from the way their faces telegraphed mutual disgust and frustration.

When Lou and Steven had arrived at the gallery, late and flustered from trying to park downtown on a weekend, Lou had looked up at the tapestry saying, "I thought you said you were weaving images of us? You changed your mind?" Alyce had smiled and shrugged. Lou didn't see what Alyce saw, but that was all right. The tapestry wasn't really for her.

An older friend who used to weave but didn't anymore came up to Alyce with a plastic bag full of beautiful, vintage silk scarves she said she no longer had use for. The material looked too old and weak for the beaters of Alyce's loom, but she accepted them graciously.

Brandon and Santiago lorded over the spinach dip, the scientist gesticulating and trying to explain something to the architect, who leaned back, his gaze both skeptical and amused. Some of Harry's friends from his private high school in Houston meandered about, nodding at Alyce and looking vaguely uncomfortable, a common response to impending divorce. A few feet away, Alyce and Harry's old Realtor stood in front of the tapestry. He looked serious, leaning back with his large arms crossed.

Next to her tapestry was a pasted white cardboard label with the piece's title in italics: *Migratory Animals*. The other walls of the space were lined with black-and-white photographs of her at the loom in the ranch studio—the fellowship had sent two photography majors from the university to take them. She thought the images turned out shadowy and formal, like old daguerreotypes taken on the frontier of stern women with beak noses and stiff black dresses. *Don't smile*, the young photographer with spiky hair had told her—*it will look better if you don't smile*.

Alyce moved toward the middle of the room, looking up at the flock looking back at her. A robin, a black-capped chickadee, a golden warbler, a finch, a tufted titmouse, a purple martin, a mockingbird, and a kingfisher. All flying, for a moment, the moment captured here, in the same direction, feeling the same swift current, powered fliers and gliders both. The mosaic flock flew in inky blackness across a strip of stars, a silver river going in the opposite direction, the two configurations poised in an X. The birds were crossing the silver river, over it, beyond it somewhere. It didn't matter where. Robin had not yet killed Bear, not yet tossed the scene in blood from his arrow. It was a story frozen en media res.

With juicy yarns and sharp colors, Alyce had used her brocade technique to make the birds themselves emerge sculpturally from the background, which was more subtly constructed with thin, slippery silks, each bird framed by a ribbony strip where the weft itself showed through, creating a halo effect. The birds seemed to be flying in a closer plane to the viewers than the rest of the scene, and it was not just a trick of perspective but of the concrete elements of yarn and weave.

Alyce had been conditioned never to touch art hung on walls, but with tapestry it was more difficult not to obey the impulse to reach, to press one's body and face directly into the cloth, absorbing it tactilely through osmosis. And this one was hers and so she could. Who would stop her? The fabric was so soft she thought about ripping it down and flinging it around her shoulders and walking out.

From up close, the birds no longer looked like a flock but were abstracted into geometric shapes, a series of curves and sharp points. The hand-dyed silks and wools were shaded with so many colors that it was impossible to tell exactly where one thread started and another stopped.

"Mom, what are you doing?" she heard her son Jake ask from behind her.

Alyce backed up, removing her face from the cloth.

The boys were characteristically disheveled but well dressed in matching navy jackets with fake brass buttons. Looking at her sons as they tugged self-consciously on their clothes, she thought maybe it was time to stop dressing them alike. "Well? Do you like it?"

"It's nice." Jake smiled shyly.

"We like it," added Ian, a step behind him, slurping on a sucker, "but birds aren't our favorite animal anymore."

Alyce leaned down to kiss them each on the forehead. Maybe the tapestry only absorbed the energies that had been put into it, neither transmitting nor refracting any of Alyce's intentions. Her own sons were oblivious. All the painstaking hours and lost stories poured into it just for them.

"Look at this, Mom," Ian commanded, showing her the chewy chocolate he'd found in the center of his lollipop, as though no one had ever discovered it before.

"Watch me, Mom. Are you watching?" asked Jake, his arms stretched wide, pinwheeling through the air, almost knocking over an older couple dressed in black. "I'm one of your birds."

Kids were always asking you to watch them, thought Alyce, to look at whatever they'd done or found. This confirmed to Alyce what she'd been lately discovering: her real job as a parent was her presence: her ability to watch, to look, to stand witness at the passage of Jake's and Ian's lives. Not for them to watch or look or stand witness to her tapestry and what it said about the passage of her own life. Maybe nobody saw what Alyce saw in the tapestry because it wasn't real. It was her own self-serving narrative. Her own subjective story used to justify her actions.

"Come on, kiddos. Daddy's bedtime," said Harry, squeezing Alyce's shoulder. He told them to say good night to their mother, and they did so reluctantly, instinctively reaching for Harry's hands. He congratulated her again on *Migratory Animals*, which in a kind-hearted overstatement he called stunning. They were still at that place, the one before the legal wrangling begins in earnest and before the small cracks of bitterness start to spread, where they couldn't get used to not supporting each other.

As he turned to leave, Harry looked over his shoulder and said, "Do you remember the metal birds you hung from my ceiling?"

Alyce smiled but shook her head no—metal birds?—fingering the glossy jet beads tied in a knot at her breastplate, the ones her mother had brought the last time she visited Austin, which must have been over two years ago now.

"I was thinking about them the other day," continued Harry. "Those birds, the way they moved when you turned on the ceiling fan. They were stunning, too, you know."

And then Harry was gone. And Alyce was alone again, with what was left of the flock.

At that moment, Alyce could almost admit what would really happen: She would move into a duplex in Duvalier Place—a neighborhood more romantic-sounding than romantic. She would be a renter again, like when she was just out of college, someone else in charge of mowing the lawn and painting the walls and calling the plumber. Her life would become less cluttered. The boys would stay with her on weekends. She would watch the light change in the kitchen from morning to evening, autumn to spring, and she would notice it because she would be alone. She would go on living.

It was a step in her most important recovery. She was a mother, which was sometimes harder than eating and exercising and drinking less. One day at a time and all that. As her therapist had acknowledged, maybe Alyce wasn't one of those women who was better off with children than she was without them. But the only way to ever know something like that for sure was to live two lives. And Alyce barely had time and energy for this one.

Migratory Animals might have been the last real piece of art Alyce would ever make. Not because it was really so different in style or staidness than the William Morris *Woodpeckers in an Orange Tree* that had been her original plan. But just because it was hers. It was all of theirs. It was finished.

From now on Alyce would only weave brightly colored table runners, blankets, and scarves with pattern names like "rose path" and "bird's eye" and sell them at festivals and boutiques around the state. She would make her own living, if not a particularly good one. She would become more efficient, warping two to four articles of clothing onto the loom at once. She wouldn't have to pay attention in the same way she did for tapestry, and could fall into a rhythm, one arm throwing the boat shuttle as the other worked the beater, her bare feet tapping back and forth on the treadles.

She would become known for a luxury shawl, based loosely on a Japanese garment she'd seen in an art house film, the stitching origami-like, the fringe feminine, the material chenille with a rayon weft, the "poor man's silk" as it was called, to give it an underlying shimmer. It would take her an average of two hours to measure the warp, five to thread and wind the loom, two hours to weave each shawl and two to tie and wash. When she took them off the loom, they would be stiff until she rinsed and blocked them, which would make them spring to soft life. The pieces would be popular among a certain set. They would be lovely. They would be satisfying in their own way.

At one of the festivals where she sold the shawls, her booth would be next to a woman hawking jewelry made from recycled glass. Customers would stop at the woman's table to say, "Oh, how pretty," pointing at a yellow or green bauble, and the woman would respond with its origin, a sake bottle or some sort of tequila they don't make anymore. There would be one necklace, a glass sliver of unreal blue, like the color of a Senegalese kingfisher in bright sun. Alyce would walk over and say, "Blue Nun," referring to a brand of wine that came in a blue bottle, and the woman would smile and ask how she knew.

Alyce would tell her that her mother used to drink it when she was young, and then she would buy the necklace, or trade for it with one of her loose woven scarves, and wear it from then on like a talisman.

Alyce wondered: Would we ever start anything if we knew how it would end? Would she have married Harry and had his children? Would she have woven this tapestry? If she'd known at the start that all she expected was not even possible? And at the start could she have believed it might still be enough?

"Snow White. You've done it," said Flannery, coming up behind Alyce in the gallery and leaning into her, letting their cheeks rub together. Flannery wore a yellow sundress Alyce had never seen before.

"Where's your sister?"

Flannery shrugged. "We sent Brandon for more booze, but I don't know where she disappeared to." Molly was on bed rest at home, but her doctor had given her permission to come to Alyce's show.

"How'd it go last week?"

Flannery shook her head. She said that the silo test hadn't worked but that they thought they knew what went wrong. "We'll try it again in a few weeks."

Alyce slipped her arm around Flannery and drew her across the floor and toward the tapestry. Alyce felt the new thin layer of flesh around her friend's waist; where it used to be all rib cage, now it was like pressing your hand into a wall that has been painted over. Alyce thought: *It's curious how age softens some people and hardens others.*

"Which one am I?" Flannery nudged her shoulder into Alyce and looked up at the flock of birds covering the wall, arced and spread and diving into the bottom right-hand corner of the room.

Alyce smiled at her old friend. "You know which one."

They stood there for a minute, touching, breath going in and out in unison, hearts pausing and finding the same rhythm; for a fleeting second, they merged into one organism and saw out of the same watery eyes. It was there, and then it was gone. But it would sustain Alyce for weeks, longer. She looked down at her hands. Knobby and thick knuckled from so much weaving, they didn't seem to match the bird bones that threaded the rest of her body. Her hands looked twenty years older than the rest of her. She didn't mind.

"I'm going for a refill," said Flannery. "Want anything?"

"Nothing. Thank you." And she meant it.

FLANNERY

*P*ale pink and fuchsia petals from a crepe myrtle tree littered the windshield of the compact car parked across the street from the art gallery. Flannery tapped on the window, and Molly, sitting with the driver's seat reclined all the way back, jumped.

She rolled down the plate of glass. "Hey."

"On a stakeout?"

"Most comfortable chair in the world," said Molly, rubbing her belly. "Leans back at just the right angle." She wore a navy-blue Mexican muumuu with flowers stitched around the neckline. She looked like a beautiful beached whale.

Flannery walked around to the passenger side and climbed in. She had made up with her sister over the last few weeks, but slowly, testing the waters. They were being careful with each other for once.

"Wanna cruise the strip and pick up Romeos?" asked Molly.

"People are wondering where you are."

Molly rolled her eyes. "Oh well." She reached to turn off the car radio. Then, her face scrunched up and her hands gripped the steering wheel. A moan escaped from between gritted teeth.

"What the hell?"

"Con . . . traction."

"Oh." Flannery counted on her fingers: her sister wasn't due for another five weeks.

Molly took deep breaths. "Might be Braxton-Hicks," she said. "How far apart?"

Molly looked at her watch. "Five minutes or so."

"I'm taking you to the hospital."

"If I have two more, we'll go."

"We're going now."

"No. We're not. We are doing things my way for once." Eventually Molly's body relaxed again. "Distract me. Tell a story."

Flannery heard a new steeliness in Molly's voice; she tried to respect it. "I don't know any stories." She knew lots of stories, but all the ones that came to mind were told to her by a beautiful man with three scars across his face and involved palm-wine tappers falling from trees.

"Remember when I came to visit you in Madison that one winter? I woke up to find your side of the bed empty because you were outside in your car watching the snow fall." Molly yawned and stretched her neck. "I was mad at you for not waking me up."

Flannery tried to recall the visit she was talking about; the only images that came up were of the two of them at a bar with stained-glass windows and a fireplace. But she remembered watching snow. "I used to do that all the time. Sit in the car watching snowfalls. All winter long in Madison I did that."

"I was surprised you weren't outside, standing directly in it. I remember thinking grad school had made you soft."

"I was protecting the snow. From my body heat. A car windshield is cold enough that when snow crystals land, the edges don't melt, not right away. It's one of the only ways to really see the designs of a lot of them at once." Flannery twisted her hair in her hand, looking at the light spray of clouds in the sky. "Sometimes they're all needles. Sometimes stars. Sometimes they're needles at first, and then stars."

"What about this one?" Molly splaying out her fingers on the inside of the windshield so they covered a constellation of the pink flower petals resting lightly on the outside of the glass. "From the shape of these snowflakes, what can we determine about the conditions outside?" Molly doubled over with another contraction.

Flannery reached out to put a hand on her sister's back, but Molly waved her away. "Let's see," said Flannery softly, pointing to one pale pink petal. "First, notice the serrations on the perimeter. In isolation, it would have grown into a plain hexagonal prism, so this pattern means it was out of equilibrium as it developed inside the cloud. Because the points stick out a little, water molecules were more likely to diffuse there and that instability created branching. Complexity."

"Beauty," said Molly through clenched teeth. They watched Harry and his sons walk diagonally across the street and toward their SUV. Brandon still wasn't back from the store.

"But these don't have the long dendrite branches, which means the humidity is not particularly high."

"You'll miss this when you go back to Nigeria."

"I've told you. I think I'm staying." Flannery's fingers found a tear in the upholstery and she had to stop herself from picking at it, making it bigger. Molly would be a mother soon, and it was important that Flan make herself clear. After her sister's contraction seemed to have passed, Flannery swallowed her own personal, useless feelings and turned to look at Molly as she said, "Maybe Santiago will even build me a glass house down the street from you."

Molly didn't respond for a few moments. She leaned forward and exhaled directly onto the glass. "There. More humidity."

Flannery leaned forward and breathed out, too. An act of solidarity.

Molly shrugged. "It's too late."

"Well, yes. By the time snow crystals reach the windshield, they're done forming. They're already dissolving." As soon as Flannery finished saying it, she shivered.

"No, Flan. I mean, it's too late—years too late—for you to convince me that you truly love Santi," she said.

Flannery grimaced. "But Santiago is not the reason to stay. We're the reason."

Molly, trying to turn despite the steering wheel's creaking protest against her belly, squeezed Flannery's shoulder. "You're the one who told me that with Kunle it felt for the first time like a square peg fitting into a square hole. That Nigeria felt like home."

Flannery didn't want to think about Nigeria or Kunle. How with him there wasn't drama or suffocation or anxiety. Easy. Normal. Love. Nothing to say about it because it just was. Kunle was like a stasis. Like a kite suspended in wind. He'd never met her family or her friends, and he hadn't understood her past. But that had been freeing in a way. With him, she was not tied to the expectations of history.

Part of her realized Molly was right, but Flannery couldn't let go of the guilt associated with making a selfish choice. With doing what she wanted to do. "People can change their minds and come back. Just like Papa did."

"Like Papa did?"

"In the journal. He left Mom when he found out, but he came back. Remember?"

"I didn't read it." Molly sighed. "But I can still tell you that's a load of shit. Our father the martyr? Is that really your model?"

Flannery turned away, not knowing how to respond. If her sister never read the journal, why had she sent it to Flan? What did Molly want? For her to get down on her knees and beg? The car was hot and stuffy; Flannery was suffocating.

"How many times would I have to exhale to create enough humidity?"

"What?" Flannery was unable to hide the frustration and resentment in her voice.

"Shhh," said Molly, stroking her. "Don't be mad. Just tell me how many times I would need to breathe out to create enough humidity for the snowflakes to grow long, dendrite branches? Really long, amazing ones."

Flannery sighed and closed her eyes, allowing her skull to sink back into the headrest. "The average person probably exhales a liter of water per day into the atmosphere. So I don't know. A lot. You'd have to spend many, many more hours exhaling." She thought of Kunle's breath on the back of her neck when they slept, spooned together.

"Okay. I can do that," said Molly. "But right now, I need you to take me to the hospital."

SANTIAGO

When his phone had vibrated, as he stuffed his face with chips and guacamole at Alyce's reception, Santiago was annoyed to see it was Flannery. They were supposed to meet to "talk" after Alyce's opening, and he assumed she was calling to cancel—again. For the last week she'd been calling to make plans and then calling to cancel them.

But when he picked up the phone, she spoke quickly. She said she was taking Molly to the hospital with contractions and Brandon needed to get there. Santiago followed orders, grabbing Brandon as he returned from the liquor store laden with booze and driving him to the hospital.

Now he wasn't sure what to do. He found a seat in the waiting room as far away as possible from the television, which was blaring the right-wing news station. He knew Flannery was inside the hospital somewhere, and so he rummaged around in his messenger bag for his book of Czeslaw Milosz poems, which he'd accidentally bought online in the original Polish, and tried to sit there looking nonchalantly highbrow. Erudite. Like someone with whom a discerning woman might want to spend her life. Though, on second thought, while this might be a look he could pull off with a stranger, Flannery knew he didn't speak Polish. To Flannery, he would only look ridiculous.

As Santi pored dumbly over the violent Polish sentences, an

enormous red balloon came floating across the room toward him. For a minute, Santiago's heart buoyed—in his mind's eye he pictured Flannery behind him, her long fingers having just released the balloon into the empty white space in a kind of playfulness that could only mean: Joy? Love?

He swiveled his head to look for the balloon's origin, but there was no Flannery. A man came bounding down the hall, chasing the now irrelevant object, his beeper bouncing awkwardly at his belt, and he tackled the balloon before returning it to the family holding more of them, all covered in cursive writing: "It's a boy!"

"Hey, hey," said Flan's voice. Suddenly she was beside him for real.

Flannery's sweaty brown hair was tied back in a ponytail that Santiago felt the urge to undo before raking his fingers roughly through the tangles. She sat down next to him and reached for his book, flipping absently through the pages and raising her eyebrows at the Polish.

"How's Molly?" he asked.

"Brandon took over." She was not really looking at him. "Thanks for finding him."

"She'll be okay?"

"They'll do a C-section, but she should be fine."

Santiago took a deep breath. He touched her hand.

She looked up and smiled a little. "How are you, Santi?"

Santiago decided to be brutally honest. "The fire station's on the market, but we haven't gotten any bites yet. I've applied to forty jobs, gotten five interviews and no offers. I have another interview next week for Whole Foods corporate, which I'm excited about because designing grocery store parking lots is really a lot more interesting than one might think."

"It is?"

"Fuck no." He shrugged. "I'd be lucky to get it, though."

Flannery dropped the book and laid her hand on his arm, her nose wrinkling like a rabbit's, her tone serious and dark as she said, "I'm really sorry." She said it like she meant it, but also like his job prospects weren't what she was really talking about. She had started wearing powder and her freckles lay beneath the makeup like stars dimmed by cumulous clouds.

"You have never judged me, and that's something I always loved about you. But I have made a lot of mistakes. I haven't treated you right. I haven't treated a lot of people right." Flannery paused, trying to convey something that Santiago did not want to understand.

Someone came running into the waiting room saying, "He's here!," but it was a stranger addressing a group of strangers, excited about a stranger's new baby. Santiago yearned to trade places with them. "Spit it out, Flancake."

"Santi, we have always had something . . ."

He spoke before she could continue, before he could lose his nerve. "Let's go to the courthouse right now and get married. Nothing's stopping us," he pleaded, as though the molecules in the air could be transformed by pure enthusiasm.

She sat up, exasperated. "We're not getting married. You know that."

"But we UNDERSTAND each other."

She stared at him.

"You're not listening," he said, illogically. These were things he'd been saving up for later, but now later was in danger. An excruciating detergent jingle came on the television in the corner. "I'm ready for a home and a family and all that stuff we used to make fun of."

He thought Flannery might be tearing up a little as she said, "We are like a family. That is the fact you don't want to face: we understand each other like siblings who speak in shorthand understand each other." Santiago's lungs deflated. A collapse. A crumbling.

But Flannery refused to stop the assault, adding, "I wish that were enough, but it isn't. You deserve somebody who loves you best."

They were quiet except for Flan's repulsive sniffling. Santiago thought about the money he'd loaned her for the snow machine, the money he didn't have. "This is not the way to break up with someone," said Santiago, and it felt like a different person talking.

"How would you do it?" she asked, turning her wide, watery cat eyes on him.

"When breaking up with someone, be sympathetic but not patronizing. Explain yourself but avoid clichés like 'I haven't treated you right' or 'I love you like a brother.'" Flannery was openly crying now, and Santiago sensed she was trying to get him to think they were on the same side when they weren't. "And whatever you do, don't fall apart. If you're breaking up with someone, you don't have the right to fall apart in front of them."

She smeared snot with her sleeve, which did nothing to convince him she hurt as much as he did. There was a shift change at the nurses' station, and a group of them walked off down the hall, purses slung over their shoulders.

Santiago stared back at the television. "Do you think they'll get the stain off? I'm worried."

She ignored him. "We'll always love each other in a way?"

He had no idea why she would phrase this as a question to him. Santiago stood.

"Aren't you going to stay and see the baby?" The crow's-feet around her eyes became more prominent as she squeezed them shut.

"I'm going to the bathroom," said Santiago, attempting a tone of stiff dignity as he walked away.

All the other times she'd left him should have prepared him for this, chipping away at his dependence on her. He told himself, this shouldn't be such a big surprise. It shouldn't hurt so much. He didn't go to the bathroom. He walked past it, all the way out the door. He grabbed the plastic Jesus lodged in the bottom of his messenger bag and tossed it into the grass.

Santiago found his car in the hospital parking lot. He popped the trunk, which was partially filled with Black Cats, Roman candles, sparklers, and a fountain called "Dark Science." The previous summer's severe drought meant a strict burn ban had gone into effect just before the Fourth of July, leaving Santiago with an ambitious cache of unused fireworks. He stared at them until his phone vibrated. It was a text from Brandon. The baby was here. Safe and sound.

He imagined lining the fireworks up in a row and lighting the fireworks one at a time in succession. Noise. Lights. Love. We are an explosion, it would say. Maybe a spectacle was needed to make Flannery see how ridiculous she was. He would look at her as she came outside, the air filled with sooty pigment, and scream into the cacophony like a wild animal. He would be bigger and better than before. He would change. He would change her mind.

When they were younger, Santiago suspected Flannery kept leaving him because he was too boring, not crazy enough. He even admitted this once to her, while they watched television in his apartment in Boston. She'd said, unconvincingly, "No, that's not it," and took his head onto her lap, pulling her stubby, bitten nails through his hair. "What does it mean," she asked another time, in that dreamy voice she used when talking mostly to herself, "that whenever I'm upset, I end up comforting you?" How long had Santiago been hounded by the slippage between what he was and what he needed to be to make Flannery happy?

He looked up at the square hospital building and calculated which windows funneled into the antiseptic room where Flannery waited.

In the dark of the parking lot he placed the fireworks carefully on the pavement, searching for a lighter in his pockets.

He decided to start big. To really grab her attention. It took him a few seconds to get Dark Science lit, but when he did, it shot a shower of gold and silver sparks twelve feet into the air, the base spinning in a circle of red and green flare all the time whistling like an oncoming train. It seemed to go on forever, and Santiago smiled in triumph.

As he fumbled to find the next fuse, Santi heard footsteps. "Stop right there! Put your arms in the air!" He turned to find a security guard, small and round. "I'm calling the bomb squad."

"They're fireworks. Safe fireworks," said Santiago. "For a woman in the maternity ward. Please. I promised her." Santiago was intentionally vague, hoping the man might think he was the father of the baby being born.

The man relaxed a little and sighed. "I could lose my job."

"Been there, done that," said Santiago, under his breath.

"What?"

"Can you just back up a few feet? I'll set them off really fast and then you can come running and subdue me. You'll be a hero."

The man shrugged and backed up.

So, one by one, Santiago set off all the fireworks until the air was filled with smoke and the acrid smell of sulfur. The security guard played along good-naturedly, saying "oooh" or "aaaahhh" after each small glittery eruption.

"Thank you. Thank you very much." Santiago bowed.

He looked at the asphalt littered with bits of paper and charred wicks like confetti. It was a letdown. When his father took him to see Fourth of July fireworks once as a boy, Santiago had asked why they didn't just set them off all at once and make one enormous explosion. His father explained to him that it was all about building up to things, anticipation and reward. Santi heard his father's words but it was not a concept he understood at the time, being a boy born ready for everything to happen.

"Come on, buddy," said the security guard. "Let's go."

Sweat poured down Santiago's chest and the back of his legs as they made their way toward the main hospital doors, light glowing from behind the sliding glass. "She's never coming back to me," said Santiago. "It's over between us."

"I have a couple of my own. Child support, all that. It's hell."

"Fucking hell."

Santiago felt the night breeze on his face. The headlights of a car turning into the parking lot seemed unnecessarily bright. As he and the security guard walked side by side, jealousy and loss breaking over Santiago in waves, he looked at the long horizon of buildings and highway billboards and radio towers. They seemed to reach and claw toward a sky that was only an absence of light.

FLANNERY

*I*n the waiting room, Flannery tilted her orange soda bottle, allowing a few drops to fall onto the white linoleum as she exhaled the words, "For Esu."

She prayed that her sister would be all right and that the child, while premature, would be healthy; she poured libations on the ground, as Kunle had taught her, to their favorite Yoruba deity, the trickster and protector of the crossroads. Then, she tossed a brown paper towel over the orange puddle on the floor.

The others trickled into the waiting room: Alyce, still dressed up, then Steven and Lou, Harry in pajama pants. Flannery never saw Santiago return, which made her feel both guilty and relieved.

It was three in the morning, and Flannery was exhausted. During the past two weeks, she and Brandon had stayed up late each night trying to figure out what had gone wrong with their snow machine in the silo. Because ski resorts were looking for acres of coverage, they required very big, very expensive water pumps and air compressors. She and Brandon had tweaked the machine from Utah to work at a smaller scale but with more complex functioning capabilities. They had created a software program to input the variables of humidity and atmospheric pressure that existed in the dry season of the Sahel and installed special insulation and climate control equipment in the silo, so it would be possible to accurately measure the output of the machine before the external air altered the chemistry. But their trial run had been a failure, and they weren't sure why. The snowflakes didn't form; instead, a cold sleet rained down inside the silo.

Sitting in the plastic waiting room chair, her neck cramped, her soda finished, Flannery was startled to attention by Brandon emerging from the flapping hallway doors saying, "In the red corner, the tough and talented Rosie Salim, weighing in at five pounds three ounces. Ten fingers and ten toes and ready to rumble."

Through the glass separating them from the NICU, Flannery stood next to Alyce and looked at the tightly swaddled newborn, breathing peacefully through her ventilator. Her milky earlobes peeking from her cap, Flan's niece squinched her eyes into adorable little slits. Flannery leaned into the window, imagining the smell of baby, powdery and sour.

When Rosie began to cry, Flannery listened as Alyce soothed her with soft chants through the glass: "You will be brave. You will be lucky. You will be loved. You will feel joy."

"A lot of pressure." Flannery wondered if what they said could slip its way into the bloodstream and the knitted fibers of muscle that bound the bones together.

"Think so?"

"Have you thought of putting it in the form of a question?" Flannery pressed her shoulder into Alyce's. "Will you feel joy, little girl? Will you be brave today? Will you learn patience and how to be kind? Will you find your way? Will it snow in the desert? Will the birds re . . . ?"

Flannery was interrupted by a loud noise coming from outside. A booming and whizzing. The two women lurched toward the window to find that fireworks were being launched above the parking lot. Bright splashes of color erupted into the sky. Pink and purple and long white stripes. It was beyond weird. As Flannery stared, some of the eruptions, when the white lights fell back down toward the earth, looked like what she hoped would happen if she and Brandon were able to fix their machine: Snow. Falling.

Snow falling at above-freezing temperatures. Glittering like fireworks. Alighting slowly toward the ground. In her fantasy, Kunle would be at the silo when they performed the successful test, wearing his Drogba jersey and jeans, face as handsome and serious as the young Soyinka, and, in this dream, Flannery would kiss him on the cheek before disappearing behind the controls and water tanks. By this time, she would have gotten up the nerve to confess to Kunle her awful breach of trust. He would be hurt, but she hoped he would also understand. Maybe not at first, she thought, but eventually. She couldn't force him, but she could beg.

Molly and Rosie (on Molly's chest in a candy cane baby sling) would also be there with Brandon. Harry would arrive with the boys, and immediately walk over to Alyce, kissing her straight on the mouth and sliding an arm around her, laughing. Steven would be sharing nuggets of wisdom with Maya and Harry and Alyce's boys, little Zen koans about farming. "What goes down must come up."

Santiago always did like an entrance, and he would make one dressed in the rattiest ankle-length fur coat Flannery had ever seen, his Russian ushanka beaming off the top of his head, grazing the door as walked through it in black boots with shiny silver buckles, a woman's muff swallowing hands and wrists.

After setting everything up, Flannery would walk over to Molly and pick up little Rosie, skin the color of strawberry ice cream, and hold her up, the older cousin to her and Kunle's future children. She would let Rosie settle onto her chest, and behind her would be Kunle, and behind him Molly moving backward into Brandon's body. Like a row of Russian matryoshka dolls nestled together to form a set.

There would be noise as the machine cranked and shook, the industrial lights covered in metal strips flickering. It would begin.

Flannery would hand Rosie back to her mother and try to remember what it was like to be a child and feel that the world was still fluid and mysterious, a place where monsters and angels waited in the wings, just out of view.

Then, they would begin to see it. Just barely. Little bits of white. Tiny. Lintlike. Cosmic dandruff. They would float from the open metal-gridded mouth of the machine, a little wobbly on their axes, as if they'd been waiting inside this mechanical prison for eons and were still getting their sea legs, air legs.

The flecks of white would grow. The next puff would blow out bigger ones, real snowflakes that you could see. Snowflakes that, as they passed through the light, looked like real snow in the yellow pool of a streetlamp in a Wisconsin winter. Watching them fly and flutter and fall softly onto the combed heads of her friends, Flannery would almost forget she had no health insurance of any kind. Almost forget about everyone they knew who'd been laid off, about her dying sister, about climate change and the religious riots happening near Kunle's mother's village. About the fact that she had betrayed him. Not forget, but almost forget.

Because when Flannery arrived in Nigeria for the first time, fearful of the chaos and danger she felt surrounded her as she stepped into throngs of people waiting outside the airport fence, it had been nighttime. The consulate driver picked her up, and they pulled onto the highway with military escorts, a lead and follow vehicle, heading into Lagos proper. There was something insane in the image of them barreling down those weaving and washed-out dirt roads in all their conspicuous, glorious first-world splendor. She couldn't imagine what the people they passed must have thought. But she thought they were beautiful. Everything was just as poor and crazy as she'd expected—plastic tables and oil lamps and people drinking and dancing, selling food, children darting through the streets—but more joyous. Because she'd forgotten to expect joy.

Flannery would continue to watch the snowflakes as they spewed out near the ceiling, before they fell, and she would cry and feel ashamed of the crying. She would see Kunle to her right and allow their eyes to latch together for a moment until the sound of laughter broke the fishing line of their gaze. She loved him. She was exceedingly imperfect and yet she hoped he would still love her back. Forgive her. Have faith that she could change. The snow would feel cool and real as it hit her cheeks. The silo would be gone, and she would suddenly be in the Sahel, a yam farm stretching into the distance.

Flannery would look around at Kunle and all her friends as they stood in the middle of West Africa, covered in the lightest dusting of snow, faces tilted upward to a God most of them didn't believe in and who probably wasn't there. Flannery might stumble under the dizzy weight of the white, cold flakes, but that wouldn't matter. It wouldn't even matter if she fell. She would be home.

ACKNOWLEDGMENTS

*T*hank you to my secret agent Emily Forland, who championed this work with such enthusiasm; to my insightful, discerning, and patient editor, Emily Cunningham, and the rest of the HarperCollins family; to everyone who read early versions of the manuscript, especially Dalia Azim, Sarah Bird, Dave Brice, Ellen Garcia, Jessica Grogan, Charlotte Gullick, Erin Hamilton, Margo Rabb, Dawne Shand, Tyler Stoddard Smith, Kirk Walsh, Amanda Eyre Ward, and Chris Zarate; to my teachers, particularly Pamela Painter, who taught me how to enter the "House of Guns"; to my students, who allow me to see the world through their eyes; to everyone who touched my life in Nigeria, especially Rome Aboh, Wole Adeleke, Rotimi Babatunde, Chris Bankole, Mr. Clement, Tariye Isoun Gbadegesin, Ayobami Kehinde, Sam Krinsky, Kunle Okesipe, Kathy Okpako, Toja Okoh, Ayo Olofintuade, Josiah Olubowale, and Krystal Strong; to my wonderful family and friends, especially Josa and the Chezmarcs, who sustained me with beer and tacos, sofas to sleep on, incredible loyalty and warmth, and who "let" me mine from their lives.

I am deeply grateful to those individuals who aided in my research for this novel: climate scientist Dr. Kerry H. Cook from the University of Texas's Jackson School of Geosciences; the talented weavers Ann Matlock and Patricia Day; neurologist Dr. Sunil Cherry; and especially, Leslie Morris, Annie Murray, and the others from HD families who shared their stories with me. Any errors or misrepresentations are my own. The Fulbright Program, the Dobie Paisano Fellowship, the I-Park Foundation, and St. Edward's University all helped make this work possible with their generous gifts of support. Thanks also to the Austin Public Library.

Most of all, I thank my parents, Alice and Joe Specht, who, with offbeat grace and humor, gave me everything.

About the author

About the book

Read on

Insights,
Interviews
& More . . .

Meet Mary Helen Specht

Erica Nix

BORN AND RAISED in Abilene, Texas, to librarian parents, Mary Helen Specht holds a BA in English from Rice University and an MFA in creative writing from Emerson College, where she won the award for fiction. Her writing has been anthologized and appeared in numerous publications, including the *New York Times*. She has been awarded fellowships from the Fulbright Program, the I-Park Foundation, and the Dobie Paisano

Fellowship Program, and she has also lived and worked in South America and Africa. Specht currently teaches creative writing at St. Edward's University in Austin, Texas. She enjoys live music, traveling by bus, goat pepper soup, elote, snorkeling in Barton Springs, paying for things with coins, receiving postcards in the mail, reading and lolling about in hammocks, hiking, meditating, bumper stickers, and drinking wine from a bota. ∾

The Seed of a Novel

Adapted from an essay first published in Bookslut.

Ibadan,
running splash of rust
and gold—flung and scattered
among seven hills like broken
china in the sun.
                                    —J. P. Clark

THE SEED OF *MIGRATORY ANIMALS* was planted during my Fulbright fellowship to study West African literature in Nigeria in 2006 and 2007. I'd come to believe that American writers and readers tended to be too insular, mostly reading and writing for a native audience. With this in mind, I embarked on a reversal of the usual migration, choosing to study at the University of Ibadan in Nigeria, an institution that many of the literary titans of Nigeria had passed through at one time or another.

In Ibadan there was a canteen called Flavours that served the best melt-your-mouth-off goat or fish pepper stews—the goat soup overflowing with juicy chunks of meat, the fish laid across the bowl from eyeball to tail in triumph. This was one of the many cafés where I came to know a circle of young Nigerian writers and lovers of books.

One evening toward the end of the dry season, clouds flirted with the scorched earth and, as dusk fell on the canteen, we watched dozens of lightning flashes streak the sky, each a slightly different shade of white, blue-white, silver-white: the Yoruba sky god Sango's fireworks extravaganza. We ordered Star beer or Guinness, pepper soup or *isi-ewu*, flares of phosphorous matches lighting Bensons or sometimes the menthols called White London.

Earlier that day the writer Rotimi Babatunde and I had been invited to speak to our friend Kunle Okesipe's students. (My character Kunle is not based on this real-life Kunle—they merely share a cool name.) I'd shown up at Kunle's school in the Eleyele district of Ibadan to discover that by "his students" he hadn't meant the students in his English class but the entire secondary school. There was no auditorium or microphone, just two hundred teenagers lined up in a field with rows marked off by white stones. We stood above them on a concrete slab. I yelled about what it was like growing up in West Texas, about writing what you know while also imagining yourself into the lives of others. Writers need empathy first and foremost, I remember saying, repeating what other writers had once taught me.

During the Q&A, the Ibadan kids were unforgiving. I'd figured they'd want to know about the United States, but they were more interested in stumping me: What is the difference between prose and fiction? How many different types of poetic meter are there? Can you define hyperbole?

At Flavours that night, I asked Kunle what the students had to say later about our "speeches." ▸

The Seed of a Novel *(continued)*

"They thought Rotimi was more arrogant than you," he said. "And some people"—he laughed—"were confused as to how your parents could possibly be from Liberia."

Despite my attempts to speak slowly and enunciate—I knew from experience my American accent would be difficult for the students to understand—I hadn't anticipated the phrase "my parents are librarians" might cause such confusion.

"They thought Mary Helen was less arrogant than I was because they only understood every third word she said." Rotimi wasn't fat but spherical—a jolly pastille—and he spoke quickly, with a slight stutter, frequently interspersing his words with laughter. He was the most successful of our literary circle, having already had several of his plays staged in London, along with awards from numerous international fellowships like the MacDowell Colony and the Rockefeller Foundation.

"Or maybe it's because the superior can afford to be self-effacing," I replied.

"See, the Liberian isn't arrogant at all."

The students at Kunle's school never asked me why I'd come to Ibadan to immerse myself in African fiction, because they knew there was no city on the continent with the charmed literary history of their hometown. It's a city that, while virtually unknown in the States, played such an important role in the emergence of English-language African literature that I was inspired to move there after graduate school in the same way writers used to swarm the *quartiers* of the Left Bank.

My first encounter with Nigerian fiction: holed up in a bone-chilling Boston winter, I was drawn into Ben Okri's novel *The Famished Road*, a frenetic, meandering novel of magical realism in which the "scumscapes," where a boy named Azaro lives in abject poverty, are permeated by the dazzling images and machinations of the spirit world. I learned that the title *The Famished Road* alludes to a poem by Wole Soyinka (which is, in turn, indebted to a proverb): "The right foot for joy, the left, dread / And the mother prayed, Child / May you never walk / When the road waits, famished." I had to find a way to get there.

In Robert M. Wren's *Those Magical Years: The Making of Nigerian Literature at Ibadan: 1948–1966*, he avers that no other university town in the world has "produced a similar cluster of distinguished authors." There are dozens of renowned writers (Flora Nwapa, Elechi Amadi, Femi Osofisan, Niyi Osundare, Remi Raji, and many more) who at one time or another have made their way through Ibadan, but the four heavyweights to whom Wren alludes are Wole Soyinka (playwright/poet/novelist/biographer—Nobel Laureate), Chinua Achebe (whose *Things Fall Apart* adorns high school and university reading lists everywhere), Christopher Okigbo (the modernist ▶

poet who died tragically in the Nigerian civil war), and J. P. Clark (known primarily as a poet, though he wrote a number of plays, one of which was first directed by Soyinka and involved the live sacrifice of a goat). Even two of the biggest names in African literary criticism had come out of Ibadan: Biodun Jeyifo and Abiola Irele.

As an anthropologist passing through town on research told me once: "In the Ibadan of the '60s and '70s, everywhere you went, literature was in the air."

The British established University College in Ibadan, or UCI, in 1948 as one of three full-scale institutions of higher education in Africa to confer degrees from the University of London. One purpose of this program was to educate an African civil service elite as part of Britain's policy of "indirect rule."

UCI became the University of Ibadan after Nigeria's independence from Britain in 1960 and attracted talent regionally and globally. The city of Ibadan was also the hub of West African publishing, and it was there in the late '50s that the German Ulli Beier and South African exile Ezekiel Mphahlele started the literary magazine *Black Orpheus*, encouraging an African literature built on indigenous models rather than British ones. Today, the publication's list of authors reads like a Who's Who of anglophone African fiction and poetry.

In May 1967, months after a bloody coup led by a northern Nigerian military faction, the eastern part of the country, calling itself Biafra, seceded, igniting a civil war that lasted almost three years and left hundreds of thousands dead. The war scattered the Nigerian writers—Achebe, Okigbo, and Gabriel Okara went east to support the breakaway state, while others, including Soyinka and J. P. Clark, remained on the federal side. Clark once remarked that the war dispersed "atoms that should have collided to make a nuclear charge."

By the time I arrived at UI, extreme financial straits—precipitated by a series of kleptocratic governments—had led to perennial strikes, overcrowding of classes and residence halls, the almost total lack of laboratory equipment or texts, and the crumbling of infrastructure. From the moment I stepped on campus—via a back road because strikers had blocked the front gate—it seemed obvious that Ibadan's "magical" years had long ago rung down the curtain.

The classrooms were stifling, despite the open windows flanked by frangipani trees; there was rarely electricity to run fans or computers. And there was the problem of books—where to find them, how to afford them. The collection in the library was old and most volumes devastated by the tropical heat. The selection at the two decent local bookstores (in a city of over a million people) was not much better: Who was going to spend the equivalent of two weeks' worth of food on one novel? ▶

The Seed of a Novel *(continued)*

Most of the graduate students passed around photocopies and abandoned the idea of keeping up on the latest scholarship. Even if they had the money, it was near impossible to order journals or books online without a credit card, or to convince international websites they were not just another Nigerian scammer/prince-in-distress.

During my first month in Nigeria, I arrived early for a seminar and pulled out a ratty paperback to read. Everybody's heads swung in my direction. Where did you get it? Can I borrow it? Can I make a copy of it? Books were valued in Ibadan in the way one values something hovering on extinction.

And yet Ibadan's important history of nurturing authors—though the facilities and intellectual support were remnants of what they once had been and the newer generation composed of what Jeyifo called "the unfortunate children of fortunate parents"—still inspired. There was the echo of myth. Of barely lingering magic.

When I got together with my Ibadan literary crew, we shared works-in-progress and argued over politics; we told bad jokes and drank too much Star beer; we sometimes left the canteen with our arms flung over each other's shoulders in affection.

I would tell Kunle I'd enjoyed his play about the pompous professor, but I thought the ending, where he threw a woman in a wheelchair up against the wall, might be taking things too far. They would critique my retelling of the Handsome Man folktale, where a village woman follows a handsome stranger into the bush only to discover he's a spirit who borrowed his human parts. In my version, the handsome man was a white woman.

"I think your dialogue in pidgin was okay," said Rotimi. "But you need to make the bird a parrot. In Yoruba tradition the parrot is always the gossipmonger."

In the fog of beer and conversation, we could almost forget that the world had changed, Nigeria had changed, and literature itself had changed. My friends sitting across the table were the inheritors of Ibadan's past, for better or for worse.

On one of those nights, I tramped back behind the canteen to piss in the only bathroom available, the gully. There, tucked into the cuff of my jeans, was a lone firefly winking against the backdrop of denim. And I remember thinking: *These days, even in this decaying city during these decaying times, are sometimes magical, too.*

On my return to the States, I lived alone on a Texas ranch for the Dobie Paisano Fellowship and continued writing about Nigeria with the goal of completing a creative nonfiction book. Several essays from this stage were eventually published, including "How Could I Embrace a Village" in the *New York* ▶

11

The Seed of a Novel *(continued)*

Times. I didn't want to portray Nigeria one-dimensionally, when in reality it is a country with rural huts and modern houses, dirt roads and concrete flyovers. I had notebooks full of descriptions from my time living there, and I combed through them, looking for details that would do the most work to reveal the country's complexity.

However, along the way, the book changed on me. I became less interested in writing about what *was* and more interested in writing about what *if.* During this time in Texas, I was also watching the economic recession ravage people, many of whom were well educated and hardworking, people who'd always expected adult lives at least as successful as those of their parents. And I was thinking a lot about place while living at the ranch, and I wondered, what if an American woman felt she'd finally found her place in West Africa but wasn't allowed to stay? What if she returned to a homeland in trouble? I was a fiction writer by training, so I shouldn't have been surprised when the *what if*s pulled me back in and *Migratory Animals* was born. I am grateful for it. ∾

Recommended Reading

IN WRITING ABOUT NIGERIA, I've struggled with the question of whether it is possible to write, as Edward Said asked, about "other cultures and peoples from a . . . non-repressive and non-manipulative perspective." This is a question I explore in my online essay "The Challenges of Writing Global Fiction," and I'm still not sure I can answer it fully; however, I *think* there is an opportunity for writers from the developed world to write about the developing world in a way that is productive, especially when these writers use the opportunity to explore their own privilege and maybe even culpability. That said, it is almost impossible to entirely escape being part of the "Western gaze" when writing about other cultures. I believe the most important action writers and readers can take to ameliorate this situation is to support—by reading, reviewing, promoting, assigning to our students—international fiction written by nonwestern writers. As Chimamanda Ngozi Adichie discusses in her amazing TED talk, the danger is perpetuating a "single story" about any given place. If there is a multiplicity of voices, native and nonnative, writing about a country or culture, then there isn't the same pressure to provide some impossible "objective" viewpoint. The beauty of fiction, after all, is in the opposite, in its subjectivity and ability to refract the world through many prisms. ▶

Recommended Reading *(continued)*

To this aim, I encourage everyone to explore the diverse and brilliant array of Nigerian authors easily available at local bookstores. If you're unfamiliar with Nigerian literature, here are some good places to start: Chimamanda Ngozi Adichie's beautiful tour de force *Half of a Yellow Sun* tells the story of the Biafran civil war through multiple points of view, from the Nigerian to the Western, the powerful to the powerless. In the memoir *You Must Set Forth at Dawn* by Wole Soyinka, revel as this very public intellectual and Nobel Prize winner holds up an Ibadan radio station at gunpoint for not broadcasting correct election results and runs into the daughter of Nigeria's most infamous dictator at Wimbledon, among other adventures. While less canonized than his more famous *Things Fall Apart*, my favorite Chinua Achebe novel is *Anthills of the Savannah*, which is set in a postindependence unnamed African state where the educated protagonists must confront the question of whether it's possible to live good lives in a country where corruption and oppression are the norm. *Political Spider and Other Stories*, edited by Ulli Beier, is culled from the pages of famed Ibadan literary magazine *Black Orpheus*, and the stories are by many of the best writers of Nigeria's independence era, including Ama Ata Aidoo. If you're looking for more Nigerian fiction writers from this "golden" period, consider exploring the work of Buchi Emecheta, Flora Nwapa, Femi Osofisan, and Amos Tutuola; if you're interested in more contemporary stories and novels, try reading Rotimi Babatunde, A. Igoni Barrett, Teju Cole, Helon Habila, Chinelo Okparanta, and Ben Okri.

Huntington's disease entered as a thread in my novel when, while driving to visit my parents, I heard Charles Sabine, the former war correspondent, speak on NPR about his family's experiences with the disease and his difficult decision to get tested. I knew about HD already from studying the life of Woody Guthrie, but I was particularly moved by this radio piece. It got me thinking about how Huntington's disease, inherently a horrific situation where children watch their parents die slowly from symptoms that they have a fifty percent chance of inheriting, is a twisted and magnified version of what we all go through on some level: watching our parents age and die, knowing that, in a way, we are watching our own futures. If you're interested in learning more about Huntington's disease, I encourage you to listen to Charles Sabine's story on the NPR website. In addition, I was aided in my research on this topic by Alice Wexler's *The Woman Who Walked into the Sea: Huntington's and the Making of a Genetic Disease* as well as her more personal *Mapping Fate: A Memoir of Family, Risk, and Genetic Research*. Huntington's disease is also a very ▶

Recommended Reading *(continued)*

powerful thread in Joe Klein's excellent biography *Woody Guthrie: A Life*.

Two other nonfiction books that I used in researching this novel were *The Noonday Demon*, a moving and informative book on depression by Andrew Solomon, and *The Bedside Book of Birds*, Graeme Gibson's beautiful anthology of literary and visual representations of birds throughout history and myth. ∽